Curing one ill…
Finding the vict…
Easing an ache th…
*   All of this and mor… you…*
After you pass through the doorways
Of the Library of the Sapphire Wind

Teg had hardly stopped speaking when the cluttered, book-lined room seemed to tilt sideways. Each woman grabbed hold of the arms of her chair. Peg shrieked.

"Earthquake?" Teg exclaimed, trying to shove back her chair from the table. "We'd better get out of—"

She never finished the sentence. Between "of" and "here" the room stopped tilting and the three women were somewhere else.

The ambient glow of the bookstore's artificial light had been replaced by a brighter, somehow colder, glow from off to one side. The walls were no longer of books but of stone: reddish brown and seemingly unworked. The three women now sat not around a scuffed table, but within a circle of intricately carved pillars or columns, some of which were slightly tilted on their bases, as if they had shifted over time.

Perhaps because they had been holding on to them so hard, the chairs upon which the three women had sat had made the journey with them. So it was from a still-seated position that the three women met the astonished gazes of those who—so it would seem—were responsible for this change. These also numbered three, which seemed appropriate, but that's where anything stopped making even the remotest sort of sense.

For one, although all three were bipedal and basically human in form, they either had very odd taste in headgear or were horribly deformed. Teg suddenly realized that neither was the case. Instead, each one of these people, although human in shape, had the head of an animal.

BAEN BOOKS
by JANE LINDSKOLD

OVER WHERE
Library of the Sapphire Wind
Aurora Borealis Bridge
House of Rough Diamonds (forthcoming)

STAR KINGDOM
Fire Season (with David Weber)
Treecat Wars (with David Weber)
A New Clan (with David Weber)

To purchase any of these titles in e-book form, please go to www.baen.com.

LIBRARY OF THE SAPPHIRE WIND

Book 1 of Over Where

JANE LINDSKOLD

LIBRARY OF THE SAPPHIRE WIND

A Baen Books Original

Baen Publishing Enterprises
P.O. Box 1403
Riverdale, NY 10471
www.baen.com

ISBN: 978-1-9821-9251-8

Cover art by Tom Kidd

First printing, February 2022
First mass market printing, March 2023

Distributed by Simon & Schuster
1230 Avenue of the Americas
New York, NY 10020

Library of Congress Control Number: 2021049577

Printed in the United States of America

10 9 8 7 6 5 4 3 2 1

❧ACKNOWLEDGMENTS❧

Through its long voyage from crazy inspiration to the book you hold in your hands, there are many people who kept me on course.

First and always, is my husband, Jim Moore. He always stayed interested in a project I wouldn't let him read until it was completed. Then, when it was done, he was my first reader. During revisions, he listened to new passages.

When the manuscript was finally completed, several friends gave their time to read the final draft. These include Paul Dellinger, Sally Gwylan, Maria Boers Morris, Julie Bartel, and Scot and Jane Noel.

Walter Jon Williams gave me research help. Chuck Gannon offered some very necessary advice.

Toni Weisskopf provided intelligent and thoughtful editorial notes, encouraging me to write a few scenes that now may be among my favorites.

LIBRARY OF THE
SAPPHIRE WIND

⚓CHAPTER ONE⚓

I wonder why I'm wondering if I'm late, thought Tessa Brown as she hurried through the front door of Pagearean Books. *After all, it's Valentine's Day. I'm probably the only one who's going to show up for book club.*

Unbuttoning her coat, she waved to the college student at the cashier's station, one of her students in the Introduction to Archeology course she taught at Taima University almost every autumn term.

"Nice to see you, Dr. Brown!" the young man called as he put his customer's order into a shiny bag printed with multicolored hearts. "Go on back. The meeting room is already open."

"Thanks!"

The meeting room was in the back of the store, a bookshelf-lined space with a large oval table in the center, surrounded by an array of the more comfortable sort of stackable chairs. Two of those chairs were occupied, with an empty one between. In the chair on the right sat Meg

Blake, a retired librarian in her midseventies. She'd moved to Taima, Pennsylvania, shortly after the death of her husband, choosing the town because it was reinventing itself as an "active retirement" destination. Silver-haired, fair-skinned, with somewhat faded blue eyes, Meg radiated a timeless elegance that her friend envied just a little.

Seated on the left of the empty chair was Peg Gallegos. Since Peg had never held a formal job, she couldn't be said to have "retired." Thrice divorced, she remained so involved in the lives of her many children and grandchildren—even those who lived some distance away—that it was hard to imagine her ever retiring. Based on things Peg said about people she'd met, movies she'd seen, concerts she'd attended, and the like, Peg was probably somewhere in her sixties, but she adroitly refused to be pinned down.

Peg had long ago given up the hair "down past her butt" of her hippy days, although, when loose, her hair still fell almost to the middle of her back. The silvering dark-brown locks had been artistically streaked, thus making, as Peg liked to say, "a virtue of reality." She had her ethnically Hispanic mother's dark hair and lightly olive skin, accented with hazel eyes that blended brown and green. The lightening of the irises common with aging made them more green than brown, an effect Peg enhanced both with cosmetics and her choice of clothing.

"Sit here, Teg," called Peg. "I can already see Meg and I are going to disagree about the value of romance novels. You get to have the deciding vote."

In the book group, Tessa had become "Teg" when a

new member had fumbled her name. Peg, who loved coining words, had been delighted, and the nickname had stuck. Tessa rather liked having a nickname, especially the sense of belonging it gave her.

She'd always been just a bit of an outsider. Her heritage mixed European, African, and Asian—a "Heinz 57" American, who didn't fit in with any culture, not even within her own family, where she had been an only child of parents who had split when she was in high school, so that her sense of having no place she belonged had been intensified. Although fairly short, years of archeological fieldwork had given Teg broad shoulders and a solid build that made her anything but petite.

"I like what you've done with your hair, Teg," Meg added.

Lately, Teg's once jetty-black hair had become a trial to her, showing enough grey to make her look older without being in the least interesting. Her most recent attempt to deal with greying had been a short, upswept punky cut that her thick hair held with a minimum of "product." This she'd had dyed a dark purple that gradually brightened to lavender near the tips.

"Thanks," Teg said, taking off her coat and putting it around the back of her chair. "Now, what's the argument?"

Usually the book club chose a specific book, or at least an author. However, in honor of Valentine's Day, it had been decided that a general discussion of romance novels was in order.

Even as Teg listened to Meg's erudite outlining of how she considered romance novels not only formulaic but potentially psychologically dangerous, given that they raised impossible expectations for relationships, Teg found herself thinking:

Of course, we three are the ones who showed up. The widow, the divorcee, and the commitment shy.

Peg had pulled a box of fancy chocolates from her bag. After offering it around, she launched into her own argument.

"For me, I guess they're a guilty pleasure, a comfort read. But the more I think about it, why should I feel guilty? What's wrong with wanting to read a story that's going to come out all right in the end? Some of the more modern romance novels are very ambitious, and even classics like Barbara Cartland and Georgette Heyer often featured women who had to make their way in a world that wasn't very receptive to female independence."

"One of the things I dislike is the reliance on misunderstandings," Meg countered. "When five minutes' discussion would clear up the identity of the young woman Our Heroine saw with her True Love, why not talk?"

"In historical romances," Peg shot back, "social constraints often meant that sort of discussion was nearly impossible to have . . ."

Teg waved a hand. "Ladies, please. How about we actually look at a sample text or two? Remember, I'm not much of a romance reader, and I lack Meg's general background."

"Great!" Peg pulled out a battered paperback. "This one is certain to hit all of Meg's buttons, but I loved it. Barbara Cartland, *The Irresistible Buck*. Wait, I'll find a good part."

A moment later, Peg handed the book to Teg. "Start with the second paragraph on the right-hand page."

Teg nodded. Years of teaching meant that cold readings didn't hold any horror for her, but what came out of her mouth had nothing to do with Regency rogues or sweet but sassy debutants:

> *Curing one ill who is not sick*
> *Finding the victim of a cruel trick*
> *Easing an ache that cuts to the quick*
>
> *All of this and more you will find*
> *After you pass through the doorways*
> *Of the Library of the Sapphire Wind*

Teg had hardly stopped speaking when the cluttered, book-lined room seemed to tilt sideways. Each woman grabbed hold of the arms of her chair. Peg shrieked. Or Teg thought she shrieked. Peg's mouth had opened in a wide O, and Peg had been known to shriek. But the sound, if there was sound, was curiously muffled.

"Earthquake?" Teg exclaimed, trying to shove back her chair from the table. "We'd better get out of—"

She never finished the sentence. Between "of" and "here" the room stopped tilting and the three woman were somewhere else. Where they didn't know, but they knew with absolute certainty that this wasn't the familiar meeting room at Pagearean Books.

The ambient glow of artificial light had been replaced by a brighter, somehow colder, glow from off to one side. The walls were no longer of books but of stone: reddish brown and seemingly unworked. The three women now sat not around a scuffed table, but within a circle of intricately carved pillars or columns, some of which were slightly tilted on their bases, as if they had shifted over time.

Perhaps because they had been holding on to them so hard, the chairs upon which the three women had sat had made the journey with them. So it was from a still-seated position that the three women met the astonished gazes of those who—so it would seem—were responsible for this change. These also numbered three, which seemed appropriate, but that's where anything stopped making even the remotest sort of sense.

For one, although all three were bipedal and basically human in form, they either had very odd taste in headgear or were horribly deformed. Teg suddenly realized that neither was the case. Instead, each one of these people, although human in shape, had the head of an animal.

Back at Pagearean Books, the three women had been seated in a crescent at one end of the large oval table: Teg in the middle with Meg to her right, Peg to her left. They retained that configuration now. As if the table was still somehow present (which it wasn't), the other three people in the room were also arrayed in a crescent, although they were standing, not sitting.

The one to the right had the head of a fox. The one to the left had the head of a deer. The one in the middle had the head of a young male lion. At least, Teg thought this last must be young, because his mane was still straggly. Even though his features were completely feline, there was something about him that reminded her of a youth in his late teens or early twenties desperately trying to grow his first beard.

When Teg took a second look at the two others, her impression of youth was confirmed. The deer-headed one had antlers, true enough, but they only had a few tines, rather than being a great rack. The fox's head offered no easy cue, but the body was slender, the breasts small and tight—those of a young woman hardly out of girlhood.

Teg wondered what these three therianthropic people made of the three humans. Did they see them as alike, since each had a human-style head, or did they notice the differences?

"Teenagers?" Teg said aloud, suddenly uncomfortable with the silent staring.

Meg laughed, a high, shrill sound more indicative of nerves than of humor. "That's your first impression, eh? I wasn't nearly as taken with their age, as in that each of them are holding weapons."

Peg snorted. "Well, I suppose if you ignore the obvious, then that's what I noticed first, too, but I think Teg's right. They're just kids."

Teg grinned weakly. "Kids with swords and spears."

They'd been talking as if the three young people facing them couldn't understand what they said, maybe from shock, maybe because those animal heads made the trio seem less human, more animal, no matter the shape of their bodies.

"We're not kids!" said the lion, thumping the butt end of his spear—or was that a staff?—on the ground. His voice went from impressively deep and rumbly to almost a question on the final word. His ears flicked, then steadied, for all the world like those of a cat trying to pretend it hasn't just been caught doing something foolish.

"I suppose 'kid' isn't the greatest choice of word," Peg admitted. "There's nothing goatlike about any of you."

"But you didn't say 'goat,'" said the deer, his voice a smooth baritone. He held a long sword with the easy confidence of one who knew how to use it. "You said 'child,' or 'youth,' didn't you?"

The fox yipped in what was clearly amusement and sheathed her twin swords. "Are we really going to worry about what word she used? These can't be the ones we were hoping for. I've never seen anything like them! What are they, anyhow, some sort of shaven-faced feline? No, that can't be it. The nose is all wrong for a feline, even if the eyes do face forward. They have teeth like equines, not a beak, or I might say they're some sort of owl."

"Whatever they are," the deer said, following the fox's example and sheathing his sword, "you're right, Vereez. They're not those we hoped to summon."

That's when, with horrible suddenness, the situation became real to the three women.

Later, they'd agree that at first they'd been too startled to think—or as Meg put it in her blunt way, they hadn't *wanted* to think. But, at that moment, with the three young adults talking so calmly about summoning and clearly not recognizing them as human, the reality struck like a physical blow. As Peg said later, "If we hadn't been sitting, I would have been groping for a chair right about then."

And it became clear that the three youths also had realized the enormous weirdness of the situation. For a very long moment, no one said anything, then the fox-woman and Peg spoke at once.

"What are . . ."

"Summoned?"

Peg's question, spoken with all the authority of her many years working with kids—her own and others—won out.

"Summoned? What do you mean?"

The lion tilted his head slightly to one side. "Is this related to the matter of goats? A word you seem to not comprehend? Summoned. Called." He considered. "In this context, used to mean calling by means of magic. Does that help?"

Peg ignored his supercilious tone. She hadn't raised numerous teenagers without recognizing the insecurity that lurked behind the need to show off. Instead she glanced over at Meg and Teg.

"Well, being magically summoned makes as much sense as anything. The only other option would be that one of you two decided to drop some acid in my tea, and that makes even less sense. The days when my friends thought putting acid in their friends' drinks without telling them was acceptable are long ago and far away."

"So we're in Narnia or something?" Meg retorted tartly.

"Not Narnia," Teg corrected, obscurely comforted by the familiar arguing. If she closed her eyes, she might even imagine herself back at the table in Pagearean Books debating the fine points of some novel. "That had talking animals and mythological creatures, like dryads and water spirits. I don't think there were any people with animal heads."

"A few," Meg shot back, "but those were monsters, like the minotaurs in the White Witch's army. Whatever else these may be, they are not monsters."

The lion, fox, and deer had been staring at the three women in undisguised amazement. When there was a pause, the fox—Vereez—cut in.

"Xerak's answered your question," she said. "Now, would you tell us what you are?"

"We're humans," Meg replied, "and before you ask what a human is, I'll add that in matters of psychology and even spirituality, that is a question we're still asking ourselves."

"Meg, stop teasing her," Teg interrupted. "I'm sorry. This is a bit of a shock for us. You at least had the idea you were going to summon someone—although apparently not us—but we had no warning at all."

"Oh," the stag said, looking embarrassed—an expression that had something to do with his posture, something to do with the tilt of his large ears. "I don't think we'd considered that. Still, would you mind explaining what a human is—physically, at least, if the other is a matter of debate? We've never seen creatures like you, not even in art. Are your faces supposed to be so, so . . . hairless?"

He'd clearly substituted "hairless" for some other less polite descriptive term, and Teg took it upon herself to answer politeness with politeness. Maybe because—unlike Meg and Peg—she'd never had children, she didn't immediately think of these three as "kids." Rather, they reminded her of the students at the field school, people with one foot in adulthood, the other still in childhood, switching back and forth with astonishing dexterity.

"Yes. Our faces are supposed to be hairless. Some of our males—we three are all female—can grow some facial hair, but that's usually reserved for the lower face. Before you ask, yes, our ears"—she brushed her fingertips to indicate her ears—"are supposed to be at the sides of our heads, rather than toward the top as with yours. We're also rather—uh—mature specimens of our type. Meg is the eldest and I'm the youngest, but I'd wager even I am at least three decades your senior, if not more."

Xerak, the lion, groaned, then quickly apologized. "I'm sorry, ma'am. I was just thinking . . ." He looked at his two comrades. "The spell got something right. We were looking for elders, those who could teach us what we need to know if . . ."

Vereez, who seemed to be the most impulsive of the three, interrupted him, "But these *can't* be who we need. They sound as if they know less than we do!"

A tall shadow momentarily blocked the light as someone else entered the . . . "chamber"? "Cave"? What to call this place?

"I warned them," quavered a decidedly elderly voice. "I warned them that they needed to take more time, but would they listen to an ancient? Oh, no. They knew far more than I, who have dedicated my life to this place and its magics, could possibly know."

The speaker had the head of an owl—the sort with tufts of feathers that give the impression of being ears. He wore a long turquoise-blue tunic, styled rather like the robes worn by Chinese mandarins, slit at the sides, and showing trousers beneath. He leaned on a tall staff topped with a crystal orb.

Oh, please, Teg pleaded with what she hoped was her own imagination gone wild. *The wise old wizard is an owl? Is that incredibly clichéd or what?*

From the looks on her two friends' faces, she could tell they were having similar thoughts. Peg was pinching the back of her hand the way she always did when she tried to suppress a desire to say something inflammatory— something all too easy to do when certain of the more dogmatic members of the book group tried to dominate a meeting. Meg had pushed her lips tightly together, deepening the network of lines around them.

The three young people stiffened when they heard the self-proclaimed "ancient" speak.

"It wasn't that we knew more," said the deer, shifting restlessly, "it's that we don't have the time to learn everything you know. If we were going to do that, we'd be as old as you by the time we finished. Stands to reason, right?"

There was a note of triumph in his voice as he reached this conclusion.

"Not precisely, young—uh—man," Meg cut in. "Much would depend on how this gentle . . . man, acquired his knowledge. If he learned it through traditional pedagogy, then you would be correct. However, if he acquired it in other ways—research or experimentation—then he might be able to relay to you in a few hours the results of years of hard labor."

For the first time, the owl turned to examine the three women. He did not bend or peer, as a human of his age would have done. Teg wondered if he had an owl's proverbially sharp sight, for he seemed to take in every detail of them.

"Wise words," he said, blinking round, dark-amber eyes with deliberation. "And true as well. Much of what I have discovered took me decades to learn but, had these three been inclined to listen, I could have related it to them in a matter of several weeks. Maybe a few months."

"But we may not have months," Xerak retorted, a hint of a roar underlying the words. "We have things we need to do!"

"Calm down, young man!" Peg rose and smoothed her hair, exuding authority. She looked sternly at the three summoners. "If, as this young woman—Vereez, I believe you said—indicated, we are not the . . ."

She paused. Teg knew she'd been about to say "droids" and had caught herself just in time.

". . . people you meant to summon, then perhaps the first step in getting what you want would be to send us home again. Then you can consult with this gentleman"— she inclined her head toward the owl—"and learn what you should do to correct your error."

"Can we?" said Xerak, addressing the owl.

"You can send them back, yes," the owl began. Then, when the shoulders of the three young people began to relax in evident relief, he continued. "However, you cannot summon anyone else. Hettua Shrine works only once for each person unless . . ."

He shook his head so hard that the long "ear" feathers wobbled. "Let's just leave it at 'This shrine only works once.' The contingencies would not apply at this time or in this situation. Even if they would"—he sniffed—"no one would care to listen to the explanation."

Teg certainly wasn't interested, but his words had

crystalized a faint sense of dread that she hadn't been aware of until this moment. "We can go back? We're not trapped here?"

She would have asked more, but Meg was looking at the three young people with the same look she got when someone at the book club started talking about a "friend" who had been in some sort of trouble, and after a few sentences you realized that the friend under discussion was the speaker.

Meg cut Teg off with a short, apologetic nod. "Then if we go back, that's it, isn't it? That's the end for whatever it is that brought you here. Maybe you should at least explain to us what you were hoping for. It is possible— just possible—that we may be able to help you."

"But let's not talk here," Peg cut in, "at least not unless you bring chairs and sit with us. This is all too Stonehenge. I keep expecting druids holding sickles or maybe carrying one of those horrible wicker baskets to come stalking in."

The four animal-headed people looked completely mystified, but Meg and Teg understood immediately. There had been a gruesome sacrificial scene in a novel they'd read the previous Halloween, so the stone circle did evoke certain memories.

"Can we leave this stone circle?" Teg addressed the owl. "Without ruining our chance to get home?"

Privately, she wondered why she was pressing the point so hard. It wasn't as if she had a lot to go home to. She was currently on a sabbatical, while she wrote up the results of her last dig. There were the cats, but it wasn't as if she had anyone in particular to miss her.

The owl replied, "No, leaving the circle will not violate your ability to return, although . . ."

When Peg attempted to cut him off, Meg raised a hand. "Please, Peg. I'd like to hear what comes after 'although.' After what happened when these three were disinclined to listen to this gentleman, I don't think we should make the same mistake."

Peg nodded and resumed her seat. Without even thinking, she reached behind herself for her omnipresent bag of knitting, picked out a project by touch, and began clicking yarn into something pale blue and fluffy—probably, if past experience was anything to judge by, a baby blanket. Even when one of her eight children (four of her body, four step) wasn't providing an excuse, Peg donated blankets to a program at the local hospital that, in turn, gave them to indigent young mothers.

Peg's reaching for her knitting made Teg wonder if her purse and messenger bag had come through with her. Had she hung them on the chair, as Peg had her knitting, or tucked them on the floor next to her? Before she could check, the owl's words as he completed his interrupted sentence wiped everything else from her mind.

"Whether you leave the circle will not violate your ability to return, although that provision will only hold for the next several hours. After that, the chance will diminish until it vanishes entirely." He stopped, saw from the expressions on the three women's faces that he had made an impression, and then continued more kindly. "However, if for some reason you do decide it is your task to assist these impulsive ones, it may be possible to arrange the means by which you can move between this place and your homes, somewhat at will."

"Is it complicated?" Meg asked at the same time Peg said, "Is it dangerous?"

"It is more complicated than it is dangerous," the owl said, "but certainly there is danger involved. There always is when performing a complex magical working."

His glower was clearly meant for the fox, the stag, and the lion, all of whom looked appropriately chastened.

"Very well," Meg said, taking the lead, as she so often did in book group discussions. "Then, before we attempt this possibly dangerous and definitely complicated procedure, perhaps we should investigate whether we intend to have commerce with this land. If we do not, then the point is moot."

"Well, put, good lady," the owl said. He looked as if he was about to swoon from admiration. Meg had that effect on a lot of people, Teg had noticed. It seemed that Meg's impressive aura extended to owls and possibly—looking at the three summoners—to lions, foxes, and stags as well.

"If we are going to have a lengthy discussion," Peg said, "may we please move from this place? I wasn't joking when I said it gave me the heebie-jeebies."

"I have an office," the owl said, a trace dubiously, "but it is crowded already and would not suit such a large group. Perhaps the terrace would be better. Yes, much better. That way our visitors can see something of this new land to which they have been brought."

"But the time," Teg pressed. "I know how all of us can get caught up in an interesting discussion. What if we overstay our time?"

"You have until sunset," the owl said, "before the option to return diminishes. Even after that, you will have until noon the next day before the option is completely gone. I would caution you to make your decision before dawn."

"Because the hours between dawn and noon will be when the chance is lowest," Teg guessed.

"And because I am really much less alert when the sun is high," the owl said. "A fact that was brought home to me quite firmly today." Again he glowered at the three young people. "You take our guests out to the terrace. I will gather some refreshments and join you presently."

He bowed to them and turned away. Trying to study him with the same objectivity she brought to archeology, Teg noted that he didn't seem to have wings, and that the transition between owl head and more human body seemed to happen somewhere around neck level, since rather than hair, his head feathers just brushed his collar.

"This way," said Xerak, his voice husky. "The terrace is this way."

"Do you want us to carry your chairs?" asked Vereez. "I believe there are seats already there, but maybe these are special to you?"

"No, we just happened to be sitting in them when your call came," Peg replied. "If there's nothing out on the terrace to suit us, we'll just send the boys back to bring us proper chairs."

Teg felt curiously insecure about leaving her chair, a reaction which was completely ridiculous, given the considerable amount of traveling she had done in her life.

But although I've been to the jungles of the Yucatan and the deserts of Egypt, I've never quite managed to go to another world.

She settled for taking her purse and her messenger bag, both of which were indeed slung over the back of the chair. She thought about taking her coat, decided that would show how very insecure she felt, and left it. Then she joined the parade out onto the terrace, noticing as she did that their hosts not only had animal heads, but also animal tails and that their clothing was tailored to let these move freely. All three wore a variation on the tunic/trousers worn by the owl, but while the fox and the stag's tunics stopped midthigh, the lion's went nearly to his ankles.

The terrace was lovely, built upon a natural shelf jutting from the side of a rock face. They were too close for Teg to tell whether the rock face was part of a mountain or part of a smaller outcropping, such as a cliff or mesa. The terrace caught the light of the sun, which seemed to be about an hour after zenith.

So the young people took advantage of the old owl probably being asleep, Teg thought. *I wonder if he sleeps in the daytime because he's nocturnal or because he's elderly? I suppose it would be rude to ask.*

The terrace proved to be furnished with an assortment of seats carved from stone, softened with thick sheepskin-like cushions. Meg, Peg, and Teg seated themselves on a long, high-backed bench that offered a remarkable view of green forested slopes through which numerous smaller watercourses could be glimpsed, falling to merge into a river lower down. As best as Teg could tell—and she was fairly good at spotting signs of habitation—there were no towns or villages within sight, not even areas cleared for farming.

The three young people took seats as well: Xerak and the stag on separate chairs, Vereez sprawled with self-conscious grace on a sort of fainting couch that allowed her to drape her bushy tail over the side.

Under the guise of settling her purse and messenger bag, Teg took a look at the back of their own bench. *There's a long slot along the back so tails can fit comfortably through. Whoever would have thought . . .*

Before setting her purse down, she took out a pack of cigarettes. "Since we're outside, anyone mind if I smoke?"

"I do," Peg said as usual. "If you insist, go sit where the wind will blow the odor away from the rest of us."

Teg moved as directed, settling on a chair off to one side. None of the three young people had rejected her request, although they all looked somewhat confused. Maybe people didn't smoke here. As she lit up, Teg made a quick count of her remaining cigarettes. Six in this pack and she'd just bought another on her way to book club.

Peg had pulled out her knitting and, needles clicking away, she said, "We should probably start by introducing ourselves. I'm Peg Gallegos. Call me Peg."

"I'm Meg Blake. It's fine if you call me Meg."

"And I'm Tessa Brown," Teg said, "but you might as well call me Teg. It will save confusion."

The three young people looked at each other. Vereez said, "Save confusion? When your names sound so alike?"

"Because Peg and Meg will end up calling me Teg," Teg explained, taking a long drag on her cigarette. "But I doubt it will matter, since we're probably going home in just a little."

"So, what are your names?" Peg prompted.

"You've heard the other two's names," the stag said in sullen embarrassment. "I'm Grunwold. Look, why are we even bothering to have this discussion? Are you afraid we won't be able to send you back? Well, even if we messed up, Old Man Hawtoor won't. So what's the reason for the delay? Just go back to your homes, so we can get on with figuring out what we need to do next, now that we've screwed this part up."

"You were looking for help," Meg said with a gentleness that by no means indicated weakness. "I've spent my life answering 'Can you help me?' in one variation or another. I suppose I'm curious."

Vereez the fox—*Or would that be vixen?* Teg thought—asked with honest curiosity, "Are you an oracle, then?"

"The next best thing," Meg said smugly. "I'm a librarian. Retired, true, but I don't think librarians ever really retire."

"Oh." Vereez looked at Peg and Teg. "And you? Are you also librarians?"

Peg shook her head. "Nope! I'm a nightclub singer turned mother of many."

Teg blew out a long trail of smoke. "I'm an archeologist."

Vereez was opening her mouth to ask another question when Peg cut her off. "And you three? What are you?"

"We're inquisitors," Xerak replied. Then, seeing the shocked expression that passed over each of the women's faces, he added, "What did I say? You all look troubled—and scared."

"Wait!" Teg held up the hand that held her smoldering cigarette. "There is something we need to clarify before we go any further." She turned her attention to Xerak, Vereez, and Grunwold. "How is it that we can understand you? I find it hard to believe you're speaking American English, but that's what my ears are hearing—except that, every so often, like just now, we have a hiccup."

"I have not..." Xerak began indignantly, then he caught on. "Ah, I see what you mean. By 'hiccup' you mean an unexpected interruption. This has something to do with the goats earlier, doesn't it?"

"I think so," Teg replied. "How is it that we can understand you so easily? How, if we're going to push the point, can you talk at all? Your mouths shouldn't be shaped right for this sort of speech."

A rattle of glass and china from the cavern heralded Hawtoor, the owl, as he emerged from the cave, pushing before him a wheeled butler's cart. Grunwold leapt up to help him with an alacrity that seemed to owe as much to the perpetual appetite of a young male as to good manners. Letting Grunwold maneuver the cart around the various seats, the owl answered Teg's question.

"You understand us by means of the summoning spell that brought you here. After all, it would do little good if aid was summoned only to be balked by the inability of the summoned persons to understand what was required of them."

"Very sensible," Meg agreed. "How will it deal with things that are in this world, but not in ours?"

Hawtoor swiveled his head to one side and looked thoughtful. "I don't know. I'm not certain we've ever had mentors from another world. I suppose you will need to discover."

"So, the translation won't be perfect," Meg said, sounding interested rather than annoyed.

"No," the owl admitted. "But then is any form of communication perfect? I was married for many, many years—happily married, as such things are judged—yet my wife and I continually misunderstood each other."

Meg and Peg both chuckled, the laughter of those who understood all too well.

Teg cut in before the conversation could be sidetracked from what really interested her. "So, we're under some sort of translation spell? Is it likely to wear off?"

"No," the owl said. "As I said, it is part of the summoning. If you are here to be of some sort of service—which is implied in the summoning—then you will be able to understand us and we you, within the limits of communication, of course."

Grunwold started eating what looked very much like carrot sticks, but he had manners enough to wheel the cart to where the three women could help themselves to the varied snacks and drinks. Xerak had knelt to examine the carafes and bottles on the lower portion of the cart.

"Wine, mead, several types of tea..." Xerak began pouring himself a wide-bowled goblet of bloodred wine, caught the reproving gaze of the owl, and added as if remembering his manners, "May I pour for you ladies?"

"Thanks," Peg said, giving him a sunny smile, "but since we don't really know what to call what's here, maybe it's best if we just choose what smells good."

"Wait!" Meg said, turning to Hawtoor. "In many of the

tales from our world, eating or drinking in another—call it dimension or plane..." She paused to see if the translation spell had handled the idea, then continued. "...can trap you there. Is it safe for us to eat your food, or will doing so bind us to this place?"

"Very interesting," Hawtoor said. "I would enjoy further discussion of the matter. However, no, to the best of my knowledge, eating and drinking here should in no way influence whether or not you can return."

"Very well, then," Meg said. "I'll take some of this. It smells rather like Irish breakfast tea, with just a faint touch of vanilla."

"I smell coffee!" Peg said and, sniffing dramatically, tracked the scent to a fat pot holding a bright purple liquid that did, in fact, smell like a good-quality dark-roast blend.

"I'll have that too," Teg said, taking a final deep drag, then stubbing out her cigarette, automatically pocketing the butt, a longtime habit from her work on archeological sites.

Coming over to join the others, she inspected the snacks. There was a nice pink-veined cheese, and something that might have been a pear from the scent and texture, except that it was crimson red and shaped like a deeply lobed peach. Whatever it was, it went very well with the cheese.

Xerak downed a good third of his wine in one leonine gulp, then reiterated his earlier question. "Why did you all look so uncomfortable when I said we were inquisitors?"

Meg set down her teacup—a deep, rounded bowl without a handle, closer to some Asian styles than to the shallower European model with its ridiculously tiny handle. "Because where we come from that word has acquired very negative connotations. Technically, all the word 'inquisition' means is to seek information. However, a few hundred years ago, there were those who used torture as one of their means of inquiry, and their acts taint the word to this day."

Peg—who had been nibbling a pastry that resembled a miniature éclair, although the frosting was pale orange, rather than chocolate—daintily licked her fingertips and smiled. "My ancestors came to America fleeing the Inquisition—or so family legend says. We're Catholic now, but there are a few odd traditions that almost certainly point back to our having been originally crypto-Jews."

Teg thought their hosts remained confused. "Let me guess," she said, considering lighting another cigarette, then reluctantly deciding against. "You understood some of that, but some of her words didn't quite translate."

Everyone nodded. Vereez added, "Yes. I heard something like 'My long-ago relatives came to my homeland fleeing inquiry. We're religious now but our family has some traditions that indicate that once we were secretly another sort of religious.'"

"Close enough," Teg said. "I'm impressed. As long as we're careful, I think we can understand each other."

Peg reached for another pastry, started to pull her hand back, then took it anyhow. The owl courteously refilled her cup—which, like Meg's teacup, was really more like a small, thick-walled bowl—leaving room for her to add cream and a sweet syrup that wasn't quite honey.

Peg nodded her thanks, then said to him, "We've

introduced ourselves to Vereez, Xerak, and Grunwold, but what should we call you, sir?"

"My title is Shrine Keeper, my name is Hawtoor. Please, call me Hawtoor." As he introduced himself, Hawtoor gave a little bow. "I was listening as I prepared refreshments, so I know your names. Now, the sun is still high, but it will wester. Perhaps, pleasant as this discussion is, we should return to the issue of what brought these inquisitors to this shrine to seek assistance."

"Don't you know?" Teg asked in surprise.

"Inquiring is not my task, teaching is," Hawtoor said, literally ruffling his feathers to show his annoyance. "Although many who come to Hettua Shrine confide in me so that I may better assist them. I have never violated a confidence."

"But our impulsive inquisitors have not chosen to confide in you," Meg said, her expression wry. "I've encountered that same difficulty in my own job. However, this is neither the time nor—quite literally—the place for such reticence. Vereez, Xerak, Grunwold, the choice is yours. Do you wish to tell us more, so that we may offer what assistance we can, or do you wish to press ahead with your inquisitions? I believe you have expressed a desire for some alacrity."

Xerak refilled his wine goblet. "That was me. Can we drop it? We messed up. We know it. If it helps make amends, then I'll tell you what brought me here."

A ripple of nods encouraged him to speak further and, with a great gulp from his goblet, he began.

"About a year ago, my teacher, Uten Kekui, went out for his daily meditation stroll and vanished without a trace.

I tracked him—and I am no poor tracker—and the trail ended between one step and the next. Since then, I have sought him. For a time, I even thought that his disappearance was some sort of test of my skills, but eventually I came to believe that he is truly in trouble. A year is a long time, though, and so I came here hoping for guidance."

So what was the rush? Teg thought. *A year gone by already?*

Vereez stretched on her fainting couch, then swiveled to sit up. "My tale is similar to Xerak's, except that I seek my little sister. She was kidnapped when she was but an infant, and would be about four now. My family has shown too little interest in finding her, but I have never been able to forget her. Until I find her or at least do the best I can to learn what happened to her, I will be held back in all I attempt."

Grunwold—who had watched Vereez stretch with appreciation—tossed a couple of something like blackberries into his mouth. He took so long crunching them that Teg wondered if he would refuse to share his own search. However, with a flick of his ears that somehow emphasized the slight smile that twitched his thin, black lips, he spoke.

"My father is ill. Very ill. He does not have long to live, but I could not move on with my own affairs without first making my best effort to find a cure. Thus far, every lead I have followed has trickled to nothing, as do streams in the driest times of summer. I came here hoping to find guidance."

Hawtoor clicked his beak in a thoughtful manner but,

other than that, silence reigned. The three inquisitors seemed to think they had said enough. The three women waited but, when the silence grew uncomfortable, Peg spoke.

"What you've told us certainly matches the first part of the summons, but what about the second verse?"

"Second verse?" The inquisitors spoke nearly as one, their confusion genuine.

"The second part of what we heard Teg recite," Meg clarified, "right before we were dropped in here from the bookstore. Teg, do you remember the precise wording?"

Oddly enough, Teg did, although usually she wasn't much for verse:

> *Curing one ill who is not sick*
> *Finding the victim of a cruel trick*
> *Easing an ache that cuts to the quick*

> *All of this and more you will find*
> *After you pass through the doorways*
> *Of the Library of the Sapphire Wind*

"You understand?" Peg asked. She'd taken out her knitting again, doubtless to forestall further nibbling on her part. "The first verse makes sense now—it refers to your three inquisitions. But what about the second verse?"

"We didn't hear any of that," Vereez said. "Xerak had a book that told how to appeal to the forces that animate Hettua Shrine. We'd designed our appeals on the boat we took to here, but we didn't speak them aloud. The book we had told us the proper way to inscribe them, even to what types of parchment and ink to use."

She looked apologetically at Hawtoor. "That's why we didn't want to listen to your instructions. Xerak said his book was reliable."

Xerak growled—a genuine rumbling lion's growl—and reached for the wine bottle. "It was reliable. My master told me he had copied the instructions himself, from someone who had been to the shrine and had successfully acquired guidance. You're not saying he lied to me, are you?"

He upended the remains of the wine into his goblet and then, when this proved to only be splash, reached for a fresh bottle. The claw he extended from his right forefinger proved to be an excellent corkscrew—as well as a reminder that one should not lightly insult a lion, even one as young and patch-maned as this one.

Grunwold snorted, nostrils flaring wide, and stamped one booted foot. "Don't you dare yell at Vereez! She only asked what all of us—even you, I bet—have been asking ourselves since these three . . . creatures appeared."

Meg cut in with the same steady authority she used to defuse heated arguments among members of the book club. "Stop it, all three of you. This is not an either/or situation. It's possible that Xerak's manual was completely accurate. It may have been written with the assumption that you would consult the shrine keeper first, for basic instructions."

"That's very reasonable," Peg added, knitting needles clicking away. "You won't believe how many knitting patterns are like that: assuming that knitters will make a gauge first and adjust accordingly, or that they understand the need for maintaining a consistent tension. Yet those little assumed steps are precisely what makes the difference between a fine sweater or sock and a knotted disaster."

Grunwold ran his hand along the tines of his right antler, and nodded. "I don't knit, but I understand what you mean. I won't apologize, though. Xerak shouldn't have yelled at Vereez."

"And you," Vereez said, "shouldn't have yelled at Xerak. Shall we get back to the real point? Who spoke that second verse? Was it you, Shrine Keeper Hawtoor-va?"

The owl shook his head. "I did not. Moreover, I can confirm that you three inquisitors did not either. I emerged from my office where I had been . . . resting my eyes after researching, when I felt Hettua Shrine becoming active. I heard you three reviewing the various steps you had taken to that point. Indeed, I felt a certain degree of hope that your appeal would be successful, despite your impulsiveness, because you did have the forms correct."

"So what does that mean?" Teg said. "Why did I say something that I shouldn't have?"

"Perhaps because," Hawtoor replied with thoughtful deliberation, "you *were* supposed to be summoned. The summoned often have insights that are granted to them by the shrine. This may be your own."

He repeated the last verse with care:

All of this and more you will find
After you pass through the doorways
Of the Library of the Sapphire Wind

"Is that right?"

Teg nodded.

Vereez frowned, an action that included a slight pinning back of her ears. "The Library of the Sapphire Wind? Why does that sound familiar?"

"Because not long ago it was the most famous privately owned repository of magical knowledge in all the land," Hawtoor said. "The knowledge it held was not restricted to written texts, but was embodied in those who served as resident scholars. There was also a vault in which, so it was rumored, magical tools of considerable power were stored."

"Then perhaps we'll find our answers there!" Grunwold said excitedly. "Surely a magical repository would be just the place to find a cure for my father. Maybe Xerak's master is hiding out there."

"Maybe," Xerak said, doubt in his voice. "There's just one problem. Something like twenty-five years ago, the Library of the Sapphire Wind was completely destroyed."

❧CHAPTER TWO❧

"It is true that the Library was destroyed," Hawtoor began, but Teg was speaking, too, and her urgency won out over the old owl's pedantry.

"Destroyed? Very little is completely destroyed. If anyone knows that, it's me. Finding traces of places that everyone believes are forever gone, that's what archeologists do."

"What? They don't break into lost tombs," Peg asked teasingly, "or crumbling temples dedicated to nearly forgotten gods?"

Even knowing she was being teased—Teg had heard variations on this theme from the time she got her first job doing salvage archeology where a road was being rebuilt in some nowhere part of the southwest—she felt a flare of annoyance.

"That sort of archeology was how it was done a long time ago. Even then the archeologists—the real ones— were interested in learning about the people who had lived there before, not just in treasure hunting."

33

"Peace," Meg said in that voice that not only suggested but commanded. "Peg, I know you're nervous. All of us are, but it's not right to relieve your nerves by teasing Teg."

Without waiting for a response from Peg, Meg turned to the others. "Xerak, Hawtoor, was this Library of the Sapphire Wind destroyed without a trace?" To illustrate her point, she picked up a small round cookie and put it in her mouth. "Or was it merely severely damaged?"

With a slightly apologetic look, she took a cookie of the same type, set it carefully on a small plate, and pressed her thumb onto it until it was smashed into crumbs.

Hawtoor blinked slowly.

Owlishly, Teg thought, fighting down a giggle that she knew was dangerously close to hysteria.

Hawtoor looked at Meg's plate of cookie crumbs. "Closer to your second example, Librarian Meg. And not nearly so completely. Ruins of the buildings remain, or so I have been told. I have not been there myself. The region is extremely dangerous, reshaped on a geographical level by the immense magical forces released when the Library was destroyed. As if volcanoes and earth tremors are not enough, the land is inhabited by creatures created or freed—the tales are unclear—from the Library of the Sapphire Wind itself."

Xerak coughed what must have been meant as a laugh, although there was little humor in it. "But, at least as my master, Uten Kekui, said, all of these reports are open to question. Very few of those who venture into the vicinity return to tell tales, so it's not even sure that what we have heard are genuine reports. The stories could just have been made up by people trying to build a reputation for themselves as bold explorers."

Peg shook her head. "If you had drunk just a little less wine, young man, you'd see that these tales, tall or not, should make you feel better about going to this Library. If the region was not dangerous, then there would probably be a lively industry in salvaged materials, and whatever it is you seek might no longer be there."

"Pot hunters," Teg grumbled in agreement. "No consideration for the real value, which is knowledge, just looking to make a buck on the antiquities market."

Xerak—who had been reaching for what would have been his third bottle of wine—stopped in midstretch and poured himself water instead.

"I am wondering," Vereez said, and there was apology in her voice, "if we did indeed fail in our summoning. These three ladies have knowledge we did not— knowledge that gives at least Grunwold a direction for his search. That's good right there. Moreover, one is a librarian, another a specialist in finding out about lost places."

Peg smiled and shook out her knitting. "And maybe I'm a mistake, brought along because I was with these two. But maybe, just maybe, I'll be of some help. You don't raise eight children—and four of them not your own— without learning a great many things."

The three humans looked at each other, then Meg turned to Hawtoor. "Is there somewhere private we three can talk? Completely private? I know we all would feel better discussing our options without an audience."

The owl twisted his head side to side, looking—quite

literally—over his shoulders. "Let me see . . . Ah, yes. My office is a complete mess, but there is a secondary office, used by my predecessor. If you close the door, you will have the privacy you crave."

"Excellent," Meg said. "Ladies?"

Teg reached and refilled her drinking bowl with more purple coffee, then scooped up a shallow saucer of nuts that looked like thumb-sized almonds, but tasted more like pecans. "I'm with you. Peg?"

Peg was stowing her knitting. "I'll just leave my knitting here and fill my poffee bowl."

"Poffee?" Teg asked.

"Purple coffee," Peg explained. "Easier to say." She turned to Hawtoor. "May I take some of those éclairs? I am sorry to be such a glutton, but we were going to have lunch after book club."

"Please," Hawtoor said, looking slightly dazed. "Take whatever you wish and follow me."

The room into which Hawtoor guided them was less dusty than Teg had expected, probably because it had been well sealed. It was also sufficiently crowded with shelves of books, a large desk, knickknacks, and furniture to make her wonder if Hawtoor needed to fly to get around his own office.

A large window with a thick pane of glass provided sufficient light for their needs. Hawtoor bustled about, finding them chairs, making sure they were comfortable, and then quickly retreated.

"He probably wants to harangue the kids," Peg said, seating herself and placing the orange-frosted éclairs where they could each reach them. Teg set the nuts down next to them.

"If I may start," Meg said, "before we discuss anything else, I would like to know if you agree with my impression that our young inquisitors were each lying."

Peg nodded. "Absolutely. Not so much lying as withholding information. I am reminded of when my daughter Emily explained how she needed to spend the night at a friend's house because they were both going to be playing a very early game in a softball tournament. Her friend lived much, much closer to the playing field, and Emily would be able to sleep in an extra hour. All well and good . . ."

Once Teg would have been annoyed by Peg's rambling way of making her point, but she'd learned that the discursive discussion was part of the point, so she played along.

"Let me guess . . . The other girl's parents were out of town, and Emily and her friend were planning to take advantage of this."

"Bingo!" Peg replied. "They were both good girls, really, and they didn't have anything terribly wicked planned—not with a tournament game the next day. But the prospect of having a house all to themselves. Well . . ."

"So," Meg asked, diverted despite herself. "What did you do?"

"I let Emily know I'd guessed, spoke with her friend's parents, and then let Emily sleep over. There comes a time when you need to make people live up to their better selves." She paused and picked up an éclair. "They played very well the next day, too. Came from behind on a triple Emily hit, if I recall correctly."

She popped the éclair into her mouth to put a period on her sentence.

"So," Teg said. "Do we challenge our young inquisitors? Let them know we know they haven't told us the whole truth?"

"Only," Peg said slightly indistinctly, "if we don't plan to join them. For all we know, they may be withholding information specifically from Hawtoor. They may tell us more later."

"Or we may worm it out of them," Meg laughed. "Each of us in our different ways can be very good at eliciting confidences. That raises the next question. Do we attempt to assist these inquisitors with their inquisitions?"

"If . . ." Teg paused. "If I knew I was covered at home, I actually would like to try. Hawtoor did say we could go back, so it's not forever. If we backed out, I'd always wonder what I'd missed."

"Can you arrange to be 'covered'?" Meg asked. "You have cats, don't you?"

"Thought and Memory," Teg said. "My friend Felicity would be happy to come in to feed them and scoop the boxes. I could tell her I'd been called away to someplace in the back of beyond, out of cell phone reach."

Meg nodded. "In my case, I believe I can manage to get away."

"Your kids?" Peg asked. Meg was a widow.

"They would be happy to know I was off travelling with my book-club friends."

There was something in Meg's voice that did not invite

further inquiry. Teg made a mental note to ask Peg for more information. Peg knew just about everything about everyone, sometimes more than they did about themselves.

"Seems as if you're going to be the difficult one to manage, Peg," Teg said instead. "What excuse can you come up with that won't leave one of your kids panicking?"

Peg smiled. "Happily, most of my kids are at the age where I've cut them loose and told them that it's up to them to make their own mistakes. If they try to get me to solve their problems for them, I bore them with long-winded anecdotes. Probably, I'll come up with some variation on the 'going on a trip with friends,' and they'll be relieved that I'm doing something with myself other than knitting and reading books."

"So we're all in?" Meg asked, sounding pleased.

"Seems like it," Teg said. "If the inquisitors want us, that is."

"Oh, they will," Meg said. "They already are apprehensive. They can't handle this on their own or they wouldn't have come to this shrine." She gestured toward the window, which showed a forested mountain slope, completely devoid of any sign of civilization. "It's not exactly on the beaten path."

"Then let's go tell them that they have three mentors," Peg said, preparing to pop the last éclair into her mouth, "and hurry home and make our excuses, then head back Over Where."

"'Over Where'?" Teg asked.

"Over Where," Peg half-sung to the tune of George M.

Cohan's "Over There." "We've got to call this place something. Over Where sounds good to me."

Teg watched the three inquisitor's faces as Meg announced that she, Peg, and Teg would "assist the inquisitors to the best of our abilities." Reading their expressions wasn't as difficult as she had thought it might be. Although the fur did mask some expressions, the ears and nostrils gave away a great deal.

She thought she read relief there, as well as a certain degree of . . . What was it? Apprehension? Well, that made sense. Now the inquisitors had no good excuse not to seek out this Library of the Sapphire Wind.

Meg was continuing. "Our agreement to come along is contingent, however, on our being able to return home. We do have other responsibilities, you see."

"As I said earlier," Hawtoor replied, "it is possible, complicated but possible. In collaboration, we will construct a key—a talisman might be a better word—that will act as an . . ."

He looked at Xerak, who was now drinking some of the purple coffee. "An extension of the summoning spell? Would you say that is an accurate description?"

Xerak nodded. "From what you described to me a few minutes ago, yes. I've been thinking about the best way to construct the talismans they'll need. First, we'll definitely need something . . . uh . . . personal."

"Not blood," Peg said firmly. "I will not have anything to do with blood. I'm not afraid of the sight of blood. I simply think cutting each other to seal a bargain sets a bad precedent, no matter all those blood-brotherhood rituals.

Although I think they've fallen out of fashion since blood types became general knowledge, but kids will be kids."

"Hair?" Xerak said, somewhat faintly. Peg had that effect on people. "Would you ladies be willing to sacrifice some? You have so little, but it is important that something of you be in the talisman."

"We certainly can spare some," Meg said, reaching to touch her own silver locks. "How much will we need?"

Xerak considered. "That will depend on the form of the talisman. Shrine Keeper Hawtoor, what do you recommend?"

"Something that can be worn close to the skin is good." Hawtoor clattered his beak in what Teg guessed was his equivalent of a frown. "A bracelet, perhaps? But several of you do not have hair long enough to braid."

"That won't be a problem," Vereez said. "We can make yarn."

"Excellent idea," Peg said. "It's been a while, but I took a workshop on spinning and weaving some time ago. As part of that, we made yarn with no more than fiber and our own hands."

After that, it was only a matter of logistics. Four of them—Peg, Meg, Teg, and Grunwold—had hair, which does not bind well. However, fur combed from Xerak's mane and Vereez's tail, as well as some fluffy plant material that Hawtoor supplied, provided a matrix into which the hair was blended. Then all six of them rubbed the fibers between their palms or along the legs of trousers until a length of rough yarn had been spun. When this had been completed and twisted to further tighten the joins, they cut the yarn into three pieces.

Finally, Peg reached into her bag and came up with a crochet hook.

"I prefer knitting, but sometimes crochet is very useful." Then, using chain stitch, she turned the seven-ingredient yarn into three lumpy cords.

Hawtoor had vanished into his study while all the trimming, spinning, and crocheting was going on. Now he emerged with three small stone beads.

"These were shaped from stone cut away when Hettua Shrine was built," he said, "for purposes such as these. The fur and hair will create a bridge. The stone bead will strengthen the link."

Teg put down the length of yarn she had been holding. "I was wondering how these talismans will work. Is it like a commuter pass—we can go back and forth at will—or is it more limited?"

"That remains to be seen," Hawtoor admitted, "but I would not think of these talismans as ferry boats to carry you back and forth simply by ringing a bell and summoning a barge. Just as a ferry cannot be placed anywhere on a river—some places the water is too rough, others the way is too wide, and suchlike—so it is with travel between worlds. This shrine is built where it is because the ways are thinner here. In many places the ways will be thicker."

Hawtoor glanced at the three inquisitors. "I doubt these three have the patience to sit through an explanation of why, so, suffice to say, that the more populated an area, the more magic actively in use, the thicker the way between places. Again, if a place has been prepared—as this shrine had been prepared—transit will be easier than in an otherwise identical place that has not been prepared."

"Thank you," Teg said. "So while we can get home, we shouldn't count on these bracelets as a . . ." She started to say "get out of jail free card," decided that was unfair to the translation spell, and changed to "means of escape if we're in danger."

"That is so," Hawtoor said. "It might work, but it is not a good idea to plan on doing so. Now for the final step. Xerak, I believe it would be best if you took lead, but I will be your second."

"I've been meaning to ask," Peg said. "Xerak, are you a wizard?"

Xerak shuffled his feet, then shrugged. "I was studying to be one. My master vanished before I was formally inducted, but I have the training, so I am, but I am not formally entitled to the '-va,' at least not in my deepest heart."

"But," Vereez protested, "I heard that you were tested by the wizards at Zisurru University and passed at what would have been the head of your class, if you'd been in any class. I'm sure my mother said that was one of the terms your parents set before they'd support your going searching for your master."

"Yeah, I graduated." Xerak's ears pinned back and he hissed like a very large cat. "I want my master to perform the final induction. I've been told I am foolish, that Uten Kekui is likely dead, that if he isn't, his leaving without taking care of such an important responsibility means that he is untrustworthy. I will not give up on him, even if I remain an apprentice in my heart until the end of my days."

Teg felt distinctly intimidated. She'd begun to think of the inquisitors and Hawtoor as a variation of "normal" and with that "safe." Now she was reminded that even if they were normal for here—wherever here was—that did not mean they were anything like safe. Peg, however, took Xerak's reaction in stride.

"Well, then, we're going to need to find this Uten Kekui, aren't we? Hawtoor, am I correct in assuming we'll go back into the shrine for the final enchantment?"

"That's right. It will take Xerak and me a few minutes to set up, so wait at your ease."

He motioned to Xerak. As they left, Teg glanced after them and noticed that Xerak's fur was slightly puffed, like Memory's when the cat had been confronting an invader to his territory.

Xerak's holding out on us again, she thought.

"Are you also wizards?" Meg asked Grunwold and Vereez politely.

"Not me," Grunwold said. "I'm about as magical as a boot."

Vereez delicately scratched behind one pointed ear. "I can do a little: cantrippy stuff, not the major workings that Xerak can sometimes pull off."

"So what..." Peg was beginning when Hawtoor emerged.

"We're ready."

When the chairs from Pagearean Books had been removed from the stone circle, there was just enough room for the three humans and the three inquisitors to stand facing each other in an irregular ring. Beneath the light of multibranched candelabra that had been set atop the carved stone pillars, the six began the ritual by each looping one finger through the stacked bracelets.

The women—Vereez included—all had fairly dainty fingers. This proved to be a good thing since both Xerak and Grunwold had massive hands. But there was no mistaking Vereez's hand for that of any of the humans. The back was lightly furred in white, and her nails were sharply tipped and slightly curved: claws rather than nails and deep black—and not from an excess of Goth polish. Xerak also had claws, although the fur—no more dense than the body hair of many a human male Teg had known—on his hands was golden. Grunwold's hands were the closest to what Teg thought of as "normal," since they had nails, rather than claws. A light coating of golden-brown hair grew smoothly over the backs of his hands, thinning as it went down the fingers.

Xerak held his spear—which Teg now realized served him as much as a wizard's staff as a weapon—in his free hand. The spear staff was a beautiful example of the woodworker's art, with intricate inscriptions worked into the length. The spearhead was quite large, flaked with elegant symmetry. The obsidian of which it was made appeared to be of a dark, translucent sort, with undertones of green. Therefore, Teg was distinctly startled when, as Xerak began chanting, the spearhead began to glow until the stone shone with a rich, flame-hued amber.

Xerak chanted a few more lines, then continued the ritual by thumping the butt of his spear staff onto the stone, an act that created no visual effects but initiated a reverberation Teg felt in her every bone and sinew.

Under Hawtoor's verbal direction, the six worked their way through elaborate steps and turns that reminded Teg of a contra dance she'd loved back in college. She was so busy concentrating on which foot to put where, when to raise her free hand to rest it on the shoulder of the person to her left (Grunwold), when to drop it, when to touch the looped bracelets with both hands, that she didn't register just when the character of the simple spun yarn began to change.

Fox fur became ruddy copper, deer hair polished bronze, lion fur brilliant gold, human hair eye-blinding silver. The beads remained grey stone, but now minute etchings, so fine that most must have been done with the point of a pin, were picked out in liquid crystal that coursed with rainbows.

At the conclusion of the ritual, Xerak ceremoniously handed one bracelet to each of the women.

"Loop it around your wrist," he said, "and I'll fasten it."

He did this by using the claw on his index finger rather as Peg had used her crochet hook, looping the ends together into a seamless whole. "The talisman should be loose enough that, in an emergency, you should be able to roll it over your hand and get it off that way. However, it should be tight enough that losing it by accident should be difficult."

Peg moved her hand back and forth, admiring the effect. "I'll need to be careful Tasha doesn't see this. She's a demon for unusual jewelry."

Meg, who rarely wore more jewelry than small earrings and a wrist watch, pushed the sleeve of her sweater down over the bracelet, as if embarrassed. However, no trace of any negative opinion she might have had about her new bit of gaudery could be found in her voice.

"If I had not been already convinced, that interesting working would have assured me of the veracity of magic, and that Xerak is a wizard."

"I am but my master's apprentice," Xerak muttered.

Meg ignored him. "Now, how do we go about returning home and coming back here?"

Peg looked worried for the first time. "Do we need to come and go through the bookstore? I don't think we ever explained. We were at a bookstore—those chairs belong to them."

Hawtoor considered. "This is a public place? I see . . . Will they be greatly inconvenienced by the loss of three chairs?"

"Somewhat," Meg said. "These are some of the nicer ones. Still, I think they would be more inconvenienced by us popping in out of nowhere."

"Then here is what I suggest," Hawtoor said. "Where do you live?"

They each started to reply, then Peg spoke over the jumble of addresses. "We don't live together. You do realize that? We're not related or anything. We're just friends. We meet once a month for a book club, then go out to lunch after. This time—probably because it's Valentine's Day—we were the only ones who showed up."

Teg wondered what the translation spell made of "Valentine's Day," but either it found a cognate or the locals were willing to accept a certain amount of garble.

Meg added. "Will the spell work to take us each back to our own homes, or will we need to pick one place to meet?"

"I think it should take you to your own homes," Xerak replied, glancing over at Hawtoor, who nodded agreement.

"Very good," Meg said. "Then I'll take the chairs. I can tip one of the retirement community's van drivers to drop them off at Pagearean Books when he does his afternoon run to the shopping center. Now"—she turned her attention to Peg and Teg—"how long do you think you'll need to make your necessary arrangements?"

"A day?" Teg hazarded. "Less if I can reach my cat sitter. I'd like time to shop for a few things as well."

She looked over at the three inquisitors. "How are we going to travel to this Library of the Sapphire Wind? What is the climate like? What sort of clothing should we pack? Will we be hiking?"

Vereez smiled, somewhat wickedly, Teg thought. "We will need to figure out how we're getting there. Until not long ago, we had no idea that would be our destination. As for clothing and climate . . . Why don't we acquire clothing for you? Honestly . . ." Her ears flickered, telegraphing that she was uncomfortable with what she was about to say. "Please don't be offended, but we're going to need to figure out how to disguise you. Your faces are very strange!"

And this, Teg thought, *from someone with a fox's head, fur on her hands, and tidy black claws instead of fingernails.*

"We're not offended," Peg said quickly. She clearly was about to start quizzing the inquisitors for more information about their world, but Teg, aware of the tip of Xerak's tail twitching with impatience, cut in.

"Is it likely," Teg asked, "that at some point we may need to hike?"

Grunwold nodded. "I have some ideas about how we may be able to travel fairly swiftly to the vicinity of the library ruins, but once we're there . . . I'm not sure how long it will take for us to find the door mentioned in your verse. That will certainly take some hiking around the ruins."

Teg turned to the others. "So, lightweight hiking boots, if you have them. Underwear—because Vereez might have trouble finding a type we'd like. Do you both have daypacks?"

Peg nodded. Meg shook her head.

"I have extras. I'll bring you one, Meg. And I have lightweight water bottles, too."

"Medication," Meg said. "I'm on a few prescriptions, and I don't think it's likely that we'll find a pharmacist who can blend what we need here."

"Extra glasses," Peg added. "Even older prescriptions would be better than none. And contact lenses could be a problem."

Meg smiled and touched the reading glasses on the lanyard around her neck. "I never thought I'd be glad I had cataract surgery! I only need reading glasses these days."

Teg had only recently started needing reading glasses. As with many people her age, the mild nearsightedness that had meant she needed driving glasses in her thirties and forties had been balanced by the farsightedness that came with age.

"We can phone each other once we're home," she

reminded them, "if we think of anything else, but the plan should be to pack light, focusing on things we don't think we'll be able to get here, and trust our young associates to cover the rest. So, shall we plan to meet here again in twenty-four hours? We can coordinate our departures so we get back here about the same time."

Hawtoor and Xerak had been moving things about, apparently preparatory to the ritual that would permit the humans to return home. Now Hawtoor straightened his shoulders and put on his lecturer mode again.

"One at a time, you'll step through this arch." He pointed, although it was obvious which he meant. "Xerak and I have told the spell to take you to your current home. When you wish to return to this shrine, choose a door in your home, grasp the handle or knob with the hand of the arm on which you are wearing your talisman. Make as if to open it in the reverse of the way you normally would— that is, if it is a door you would normally push in, pull. If you would normally open it toward you, push."

"Very neatly arranged," Meg said. "Which of you ladies wants to go first?"

"Wait!" Peg grabbed Meg by one shoulder, as if afraid the older woman would go racing through the gate. "Time! I was remembering old stories . . . Remember how in *The Lion, the Witch, and the Wardrobe* when Lucy first goes through to Narnia she comes back thinking everyone will have been worried about her, but instead they laugh at her because, although from her point of view she's been gone for hours, only a few minutes have passed at her home?"

Meg and Teg nodded.

Peg continued, panic making her voice rise. "Do we have any idea if time passes at the same rate here and there? What if it's like Rip van Winkle and we return to find hundreds of years have gone by? We might not even have homes!"

"Are either of you wearing a watch?" Meg asked.

Teg shook her head, but Peg pushed up her sleeve to show a neat electronic model. "A smart watch," she said, touching the button on the side. "A gift from young Henry. But it seems to be dead."

"My watch is an old mechanical model," Meg said, "an anniversary gift from my late husband. It was about eleven when we were summoned. A fair number of hours passed while we prepared the talismans. My watch now reads 6:00 p.m., which would be about right. However, that does not mean that time has passed at the same rate as at home."

"Off the topic, but Meg's smart watch frotzing does confirm something I'd been wondering," Teg put in. "Looks as if we shouldn't bother bringing computers or anything electronic. Even if we could figure out how to recharge the batteries, they probably wouldn't work here. We'd probably better pack mechanical timepieces, too."

Peg nodded to acknowledge Teg's point, but asked anxiously, "Hawtoor, Xerak, is there any way you can check how much time has passed at home?"

Hawtoor clacked his beak in agitation. "Not in advance," he said, "but if one of you go partway through the gate, once our worlds are connected, Xerak and I may be able to calculate something."

"Oh!" Peg said anxiously. "Let's get on with it. I don't know what I'll do if everyone back home is dead!"

The three inquisitors looked equal parts guilty and frightened. Clearly, they hadn't thought through the implications of pulling other people from their lives and worlds, only about their own needs.

"I'll go first," Teg said. "Hawtoor, when you have the information you need, should I step back or go ahead?"

"Back if you can," Hawtoor said. "That way you can learn the results of our calculations. I'll call for you to step back into Hettua Shrine when we have gathered enough information."

"Right," Teg said, shouldering her purse and her messenger bag, just in case. "Through the arch, right? Tell me when you're ready."

"Ready," said Xerak, touching one hand to the side of the arch as he braced his staff on the stone floor.

"Ready," said Hawtoor, also touching the arch. Instead of a staff, he held a classic hourglass in his free hand. "Go!"

Teg did. For a moment she saw her bedroom, Thought and Memory curled asleep on the bed. Then, almost instantly, she heard Hawtoor say, "Back, Teg-lial!"

She felt a pricking in her shoulder, and realized it was Xerak's clawed hand reaching to pull her back. Feeling as if she was pushing against a strong current, Teg stepped back into the shrine.

"Thanks, Xerak. The hard part was turning. Actually, going toward home was harder."

Hawtoor was studying the hourglass he held in his hand, comparing it to another that rested on the floor just outside the stone circle, and scribbling calculations on a slate. He spoke in stops and starts as he worked his equations.

"That is because you were doing the equivalent of moving against the current. Apparently, time moves more slowly where you come from, more rapidly here."

"Like Narnia, again?" Peg said. "I'm not sure I like that. Didn't the four children—Lucy, Peter, Edmund, and Susan—grow up in Narnia, rule for decades, then go home again?"

"Yes," Meg said. "That's how the story went. However, when Lucy and the rest of them returned home, they were children again. I would guess that somehow they were rooted in the place in which they originated."

"Rip van Winkle was rooted in his own timeline too," Peg said. "Except in his case, he thought he was gone just overnight, but apparently overnight there was decades at his home."

"There are a lot of stories like that," Teg said thoughtfully, "in many cultures. I suppose we'll just need to find out how the passage of time affects us in our own situation. That or quit and somehow—and I realize it's different for you two, because you have families and all— but I don't want to quit."

"Me either," Meg said quietly. "This is the most interesting thing I've done since I retired."

"I don't want to quit either," Peg said, then added, "As I was telling Roberto the other day, we do our best to plan for old age—take out insurance, eat right, get exercise— but there's no certainty that we won't get hit by a bus. I could pass up helping these young people, then find out that I have cancer and don't have long to live anyhow. Sometimes, you just need to take a risk."

"So, what's the time difference?" Grunwold asked

Hawtoor, who seemed to have concluded his calculations and was now hooting softly to himself as he studied the results. "I hope it isn't like this Rip van Winkle they keep mentioning. If a day there is a hundred years here, well, either they'd better do without their fresh underwear and spectacles or we might as well do without their 'help.'"

His inflection on the final word made clear that he still wasn't at all certain what help three old ladies might have to offer.

"There is a time difference, but it's not that extreme," Hawtoor replied. "Xerak, I'd like you to check my work, but I think that the difference is about one to seven. The time these ladies have spent here—even with the delay to make the yarn for the talisman—should have cost them about an hour in their own world."

"That will make our being gone much easier to cover for as well," Peg said. "If we go home for a day, that will give you young people a week to make arrangements for our journey, yes?"

Xerak looked up from the figures and nodded that he agreed with the old owl's calculations. He looked frustrated, doubtless kicking himself for insisting on rushing the summoning since they would be delayed anyhow. However, Grunwold looked pleased. Teg wondered if this would give him time to make the travel arrangements he'd mentioned.

Vereez said with a cockiness that Teg was coming to think was typical of her, "If you ladies will delay long enough for me to get your measurements, a week will definitely give time for us to get clothing for you."

When Hawtoor supplied a measuring tape, Teg

realized that, if she didn't think about it, the tape seemed to be marked in standard Arabic numerals. However, if she concentrated, she could almost make out the "real" numerals. Trying made the space behind her forehead ache, and she thought she'd settle for being grateful that the translation spell seemed to extend to at least some basic reading.

"Then we'll see you in a week, your time," Peg said when Vereez had finished. "Since my watch isn't working, I'll check the time as soon as I get home. Teg? Still want to go first? I'll follow. That will get me out of the way while they figure out how to get the chairs to Meg's."

Teg nodded. "Talk to you in just a bit."

Then she stepped forward, pushed, as if indeed moving against a current or a strong wind, and found herself in her bedroom once more.

Neither Thought (a longhaired grey-brown tabby) nor Memory (a pale golden shorthair) were very surprised to see her. After all, for them, Teg had been only gone for a couple of hours, and they'd had an early lunch.

Nonetheless, Teg paused long enough to hug each one tightly. Then she checked the clock on her dresser and noted the time: just past noon. On a normal day, they would be winding up the book club meeting, and deciding where to go for lunch. Methodically, Teg made a note of the time in one of the small blank notebooks she intended to pack, then checked the status of her wardrobe.

She'd just finished tossing a load of laundry into her machine so she'd have enough clean underwear when her phone rang.

"Teg? Meg. How large is the daypack you are going to loan me?"

"I've an assortment. How about I run over there and bring you a few choices? We can also check what style of straps fit you most comfortably."

"That would be kind. I would like to wait here for the people who are coming over to get the chairs."

"How did you manage to carry three chairs?"

"Hawtoor put them on a platform with wheels—sort of a primitive moving dolly—and I pushed them in front of me. I won't lie. It was tough going, but I managed. I'll bring the dolly back with me when we return. Anomalies would not be a good idea, just in case . . ."

. . . *we don't make it back,* Teg finished in her thoughts.

"Right. I can be to your place in about an hour. I need to get a couple cases of cat food. I also want to drop by a drugstore for some basics like extra-strength aspirin, muscle rub, and bandages." *And cigarettes.*

"Good. I've been wondering. Do you think we'll need to take our medication based on time there or time here?"

"I have no idea," Teg said. "Do you take anything that will kill you if you get the dosage wrong?"

"I don't think so. I've been blessed with good health."

"Me, too. My biggest problem is thyroid and I'm on a low dose of meds. I was thinking about splitting the difference. It'll make the pills last longer, too. I never thought I'd be grateful that my insurance insists I buy three months at one time!"

"That seems like a sound compromise. See you in about an hour."

Teg packed with her phone at her ear, making calls (Felicity the cat sitter *was* available and had no problems with Teg not knowing exactly when she'd be back) and taking calls when either Peg or Meg phoned to consult over some point or another. She dashed over to Meg's and was able to outfit her friend with a lightweight pack with numerous outside pockets. At the store, she added cough drops and a freshly stocked first-aid kit to her list. Then she hurried home.

Teg had a lot of practice getting ready for fieldwork, but it had been years since she had to think about packing only what she could carry. Nonetheless, old habits reasserted themselves. Despite Vereez's assurances that she would arrange for appropriate clothing, Teg had packed (and suggested the other two pack) lightweight rain ponchos; sturdy, flexible gloves; collapsible umbrellas; and a few other of those items that made modern life so much more comfortable.

At the appointed time, Teg shouldered on her sturdy daypack overstuffed with useful items and strategically placed crushable packs of cigarettes. Then, after hugging Thought and Memory, Teg grasped the knob on her closet door and pushed. She stepped into what felt like a rapid current, pushing her into her unlooked for but not unwelcome adventure.

When Teg arrived she was struck by the oddness of seeing Meg and Peg made unfamiliar by being wrenched out of the context in which she'd always known them. She'd never seen Meg wearing anything but a dress. Peg's attire varied more, but she was always stylish in a slightly bohemian fashion, as befitted someone who claimed to have performed at the Fillmore West in San Francisco.

Peg liked to say that when the band Jefferson Airplane had been looking for a new female vocalist when Signe Anderson was planning to retire, the choice had been between Janis Joplin, Gracie Slick, and herself, only she'd still been a minor. Teg often wondered if this was true.

Today the elegant librarian and the once-upon-a-hippy were gone.

Both women wore work pants. Meg's were cargo pants, somewhat dirt stained around the knees. Peg's were jeans: not the lightweight, useless sort usually sold to women, but made from the thicker fabric reserved for men. With her cargo pants, Meg wore a practical ensemble of tee shirt, pocketed work shirt, and jacket. Peg's tee shirt was topped with a heavy, hand-knitted cardigan. Both wore lightweight hiking boots, again showing evidence of prior use.

Meg had swept her silvery-white hair back into a neat ponytail, clipping the trailing wisps near her face into place with flat barrettes. She wore just a little makeup.

Given the lightning-strike sharpness of the streaks, Peg had probably taken some of her twenty-four hours to go to the beauty parlor and have her "do" freshened. Peg also wore makeup, but more subdued than what she wore to book club.

Like Meg, Teg wore cargo pants, hers reinforced at the knees with heavy patches. She also had gone for layers on top—long-sleeved tee shirt, canvas shirt, Army-surplus leather jacket. Her belt was hung with numerous sheaths, including ones for a trowel, knife, compass, tape measure, and cell phone. The phone would definitely be outside its service area, so she'd left it, but she'd figured the case might come in handy.

Unlike the others, Teg didn't bother with makeup, having grown accustomed to not wearing any except for social occasions. She wished she'd thought to freshen up her hair dye, though. For the first time, Teg realized that the inquisitors and Hawtoor had probably taken purple to lavender for her natural coloration. Well, the shades did go with her dark brown eyes.

The inquisitors and Hawtoor were looking at the three humans with astonishment.

"You are very altered," said Vereez at last. "Did you not believe me when I said I would provide attire for you?"

"We did," Meg said speaking for them all since they'd discussed this point at length on the phone, "but from what you said, this Library of the Sapphire Wind is in an isolated area—and a dangerous one. We thought it would be wise to have at least one complete change of our own attire suited for that environment."

Vereez clapped her hands in delight. "Wise! Very wise! Now, if you will accept the clothing I have selected for you, we will explain to you the plans we have made this past week while you were away. I have set your new attire in the office you used once before—I even cleared up some of the mess so you can move about despite the clutter."

Peg looked as relieved as Teg felt. She'd done her share of locker-room changing. On field projects where water had been limited, she'd even shared mixed-sex showers, but as she had grown older, she'd realized that the nudity taboos ingrained into American culture had not passed her by. Changing in front of strangers would have made her very shy. It was going to be hard enough in front of Peg and Meg.

Maybe because I know I'm not young and—if not "pretty"—my body shows the passage of time. These days I'm fit enough, but still . . . I'm not a strong, young animal anymore. I guess I feel more vulnerable.

Vereez led them into the office. "That stack is for Meg, this for Teg, this for Peg. Don't open the boxes quite yet. The contents will take some explaining."

The fox woman was obviously very pleased with herself. Glancing at the three heaps, Teg thought she had every reason to be so. Her shopping expedition had doubtless involved a hike into civilization, then a visit to a tailor. Or did this world have off-the-rack clothes?

"If you need any help figuring out how something fits on," Vereez said, pulling the door shut behind her, "just call."

Vereez had hardly completed her polite withdrawal when Grunwold's voice came from the other room, slightly muffled by the door but perfectly understandable.

"After a great deal of discussion, we've agreed that our best option would be to use a conveyance belonging to my parents."

The word "conveyance" sounded awkward, as if the translation spell had searched among numerous options and come up with the least incorrect.

"It will carry all of us and, even better, can travel well on both air and water. It is less suitable for land, but there is a conversion package. Even better, it has lockers above deck and several roomy cabins below, so we will be able to travel with ample supplies and in some comfort."

By unspoken consent, the three women had taken their assigned pile of clothing, turned to offer each other a modicum of privacy, and were now stripping off their field gear. From the corner of her eye, Teg could see Peg pause in the act of pulling off her tee shirt.

"That sounds ideal, Grunwold. Why do I hear a 'but' in your voice?"

Grunwold laughed. "Because if we are to use *Slicewind*, we will need to steal it."

"What!" The exclamation was general and, if Teg heard correctly, included Hawtoor.

"Didn't I tell you? My father has expressly forbidden anyone to attempt to find a cure for him. He says he doesn't want anyone at risk."

"I don't suppose you could make an excuse for borrowing this 'conveyance'?" Peg asked.

"Would you believe any of your children if they said they needed to borrow a craft such as I have described for any routine purpose?"

"No. You're right. I wouldn't." *Sotto voce*, Peg addressed the other humans. "I can't believe it. We're going to start this crazy quest, or whatever you want to call it, by stealing the family sports yacht."

"It is a wise solution," Meg said, her voice pitched to carry. "I am not certain I could walk more than a few miles at a time, and it has been many years since I have ridden."

Teg—remembering deer ears, lion ears, fox ears—wondered if raising their voices was necessary. Quite likely the three inquisitors—and maybe even Hawtoor, although she had no idea how well owls heard—had caught Peg's comment.

"Riding animals don't travel all that much faster than do people afoot," Vereez explained, "at least over a long distance, although they do carry a great deal more weight. We did discuss the possibility of taking boats for much of the distance, then switching to mounts, but then we would need to worry about food for our mounts. We cannot count on good grazing in the area into which we are going. Foolhardy as it may seem at first glance, stealing *Slicewind* is the most practical way to travel."

Grunwold took up the briefing, explaining more about what they should expect. Although Hettua Shrine was isolated, there was an arrangement with a village downriver that would ferry pilgrims to the shrine, then return for them. The plan was for them to leave the shrine that very day. The inquisitors had already booked passage on a larger boat that would take them to where they could travel to Grunwold's family estate.

Even as she listened, the anthropologist part of Teg was busy trying to figure something out about the culture from the clothing she was now putting on. The bottom part of the costume—she couldn't get away from the feeling she was getting dressed for an elaborate Halloween party— consisted of trousers that were loose without being baggy. She recalled that all four of the natives they'd met had worn trousers. No skirts or robes, although both Hawtoor's and Xerak's over tunics had been ankle length.

The trousers had a neat slit at the back, probably for a tail, but Teg couldn't get away from the feeling that she had a tear in the seat of her pants. The trousers tightened at the waist with a drawstring, eliminating the need for a belt.

Next came a shirt, long sleeved and slightly blousy in the cut of the sleeves. Not quite pirate or Regency dandy, but something like. Over this came a sleeveless tunic that fell to midthigh. This also possessed a tail slit.

There was a belt to go over the tunic, with a neat leather purse that slid onto the belt. Teg thought she could probably get some of her tool sheaths onto the belt as well. The final touch was a garment that was too loose to be called a jacket, but it had sleeves, so it wasn't really a cloak or cape. It did have a hood. Teg guessed that she'd be wearing that to help hide her physical oddities.

The boots were beautiful works of tooled leather, coming to just below the knees, and lacing up. Teg had noticed that the three inquisitors all wore their trousers tucked into their boots, so she followed suit, noticing that the trousers were tailored to fold in without causing undue bulk.

The cut of the clothing was a sufficient hybrid of what Teg thought of as Asian and European elements to be their own style. Nonetheless, there were only so many practical ways to cover a bipedal frame, and many of those choices had more to do with how easy it was to manufacture large pieces of fabric. If this took hard labor, you didn't cut it into little bits. Instead you wore drapes, robes, tartans, and the like. Many of the flourishes of costume that made for fashion had nothing to do with need, were instead the result of custom, social role, and, frankly, the desire to show off.

So, Teg thought, looking at her still unopened box and

wondering what it held. *We have a culture in which textile production has reached at least that of the large loom. There must be a good trade network or Vereez wouldn't have been able to lay her hands on fabrics as nice as these in what the translation spell is calling a "village."*

She slipped on her jacket and turned to inspect her friends. Teg had noticed without thinking much about it that the colors of her own costume were dominated by darker blues and purples. Now she saw that Peg's ranged through the darker greens—emerald to forest—accented with golden yellows. Meg's costume was built around charcoal and lighter grey, touched here and there with a cobalt blue that drew out the color of her eyes.

"Wow," Teg said. "If Vereez ever wants a job as a fashion consultant, I know where we could get her one. You ladies look great!"

"You don't look too bad yourself," Peg said, patting her hair into place and trying to get a look at herself with the mirror on her compact. "I wish I had a full-length mirror."

"Are you ready to see what's in your boxes?" Vereez called from the other side of the door. She peeked around the edge, and then, seeing Meg's nod, came in. She frisked between them, straightening a hem here, raising a collar there, but mostly looking very pleased.

"Go ahead," Vereez prompted. "Open the boxes and I'll explain."

Teg did and found herself confronted with a lynx-faced mask, a set of gloves, and a stubby tail that coordinated with the mask. Meg's mask was of a black-and-white badger, Peg's of a pronghorn antelope.

"Sometimes the people who come to the shrine don't

want to be recognized," Vereez explained. "After all, not everyone who comes here is a holdback looking for guidance. After you left, Hawtoor recalled that there was a chest with masks and prosthetic tails in one of his storerooms."

"You'll find the masks are fairly comfortable," Xerak said. "Given how flat your faces are, you can even slide food under them to eat, although drinking will work better if you use a straw. We have some packed."

"We were lucky to find some sets without long tails," Grunwold added. "We didn't think you could handle long tails at all naturally."

"Won't anyone notice that we did not arrive in these disguises?" Meg asked, lifting the badger mask to her face and peering out through the eyeholes. Framed by the dark stripes, her pale blue eyes were startling in contrast.

Hawtoor shook his head. "If they do, they will not ask. They will assume that I advised you to change your appearance. I do, sometimes. That is how I acquired these."

"This certainly will work for departing the shrine," Peg agreed. "But what about after we arrive at the village?"

"We thought of that," Grunwold said, sounding put-upon. "We came up with a bunch of possible options for why you'd stay masked, then settled on telling anyone who asks that you had suffered greatly in a fire. We are your assistants as you go to seek healing."

"That's clever," Peg said. "Burn injuries are ugly. Very few are likely to even try to peek."

"Even those who are rude enough to be curious," Vereez said, "won't have much of an opportunity. When we arranged for the ferry, we also reserved a suite at a dockside inn. You will stay in your rooms until it is time for us to catch the boat the next day."

If she noticed the three humans staring at her in utter astonishment, Vereez did a very good job of pretending not to notice.

{CHAPTER THREE}

"Well," Peg said when some hours later the humans were alone in the promised suite at the inn, "at least we weren't sent to our rooms without dinner."

"Just sent to our rooms," Teg grumbled. She positioned herself where she could look out the window without being seen. "Here we are in another world and we might as well be looking at illustrations."

"You're just peeved because you can't have a cigarette," Meg retorted, not at all incorrectly.

Teg had already been asked not to draw attention to herself. Apparently, the animal-headed people did not smoke cigarettes, and objected to the odor—reek, was the word Vereez had used—of Teg's. No one had commented when Teg had lit up at Hawtoor's because they hadn't realized that this was an optional behavior on her part. But when Meg and Peg's distaste had made it evident that it was . . .

"I'm not quitting cold turkey," Teg warned. "I've done

that once, when something got into my supplies during a field project. I didn't like it at all—and neither would you."

"So I can believe," Peg said mildly. She moved to where she could join Teg viewing the people moving up and down the street. "When I was home, I thought about trying to explain this place to my kids—to anybody, really. I realized they'd think of some Disney movie, maybe that *Robin Hood*, where Errol Flynn is played by a fox. The thing is, they wouldn't get it . . . These people aren't cute at all. They're . . ."

She trailed off, at a loss for words.

Teg looked down at the street. The inn faced the river, and the street below was busy with people going back and forth, carrying bales and bundles, wheeling carts. Not everyone was a porter, of course. There was a riverside market, even people selling directly off their boats, so there were shoppers, gawkers, idlers.

She narrowed her focus to a young couple walking along holding hands. One had a leopard's head, the other a koala's. She couldn't tell which one was male and which female—maybe they were the same sex. They were not like bipedal renderings of their animal counterparts, more like artistic renderings of Egyptian or Assyrian deities—human except where they were not. She'd already observed that the inquisitors' hands were somewhat of a hybrid, with light fur coming down the backs and nails more like claws.

Then again, how different was that from humans? She'd dated a man who had so much body hair that if he wore a close-fitting shirt, it hardly touched his skin. You could gently pat his shirt and feel the springy hair beneath. Still, she'd like to know more. Vereez clearly had breasts along the human model, so apparently she didn't have litters . . .

"There's so much we don't know," she muttered.

"And you're not likely to learn the answers by going down there and cross-examining the townsfolk," Meg said tartly. "More likely, you'd start a riot. Make a list, and when we're on this sports yacht Grunwold intends to steal, you can start asking questions."

"I did bring a notebook or three or four," Teg admitted. "And pencils and a sharpener." She didn't budge from the window, though. The view was just too fascinating. She'd lost count of the variations of people she'd seen. Were the types cross fertile or was the koala/leopard couple down there setting themselves up for a local variant on Romeo and Juliet? Were certain jobs more commonly taken by certain racial types? The ferryman had had the head of some sort of otter, but the person working the oars of a fishing skiff down there looked like a wild boar, complete with curling tusks. How about diet? A doe was busy negotiating for fish at one stand, but maybe she was buying for a friend . . .

It was almost enough to make Teg forget how much she wanted a smoke. Almost.

Meg had obviously been considering Peg's comment. "They're not cute—or no more than average. Vereez is actually quite cute, if you like the mischievous sort. Grunwold may actually grow to be quite a majestic man— or male—whatever the correct term would be. I fear Xerak may remain scruffy. No, they're not Disney creatures—or Redwall or Animorphs or anything like that.

They're people, and we'll be wise to remember that. I would like to know how the Library of the Sapphire Wind came to be destroyed."

"You have a good point," Teg said. "Did you notice that the kids talk about it as past history, but not Hawtoor? That would argue that it was destroyed before they were born but within his lifespan so, as history goes, recent."

"Like World War II," Peg said, "when I was a girl."

"Or even for me," Meg said with a smile.

"Or the Korean War for me," Teg said. "Something I knew more from watching *M*A*S*H* on TV than because I knew anyone who'd been involved."

Meg tapped a neatly manicured index finger against her chin. "I think Xerak said it happened about twenty-five years ago. So that gives us an idea as to an upper limit for their ages."

"And," Peg said cheerfully, "we now know that we were right that Grunwold, at least, was only giving us part of the story about his holdback. This is going to be fun!"

A few of the mentors' questions were answered once they were on the riverboat—a multimasted sailing vessel that, at least for now, wasn't using the sails because the current from the various mountain streams was strong enough to carry the vessel at a comfortable clip.

The captain had a wolf's head, while his first mate, who was also his wife, was a jackrabbit, with long, dark-tipped ears.

After a few meals, Teg decided that whatever their heads looked like on the outside, the mouths must have some adaptations, because everyone seemed omnivorous.

Watching Grunwold eat meat was startling, while Vereez turned out to have a liking for melon. Long-bladed knives were the usual tools, and when a food didn't fit the shape of a mouth, it was cut or trimmed so automatically that Teg figured the locals must learn the skill along with that of using the fat-bowled spoon and three-tined fork that were ubiquitous tableware.

She watched to see if anyone ate what she would have thought of as "themselves"—like Grunwold eating venison, or the rabbit *hasenpfeffer*, but didn't have the chance. Shipboard meals were largely built around fish, domestic poultry (or more usually eggs), and occasionally some sort of waterfowl. Clearly the frugal owners did not believe in buying what they could raise or forage for themselves.

The voyage took several days but, since the three humans were kept more or less cloistered, they didn't learn much more about the world around them. Peg tried to get the three inquisitors to answer some of her many question, but they refused on the grounds that if any of the crew or passengers overheard, there could be trouble.

Eventually, Meg and Peg pretty much kept to the cabin, playing an endless tournament of gin rummy. Since the area was relatively unpopulated and magic-free, each used her bracelet to slip off home and make a few phone calls or send some e-mails, thus alleviating any anxiety that would be felt by family members and close friends when they didn't touch base.

For her part, Teg didn't feel any need to check in. Her family and friends were used to her "disappearing," although never as literally as she had this time. Her one problem was getting a chance to smoke. Meg and Peg refused to let her smoke in the cabin, and she really didn't blame them. However, she insisted that if they wouldn't let her smoke in there, then she needed to get out and indulge her vice.

"Tell them it's for my health," she suggested to the horrified inquisitors. "Or a religious ritual. Or a penance for past crimes. Tell them whatever you want, but you'd better tell them something because I'm not quitting cold turkey."

Oddly enough, Xerak was her champion on this matter, saying that if she sat upwind the smoke would be carried away. "I'll tell them you belong to an obscure religious sect. That should do it."

However, in order to cause as little disruption as possible, Teg tried to smoke mostly after dark. It was peaceful to sit in some secluded corner, looking up at the stars or at a moon that looked pretty much like the familiar one at home.

"Just one moon here?" she asked Xerak, who often joined her, although whether to make sure she wouldn't start asking questions of the crew, or because she didn't seem to mind his drinking, she wasn't sure.

"Just one," he said. "More where you live?"

"Nope, just one. I was just thinking about John Carter on Barsoom..."

She cut herself off, suspecting the translation spell wouldn't manage an explanation of John Carter and Barsoom. Anyhow, that was a lousy example, because Barsoom was really Mars, so the two moons were science, not fiction.

"The stars seem different though," she continued. "I'm no astronomer, but I can usually find the Big Dipper and Orion without even trying. Constellations, you know."

"I know constellations," Xerak agreed. "Not those. Want me to show you a couple? To the right and a little higher, that's the Bow. Over there is the Reaper's Basket. You can see it best during the summer, like now."

So it's summer, Teg thought. *And so they have seasons here. Live and learn. Live and learn.*

Teg was nursing her second-to-last cigarette of the day (she'd been carefully rationing them), and so was the first to see the high towers that were their first indication they were getting close to their destination. Xerak was hovering nearby, as he often did, possibly to make sure she didn't say anything unwise. There was a chance he had an ulterior motive, since there was often something furtive about his manner. Glad to have an ally, Teg didn't try to ferret it out. Time enough for that later—and only if absolutely necessary.

"Is that a city?" she asked.

Xerak coughed a leonine chuckle. "Not really. KonSef Landing is just a port town. Those are grain silos. Impressive, aren't they?"

"Astonishing!" Teg agreed. "They're beautiful, too. Where I come from, such things are constructed with practicality in mind, nothing more."

"They're boasts," Xerak explained, "as well as landmarks. From what Grunwold said, KonSef Landing used to only be busy after the harvest. Then his parents started buying up land and farming on a huge scale. Now they usually have surplus, and trade goes on pretty much year 'round."

Anthropologist Teg wanted to ask questions about types of crops, processing, and drying procedures. A more important question came out instead.

"So that's where Grunwold's family estate is?"

Xerak nodded. "We've been discussing plans for days— arguing. Grunwold wanted to avoid his family entirely, but that would make—uh—borrowing *Slicewind* a lot harder. Instead, he's going to go back, as if he's just reporting about his pilgrimage. That will let him check out the lay of the land, make sure where *Slicewind* is berthed. He'll send a message, so we'll know when to be ready."

Teg nodded. "Do you and Vereez live near here?"

Xerak coughed another laugh. "Not even close. We live in Rivers Meet, a large city way downriver from here."

"Have you known each other long?"

"All three of us have known each other since we were children. Our parents were good friends and we were all born in Rivers Meet. Then, when Grunwold was little, his parents bought KonSef Estate and moved, so after that, we three only saw each other a couple times a year." He laughed. "But those were intense times. We're all only kids, so we sort of adopted each other."

Teg nodded. "I had cousins like that. We didn't see each other often but, when we did, we just picked up where we had been before. How about lately?"

"The last several years, we've been finishing up our educations, so we hadn't seen each other that often. I was living with my master well outside of Rivers Meet, and didn't leave often. I think Vereez went abroad for a year or so. Grunwold was stuck out here. The KonSef estate is massive and deals with more than raising grain. There's a brick-making facility, for example, and a sideline in raising vikrew, especially the heavy draft breeds."

The word "vikrew" meant nothing to Teg, but she didn't want to get sidetracked.

"So when you met up on the boat on the way to the shrine, that wasn't by accident?"

"Not at all. Each of us are holdbacks. Eventually, we decided to make pilgrimage to the shrine. Me and Vereez decided first, then we got in touch with Grunwold."

Teg wanted to ask more. She could guess what a holdback was—each of these young people had admitted that there was something that was keeping him or her from moving along with their lives. But didn't the kids' parents worry about sending Vereez off with two young men? Xerak treated her like a sister—alternately affectionate and argumentative—but Teg would have sworn that Grunwold was nursing a serious crush. On the other hand, Vereez didn't seem to return Grunwold's affection, and he didn't seem like a rapist, so maybe she was safe after all.

Maybe even safer than if she was travelling with a chaperone, Teg thought, *since Grunwold hanging about is going to be a serious obstacle to any rivals.*

She stubbed out her cigarette, carefully putting the butt in her pocket. She didn't want to leave any weird artifacts for future archeologists.

"Aren't you going to be expected to go up to the estate? Won't it be considered rude if you stay away?"

Xerak shook his head. "Not with Konnel-toh so sick."

Interesting, Teg thought. *This language seems to use suffixes rather than prefixes. We've heard "-va" for wizards, and "-lial" seems to be a general term of respect. I wonder if "-toh" indicates respect and affection, rather as in English a child might call an adult "uncle" or "aunt," even if there is no blood relationship. In English there's always the confusion as to whether or not blood relationship is included. Very sensible, having a term more intimate than "mister" or "sir," but without familial baggage.*

Xerak went on, "He'd feel required to at least meet with us. By staying away, we're actually showing respect."

Since this was quite literally *his* home port, Grunwold left the barge separately from the rest of them. Otherwise it would have been impossible for the three humans not to attract attention.

"Grunwold said to look for a message from him this evening," Vereez said when they were ensconced at another inn, this one set back from the bustle of the waterfront, run by an older couple who seemed interested in little other than proof that the group could pay for their suite. "Personally, I think he's being optimistic. Still, don't unpack too much. We may need to leave quickly. Xerak, you and I should go out and shop for some supplies."

Xerak nodded, then turned to Meg, Peg, and Teg. "You three, please don't go anywhere. Don't talk to anyone. We're going to tell the innkeepers that you seem to be coming down with a cold, and might be contagious, so they shouldn't bother you. However, if someone comes to the door, remember to put on your masks."

"Does anyone else feel like a prisoner?" Peg asked

when the pair had departed. She pulled out her knitting and set to work, this time on a sock.

"A little," Teg admitted.

Meg shook her head. "Not really. They have good reasons for their requests—and they expect us to understand. When you think about it, that's really an honor."

"Mm," Peg said noncommittally, although it was possible she was concentrating on something complicated she was doing around the toe.

Meg pulled a notebook and pen out of her bag. "I've noticed that the translation spell has a tendency to break down when encountering specific items."

Teg, who had been staring out the window, idly watching the people on the street, and trying to figure out if she could sneak a smoke, nodded. "Me, too. It's fine if someone says 'Do you want a piece of fruit?' But if they offer a specific type of fruit, then the translation gives what I've been assuming is the name for the fruit."

"That is my conclusion as well," Meg said. "I thought we should start making a lexicon of these words."

"Good idea," Teg agreed. "We can always point, but I'd like to be able to use the right word. There's another advantage, too. We may see relationships between words that will tell us something about the culture."

Peg tilted her head to one side. "Okay. I admit, I managed to graduate college, but I mostly majored in student protests and partying. How would the names of fruits tell us anything about the culture?"

"Pluot," Teg replied promptly. "That's a hybrid of a plum and an apricot. Not only does that tell you that apricots and plums—for all they look really different—are closely related, it tells you that the culture that created them is advanced enough to breed stable hybrids."

"Groovy," Peg said. "I'm all for anything that will help me rap, like on the level, with the locals."

"Hippy chick," Teg said with exasperated affection. "Meg, there's something else we should note. They seem to use suffixes instead of prefixes for honorifics. I caught a couple. 'Va' seems to be for wizards, from what Xerak said about not feeling he could use the '-va.' I've heard '-lial' used, too. And Xerak referred to Grunwold's father as Konnel-toh."

Meg started scribbling. "I think there are others. I'm sure the riverboat captain addressed Grunwold as 'Grunwold-kir,' but I couldn't get the context."

"I asked about those forms of address," Peg contributed unexpectedly. "'Lial' is a polite respect term, sort of like we use 'Mr.' or 'Mrs.' 'Kir' is more like 'my lady' or 'my lord.' As best as I could tell, neither has a gendered form or one that indicates marital status. Xerak seemed completely confused when I asked, so I dropped the subject."

"Interesting," Teg said. "That seems like a confirmation of Meg's theory that when the translation spell can't find an equivalent, it doesn't translate."

"Perhaps we should stick to nouns for now," Meg suggested. "Although I will have questions for our inquisitors about forms of address. I have no desire to cause difficulties by being impolite or incorrect."

Teg nodded. "All right, Meg. That fruit that tastes like a peach with cherry overtones is an 'umm-umm.'"

Peg chuckled. "Umm-umm good. Wasn't there a commercial for something that used that as a slogan?"

"Campbell's soup," Meg said absently as she wrote, then tapped her pencil eraser on the page. "I'm trying to decide how to organize these . . . Should I put food items on one page or perhaps plants on one, animals on another? Place names on another? I can't believe how much I miss my laptop!"

Peg grinned. "Start with a general list, then divide it up when you have a better idea of categories. I mean, sometimes we use different words for the animal and the food item—pig and pork, or cow and beef."

"I agree," Teg said. "Create a column on the far left where you can draw icons for categories. A little apple for fruit or a stick-figure animal for an animal."

While the linguistics exercise didn't exactly remove Teg's desire for a smoke, it was a good distraction. She started pacing back and forth, making suggestions, arguing about spelling conventions. She was so absorbed that when a tap sounded against the window, she jumped and gave a soft shriek.

"Meg, Peg, there's a sort of mini pterodactylish thing out on the windowsill. It looks as if it expects us to let it in."

"Don't," said Meg, just as Peg said, "Go ahead."

Teg considered. The window had numerous small panes and swung like a door, rather than pushing up and down. The pterodactyl creature was teetering on the windowsill, apparently having difficulty keeping its balance. When it tapped again, Teg saw it was holding something in its beak, and reached to open the window.

"Teg!" Meg exclaimed. "Stop!"

Teg kept swinging the window. "It's holding a tube of some sort in its beak. I think it's a carrier pterodactyl."

She tentatively put out her hand but, rather than dropping the tube into it, the creature hopped onto her forearm and clung there with talons that poked right through her shirt sleeve. Teg stifled another shriek. At the sound, the creature swiveled its neck and inspected her carefully from cherry-red eyes with a sun-yellow iris. This gave them all a chance to study it as well.

The creature was about the size of a raven, with a long neck balanced by an equally long tail. Its head was what made it look so much like a pterodactyl, shaped with a long, toothy jaw that was balanced by a long, tapering crest. Its wings were leathery, rather than feathered, adding to the resemblance to the winged dinosaurs, but none of the pterodactyls in the illustrations Teg had seen had been bright lime green on their upper surface, eye-searing orange beneath.

Turning to tuck the tube under its wing, the creature spoke, "You've got to be the odd ones."

Somehow, even with the translation spell in place, Teg gathered that the bird spoke with an accent, so that the words were more like "Yuv got t'b th' od-wonz." But equally clear was that the bird had *spoken*—not echoed a phrase learned by rote.

Teg had thought she was getting jaded. She'd noted the innkeeper's lack of interest in his masked guests before she had registered that he had the head of a black bear. Apparently, jaded only went so far, and a talking miniature pterodactyl set her process of acculturation back several days.

"You came from Grunwold," Teg guessed, hearing the stag's casual rudeness in the wording. "Do you have a message for us?"

"If th' real p'pl aren't here," the bird agreed. "Yep. Here."

It retrieved the tube from under its wing, then poked its neck out toward her, head slightly cocked as if doubting her intelligence. Teg took the capsule, then handed it to Peg, since the bird didn't seem inclined to get off her arm, and Meg was unconsciously backing away, her journal held like a shield in front of her.

Peg pulled apart the halves of the tube to reveal a tightly rolled spill of paper. "I wonder if we can read the local language?"

The answer proved to be yes, although Peg tutted over the quality of Grunwold's handwriting as she puzzled her way through.

"Grunwold writes: 'Tonight. Definitely. Otherwise I may be stuck. Be at the boathouse at midnight with all our gear. I'm going to need at least Xerak's help.'"

"I hope the others know precisely which boathouse Grunwold means," Peg said, coiling the paper and returning it to the tube. She looked at the miniature pterodactylish creature. "Are you expected to bring a reply?"

"Nope. Grun's nested w' his kin, serious talk."

"So you're staying here?"

"Sure. Why not?"

Teg motioned toward a nearby chair. "Would you mind sitting there?"

"Don't 'cha like me?"

"I like you just fine, but I want to close the window. I can't do that if you're on my arm."

"Okay. Gotcha."

Teg moved over and the miniature pterodactyl hopped off onto the seat of the chair. She wondered if it would poop as randomly as birds did in her world, and decided that, at this moment, she didn't care.

"I wonder what . . ." Peg was beginning when Xerak and Vereez returned, burdened with packages and parcels, most tied up in coarse burlap, rather than being bagged.

Teg hurried over to help them. Xerak, in particular, looked as if he was about to drop something any moment.

"We have a . . ." she paused. What did one call a talking pterodactyl? Were they considered people here or tools? She decided to opt on the side of "person" until informed otherwise. ". . . visitor. Over there."

"Heru!" Vereez rushed over and gracefully knelt in front of the chair, where she reached up to scratch the creature along its long neck. "Did you bring a message from Grunwold?"

"Gave it t' her," Heru replied, honking through its crest, and pointing toward Teg with its jaw. "'Tas a her, right? Has chest bumps."

"They are all hers," Vereez confirmed. "Have they introduced themselves?"

Meg interjected tartly, "Heru—if that is this person's name—only just arrived."

"'Tas right," Heru said. "They offered me a chair."

"Then let me do the honors," Xerak said. "Peg, Meg, and Teg, this is Heru. Grunwold raised him from the egg, and they've been together since. Heru, the lightest-colored female is Meg, the middle one is Peg, and the darkest one is Teg. They're our mentors, sent to us from a distant land when we made our inquiry at Hettua Shrine."

"Pleased t' meet 'cha," Heru said, bobbing up and down and whistling through its crest.

While Xerak had been handling introductions, Vereez had been reading Grunwold's note. Now she frowned, and passed the note to Xerak.

"The weather is going to be bad tonight. I wonder why Grunwold's worried about being stuck? I hope Konnel-toh isn't worse."

"Can't be that." Xerak lashed his tail. "Grunwold wouldn't leave if his dad was dying. He says he's going to need at least me, which I suspect means that there are wards to be taken down before we can get to the vessel he told us about. I'd better get some rest. Speculating won't get us anywhere."

Both Xerak and Vereez had the sort of ability to see in the dark that Teg associated with their "animal" selves. Since showing a light didn't seem wise, once they had left the town and entered the outlying lands of KonSef Estate, the inquisitors guided the humans along a twisting trail through an orchard that bordered a field of something that rustled like corn in the rising wind.

Heru flew overhead, flapping his wings very much as a bird would have done, although perhaps tending to glide more often. The xuxu—which turned out to be what Heru's species was called—were apparently very dexterous, and the neatly planted orchard gave Heru no difficulty.

By the time the boathouse was a tall, dark shape bulking at the edge of the field, the storm Vereez had predicted was holding off, but—from how they kept getting hit by periodic gusts, often damp with rain—it wasn't going to do so for much longer. As they stepped from cover, Xerak released Teg's hand. At the same moment, a spikey shadow separated itself from the warehouse, turning into Grunwold, overburdened with bundles and bags.

"I thought you guys would never get here," he grumbled. "Here's the deal. Security's been upped on the boathouse since I was last home. If Xerak can't defuse the wards, we're going to need to figure out some other way to travel—and we've gotta hoof it out of here tonight, no matter what. I'm due to get shipped to supervise the brickworks come morning."

"Brickworks? Then I'd better deal with the wards," Xerak said with deceptive mildness. "Show me?"

"I've gotten a side door open," Grunwold said, "and a few windows. It's the main door, the one we'll need to sail out through, that's going to be a problem."

Vereez looked up anxiously. "Hurry! The storm's nearly on us!"

She turned to the humans. "Can you mentors get the luggage belowdecks? I'm not the wizard Xerak is, but I know a few tricks. I'd like to go help him."

"Will do," Peg said, moving toward the shape that bulked in the boathouse. "Grunwold, dump your gear. We'll get it aboard."

When they got closer to *Slicewind*, Meg gasped softly. "It seems our 'conveyance' looks very much like a sailing ship. But didn't Grunwold say it could fly?"

"I guess we'd better hope it can fly," Teg replied, half-running to the steps shoved against one side of the ship, "since there isn't any water closer than the river, and the hull's not resting on a trailer."

Teg's knowledge of sailing ships ended with some small-craft sailing when she'd been in her twenties, but she knew enough to remember that sailing ships were first classified by the number of masts. *Slicewind* had a single mast, as well as various lines she thought indicated that extra sails could be set. Once Teg had climbed aboard, she could see there was a wheel rather than a tiller. The wheel was on a slightly raised platform, protected by a partially open wheelhouse, but otherwise there were no cabins above deck. There was a single hatch, roughly near the middle of the deck.

"We'll learn if *Slicewind* can fly soon enough," Peg said. "Let's just make sure we're on board when it leaves. Teg, let Meg and me hand things up to you. That'll be faster than all of us crowding that stair."

Someone—Grunwold, presumably—had activated low-level lights along the waist-high rail that ran around the upper deck, providing enough illumination to make it possible for the mentors to get the luggage aboard without stumbling. The hatch was also lit, revealing a sturdy ladder going belowdecks.

Once they had the luggage aboard, Teg scrabbled down to the lower deck, then reached up to grab the luggage the other two handed down. Since she had no idea what should go where, but figured that leaving stuff scattered around was a bad idea, she shoved everything through the nearest open doorways.

As the mentors relayed bags and bundles, what they overheard of the three inquisitors' conversation was far from comforting.

Grunwold: "Out of the way, idiot!"

This was followed by a loud cracking noise, like a short string of firecrackers going off.

Xerak: "Sparks! Scorched my mane."

There was a loud rumble, presumably as the heavy boathouse doors were slid back, then a brilliant flash of crimson light.

Grunwold: "Well, that probably set off an alarm or three. Good thing the boathouse is on the fringes of . . ."

"I look if trouble, Grun." That last was definitely Heru.

Vereez: "Hurry. Storm's coming!"

Teg was still below when there was a thunder of booted feet, then a sound that she identified as the moveable staircase they'd been using to get up over the side being hauled up. A few moments later, she was flung against a wall as *Slicewind* surged into motion. She groped her way up the ladder to the main deck. Once she was there, she froze in place, trying to figure out what was going on. Most of the action seemed to be at the ship's stern, but Grunwold and Peg were in the wheelhouse, about five feet back from the hatch.

Unsurprisingly, given that one of the participants was Grunwold, the pair were arguing.

"Shut up!" Peg snapped. "Look, does this thing sail like a normal boat? I mean, except for the in-the-air part?"

"More or less," Grunwold replied. His eyes were wild, the whites showing all around the dark brown.

"Fine. I know something about handling single-masted

sailing craft. My stepson Wilson . . . Never mind that for now. I'll take the helm. Teg, get over here. If I remember when we were reading Patrick O'Brian, you said you had done a little sailing."

"A long time ago, but yes."

"Stand by to cast us off."

"Aye, aye!"

Grunwold gaped as Peg shoved between him and the wheel. "Are you serious?"

"As death," Peg said. "I don't have a spear or a sword or whatever you're going to use to get rid of your family's watch horrors. Presumably, you know what to do."

Grunwold nodded crisply. "All right. You have a point. *Slicewind* sails more or less like a watercraft with one addition. See that lever on your right? Pull back to gain altitude, push forward to go down. As long as you change altitude gradually, the ship will adjust to keep the wind in her sails. I've already got her set to hover, and at the right height to get us through the doors. *Slicewind*'ll help you along."

"Right," Peg said. She tried the wheel. "Not very good power steering on this but . . . Oh, groovy! Grunwold, is that a navigation screen in the middle of the wheel?"

"Of course," Grunwold replied. "You're going to be sailing in three dimensions. That will show a simplified version of what's under the hull, as well as around you."

"Lovely," Peg sighed. "I always hated trying to see around the mast and sails. I'm set. You go and disable the guards."

Grunwold gave her a worried glance, then ran to join Vereez and Xerak.

Peg called, "Meg, can you handle the up-down control thingie? I don't want to take my hands off the wheel."

Even in *Slicewind*'s dim running lights, it was evident Meg was scared stiff, but she stalked over to the lever, then grabbed hold as if her life depended on it—which it just might.

The only good thing about the rising storm was that they didn't need to look for a wind. It was there in force, gusting through the windows Grunwold had opened.

"All right!" Peg yelled. "Teg, cast us off!"

As soon as Teg had done so, *Slicewind* jumped forward, passed through the now-open boathouse doors, then out under the skies, from which rain had begun falling. They skimmed off over the field of the something-like-corn.

Peg shouted. "Meg! Give us some lift, gradual and steady. We've got to clear the trees. I'll let you know when to stop pulling back on the lever."

Teg stood by, feeling useless once she'd coiled the line. *Slicewind*'s sails were adjusting to keep and catch the wind far better than any of the sailboats she'd been on. In fact, it seemed as if the mast was actually bending... The sight made her queasy, so she concentrated on what the three inquisitors were doing.

Grunwold was running toward the stern, readying a bow. Xerak stood a few paces back from the stern rail, hands gripped tightly around the shaft of his spear staff, chanting something. Vereez had both her swords drawn and waited slightly to one side and a little in front of Xerak, covering the young wizard.

Okay. They know something's coming up from behind.

Xerak's preparing a spell of some sort. The other two are going to protect him.

What Xerak was preparing became evident a few moments later when he leveled the tip of his spear staff— once again glowing that flame amber—and a series of fireballs, each about the size of a baseball, shot out. By their light, Teg could see that he had neatly targeted three sections of an approaching flock of whatever it was that was chasing them.

Teg glanced ahead. The tops of the trees they were racing toward were tossing in a wind she didn't feel.

Of course. We're being pushed by that same wind, so we're going to feel it a lot less intensely.

Whatever was pursuing them sounded like a swarm of really, really large bees. Heru dropped to the deck. Teg saw that the mini pterodactyl had caught something nearly as large as he was: insectoid, rather than avian, with four wings and a stinger at each end. As she watched, he crunched one stinger, then the other; dropping the still wriggly body, the xuxu launched back into the darkness.

"Tranquilizer darters!" Grunwold shouted. "They won't kill us, but if they knock us out, my mother will gladly do the killing. Don't let them sting you!"

Teg looked nervously around, but the darters seemed to be emerging from the upper loft of the warehouse, and would offer little or no immediate threat, at least until they caught up. She had just convinced her shoulders to stop tensing when she heard the scream: a shrill cry, like fingernails on a blackboard focused down so that all ten fingers reverberated within a single throat: Worse, the sound was coming from the forest that they were about to sail over.

Deciding Meg and Peg could handle *Slicewind* without her, Teg ran to where she'd noticed a boathook. Grabbing it from its brackets, she hefted it once to get a sense of its weight and balance, then thudded across the deck toward the bow, hoping to get a glimpse of whatever was making that ear-searing racket.

It had been a long time since Teg had run with the thoughtless energy that she now found almost unbelievable in small children and young dogs, but she could still move quickly enough if she put her mind to it. With that horrible screeching ringing in her ears, moving was the easy part—the hard part was not giving in to the impulse to dive down the hatch and cower belowdecks.

Teg spared a moment to glance over her shoulder, hoping to see one of the three inquisitors rushing to join her, but they were still occupied by the approaching swarm of darters. Xerak was muttering and gesturing with both his hands and his tail, but the fastest of the tranquilizer darters had already reached the stern and were trying to get at him—a choice of target that made Teg wonder if they were smarter than they looked or if something was guiding their actions.

Neither thought was particularly comforting, but Teg forgot the battle off the stern when she got her first look at what was rising from the forest. She didn't think she'd had any expectations as to what could be making that horrible screeching, but when she saw their attacker she knew she must have—or else she couldn't have been so completely shocked.

The hull lights that enabled the pilot of the flying ship to assure that she was clearing any obstacles below now illuminated what looked like an enormous section of grey-green shag carpet rising from the trees and undulating through the air toward them. The impression of "shag" came from thousands of cilia, each roughly the diameter of Teg's fingers and some eight inches in length. These covered both sides of the thing. The front edge gaped open in the middle, revealing a toothless oval opening, the size of which varied randomly, sometimes barely the width of her hand, other times easily large enough to engulf her entire body.

The illumination from the ship wasn't sufficient for Teg to tell how large this thing was, but she thought it might possibly be able to engulf *Slicewind*'s bow.

"Peg! There's a gigantic bathroom rug coming in at twelve o'clock! Looks like it wants to swallow the ship. I'll do what I can to fend it off but . . ."

Teg didn't have time to pursue the "but." The "rug" was unzipping its toothless mouth to its fullest extent. Weirdly, she found herself thinking of a pillowcase.

Right. We're being attacked by the love child of a pillowcase and shag rug, she thought wildly. *It's bigger than I thought. What to do?*

Meg operated the lever to raise *Slicewind* higher in the air. This helped some but, since Peg had to take care she didn't lose the following wind, she couldn't do much to change their direction.

Teg climbed out onto a cabinet built into the narrowest part of the ship's bow. From that precarious perch, she shoved out with the boathook, hoping to fend off the creature. It dodged. As it did, she saw that the cilia closest to the boathook had parted and flattened.

Okay. It doesn't like the idea of being hit. I'm with it on that. It doesn't want to get hit. I don't want to get swallowed.

Kneeling, so she wouldn't be as likely to topple over the side, Teg leaned forward and poked again. This time she managed to hit a portion of the thing's "lip." The creature veered, letting out an offended shriek that made a cluster of cilia extend straight up in the air.

"What? Do you expect me to let you swallow us?"

Grunwold's voice, from close behind her, said, "Actually, it does. It was bred to move bulk cargo. Keep waving the boathook at it. It's used to being steered by pokes from tools like those. At the least, you'll confuse it. They're determined, but not very smart."

Teg didn't dare turn, but she could hear Grunwold rummaging in the cabinet on which she knelt.

"Fantastic!" he said. The word was followed by a sound not unlike a slide whistle, a series of liquid notes rising and falling, although not in any melody Teg could recognize. The shag rug hooted what Teg took to be a question. This time Grunwold played a pattern. Teg expected the creature to drop or retreat, but instead it began to expand, stretching its mouth open wide.

"Hot-weather sweat eaters!" Grunwold cursed. "Change the command sequence, then not tell the heir to the estate?"

He tried playing a different sequence. This time the rug made a flat, blatting sound. Vereez was shouting something that Teg couldn't quite make out but, in response, Peg was hauling at the wheel, turning them hard to the right. The sail began to flap as it lost the wind, and Teg felt herself buffeted as she hadn't been when they'd been moving with the wind fully behind them.

Grunwold tried a third sequence on the slide whistle, repeating the final "foo-whoop" as if the sound alone could bully the vast thing in front of them into obeying. Maybe it could, for with a hiss of damp breath that smelled faintly of beer, the rug reluctantly closed its mouth and went flat.

Grunwold yelled. "That wind, Vereez? Any time now would be really good . . ."

"Did you put the creature to sleep?" Teg asked, adjusting her grip on the boathook and keeping careful watch on the rug. The ship was gliding alongside and slightly over it now. As it did, myriad cilia shifted as if watching.

Grunwold grunted. "Sort of. Only for a short time. Someone changed some of the commands, but whoever it was forgot the one for 'await new orders.' That will only give us a few minutes at most."

He shoved the slide whistle into his waistband, then bounded aft to help Vereez, who was struggling to drag something cumbersome from one of the lockers. Teg wanted to see what it was, but she thought someone should keep an eye on the rug in case it decided its waiting period had ended.

Shortly thereafter, Teg felt a fresh wind catch the sail, heard Peg shout an enthusiastic "All right!" and *Slicewind* began picking up speed. Only once they were well clear of the still-drifting rug did Teg put the boathook back in its brackets and join the others where they were gathered near the stern. The rain had ebbed, suggesting that they'd sailed out of the range of the storm.

Grunwold had taken over at the wheel. Xerak—smelling distinctly of smoke—was butt down on the deck, drinking deeply from a leather bottle of what Teg suspected was wine. The others sat in a row on a dry tarp that had been folded to cover one of the cabinets—doing double-duty as bench and storage—that was built along the stern. Peg was knitting. Vereez sat shoulder to shoulder with Meg.

"Are we clear, then?" Teg asked. "Or will something else come after us?"

Grunwold said, "I think we're clear. When we crossed that river, we also crossed the borders of my family's estate. I've set course for the city of Rivers Meet. We'll be able to get both supplies and news there. Dad's not going to want to advertise a family squabble by sending anything after us, so if we're careful . . ."

He shrugged. Meg had regained a great deal of her composure, but nonetheless a prickly note underlay her voice when she spoke.

"Don't you think it's about time you filled us in—both on the situation with your family and about what we are likely to encounter next?"

❧CHAPTER FOUR❧

When none of the inquisitors replied, Meg pressed her point. "We have many questions, and to this point you inquisitors all have avoided answering them because you did not wish to be overheard. Unless we have a stowaway or Heru is likely to carry tales back to your family, I believe we are as private as we are likely to be."

"Heru's good," Grunwold said defensively, letting go of the wheel to stroke the xuxu along its back. "I raised him. He's imprinted on me. The night before the barge reached KonSef Landing, he flew out to meet us. I sent him off to tell my folks I was coming home, because I knew I'd need to go up to the main house to get some supplies and I figured it was better to go openly. That last turned out to be a mistake."

"Mistake," agreed Heru in a croaking voice.

"I agree with Meg," Vereez said. "The time has come for us to answer some questions. The rain has let up, and the way we're going, we're not going to hit another storm."

Teg noticed that neither of the young men questioned Vereez's certainty about the weather, but put that thought away for later.

"Let's start with your situation, Grunwold," Vereez went on. "I know you told us your father didn't want anyone looking for a cure for his illness, but I have the impression that something has changed since the last time you were home."

Grunwold nodded. "It has. Turns out that shortly after I left for Hettua Shrine, my father took a turn for the worse. When I came home and said I planned to keep travelling, I was told I couldn't. I'd even thought about asking for a loan of *Slicewind*, figured I'd say I needed it to help Vereez or Xerak get somewhere. I didn't even get a chance. I was told I was going to manage the brickworks, starting tomorrow—today, now."

"The brickworks?" Xerak said. "You?"

"Yeah, me." Grunwold snorted, making clear that he agreed with Xerak that he wasn't fit for the job. "As it was explained to me, it would be bad for business to let on that Dad wasn't doing well, but they wanted me to stay home just in case the heir was needed. They can't lock me up without raising questions, so they decided to do the next best thing—put me to a job where one of Dad's most loyal flunkies would be able to supervise and make sure I didn't screw up completely."

Peg frowned, then looked up from her knitting. "Aren't you worried about your father?"

"Of course, I am!" Grunwold snapped. "That's why I want to find a cure for him. I don't want to sit around and supervise the brickworks, and wait for him to die. I'm not needed to run the estate—my mother has been doing so for years, and she'll keep doing so if something happens to my dad. Even if I'm there, it'll be years before I'm more than a figurehead. What I need to do is save him."

"But even though you didn't say anything in advance, someone anticipated your wanting to take *Slicewind*," Teg said, "and changed the security arrangements, am I right?"

"Seems like it," Grunwold said, "though it could have been routine. Whatever. If Xerak hadn't been here to undo the wards, I couldn't even have gotten the ship out of the boathouse."

"If Xerak," Xerak added from where he now sprawled on the deck, looking more like a sleeping cat than a young man, "hadn't been here, the darters would have put us to sleep and the cargo hauler would have dragged us home. Don't forget that."

Grunwold said nothing, but his shoulders tightened.

"I've been meaning to ask about that," Peg said, her tone of mild interest defusing the tension as it so often did. "Xerak, you're quite good at this magic, aren't you? Better, I would guess, than Grunwold's parents might suspect?"

Xerak nodded, but he didn't look particularly proud of his achievement. "My master was wonderful. I learned more from Uten Kekui in the four years I studied under him than I would have in eight at one of the colleges. He encouraged me to think up solutions for myself, hybridize spells, and even gave me free run of his library.

"After he vanished, as I told you, I spent a long time searching for him. Since I played with the idea for a while that Master's vanishing might be a sort of test for me, any time I came up against an obstacle, I studied up a way around it. I didn't realize how much I'd learned until recently, when I went by Zisurru University in Rivers Meet to see if anyone might be able to give me a lead. The stuff the other students my age were doing... It seemed pathetically simple."

"That's interesting," Peg said. "So it seems as if Grunwold's parents would have every reason to believe that they'd taken adequate precautions to keep *Slicewind* locked away. Grunwold, those other things that attacked us—the darters and the cargo hauler—they couldn't have been specifically meant to stop you, could they?"

Grunwold's shoulders started to rise in his habitual sulky shrug, but Vereez snapped, "Grunwold, if you shrug one more time, I'll bite you! Give us a straight answer. Something's not right here."

Grunwold let his shoulders sag. "Something is definitely not right. The thing is, I'm not the best person to know what. I've been away at the academy for most of the last five years. I'd come home on holidays—get told, 'Someday, son, all of this will be yours.' Then I'd get reamed out for being better at poetry and weapon arts than I am at agriculture and accounting. Usually any chat over the how things are going at KonSef Estate stopped there."

Vereez softened, then got up so she could pat his shoulder. "And thank those we've been before that you're good at weapons arts. You play a pretty mean slide whistle, too."

Grunwold laughed. "I had to learn the whistle commands when I was home for harvest. We use the cargo haulers to carry grain to the silos. They can lift a surprising amount as long as they don't need to go too fast or too far."

"Is hauling cargo all those flying shag rugs do?" Teg asked, trusting the translation spell to make sense of her words.

"That's right. We use them as rudimentary guards during harvest, too. They swallow and hold. Usually, the only thing the thief risks is suffocation. I don't ever remember them being used to guard the grounds though."

"But those others—the darters?" Meg asked. "The ones Xerak said put people to sleep? Those are typical?"

"Tranquilizer darters," Grunwold said. "They're pretty typical. Ours are usually charmed to go only after unescorted strangers. I guess our taking *Slicewind* overrode that I was escorting you."

"Or you weren't supposed to leave the grounds again," Xerak added gloomily. "Now we've stolen both you and *Slicewind*. You're really sure Konnel-toh and Sefit-toh won't do anything?"

"I've told you. I don't think they can without making clear that Dad's worse. I've been allowed to take *Slicewind* out before—that's why I'm so good at sailing her."

He turned and bowed his head to Peg, a courtly gesture at odds with his usual temperamental sullenness. "Thank you for taking the wheel. I didn't expect that—or that you'd be so skillful. If you'd like, I can teach you more about piloting her."

"I think," Vereez cut in, "all of us should get those lessons. We can't always rely on stored winds for a quick escape."

"I'm sure we can't," Peg agreed, "but I was glad you had the one you pulled out. I know there are ways to sail against the wind, but I had enough to do without trying to remember how to direct Meg and Teg to reposition the sails."

"Meg," Teg said. "Remember, I wasn't there. I was poking a boathook at a flying shag rug."

"I'd be happy to learn what sailing I can," Meg said, "but please remember. I am in my seventies. The spirit is willing but the body can't always keep up with what I desire—and hauling ropes for more than a short time may be hard on my old limbs."

Grunwold smiled. "You might be surprised. *Slicewind* is an amazing craft. She has a few tricks I couldn't explain earlier but . . ."

The conversation became technical after that. It turned out that if *Slicewind* knew its course, the ship could adjust its own sail settings. When *Slicewind* sailed through the air, it sailed faster than it did on water because the drag was minimal. It could also move on land, using skids, although speed would depend on terrain and would definitely be slower than either on air or on water. Usually, this option was only used when either air or water cruising was impractical.

Additionally, there was a sort of autopilot that could be used for routine cruises.

"Even when the autopilot is activated," Grunwold said, "someone should be nearby in case problems arise, but the autopilot means that one of us shouldn't always need to be at the wheel."

"While that's wonderful," Peg said, "when there is a

crisis, someone will need to be at the wheel. I nominate me. I've proven I can wrestle the wheel. With some practice, I'll be able to handle the elevation control at the same time. That frees up Teg and Meg for other jobs."

"I second Peg's suggestion," Meg said. "I tried the wheel and it takes more muscle than I have. I could certainly handle the wheel short-term, but I'd do better as a lookout, perhaps. Ever since my cataract surgery, my distance vision is excellent."

Teg nodded. "I think I'd better learn how to handle the helm as well, just in case something happens to Peg. I'm no specialist in the fighting arts like Grunwold is, nor am I a wizard, but maybe you can teach me enough about handling a sword that I can help out if we're attacked again. I'm already a mean hand with a machete, although all I've cut with that is brush."

Vereez yipped satisfaction. "You've shown that all of you keep your heads beautifully in a crisis. I'll admit, I had wondered. There are six of us. We should set up watches with one person capable of handling the helm on each. Xerak, can you sail?"

"Not much," the leonine wizard admitted, "but I'll learn."

He didn't sound precisely thrilled.

"I have some experience," Vereez said, "although my family doesn't own a flying yacht, so mine is from watercraft."

The watches were set up to pair Grunwold, as the most skilled sailor, with Meg, who was likely to be the worst. There was some debate as to whether to pair Xerak with Teg or Peg. In the end, they settled on Peg, since she was eager to sail and he was indifferent. That left Teg and Vereez as the final pairing.

"We'll shift around," the fox said, "once we are all more skilled, but this will do for now."

"Now," Meg said. "All of us napped in expectation of this expedition, and I doubt any of us wishes to rest until we are certain we have indeed achieved our goal and successfully stolen both Grunwold and *Slicewind* from his family estates. Perhaps now would be a good time for you three inquisitors to tell the three of us everything you know about the destruction of the Library of the Sapphire Wind."

"I'm glad you're so eager," Grunwold said, "but how about I give you a tour of *Slicewind* first? I think I have cabin assignments worked out, but I want to clear them with you."

"That does make sense," Meg said, rising a little stiffly. "And now that we're no longer in crisis mode, I realize I am still damp and a bit chilly. I wouldn't mind a chance to get into dry clothes."

"I'll take the helm," Vereez said. "Go on, Grunwold. Show off your precious ship."

Once they were all below, Grunwold began his tour by showing them where the light controls were. The lights themselves looked so modern that Teg had to remind herself that the streamlined panels were not illuminated by electricity.

Or if electricity, then magical electricity or something.

"This area," Grunwold said, making a flourishing gesture around an area about five meters by five meters, "is the shared public area, the lounge. Wherever possible, the built-in furniture does double-duty as storage. My mother likes multipurpose spaces, so permanent furnishing is limited, but there are extra chairs and small tables we can pull out if needed."

"Nice high ceilings," Peg commented with approval.

"My dad has antlers, just like I do," Grunwold said. "We need high ceilings."

"Your dad's antlers," Xerak commented, "are a lot more impressive."

Grunwold shot his friend a look, but otherwise went on with his tour-guide spiel without acknowledging the jibe. "To the stern is the master bedroom suite, which has its own bathroom."

He slid open the door so they could look inside. A somewhat longer-than-usual double bed dominated the space, but once the various bags and bundles that Teg had tossed in were cleared up, there should be enough to move around comfortably. For Teg, who had done her share of living in tents, the space was even roomy. The promised bathroom had a small shower enclosure, a toilet, and a sink.

"I thought you three mentors could use this cabin," Grunwold went on. "Since we plan to keep three watches, it would be unusual for all three of you to need the bed at the same time."

The three mentors—each of whom lived in her own house or apartment—exchanged glances, but wordlessly decided to withhold any comments until the tour was over.

"Over here, across the lounge," Grunwold said, "is the other bathroom. That's the one we three will share. If someone's asleep in the master suite, it's also the public bathroom. Around the corner here, more or less part of the lounge, is the galley."

He indicated a long counter with an inset sink, and a small stove with oven beneath.

"We even have an ice box," he said, opening a cabinet beneath the counter, at the far end from the stove. "It isn't large, but it means we can carry some perishables."

"Oh, good," Peg said. "I'd hate to go without milk for my poffee or tea!"

The galley space doubled as a hallway leading toward the bow.

"Through here," Grunwold said, leading the way forward, "we have the other two cabins. "The one to port is oddly shaped and a little cramped because it works around the mast. It has a bunk bed, so could sleep two in a pinch. I thought we'd put Vereez in there. If she's on watch, and one of you need privacy, you could go in there. This last door leads to the bow cabin."

He slid open the door, revealing a roughly triangular room. Two single beds were set along the sides of the triangle, and were, again, somewhat longer than Teg would have expected.

Of course, she thought. *Antlers. It's either make a longer bed or sleep with your rack hanging off, which probably isn't all that comfortable.*

Once again, the room was fitted with cabinets, often cleverly tucked into what would have been wasted space, doubling as nightstands and bedframes.

Suddenly, impulsively, Teg decided she liked *Slicewind*. She completely understood why Grunwold was so attached to the ship. It was not only functional, it was cleverly designed, and full of little grace notes, like reading lights and carvings on the woodwork.

Grunwold mentioned his mother likes flexible space. I wonder if she did a lot of the design here. If so, no wonder she's the type of person who can run a large estate while dealing with her husband's declining health. I've wanted to help Grunwold, but now I want to help her and his dad, too.

"There's a hatch under the lounge carpet that gives access to the hold," Grunwold said, shooing them out into the larger area again. "Clean and waste water storage is there, as well as extra ropes, sails, and fittings. You shouldn't need to go down there, though."

"*Slicewind*'s layout is impressive," Peg said. "You've been very generous giving us the master cabin. I think we can manage to share."

"I agree," Meg said firmly, "especially if Vereez will let us use her cabin from time to time. I have lived alone for many years now, and sometimes I need a bit of privacy."

Teg nodded. "I'm good. I live alone except for the cats, but I've lived in enough field camps that just having a place with hot and cold running water, showers, and real toilets is luxurious."

Grunwold looked both relieved and happy. "Then how about you ladies get warm and dry, and handle your unpacking?"

"And after that," Meg said, "perhaps while we have a before-bedtime snack, you can tell us more about the destruction of the Library of the Sapphire Wind."

✳ ✳ ✳

"I don't know much about the Library," Vereez began, once they were back on deck with mugs of hot tea and poffee. "Once Xerak mentioned it, I remembered hearing that it had happened. That's about it."

Grunwold started to shrug, glanced over at Vereez and visibly restrained himself. "Me, too. My father went there when he was younger. Whenever he talked about that visit, he'd talk about the Library as if it was still open for business."

"Xerak?" Peg prompted. "From what we were told earlier, I gathered that this place was associated with the magical arts. Surely you must know something."

"Only," Xerak said, lazily combing at his mane with his claw tips, much as a man might toy with his beard, "that my master occasionally mentioned it—usually when he was annoyed by how much harder it is to research arcane matters since the destruction."

"So the Library of the Sapphire Wind was open to the public," Meg said.

"Not quite the public," Xerak clarified. "It wasn't a members-only sort of club, but you needed a reason to have access to the collections. They had lots of rarities there—one-of-a-kind books and artifacts."

"How large was the support staff?" Peg asked.

"I think . . ." Xerak began, but Grunwold interrupted.

"Why does any of this matter? The place has been a ruin since long before we were born."

Peg tsked at him. "Fold your ears down and don't listen if we're boring you, young man. I realize you're under a great deal of stress, but that's no excuse to be rude to people who have come an inconceivable distance to help you."

Grunwold's big ears did droop. "Sorry. But I still don't see why . . ."

Teg cut in. "Having a sense of what the Library of the Sapphire Wind was like before it was destroyed will help us to more effectively explore the ruins when we arrive. For example, if it had a large, permanent staff, then there will have been places for the librarians and support staff to live—that is unless the librarians did their own laundry, cooking, cleaning, and all the rest. Was there an associated village or did everyone live in the library buildings themselves? Would you like to spend days searching the ruins of a building only to find out that it had been a laundry?"

"Oh . . ." Grunwold paused. "Sorry."

He sounded as if he meant it this time.

Xerak looked thoughtful. "I believe the Library did have a resident staff. Knowing what I do about wizards, I can't imagine they would have wanted to do their own chores."

"That's what apprentices are for, right, Xerak?" Vereez teased.

Xerak tossed his mane and ostentatiously ignored her. "But as to where they lived, who did the work . . . I couldn't say. Grunwold, do you remember anything from your father's stories?"

"Not about that sort of thing." The young stag was clearly trying to be conciliatory. "I remember Dad was very impressed with a domed ceiling that showed the constellations." Grunwold looked sad. "I guess that's gone now—weird. Dad always talked about it as if we might go visit it someday. Anyhow, that's why we have the constellation mosaic in our grand dining hall at home.

When people praise it, Dad always says it's nothing like the original. Ours just shows the summer constellations. He said the constellations shown in the mosaic at the Library of the Sapphire Wind changed with the seasons, and could be commanded to show the sky as it looked in any part of the world."

"How long did the Library exist?" Meg asked. "Decades? Centuries?"

"At least a century," Xerak replied promptly, "more, I think. My impression is that it was built around the private library and associated property of a wizard who didn't want to see his collection of rarities broken up when he died. Others came to him in the years that followed and asked if he'd take their collections. A hefty donation was required to have your works archived, so not all collections ended up there, but many did. Eventually, the Library became second only to Zisurru University in the prestige of its collection."

"If the Library was both famous and in place for at least a hundred years," Teg said, "then we should be able to find drawings or prints depicting it. Even if the renderings are more artistic than accurate, still they would give us something to start from. Grunwold, you said you'd set course to a city called Rivers Meet? Would we be able to buy something like that there?"

"It's a good-sized city," Grunwold said. "Lots of shops."

He looked as if he was going to start describing his favorites with the wistful enthusiasm of someone who didn't get to visit often, but Vereez cut in.

"There might be something about the Library of the Sapphire Wind in my family's library."

"We're going to your home city?" Peg asked. "Are you going to have problems getting away from home like Grunwold did?"

Vereez shook her head. "I can't see why. I didn't tell them exactly why I wanted to go to Hettua Shrine. Or rather, I did. I told them I was looking for guidance as to how to direct my studies. I'll tell them Hawtoor-va set me a task."

"Let me guess," Peg chuckled, "helping three badly burned pilgrims."

Vereez bared her teeth in a smile that was as much defiant as cheerful. "Why not? I've always had an interest in helping people. I don't think I'll mention just how dangerous an area we're going to, though."

"That's a good idea," Meg agreed. "A very, very good idea."

As they continued laying their plans for getting to the Library of the Sapphire Wind, once again Teg wondered at the protocols of the culture from which the three inquisitors came. Why would Vereez's family, which had already lost one daughter, let their remaining child run off to Hettua Shrine, especially with such a minimal escort?

Then again, what did Teg know? Some families became so obsessed after a loss that they didn't pay attention to what they still had. Or Vereez's parents might be in severe denial. Given that Vereez had indicated that they'd given up on finding Vereez's little sister, that might be even more likely.

"If you're sure your parents won't mind," Peg said, her mother-self obviously at war with her sense of responsibility to the inquisitors and their searches. "All this stealing and running off into the wilderness does not fit my image of what a good mentor should be encouraging. What would Gandalf do?"

Teg, who had been moving to where she could light up without offending anyone, laughed. "Let's see ... Send a hobbit who'd barely been out of his hometown off to deal with trolls, wild elves, and dragons in the company of a bunch of grumpy dwarves? Dumbledore was no better— he let a bunch of kids fight the evil forces that had everyone paralyzed in terror because of some stupid prophecy. At least we're going to stick with these kids, and not vanish when the going gets bad."

The three inquisitors looked completely confused. In her best "librarian" voice, Meg explained. "Teg is citing precedents from the lore of our world. Many times the mentors act in a manner that is puzzling because it leaves their charges with a minimum of guidance. We may lack the powers of a Gandalf or a Dumbledore, but we'll make up for that by staying with you."

Xerak obviously took this as a slight on his beloved master and began to snarl, lips peeling back to show impressive fangs. Peg, with a great deal more courage than Teg would have had if their places were reversed, stopped knitting long enough to tap him on the nose with a spare needle.

"Enough of that, young man. We know this Uten Kekui was admirable. We've had evidence of that in how you saved us all from the darters. We have enough problems without bickering over imagined slights."

Grunwold glanced back over his shoulder. "Vereez's

family library might be useful, but Xerak, doesn't your family have a business dealing in curiosities? Their shop might have some excellent old maps."

"Maybe," Xerak said, "but I'd need to be careful about how I asked. When I stopped in last, they were talking about formally terminating my apprenticeship and having me enroll at Zisurru University for advanced studies. I argued them out of it but, even though I'm in something of a grey area legally, I don't want to push the issue."

"Grey area?" Peg asked.

"Apprentices are legally governed by their masters," Xerak explained, "not their parents. However, since my master has vanished, there has been a debate as to whether my parents should take back their rights. The longer my search goes on, the more they have doubts regarding how I've been spending my time."

"Or," Vereez said wisely, "what you've managed to do so far is giving them a sense of how talented you are, and they want you to get some additional training before you blow off a hand trying to throw lightning or create rain showers."

"That raises an issue I've been wondering about," Meg said. "Precisely how old are you three and what is your legal status?"

"I'm twenty," Grunwold said. "Xerak's a year older than I am, and I'm a year older than Vereez. Roughly speaking, I mean. We don't have birthdays at precisely the same time."

"Xerak said he's in a grey area legally," Teg said. "What about you others? Are you old enough to be considered adults?"

"Old enough?" Vereez said. "What does age have to do with adulthood?"

Peg blinked. "Where we come from, a child is considered a legal adult at eighteen years old, although in some places legal adulthood is twenty-one."

"So just living a bunch of years is enough to be considered an adult?" Grunwold said. "Oh, I wish it was so simple here."

The discussion that followed showed how very different this culture was from the modern United States. Marriage conferred adulthood—but only if the marriage was entered into with the approval of both sets of parents; they, by granting approval, indicated that they considered their child to be able to assume adult responsibilities. Graduation from an apprenticeship conferred adulthood, but only if the apprentice then passed a review by an appropriate board or guild. Graduation from a university or certain trade programs also usually conferred adulthood, although, again, there was an exam of some sort to pass.

Neither Vereez nor Grunwold had yet graduated from either a university or trade program—although Grunwold had been in the middle of the equivalent of a university program before he'd been called home. Vereez had been just starting a university program when she decided to go to Hettua Shrine. For this reason, neither could be considered adults.

There were further refinements. After these had been discussed in detail, Meg gave a crisp nod.

"So," she said, "if I understand correctly, it is completely possible that an unambitious person might remain a minor until the death of his or her parents. Those who cannot support themselves might become adults by default. However, if someone in their family wishes to file for them to be declared incompetent, they could find themselves appointed a guardian and remain minors. This does provide an incentive to learn responsibilities or get an education, doesn't it?"

Peg chuckled. "I can't imagine that my children would have much liked the rules over here. They looked toward turning eighteen as freedom from anyone being able to 'try and run their lives,' as I've heard many times."

"Mine as well," Meg added very, very dryly. "Nonetheless, so often, these 'adults' still expect you to supply a home, food, and pay for higher education. This world seems to have a much more sensible system. The parent is only left in charge of the child if the child refuses to take on adult responsibilities."

Peg sniggered. "No 'gap year.' No 'finding yourself.' Ah, well ... Still, I'm sure I was a trial to my parents. I shouldn't be so unkind to my own kids."

Teg nodded. "If only half of the stories you tell about your own youth are true, you definitely were a trial to your folks, hippy-chick. Now, returning to our current situation. If I understand our inquisitors' situations correctly, they are all still not yet full adults—in Xerak's case, because he feels he is still an apprentice, even if Zisurru University has given him a certificate. Grunwold and Vereez are basically still minors. For the moment, we've gotten Grunwold clear of his family, and Vereez thinks she's not going to have any problems getting away from her parents."

Vereez flattened her ears. "As long as I don't mention that I'm looking for my sister, I won't. That's got to be kept quiet."

"Why?" Meg asked, packing the single syllable with all of her considerable personality.

Vereez looked her squarely in the eyes. "I don't know. All I know is that my parents solidly deny that I ever had a much-younger sister. You won't find her listed in our genealogy. Her fate is a closed book. Only I seem willing to open it."

Peg spoke gently. "You said your sister was an infant when she vanished. Are you certain she didn't die, and that they are trying to spare you pain?"

"I'm sure," Vereez snapped, then became terrifyingly serious. "If she had died, they would have listed her in our family tree. We would remember her on the appropriate festivals. Instead, they've done all they can to make it as if she never existed."

"That is a mystery," Peg agreed. "Very well. Shall we all agree not to let on why Vereez is really travelling with us? She is simply fulfilling the somewhat cryptic commands of an ancient oracle."

Nods all around, and Vereez brightened. "Excellent! Then I'll go home and inform my family about Hawtoor's command. While I'm there I'll pillage the family library for maps. Xerak?"

"I'll check the shop for maps, pictures, whatever," the young wizard rumbled. "If my parents insist on discussing having my apprenticeship terminated, then I will insist on being tested by the Wizard's Guild. They only test twice a year, so that will not only delay things but, if and when I do enroll in Zisurru University, I will have a neutral assessment of what courses I need to take. Whatever I am, I am certainly not"—he snapped his fingers and a small ball of light appeared in his palm—"a beginner."

When they arrived in Rivers Meet some days later, the city as seen from the sky proved to be a shimmering spectacle of towering stone structures in hues ranging from pale golden brown to deep burnished bronze. Windows were often of multipaneled stained glass, so the overall impression was less of buildings than of jewelry inset with elaborate gemstone mosaics.

"I hadn't expected the buildings to be so tall," Meg said. "That one looks at least fifteen stories high."

"The buildings are sort of like pyramids, aren't they?" Peg asked no one in particular. "Both the smooth-sided sort and the step ones. The shape is all over the place, both on the ground and capping the skyscrapers."

"The roads are nicely laid out," Teg commented, "on a grid. This city was planned. It didn't evolve."

Slicewind was not the only flying ship visible over the city, but flying craft didn't seem precisely common either. Grunwold had brought them in too high to see much about the nature of the traffic that thronged the wide boulevards, but that didn't keep the three humans from trying, aided by a couple of pairs of binoculars that they'd brought from home.

Teg had relinquished her set to Meg, and was skulking to where she could have a smoke without offending most of her companions, when she overheard a snatch of conversation that brought her up short. Vereez was speaking to Grunwold, who was at the helm, carefully guiding *Slicewind* into the city along what seemed to be the equivalent of aerial "streets," indicated by markings on rooftops and the sides of buildings.

"If you drop me on the top deck of the city center," Vereez was saying, "I'll get a carriage home from there. Then go on to the hotel. Heru should be back soon with confirmation of your reservation. I'll send you a message indicating when I'll be ready to depart. I'm guessing that, like me, Xerak will only want to make a brief visit with his folks."

Xerak, who was lazing on the deck, writing in a journal, nodded. "I'll get off at the city center, too. That will let me hit a couple of stores on the way to my parents' house."

With what attention he could spare from his piloting, Grunwold managed to look grumpier than usual. "And I get to play babysitter?"

"Eldersitter," Vereez chortled. "Why not? It's probably better that you stay indoors anyhow, just in case your parents aren't as neutral as you think about your running off with *Slicewind*, rather than going to supervise the brickworks like a good little buck."

Teg paused, any desire to have a smoke vanishing. "Wait. You're not planning on keeping us locked up in some lousy hotel while we're in Rivers Meet are you?"

Vereez looked hurt. "It's not a 'lousy' hotel, I will have you know. It's the finest one my family owns. If Heru doesn't fail us, I'll have reserved the penthouse suite with its own private dock. You'll be in the lap of luxury."

"So we're still prisoners?" Teg asked, stabbing her unlit

cigarette at the three inquisitors. "If that's the case, I may just go home and to hell with helping you out."

The young people looked shocked.

Xerak rolled to his feet, tucking his journal into its case as he did so. "We're just doing as Hawtoor-va suggested. He said that it would be best to keep you three safely away from where your—uh—oddities could be detected. He said that trouble might arise."

Meg and Peg had heard Teg's questions. It would have been hard not to, since she'd been all but shouting. They turned from the rail and hastened over to join the impromptu conference.

"Hawtoor suggested?" Teg repeated. "And what does a near hermit know about anything?"

"He knows," Grunwold said sharply, turning the wheel with unnecessary force, "that people from other worlds do not routinely appear here, not at his shrine, not in others. He's very concerned that our"—he all but spat the word—"'impulsiveness' may have catastrophic results."

"But Hawtoor doesn't know," Peg said, her usual conciliatory manner less effective than usual because of the acid in her tone. "He just wants us kept close as a safeguard. I wonder if his motives are as altruistic as he makes them out to be? He was obviously negligent— literally asleep on the job—or you three wouldn't have been able to do what you did."

Meg nodded. "That's a very good point, Peg." She shifted her attention to the three inquisitors. "Tell me. Why did you go to such trouble to provide us with disguises if you were going to keep us concealed? To this point, you have given us the impression that once we were away from the smaller settlements and the close confines of the barge on which we travelled to Grunwold's family estate, we would be able to be out and about. We have honored this restriction because we assumed that at some point we would be permitted to see more of your world."

"That's right," Teg said. "No one may have said so directly, but it was certainly implied. I hate to sound like a brat but, seriously, if we're going to be prisoners, I'm going to use my bracelet and go home."

She wasn't sure she meant it but, based on the reactions, her auditors believed that she was sincere.

"Wait!" Vereez said, placing one hand with those oddly dark nails on Teg's arm. "Please . . . I don't know what the boys think, but I believe you were meant to come to us. If you leave, I may never find my . . ." Her voice caught, broke. "My little sister."

Vereez had shown herself quite capable of theatrics, but Teg believed her emotions were sincere. Before she could respond, Grunwold cut in.

"Look, I didn't like how that old owl sneered at us, not one bit, but I'm not willing to risk losing my opportunity to find a cure for Dad on the chance that we cause some sort of riot because we have three alien monsters with us."

"Grunwold!" Vereez and Xerak spoke as one, horrified—not so much, Teg thought, at what he'd said than that he'd said it openly.

Meg smiled the polite, meaningless smile with which she'd doubtless responded to numerous annoying library clients. "So you are saying that the disguises you provided are inadequate."

"No, they're . . ."

Meg cut him off. "Then if they're adequate, you're saying you think we're too stupid to remember to keep them on and to maintain the charade when we're out in public."

Grunwold tried to retort, but Meg talked right through his sputtering.

"If that's the case, then I think Teg is correct. We should all go home. I regret it, certainly, but if we are too stupid to maintain a simple charade in a strange city where everything we see, every word we hear, will remind us how vulnerable we are, then Teg is correct. We are too stupid to be able to assist you."

Peg chuckled. "In fact, we're so stupid that it's a miracle we've lived as long as we have. Even young Teg has more than five decades behind her."

Silence reigned except for the snapping of the sail as Grunwold turned *Slicewind* toward a tall, many-windowed building that was topped with a step pyramid mosaicked in shimmering deep violet-purple tiles that dazzled the eye when the sunlight reflected off them.

Grunwold was the first to start laughing. "You ladies have a point, a definite point! I concede. Very well, I hate sounding like a parent making rules before taking a small child on an outing but, if you agree to keep your disguises on and to not ask any questions—better make that 'talk'—where anyone might overhear you, then I'll take the risk."

Teg grinned. "Excellent! You may find letting us get a look at Rivers Meet will have advantages beyond keeping us from getting cabin fever. We'll be a lot more useful when we have a larger context—a better sense of your culture. Without that, we won't know a rarity from the routine."

Vereez and Xerak looked worried but, since they couldn't very well stop Grunwold, not if they were going to fulfill their part of the plans, they had to give in.

It's not as if we're Merry and Pippin, and are going to drop rocks down a well in Moria.

Nonetheless, once they were out on the streets, it was hard to remember not to talk. They'd told Grunwold in advance the sort of places they wanted to see—temples or churches, shopping centers, libraries. This last, very sensible suggestion, had come from Meg.

"After all, if we're going to be investigating the ruins of a library, it would be helpful to have a conception as to the basic layout of libraries in this culture. Otherwise, we may entertain misconceptions."

Her suggestion turned out to be a good one.

I might have expected scrolls, Teg thought, *and even deduced what a scroll rack was once I got beyond the initial impulse to think of it as a wine rack for unduly slim bottles. However, I never would have known about those cool data crystals or how useful they seem to be. I'd have just thought they were decorations.*

The temples had been interesting, not only as architectural specimens, but for what they said about the culture. Most human religions had, at their base, the need to deal with death. Here there was a widespread belief that the spirit continued on after death.

"Belief," Peg said later, when Grunwold had taken them back to the penthouse and gone to get takeout for lunch—eating out had been rejected because it would require the three humans to fuss with their masks—"is almost the wrong word. They *know* life continues on after death."

"And how they know is not exactly reassuring," Teg said. "Grunwold takes ghosts manifesting, as well as the ability to communicate with the recently deceased, completely for granted. When I wrote him a note asking if we should expect ghosts at the ruins, he looked at me as if I'd asked him if we should expect to be breathing air."

Peg chuckled. "Grunwold's expression usually says that he thinks that most other people—even his friends—are mentally wanting. It occurs to me that we should check if these ghosts are necessarily nasty."

Meg sighed as she unbent from tugging off her boots. "I did while you were in the bathroom and Teg was having a smoke. Sometimes they are, sometimes they aren't. Grunwold did admit that the chance of our encountering malevolent spirits was much higher in a place that had been destroyed by violence. What interested me was the dominant belief in reincarnation."

"Me, too," Teg agreed. "Most of the religions here seem oriented around assuring optimal reincarnations. The question seems to be what 'optimal' means. Sooner. Later. With friends and relations. I'm sure there are other refinements. I rather liked the Temple of the Exploring Soul. Best as I could tell, it seemed to be promising its advocates a sort of Grand Tour of all the world through many lifetimes."

"I thought you'd have gone for the Church of the Timeless," Peg teased. "That one seemed to be promising the ability to go backward as well as forward in time."

"Naw," Teg laughed. "Knowing for sure would take all the fun out of excavations."

"What is interesting," Meg said, "is that there seems to be no sense of a permanent heaven or hell. Some religions apparently advocate something like a rest stop, but there's no sense of an end."

"We only looked at a few temples," Teg reminded her. "Judging based on that—even on what our young inquisitors can tell us—would be like judging all of Earth based on a stop in London in, say, the eighteen hundreds. You'd miss so much."

Meg nodded. "Point taken. And, dominant belief in reincarnation or not, grief at separation from loved ones is just as real here. Death remains an end, I suppose, whether you hope to meet your loved ones in heaven or in the next incarnation."

Grunwold returned soon after with lunch. The prospect of bodily satisfaction in the here and now did a great deal to banish the increasingly solemn mood. Teg was partway through a sort of chicken burrito with a sweet-spicy sauce that brought tears to her eyes when she remembered a question she'd been wanting to ask.

"Grunwold, what are the ethics involved in eating the animal that—well—that your head came from?"

Grunwold stared at her as if she'd gone mad. "My head didn't come from any animal. You don't think I've been wearing a mask all this time, do you?"

"No, but your head—it's a stag's head, isn't it?"

Grunwold shook his head. "It's my head. It isn't the head of any male quadruped. At least that's what the translation spell says you're saying. Although for a moment it sort of stammered over 'only male,' as an option."

Teg sighed. Grunwold could be incredibly annoying, and seemed to really enjoy it.

She took another bite of her burrito, pulled out her notebook, and with a few quick lines produced a sketch of a standard white-tailed deer. It wouldn't have won any art prizes, but it was perfectly recognizable, even as to type. No one who knew deer would take this for a mule deer or an elk.

"The translation spell is obviously messing with us again," she said. "By 'stag' I meant this—the male of this particular creature. The female looks very similar, but lacks the antlers."

Grunwold stared at the drawing. "That's incredibly creepy! It looks like you took my head and put it on the body of a kubran, though a kubran is a bit more stocky than that and has dark barring in the coat."

Teg knew what a kubran was. They'd eaten a roasted haunch of one on the riverboat after the ship's captain had managed a lucky shot when the riverboat had been at anchor. They were heavy-bodied ungulates, with broad, almost triangular heads, and dark barring on coats that ranged from light grey to medium brown.

"Quick, Teg," Peg urged. "Draw a fox, then a lion. Can you?"

"Sure," Teg said. She did, then held out her notebook for Grunwold's inspection. He took it, then spent a long moment studying the pictures.

"Why do you keep drawing these weird hybrids?" he finally asked. "It's harder to tell what the body is meant to be on the creature with Vereez's head and tail, but it's just not right. As for Xerak... He'd love to have a mane like that, I'm sure. He might even end up growing one someday, but that body... It reminds me of several feline types, but doesn't match any cat great or small that I know—beyond the similarities most felines share. Could that be an aspect of your drawing?"

Meg shook her head decisively. "It is not. These are perfectly adequate sketches, especially given that Teg was drawing from memory. The proportions are good. She could indicate coloring only a little in pencil. Both the stag and the fox would be in reddish hues—similar to your coloration and Vereez's. The lion would be a rich golden brown, rather like Xerak's fur."

Grunwold frowned. "So these are real creatures from your world. Not people—more like animals?"

"That's right," Teg said. "We'd assumed that they were creatures here, too, but that we hadn't seen them yet."

Peg nodded. "After all, we've been fairly restricted in our actions, and one would not expect to see a lion or a fox—or even a deer—in most of the places we've been. It's not as if they're domesticated creatures."

"'He's not a tame lion,'" Meg quoted so softly that Teg wondered if she realized she'd spoken aloud.

"Well," Grunwold said, clearly shaken, and therefore less argumentative than he usually was, "I can't say I've ever seen creatures like them, or pictures of them, or anything like that. Your drawings look like real animals. I'll give you that, but they don't belong to any reality I know."

"Slowly now," said Meg. "How many different sorts of heads do people here have?"

For a moment it seemed that Grunwold was going to become truculent once more, but he took another long look at Teg's drawings and stopped himself.

"I really don't know. It's not something I've ever thought about."

Meg persisted. "But are there any sorts of heads that match—precisely, mind you, not just by being feline or canine or whatever—any sort of creature that doesn't have what I'm going to call a basically human body: bipedal, no fur or lightly furred. Bodies like you and Vereez and Xerak and all the other people have. Bodies more or less like ours."

"Not that I know of," Grunwold said. "There are similarities, of course, but no . . ."

"All right, a related question. We've seen mixed-type couples," Teg said. "Like the owners of the riverboat. The wolf and the rabbit. Is that common?"

"Of course," Grunwold said, vaguely disgusted. "Sure, some people fall for people who look more like them, but only perverts choose someone just because of what sort of head they have. If I refused to date anyone except girls with heads like mine, my parents would give me a stern talking to, make sure I hadn't gone completely egocentric, so that I couldn't admire anything but myself."

"How—" Teg began, but Grunwold cut her off.

"Wait! My turn for questions. We've been wondering why you three look so alike, except for little differences in coloration and height and such. We thought it was really strange that the three of you had such similar heads, but it seemed rude to ask. Now . . . Am I right? Do people where you come from all look the same?"

The three humans looked at each other, oddly astonished.

Then Peg said, "Well, we don't think we look very much alike, but I can see what you mean. Yes. All humans look more or less like we do. There are some variations: skin color, texture of hair, shape of the nose ... I guess those are the most obvious. Teg, you're the anthropologist. Am I right?"

Teg nodded. "There are differences in build as well, but those often even out with changes of diet, health care, or exercise. The Japanese, for example, started getting taller when their diets shifted to include more protein. The change happens over generations, of course. An adult who eats more protein isn't suddenly going to start growing."

Grunwold said, "You really think you look all that different from each other? I mean, your hair grows in the same places on your heads. None of you have fangs. None of you have fur or hair on your faces. All of your eyes are frontally set. Does a little difference in coloration or hair texture really matter?"

Teg said sadly, "Oh, yes. Our history is full of examples. Even in modern times, when I know we've made some progress—especially when I remember what my parents put up with, not to mention my grandparents—the fact that I have darker skin causes people to sometimes treat me badly."

"Are there places where Meg—who is the lightest of you—would be treated badly?" Grunwold asked, clearly trying to grasp what, for him, was a very strange concept.

"Yes, but it's not a simple matter of lighter or darker

skin," Teg said. "We'd need to give you a very long lecture—worse than one of Hawtoor's—to explain why."

"Worse than Hawtoor's?" Grunwold grinned—an action that had more to do with how he moved his ears than with his mouth. "Then I'll pass. You had a question for me, I think."

"If two people have children"—Teg had been about to say "If you and Vereez were to have children," but caught herself in time. They were all playing very dumb about Grunwold's unrequited crush on Vereez—"does what sort of head the children have just happen at random?"

Grunwold shook his head. "No. Often the children take after one or more of their parents. I look a lot like my dad; Vereez looks a lot like her mom, although Inehem-toh's fur is a really pretty snowy white. If a child doesn't have a head type that can be accounted for by going back a few generations, then there start to be questions about, uh . . ."

"Marital fidelity?" Peg suggested. "We have the same problem—or did until DNA testing became an option."

"How can anyone tell?" Grunwold said. "Do you have that many different shades of hair and skin?"

"Not really," Teg said cheerfully, "but just like with you, there are certain patterns in the blending. Darker hair and eyes tend to dominate lighter. So if I were to have children with Meg's son . . ."

"Please!" Meg said. "Don't wish that on yourself! Charles is sweet in his way, but too stuffy for you!"

Teg persisted, "Then my darker looks would likely assure that most of our children would have dark hair and eyes. I will spare you a lecture on recessive genes and the rest."

"So why isn't everyone on your world dark then?" Grunwold asked reasonably.

"Originally for reasons of geography," Meg said. "In our world, the lighter skin and hair colors evolved as beneficial in colder, darker climates. Darker skin and hair offered protection against strong sunlight. I realize you'll probably find this 'perverted,' but in our world it's still more common for people to marry people who share their basic coloring—although that often has more to do with shared culture than with egocentrism."

Peg nodded. "My father was of Spanish heritage and quite dark. My mother was a red-haired Irish colleen. However, they both were Catholic, met at church, and fell in love—resulting in me and my brother, who take more after our father in coloring, and my sister, who has red hair."

Grunwold rubbed the finger of his right hand between his brows. "You make my head ache worse than when my antlers budded," he said good naturedly. "Have you played tourist enough for today? If I went up to check *Slicewind*'s stores, then made a list of what we need to lay in before we leave, will you promise to stay put and not shock the hotel staff?"

"Promise," Meg said, speaking for all of them, but Grunwold waited until both Teg and Peg added their own promises.

Unnatural silence fell after Grunwold departed. Eventually, Teg went and picked up her notebook from where Grunwold had left it. She studied the pages thoughtfully, then began sketching a kudu from memory, setting it alongside the white-tailed deer for contrast.

"I think," Meg said, "that in addition to our vocabulary, we might enjoy making a list of all the different types of animal heads these people have. I'm not sure if we'll find a pattern, but we might learn something."

"I'm for it," Teg agreed. "I keep thinking of how many cultures on Earth have legends about animal-headed humans. Egyptians. Assyrians. Celts. Japanese. Many Native American groups. When you add in cultures with stories about shapeshifters, I don't think you'll find one without some use of the motif of a blending of human and animal traits. Such tales of animal-head humans are usually attributed to a desire to take on the qualities of an admired animal or, conversely, out of fear of the beast both within and without—but I wonder . . ."

"We might be the first humans to come here," Peg said, her knitting needles clicking quickly in her excitement, "but maybe, long ago, people from here came to our world and left their mark."

※{CHAPTER FIVE}※

Xerak returned that evening. Vereez dropped by the hotel the next morning to announce that she should be able to get away by midafternoon, after lunch with her parents.

"By the way," she said, "when I went through our library, the only mentions I could find of the Library of the Sapphire Wind were in general references. I found one or two drawings, but nothing that would be any help. What's weird is that I'm pretty sure my parents have both been out to that part of the world. You'd think there would be something!"

"Not necessarily," Meg said. "Often people don't bother with owning references for places they feel they know. Xerak, did you have any luck?"

Xerak shook his head. "None. Not at the house. Not in the antique shop. Maybe there was a run on material about the subject. That sort of thing happens. All it takes is one enthusiast coming through, and every shop in the city will be stripped. I started to ask, then I had a better thought. My master has a friend—an older scholar with an interest in cartography. In his younger years, Kuvekt-lial traveled a great deal. These days, he's much more sedentary—I think there was an accident, but no one talks about it. He now devotes himself to writing about various areas of interest. He also draws maps."

"Sounds perfect," Teg agreed. "A historian and cartographer. You say this Kuvekt-lial is a friend of your master. Is he a friend of yours as well?"

Xerak shrugged. "He considers me obsessive, but that hasn't stopped him from selling me some of his travel guides. I can't see why he'd stop now."

"Is where this Kuvekt lives too far out of our way?" Grunwold asked. "Not to sound pathetic or anything, but my dad isn't getting any better."

For answer, Xerak went over to his satchel and pulled out a worn atlas, doubtless one he'd used repeatedly during his year-long search for his missing master.

"If the weather cooperates, we won't need to go much out of our way." When everyone had crowded around, Xerak opened the atlas to a previously marked page. "We're here." He drew a claw tip in a line a little west of north. "If we were on foot, the detour would be considerable because of the need to find a river crossing, but since we have *Slicewind*, it's hardly a diversion at all."

"I'm for it," Teg said. "Researching a site before you start digging saves a lot of time."

There was some further discussion, but everyone agreed. The topic shifted to supplies purchased, to be purchased, and who would do what. The inquisitors rapidly found themselves eager to let their mentors help with the shopping.

Vereez ran a claw tip down one edge of the list. "I'll take care of this part from my family's stores. It won't be missed. Xerak, how about you take Teg to get the stuff for digging? Grunwold, you can take Peg and Meg to get the rest. Just pretend they're elderly aunts from the country bossing you around."

"I won't have to pretend the last bit," Grunwold grumbled, but he held his ears wide, which Teg took to mean he was teasing.

"I'll be back by late afternoon," Vereez promised. "Have fun!"

Teg did, actually. Xerak's travels hadn't included archeology, of course, but he knew the right sort of stores. Vereez had supplied them with access to a credit line, and Xerak clearly had fun taking advantage of it.

"My family," he explained, "isn't poor, but we aren't as rich as either Vereez's or Grunwold's. Lately, my folks have been tight with my spending money, saying that they'd signed me over to an apprentice master, so he should be paying my expenses. I've promised that either Master will reimburse them, when I find him, or I will when I have been formally inducted. They've taken me at my word."

But it's good not to feel you're running up the debt, Teg thought. *I get that. I've never had a grant that seemed large enough for everything I wanted to buy.*

When they returned with shovels and picks, various smaller tools, and an assortment of belts, carry bags, and buckets, they found Meg, Peg, and Grunwold aboard *Slicewind*, stocking the galley and putting excess supplies in the hold.

Vereez returned somewhat later in the afternoon than

promised, accompanied by a porter who wheeled in a heavy trolley burdened with a large enough heap of parcels and bundles to make it a good thing that *Slicewind* had ample storage space. They set up a relay, Grunwold and Xerak doing the heavy hauling, Teg—lynx mask in place—operating the winch, while Peg, Meg, and Vereez stowed items in lockers, hold, or cabins.

Loading the ship provided the mentors with their first good look at the exterior of the craft that had already come to seem a home away from home. The hull was a light golden wood, glazed with a translucent blue that Grunwold explained was enchanted so that, if given the right command, the ship would blend into the surrounding skies. A pair of large eyes were painted near the bow. *Slicewind* lacked a figurehead, but did have a sort of curving projection that looked like a bird's beak. Combined, eyes and beak created the impression that *Slicewind* was some sort of natural flying creature, as well as being a person, not a thing.

They'd already observed that the mast could bend so as not to completely dump the wind when the ship changed elevation, and that, if necessary, extra sails could be run up, using lines.

"It's even possible to set up a second mast," Grunwold said, "but most of the time we don't bother. It makes the deck too crowded. *Slicewind* is meant to be sailed by a minimal crew, which is why I thought of her. I can even handle her alone, if I must."

"I've been wanting to ask about the crow's nest," Meg said, "especially since I've volunteered to be lookout. Is the mast really strong enough?"

"Plenty strong," Grunwold assured her, patting the ship's side as if it were a cat or dog. "The ship's eyes do help with avoiding obstacles, but it's always good to have someone able to see what's going on above. If we're climbing at a sharp angle, you'll need to hang on, but the same is true for those on deck."

Meg nodded and looked thoughtful, but when the time to depart arrived, she donned an extra sweater and her mask and took her post.

They lifted off after nightfall, Grunwold at the wheel, the remainder taking advantage of the clear night weather to enjoy being on deck. Teg—who felt she'd earned an extra cigarette after all that shopping, fetching, and carrying—checked the wind and moved to where her smoke would be carried away. She was mildly surprised when Xerak came to join her, thrusting toward her a box a little smaller than a shoebox.

"I got this for you today," he said. "Figured you might like it, and it might help if you ran out of those 'cigarettes.'" He said the final word carefully, as one does a foreign word learned by sound alone.

Teg opened the box and held it near one of the running lights, so she could see the contents. This proved to be a fat, round pipe bowl carved from a warm red stone into the shape of a flower that reminded her of a peony. The box also held several spare stems, and all the paraphernalia for cleaning and packing that delight a pipe-user's heart. To one side was a bag that held what, at a quick sniff, smelled almost like tobacco—although without the rank "upper nose" odor that is so distasteful to the nonsmoker.

"I thought you people didn't smoke," she said, astonished. "This is beautiful!"

"Smoking has fallen out of fashion," Xerak admitted, shuffling his feet shyly, "but a few hundred years ago, there was a fad. That herb was the closest in scent I could find to what yours smells like, so it likely has some of the same properties. The herbalist thought it might, based on the sample I brought her."

"You swiped one of my cigarettes!" Teg said with mock rage.

"Your leavings often have a little unburnt material in them, so I collected some of the butts from the trash and pulled the scraps out."

"Clever!" Teg said. "Gracious, and generous. Thank you. Now I need to see if I remember how to smoke a pipe. It's been a while. I bet Peg can give me tips if I can't get the hang of it."

Ears perked in obvious pleasure at her reaction to his gift, Xerak moved to where he'd be upwind of her smoke, leaned on the rail, and pulled out a wine flask.

The bonding of two substance abusers, Teg thought, wishing she felt more amused. Xerak definitely had an addiction to drink, but so far it wasn't affecting his ability to function. *I'll keep an eye on him, though I don't much like the idea of taking a flask from a lion of any sort at all.*

During the day and a half it took for them to reach the home of Kuvekt the cartographer, Peg and Meg both took the opportunity to return home and check in. It was decided that they should do so whenever the group was in transit, to reduce chances of anyone at home worrying.

"But the seven-to-one time difference does help," Peg said. "I need to start keeping some sort of journal so I don't call the same kid what for me is a few days apart, but for them is only a few hours! That would create worrying of a different sort!"

Although he drank a fair amount during the voyage, Xerak was sober when Grunwold brought *Slicewind* down on the grounds of a prosperous estate on the edge of a town larger than that near Grunwold's family farm, but much smaller than Rivers Meet. Not only was the young wizard sober, but he had spent a portion of the morning getting ready. As *Slicewind* settled to a berth on a grassy field, he emerged from the cabin he shared with Grunwold well groomed and attired in a magnificent outfit that looked vaguely Egyptian, depending as it did on a stiff kilt below and a wide, metal collar above. The collar covered Xerak's shoulders while leaving his chest (lightly furred in golden brown) bare. He'd donned bracers that went from his wrists nearly to his elbows, ornamented with a motif that was echoed in the patterns embossed on his calf-high boots.

"Yum!" said Peg, pausing in her knitting to patter applause. "Whatever else, I like the fashions here. If I were twenty years younger . . ."

Xerak couldn't blush, but he could pin his ears back, and he did so now—but only for a moment.

"You'd still be cradle robbing, Peg," Teg said dryly.

"How do you know I was talking about the handsome young man and not stealing his clothes?" Peg asked with unconvincing innocence.

Teg rolled her eyes and made shooing gestures at the

young wizard. "Good luck, Xerak. Don't worry. We'll stay aboard *Slicewind* and not scandalize the locals."

"I do hope you can acquire some documents for us," Meg said. There was something distinctly wistful about her posture as she stood, badger mask in hand, clad in her "good clothes," obviously hoping for an invitation to meet the scholar and cartographer.

After they had stolen *Slicewind*, the three humans had either worn the clothing they had brought from home or, if there was any chance of being seen, some sailors' slops Grunwold had found in a locker. In Rivers Meet, Vereez had purchased them more daily wear—the local equivalent of jeans and tee shirts—so Meg's donning of her finery was definitely a statement.

Perhaps Xerak took the hint. Perhaps there was something in his tale that piqued the cartographer's curiosity, but after about an hour, a self-effacing servant (incongruously with the fierce head of a bald eagle), came to invite them to join her master and Xerak.

They did, and discovered that their host was a round-bodied man with the head and bushy tail of a raccoon. He leaned heavily on a staff when he rose to greet them, shaking hands with each as Xerak offered names.

"I am Kuvekt," he said. "Welcome to my home. Will you have some refreshments?"

The eagle-head servant handed around plates holding a variety of canapés, and offered a choice of drinks. Then, in response to a subtle signal from her master, she departed.

When the door clicked firmly behind her, Kuvekt said, "Meg, Peg, and Teg, if you wish, you may remove your masks and gloves. Young Xerak here gave away a little more than he intended, and I wormed the rest out of him. I promise you that I will say nothing about your very interesting origin, but I have travelled widely and I would like to check if I have seen people like yourselves anywhere in my journeys. It is possible that what is alien to these three inquisitors and to Hawtoor-va in his secluded aerie will not be as strange to me."

However, when the three humans hesitantly removed their masks, Kuvekt only shook his head in astonishment. "No. Never have I seen people like yourselves."

Teg pulled out her notebook. In anticipation of further discussion with the inquisitors, she had drawn pictures of Earth primates, choosing from both Old World and New World variations.

"How about these?" she asked. "Have you seen any creatures like these—or any people with heads like these?"

Kuvekt carefully studied the drawings but, once again, his reply was to shake his head. There was wonder as well as negation in the gesture. "There are creatures with bodies like these"—he indicated some of the long-limbed, long-tailed monkeys—"but they lack the flatter faces, the side-positioned ears. The features tend to be sharper, like my own or Vereez's."

Teg drew a rough sketch of a ring-tailed lemur. "Like this?"

"Smoother tail," Kuvekt said, "larger paws, but not unlike. I could show you some pictures."

He half rose as if to get a book, but Grunwold thumped down his drinking bowl—he'd been drinking a sweet-smelling beer—and said, "Please, Scholar-lial. I realize that these three humans offer a fascinating puzzle. I'll admit, the more I learn, the more intricate that puzzle becomes. However, if Xerak let slip the nature of our mentors, then perhaps he also mentioned the questions we seek to answer. Xerak and Vereez might not feel any time pressure, but my father has only recently taken a turn for the worse. Time may be of the essence."

Despite the formality of his language, Grunwold's intensity came through as well.

"I understand your anxiety," Kuvekt replied, "although at my age I have learned that rushing is rarely as useful as it might seem. I thought you might have learned that lesson at Hettua Shrine."

Vereez softened her ears and widened her eyes, looking very childlike and appealing. "We may have learned, but whatever illness Grunwold's father has might not have received the same briefing. Please, can you help us?"

Whether her words or her manner convinced him, Kuvekt allowed himself to be swayed from his curiosity about the humans.

"Xerak said that you planned to go to the Library of the Sapphire Wind. Something about a verse?"

Teg nodded. She began to recite:

Curing one ill who is not sick
Finding the victim of a cruel trick
Easing an ache that cuts to the quick

All of this and more you will find
After you pass through the doorways
Of the Library of the Sapphire Wind

"'Through the doorways of the Library of the Sapphire Wind,'" Kuvekt repeated. "You said this without knowing anything about the Library, even that it existed or had existed?"

"That's right."

"Did you know that when the Library of the Sapphire Wind was destroyed, it was reported that the largest part that remained intact were the enormous main doors?"

"You're kidding!"

"I am not. I have a reliable report—a journal written by one of those who fled the area soon after the disaster."

"That bit about the doorways is creepy," Peg said, "but heartening, too."

"Indeed," Kuvekt said, but his tone was absent, as if his thoughts were far away. "Once upon a time, several young people came to me asking for information about the Library of the Sapphire Wind. Ah, but perhaps I should not say more, lest my words somehow influence your search. I may have said too much already. Let us simply say that I am old and wise enough to see Fate's workings. Very well."

"You'll help us?" Xerak asked eagerly.

"I'll help you on one condition. I would very much like updated maps of the area. I have often doubted the veracity of some of the reports I have received, and none of the maps I have provide the view from above."

"The Library is isolated and in dangerous territory," Grunwold said dubiously. "We may not have the leisure to make complicated maps."

"True," Kuvekt agreed, "but any map, no matter how rough, would be a prized addition to my collection, especially since in your case I would have no reason to believe I was being given the creation of someone's imagination."

Teg cut in. "I'm a fair map maker. I'll do what I can, but it will take time. Is that all right with you?"

"As long as I am not kept waiting years," Kuvekt agreed. "I don't need works of art as much as accuracy."

"Good." Teg chuckled. "I can promise to be as accurate as the situation permits, but I can't promise fine art."

"Then it is settled," Kuvekt said. "Maps of the area surrounding the ruins of the Library of the Sapphire Wind, as well as of the ruins, if at all possible. In return, I will give you free run of my archives, and permission to make copies of any documents, if I don't already have duplicates."

Peg, who had left her knitting behind in honor of the formality of the occasion, asked, "Kuvekt-lial, do you need us to swear or something?"

"Your word should be enough," Kuvekt said, eyes twinkling from within his dark mask. "After all, your word is all that keeps you here."

Kuvekt not only supplied maps, most of which they had to copy, but an old brochure from the days when the Library of the Sapphire Wind accepted applications from scholars who wished to apply to use the facility. While Meg was browsing through Kuvekt's shelves of books, they learned of a limitation to the translation spell. As long as a text was written in one of the more modern scripts, the three humans had no trouble reading it. However, if the text was highly stylized or archaic, they had more difficulty reading it. In some cases, they couldn't read it at all.

However, since the Library of the Sapphire Wind was

a more or less modern concern, most of the materials were easily understood. Only a few of the brochures, which had used elaborate scripts for artistic effect, were beyond the mentors.

Most of the maps had to be copied, but Xerak and Teg were both good at drafting. Meg and Peg both proved to be admirable proofreaders. Nonetheless, nearly two full days went by before they had completed their work. When they had done so, they possessed several maps, both predating and postdating the Library's destruction.

Kuvekt cautioned them about relying overmuch on any of the maps. "I paid well for those maps, true enough. However, there are rumors that the area around the Library has changed considerably since the disaster. Some of the journals claim that the land has continued to change since. That is why no attempt to excavate or explore has ever been successful."

He turned to Meg, holding up a cloth-wrapped bundle that had been knotted at the top to create a handle. "I can tell that you are a scholar, so I would like to loan some books to you. They are journals describing the surroundings of the Library of the Sapphire Wind, as well as some of the hazards that may be encountered there. I will not vouch for their accuracy, but they make for fascinating reading."

Meg eagerly reached for the bundle, then pulled her hands back.

"Kuvekt-lial, these must be incredibly valuable, even if they are mere works of fiction. Why would you loan them to me?"

"Oh, I have ulterior motives," Kuvekt replied,

cheerfully. "Of your company, you are the one I believe would be likely to write an account of what you find. I am merely attempting to entice you to do so, and to perhaps, someday, offer me a copy of your own book."

Meg still looked uncertain. "Teg takes more notes than I do."

Kuvekt snorted. "I am sure she does and, like her maps, they will be accurate, precise, and almost certainly incredibly dry. You, I think, will strive to include the spirit of adventure and discovery, as well as mere facts."

He pushed the bundle toward her again, and this time Meg accepted it with a deep bow.

"All I can promise," she said, "is that I will return these in as good condition as I can." She paused, then relented, "And, if I do write an account, I will share it with you."

Since they were well supplied, and Grunwold had topped off their drinking water while they had done their research, there was no further delay. Once again, *Slicewind* leapt into the skies, caught the breeze, and raced toward their destination.

"Thanks to *Slicewind* we can fly above what looks like some very broken terrain rather than having to hike in," Teg said, reviewing her and Xerak's map with pride. The group was gathered above deck, enjoying the pleasant weather. "The wizard—Dmen Qeres, I think you said his name was—certainly chose a nasty area for his estate."

"They say," Xerak reminded her, "that when the Library was destroyed, there were not only earthquakes and flooding, but also rampaging hordes of creatures freed from magical bondage."

"Charming. Thanks for reminding me. I think I'd been trying to forget."

"How common are these flying ships?" Meg asked.

"Not common," Grunwold replied. "They're expensive, so not usually in private hands. My parents use ours both for work around the estate, and for transport."

Meg nodded. "I was wondering, because we glimpsed a few in Rivers Meet."

"Likely owned by transportation companies," Grunwold said. "Or by the very wealthy."

"Like airplanes in our world," Teg put in.

"So treasure hunters wouldn't have been likely to have access to a flying ship?" Meg continued. "I've been reading these journals, and they either seem to come in by land or over that enormous lake."

"Not likely," Grunwold said. "At least not the sort of people who wrote those journals you've been reading bits from to us. A major concern or a university might have such a ship or charter one, but for some reason no one has."

Xerak laughed as he helped Teg roll up the map. "Too smart to take on the risks. Maybe in another twenty-five years, when some of the magical upheaval has settled, but not now. Even if some of the accounts Meg has been reading us are more than half made up, the other half would be enough to give the liability geeks nightmares."

"Found any good new bits, Meg?" Vereez asked. She'd been practicing swordplay with Peg on the foredeck, using wooden swords, rather than the coppery bladed weapons she'd been holding when they'd first met at Hettua Shrine.

When Peg had first seen Vereez and Grunwold at weapons practice she admitted, almost sheepishly, to having been both an apt fencer in her younger days ("*Lord of the Rings*, you know?"), and then having taken the sport up again some years ago when one of her grandchildren, "Samantha's Bobbi," had joined her school team.

"Fencing is fun," she'd explained cheerfully. "Lower impact exercise, like ballroom dancing, perfectly doable as long as your knees aren't shot. When I moved to Taima, I found a class and have kept up with it. It's a whole lot more inspiring than aerobics."

Peg put the wooden sword Grunwold had loaned her in its case, then started stretching.

"I'm up for more tales of horror and woe," she said. "It'll keep me from thinking about my aches. Vereez works me a lot harder than my instructor did."

"All right, then." Meg, who was seated on one of the stern benches, pulled one of Kuvekt's journals from the pocket of her jacket. "I have been saving a part. It's from an account written by a member of a group who chose to sail in on the lake. Let me see, where was that bit? Ah, here."

She cleared her throat and began to read.

"The land breezes were freshening. Astern of the good ship Prospector, *the mainland dwindled. Stretching before us was the green tangle that had sprung up with suspicious alacrity where once there had been the manicured environs of the Library of the Sapphire Wind.*

"Shock and terror have swept from my mind the memory of which member of our crew first realized that, although the sails belled out no less full, the shore was

growing no closer. However, I shall never forget the shriek from belowdecks that foreshadowed our expedition's doom.

"'We've been breached!'" came the voice of Docan, the quartermaster. "'The claws! The claws!'"

"Docan's words were followed by a scream cut off, as it were, in midbreath. With its cessation, I could hear the sound of wooden planks splintering and felt Prospector *begin to settle lower in the frigid waters of the lake. Several of our number scrabbled toward where the lifeboat hung to stern. I would have joined them but, at that moment, there thrust up from belowdecks a claw not unlike that of many crustaceans, although larger than a person, and colored a bilious yellow. In its grip dangled the body of the unfortunate Docan.*

"I leapt back, and in my panic misjudged, a misjudgment that may well have saved my life, for I hit the side rail and spilled from Prospector *into the lake. Nearby floated one of the crates in which we had intended to stow the treasures we felt so certain we would find. Now I used it to preserve what I suddenly realized was a greater treasure than any other: my life. Using the crate as a float, for I was not—still am not—much of a swimmer, I kicked myself away from the foundering ship. Glancing back, in dread of pursuit, in hope that one of my comrades might also have escaped, I saw nothing but swirling waters, the foam of which was tinged with blood, and fragments of planks and spars. Of* Prospector *and her bold crew, nothing else remained."*

Meg looked up, cheeks a little pink. Teg guessed this wasn't quite like doing a reading for a school group.

"After that," Meg went on, "there's a lot about how the

writer barely made it to shore, and from shore back to civilization."

"I'm glad we aren't sailing on water," Vereez said. "I just hope there aren't similar threats up in the air."

"*Slicewind* should carry us there safely enough," Grunwold assured her. "However, once we arrive, it would be best if we berthed *Slicewind* at ground level."

Peg chuckled. "Oh, absolutely! Otherwise we're going to look like one of those used car lots that anchors a blimp right over the parking lot, as if you could miss acres of shiny cars and trucks!"

Either the translation spell did a remarkable job or— as Teg suspected—the young inquisitors didn't want to ask, yet again, for an explanation.

Grunwold simply rubbed one of his antler tines and said, "We certainly don't want to advertise our presence, but my reason is more practical. A flying ship is too vulnerable to damage if kept aloft. That's why my father stowed *Slicewind* in a boathouse. Even city docks, such as we used in Rivers Meet, are considered temporary berths. Had we been there longer, I would have arranged for a hangar."

Peg reached up and patted his shoulder. "I was teasing you, dear boy. I'm just as glad not to need to climb up and down a wobbling rope ladder to get to our cabins each night."

They sailed both night and day, navigating by the stars, which seemed extraordinarily clear and bright, even to Teg, who had done much work in isolated areas where there was little or no ambient light to wash out the celestial panorama. The course Grunwold had charted took them over forests or fields or even along—if high above—the course of rivers.

"There's nothing illegal about what we're doing," he explained when Meg questioned the need for such care to avoid attracting attention, "but as Kuvekt-lial indicated, periodically, treasure hunters do try their luck at the Library's ruins. I'd rather be as little noticed as possible."

Although the maps had prepared Teg intellectually for the ravaged condition of the region surrounding the Library, she was still startled when, sharing a night watch with Vereez, she looked down and glimpsed a network of red and orange cracks making a crazed pattern of the land far beneath their keel.

"Volcanos?" she asked, taking a final drag on her cigarette, barely resisting the urge to drop the butt down into the fires below.

"Maybe," Vereez said, checking their heading against the rough map. "I doubt it, though. I think Kuvekt would have told us if there were reports of active volcanos. It's just the earth bleeding from the damage done to her. When I was studying magic, they warned us of the damage a single spell gone wrong could do."

She set the wheel on autopilot, then padded over to join Teg. The two of them leaned over the rail, staring down.

"It's incredible, though. Do you think anything of use will have survived?"

"I think so," Teg said. "I can't think why else that verse would have sent us here. Whether what we want will be easy to find, that's another matter completely."

"And no matter what we find here," Vereez went on, her voice so quiet that if Teg had not grown accustomed to how sharp the therianthropes' hearing was, she would have thought the girl spoke to herself, "that's just the start. I mean, I'm not going to find my . . . sister here, nor is Xerak likely to find his master. I suppose Grunwold might find a cure for his father's illness. But my search will just be beginning."

Teg didn't normally think of herself as an insightful person. Any intuition she had was reserved for archeological sites, and that was more the result of hundreds of hours of experience rather than anything else. But this time she spoke her thought aloud, knowing she was right.

"Your daughter," she said. "You're looking for your daughter, not your sister. Am I right?"

Vereez wheeled on her, lips pulled back from her teeth in a snarl, ears flat to her skull. Over the days they'd traveled together, Teg had grown accustomed enough to the three inquisitors' odd hybridization of human and animal qualities that the relatively greater mobility of Meg and Peg's human features could look unsettling by contrast.

Now, however, there was nothing usual about Vereez's fox face. She looked canine, ferocious, and wild. Her words were underscored with a rumbling growl.

"How did you know? Have you been reading my diary? I thought someone had been in my pack but, when I asked, only Peg admitted to anything and she said she'd just been looking for dirty laundry."

Fleetingly, Teg wondered if Peg had been speaking

metaphorically, taking advantage of the translation spell to tell the truth with a twist, but what Peg might or might not have been doing was of scant interest when faced with the furious young woman who now looked as if she might—quite literally—bite her.

"No. I haven't. I wouldn't. But we've stood a few watches together now and, well, there's a focus, an intensity about you when you speak about your missing 'sister' that..."

Teg let herself trail off because, in truth, she really didn't know where her thought had come from. When Vereez still didn't speak, Teg said softly, "You want to talk about it? I promise, I won't tell anyone."

"I...I would like to tell someone. But I'm not ready for..." Her pause was long enough that Teg wondered if she was thinking of someone in particular. Grunwold maybe? "I'm not ready for the boys to know. It's uncomfortable."

"I promise I won't tell anyone," Teg repeated. "If you want, I'll even go further and play dumb if someone asks me directly if I have any suspicions."

"I'd like to tell someone—you," Vereez repeated.

"Then let's go over by the wheel," Teg suggested. "That way we won't forget that we have a course change coming up."

Vereez nodded. Her ears, Teg was relieved to see, had resumed their normal upright position, though there was still a hint of a snarl in the curve of her mouth.

"It was nearly five years ago," Vereez began. "I was just a kid, though I thought myself pretty much grown up. There was a guy... He was three years older than I am.

Funny. I never thought about it, but that's younger than I am now. Anyhow, Kaj's mother came to the city on business. I'll admit, I didn't pay much attention to what business, though I did have the impression that Kaj's mom had known my parents really well when they were all younger, and that she was hoping to play off that to ask my parents for a loan."

"Your parents are bankers?" Teg asked, more to show that she was listening than for any other reason.

Vereez nodded again. "Investments, rather than just money exchanging. Anyhow, for whatever reason, we saw a lot of them and that's how I met Kaj. I fell for him hard. Really hard. He was handsome, sure, but even more than that, he was everything I'd never encountered before. There was an aura of danger about him. From the stories he told, I gathered he'd travelled a lot, seen some amazing places. I didn't think he'd even notice me. I mean, I told you I thought of myself as pretty much grown up but, at the same time, he made me feel what a kid I was, how protected I'd been, how limited my contact with people outside my parents' social circle had been."

"But he did notice you," Teg said.

"He did . . ." Vereez sighed. "Oh, he did. He made me feel so important. I'd never had a boyfriend, not even a serious flirtation. My parents wanted to introduce me to society in a big way when I turned fifteen. I went to an all-girls school."

And then James Dean, bad boy supreme, shows up. Where were her parents?

Teg pinched her lip so she wouldn't say anything. Vereez misinterpreted the gesture and said, almost shyly,

"If you want to light up that pipe Xerak gave you, that would be okay. It doesn't smell as horrible as the cigarettes."

Teg fumbled for the pipe and busied herself with the ritual of packing it, then getting it to draw. Meantime, Vereez, her voice dreamy, kept talking.

"I didn't know Kaj was trouble. I didn't know he was probably simply bored, stuck in a city with a lot of stuffy people. Maybe he was just in hunting mode. I don't know. But he seduced me—or maybe I did him. I was so incredibly crazy for him, I lost all common sense. This was it, LOVE, capital letters, Forever And Ever, Fate, Destiny. Never mind that our worlds were so different, that his mother wanted a loan . . . We were forever."

Vereez threw back her head and for a moment Teg wondered if she would howl. Did foxes howl? Then the beautiful head drooped, the ears folded in dejection.

"Except it wasn't. We had a glorious month. Maybe it was glorious only for me. Maybe he was humping every girl in sight, and I was just a frilly little sweetshop treat added to the mix. I don't even know if Kaj's mom got her loan. I think she did. Between one day and the next it was 'good-bye.' He didn't even write. And then . . ."

"You found out you were pregnant."

Vereez's ears and tail drooped. "When my parents figured it out, I was sent away to 'study abroad.' When the baby came they took it away from me before I ever saw it. I only know it was a girl because someone said 'she' in my hearing, otherwise I might have just gone to a weight-loss spa for all anyone acknowledged what I'd been through. Before the next school year, I was sent home and back to my former academy. The only thing that changed was that I didn't get that fancy coming-out party, and I had acquired a chaperone."

Teg tried a smoke ring, failed, and asked, "Chaperone?"

"Until I finished school. After that, my parents really couldn't continue making me have one without raising questions, and questions . . . They never, ever want questions. Questions aren't proper."

"When did you start looking for the child?" Teg asked.

"Not right away." Vereez sounded ashamed. "I should have, but I was overwhelmed. About a year ago, when graduation was coming up, I realized that there were only two things I cared about—finding out what happened to my baby, and learning what happened to Kaj. My parents wouldn't even talk to me about it. I wasn't lying when I said they acted as if it never happened. A few times I thought I had leads, but those always petered out."

"And so you decided to consult Hettua Shrine."

"Yeah. Xerak got me thinking about it, actually. There was a lot of gossip about him. Everyone knew he'd gone completely nuts since his master vanished, but I thought what Xerak was doing was great. I sought him out when I heard he was in Rivers Meet. He told me he'd been thinking about going to this obscure shrine, seeking mystic guidance. Grunwold's family estate was on the way, so we wrote him, told him we'd be coming through, did he want to meet us for dinner or something. Instead, he insisted on coming along."

Teg couldn't hold back any longer. "And your parents— they didn't try to stop you? Even after what you'd been through, they let you go off with two boys? Young men?"

Vereez laughed, but a hard, ironical note underlay the humor. "Oh, they said things, but by making my choice to consult the oracle . . . Remember what we said about how there's no one 'age of majority'? Anyhow, I was making a responsible choice, trying to find a goal in life. If my choice of companions was a bit strange, well, Xerak and Grunwold were also boys I'd known since I was little, the closest thing I had to brothers."

"I bet . . ." Teg studied Vereez thoughtfully, sensing that she was still holding back part of the truth. "You threatened your parents, didn't you? You told them that if they made a fuss, you'd tell about the baby."

Vereez looked over, startled again. "You are incredible! How did you guess?"

Teg shrugged. "Something about how you kept mentioning that they hated questions, how careful they were of their social status. I realized you could use that against them."

"That's it. I was surprised how well it worked. I thought that they'd at least insist one of my girl cousins come along or something. But no. I think they were more afraid I might confide in someone, then my scandalous past would get to the wrong ears."

"Maybe that's it," Teg agreed. She had a gut feeling there was more to Vereez's parents' peculiar behavior than that, but she didn't think Vereez was being coy. The young woman looked visibly relieved to be talking.

"Have you ever told anyone any of this before?"

"No one. First I was too embarrassed, not so much about the baby—that somehow doesn't seem embarrassing at all—but that I'd been used and dumped. When I got older, saw other girls flinging themselves at guys, and realized how my behavior seemed from the outside, I knew what a fool I'd been. My tail drooped at the thought of how I must have looked, frisking around Kaj all big eyes and romantic dreams."

Vereez shuddered dramatically. "Even when I decided to find my daughter, I didn't want to tell the story except to people who could help me."

"Like me?"

"That's it. Like you. But I don't think I would have said anything unless you'd guessed, not for a while, at least."

"I won't say anything," Teg promised, "but I should warn you, Peg and Meg may figure what's going on even if I don't drop any hints. They both have a lot of experience with people—more than me, I think."

Vereez shrugged. "I'll deal with that as it happens. Right now, we find our way into the Library. For the first time since I started looking, I feel as if I have a chance. That's enough . . . for now."

By the time the sun had risen, *Slicewind* had sailed beyond the lava field and was racing over what must be the ruins of the library complex and the associated town— an area roughly a couple of miles both wide and deep, although not a neat square by anyone's estimation.

Teg stood in the bow, leaning over the side, scanning the area below for a landmark that would correspond with something—anything—on their maps. All she was finding was a tangle of green, interrupted by heaps of masonry. Where buildings could be seen, the devastation was horrible. Teg had seen pictures of cities after aerial bombing raids but, although there were similarities—hardly an intact wall, evidence of fire damage—this was different. There was something about the damage that reminded Teg of what she'd seen in post-earthquake photos—as if the breaking force had come from beneath, not above. But even that wasn't quite right.

"Anything?" Grunwold called from the wheel. He'd been meticulously sailing *Slicewind* in an unbelievably precise search pattern, first around the perimeter, then patiently back and forth in a grid. The first thing they'd confirmed was that the lava field didn't encircle the entire area. Instead, a large lake commanded one side, a jagged, up-thrust mountain range cut off another.

According to the journals Meg had been reading, the earliest explorers of the ruins had chosen to sail in over the lake. This had proven to be a mistake, for what had been a placid body of water in the glory days of the Library of the Sapphire Wind, barely justifying the term *lake*, had more than tripled in size, and become much deeper, hosting some curious creatures beneath its surface. However, the lava field had been judged impossible to cross on foot, leaving either the mountains or a sterile strip where lava met lake and created a plain of glass. *Slicewind*'s ability to sail over these obstacles definitely gave their own group an advantage.

"Nothing yet," Teg replied. "I was hoping to spot something distinctive... Maybe that colonnade that's shown in so many of the pictures, or a chunk of the big dome, but so far, *nada*. Also, there are plants that prefer disturbed areas or need less soil. These will grow over areas where buildings have fallen. Trees need greater soil depth, but benefit from how buried structures trap and hold moisture, so saplings will grow up around foundations."

"Huh." There was a long pause, then Grunwold said, "Actually, I get that. I should, given all the lectures I've had in my agriculture courses about growing conditions for different plants, but I never would have thought of plants as a clue to finding ruins."

"If we don't see anything at this elevation," Teg went on, not pausing in the steady sweep of her binoculars over the ground, "we may need to go up higher and look from there."

"Higher?" Grunwold's tone made clear that he thought he'd misheard.

"Higher," Teg repeated. "Sometimes you can pick out shapes from a higher perspective that you can't from ground level. Up close, you can't pick out the differences, but from a higher elevation, you see the patterns."

"Do you want me to take us up now?"

"Let's finish our grid first," Teg said. "I haven't given up hope we'll find something significant."

She didn't say that she was also scouting for evidence of the many dangers they'd been warned about. So far she'd seen many flying creatures, both large and small. She was pretty certain what she'd seen had all been birds, although some of the flyers had seemed to fit the "winged-dinosaur" classification, like Heru. Anyhow, their presence made sense, since none of the geographic barriers would offer creatures with wings any more of a challenge than they had *Slicewind*. She'd also seen an assortment of rabbit-to-deer-sized creatures, but so far none of the monstrous creatures the journals had warned about.

Not seeing worried her. Did these creatures only come out at night? Were they even real? Maybe they were just something the journal writers realized would make their accounts more exciting—and explain their utter failure to find any of the treasures they sought.

Teg wished she believed that. They finished their first series of passes over the library grounds without managing to make a definitive match with anything on their map, so Grunwold took *Slicewind* higher. Only when they reached a height where the terrain seemed more like a model than a real place did they find possible matches.

"Despite the lack of buildings," Meg said, lowering her own binoculars, "that hill could be where the main library building was. See? If you trace down the slope that direction"—she pointed—"there are remnants of walls that could represent the remains of what the brochure calls the Central Facility and Repository."

"The hill doesn't seem central enough," Xerak protested. "It's too close to the lake."

"We know the lake waters have risen," Meg reminded him. "Your protest reinforces, rather than disproves, my theory. Water does not flow uphill . . ."

"At least not where we come from," Peg quipped.

". . . and so the rise of the land would have been an impediment to the water's spread," Meg continued placidly. "This would also explain why the hill seems lopsided, rather than relatively symmetrical, as it is in the various artistic renderings we have."

"If Meg is right," Vereez said, "then that meadow is probably what remains of the cultivated lands and pasture. The village would be where that tangle is."

Grunwold said, "I've been considering anchoring *Slicewind* in that meadow for the simple reason it's the largest open area I've seen—unless we want to anchor in the lake."

"No!" came simultaneously from five throats, causing a general round of uneasy laughter, as everyone remembered Meg's dramatic reading.

"The meadow it is then," Grunwold said, adjusting the elevation shift. "Help me find a place without too many saplings."

"Or too many monsters," Peg added in a sepulchral tone, then laughed.

❧CHAPTER SIX❧

"I wish every field camp was this easy to set up," Teg commented a short time later.

Grunwold had brought *Slicewind* down over a promising spot, held it in place while Vereez and Xerak scouted to make sure they wouldn't land the ship on something's nest or burrow, and that the ground beneath the thick grass was relatively level. When the scouts gave the okay, skids were attached to brackets on the outside of the hull, so that *Slicewind* could rest on the ground without damage to the keel. The set of portable steps made going up and down easy.

"It is rather like having a deluxe RV," Peg said.

"That flies," Teg said, patting the ship affectionately. "Even if the field school could afford an RV, we wouldn't be able to get it to most of the places where we need to camp on-site."

Their chosen campsite was near a freshwater stream with a pool deep enough that a siphon pump could be dropped in, making getting water into the ship a simple and civilized matter.

"We'll need to lock up, then trust to *Slicewind*'s wards when we go exploring the ruins," Grunwold said. "I wouldn't want to leave any fewer than two people behind, and that would leave only four to poke around. Given some of what Meg has been reading to us . . ."

Peg looked unwontedly worried. "Better we stay together."

Xerak said, "I know we brought supplies, but how about we set a few snares, Grun?"

Vereez cut in. "I'd love to have fresh meat as much as anyone, but what if we caught some monster? How about we settle for fish and what green stuff we can forage for here?"

"If you can acquaint me with the equipment," Meg said, "I would be happy to sit and fish. Charles, my late husband, loved to fish, and I acquired the skill—and the patience—over many a summer trip."

Teg also was good at fishing, but she was itching to explore, and was relieved when Peg—whose ex-son-in-law, Arnold, as it turned out, had also loved to fish—offered to join Meg.

The inquisitors were clearly surprised that genteel Meg was skilled in something as smelly as fishing, but they took her up on her offer. Before long, Meg, and Peg were casting glittering lures over the water. This world didn't have fancy fiberglass rods or the like, but a flexible plant whose name translated as "whipweed" served very well. The fish must have liked the brightly colored yarns Peg used to augment their lures, or maybe there hadn't been any fishing here for so long that they had lost any suspicion. For whatever reason, the catch was ample and the fresh fish, augmented with greens and tubers gathered by Xerak and Grunwold, tasted great.

Over dinner, they finished refining their plans.

"The trail we'll be following is pretty narrow," Grunwold began. "Since I'm fairly good with a sword, I'll take point. Xerak, how fast can you get your magic into play if we need it?"

"If I prepare in advance, like I did before we got *Slicewind* out of the boat house, fairly fast," Xerak said. "Just remember, if I do too much, I'm going to be useless."

"More useless," Grunwold shot back, automatically mocking. "But seriously, it's good to know we can count on magical support if something goes wrong. Vereez, can you take rear guard? We hear better than the humans do. Catch scents better, too."

"No problem," Vereez said, looking up from where she was carefully inspecting her twin swords, cleaning them as if her life might depend on the sheen of the copper blades.

"I've been meaning to ask," Teg interrupted, "but how useful will swords with copper blades be in an actual fight? I'd think copper would be too soft to hold an edge well."

Vereez bared her teeth in a smile. "Oh, these blades are made from copper that's been magically hardened. They'll hold an edge as well as steel, better even, if I take proper care of them."

"That's good then," Teg said. "I'd gathered from some

of our chats that you haven't had the military training Grunwold has had, but you're kickass when you and Peg have been fencing."

"I haven't had military training," Vereez admitted, "but I took a class back when I was small enough that my parents both thought that their little girl waving a sword about was cute. I turned out to have a knack for swordplay, and have kept up with it since. I've even represented my school at tournaments. But I've never cut anyone except by accident. I don't even like hunting."

"Thanks," Teg said. "Sorry, General Grunwold, pray, continue."

"I thought we'd put you three humans in the middle," Grunwold said. "Any suggestions as to order?"

"I'll take the next-to-rear position," Peg said promptly, "since I have some skill with a sword—although, like Vereez, I've never cut someone in anger."

Something about the way Peg stressed "cut," made Teg suspect that if angered, sword in hand or not, Peg could be formidable. Remembering a few arguments at book club, Teg decided to upgrade "could" to "would."

"Let me have the fourth position," Meg said. "As Teg demonstrated earlier, when we were cutting brush for the cook fire, she at least can use a machete, so she could back up you, Grunwold, while Xerak gets his spell ready. I fear I would be needing protection, rather than otherwise."

"Good then," Grunwold said. "That leaves the question of what other supplies we'll bring, and who should carry what."

They went over their plans with such care that when

they actually set out, shortly after dawn the next morning, Teg had a curious sense that they'd gone hiking together before.

In addition to his sword, Grunwold carried a long spear with which he probed the ground whenever a fallen tree or some other obstacle meant that they had to venture off the narrow trail that, based on their maps, might be the remnant of what had once been a broad, paved road. A few times, his care saved them from stepping into holes or, one time, a nest of something like snakes. Xerak strode alertly along, his spear staff held with familiar confidence in his right hand. He wore a machete at his belt, both as a tool, and as a backup weapon.

The three humans—clad in the hiking clothes they'd brought from home—came next. Teg's daypack held a variety of small tools, including a whisk broom. They'd debated bringing shovels, but had decided those could wait until they'd done their preliminary scouting.

Next came Meg, who shouldered a light pack holding what they hoped would be the most useful of the books and maps, then Peg. In one hand, Peg held a light, flexible sword from *Slicewind*'s stores. Peg also carried the pack holding lunch—and a pair of socks she was knitting: "In case we end up sitting around while Teg does something archeological." Vereez brought up the rear.

Their first day among the ruins, they didn't find the hoped-for door. They didn't even find the main library building. However, they did establish several encouraging data points, including that the trail they were following was definitely the same road which had led between the library complex proper and the village where (as their research had confirmed) the support staff and junior librarians had lived.

They also established that, despite the seemingly complete destruction as seen from the air—something they all had found discouraging—more of the complex was at least partially intact than had seemed possible.

"It's as if portions of the ground simply dropped straight down," Teg said, hunkering to inspect a section of wall from which they'd trimmed the enshrouding vines. "From above, this seemed like the remnants of a wall, the upper portion of which had broken or crumbled away. Up close . . . I'm guessing this is the top of the wall, probably adjoining the roof. See there? That's where the roof supports would have gone."

Grunwold—sweaty but without the rank body odor Teg was familiar with from many a young archeologist—crouched next to her and peered down. "Do you think the roof caved in?"

"Probably. I'd love to look but"—she sighed and pushed herself to her feet—"this isn't the doorway into the Library, and I'll save the risky stuff for excavating that."

Meg had kept busy making notes on a rough map. "Not that we'll be likely to miss this place—not with all the pruning you have done—but better to be meticulous."

Peg chuckled. "You don't fool me. You're taking notes for when you write your own addition to Kuvekt's collection of explorer's journals."

Meg's pink-and-white complexion was no good at hiding blushes. "Well, I did think . . . I mean, don't you think Kuvekt-lial would enjoy a less sensational, more practical, text?"

Peg gave Meg a quick hug. "He would and, like every librarian I've ever met, you secretly want to write a book of your own, don't you?"

"I'm all for Meg writing the star volume of Kuvekt-lial's collection," Teg agreed. "Let's work from here long enough to get a general sense of how large this building is, its relation to the road, and to other structures. We can then compare that information to the maps we have back on *Slicewind*. That will help us refine our search tomorrow."

Both that day and the next, they continued in this fashion. Their course took them gradually uphill, into an area where towering trees—possibly the remnants of the Library's original ornamental plantings—competed with secondary growth of vines, smaller shrubs, and a wide variety of opportunistic plants.

Grunwold, now that he was aware of the significance of plant growth, noted wherever a seemingly solid patch of growth was likely to indicate a hidden or collapsed structure.

"I feel like Indiana Jones in the first movie," Peg said, slapping at something multilegged and emerald green. The local equivalents of mosquitoes and biting flies didn't care for the taste of human, but that didn't mean some of them didn't sample. "The one that starts in the jungle. I hope we don't find a pit of snakes, next."

On the fourth day of exploration, they confirmed the location of the main library building. They also met their first taste of the dangers that they had begun to believe were nothing more than travelers' tall tales.

It wasn't that they hadn't encountered some nasty creatures. When fishing the second evening, Meg had pulled up something that looked like the offspring of a lobster and a circular saw blade. The crustacean hadn't been much larger than a salad plate, but it had buzzed its claws so threateningly that Meg—normally preternaturally calm—had shrieked at the top of her lungs.

Upon seeing what had startled her, Vereez had yelped in delight and netted the noisy little horror, which turned out to be considered something of a delicacy. Vereez had caught several others, and couldn't stop thanking Meg for her find, speculating that the lake might have been stocked with them, since they weren't usually found far inland.

The "lobsaws," as Peg dubbed them, *were* tasty, but after that the three humans restricted themselves to paddling in the clearest sections of the stream, where the pale beige sand clearly revealed anything that was sharing the water.

Heru had had several nasty encounters with something the inquisitors called "efindon," and which Peg dubbed "lizard parrots." Only the fact that the lizard parrots were more gliders than flyers, and that they seemed genetically adverse to cooperation, saved the mini pterodactyl from serious injury. After that, Heru decided that staying near *Slicewind* and trying to steal Peg's yarn was more amusing than solo exploration.

Xerak drifted off the third evening—probably to drink, Teg thought, for although he hid the signs well, she had experience with more than one secret drinker. He came jogging back, tail lashing, eyes wide and scraggly mane wild, to report that he'd had a brush with a small pack of qwesemu, creatures built more or less like a wolf, but with quills like a porcupine. He'd frightened them off with a pyrotechnic scatter, and taken to his heels. Peg dubbed these "spike wolves."

Peg—especially since the translation spell actually adopted her terms—became annoyed when Meg, who had been carefully recording the creatures' actual names, tried to get Peg and Teg to use them.

"Why can't you call a qwesemu a 'qwesemu,' not a 'spike wolf'?" Meg said with a quiet patience that did not hide her exasperation.

"Because the one is just a funny-sounding word, and the other is descriptive," Peg replied sharply. "I need to remember why I'm supposed to be scared of something, not try to remember if it's pronounced *qweh-semu* or *qwes-eh-mu* when I glimpse one lurking in the underbrush."

"You have a point," Meg admitted, but she persisted in her efforts to learn the local language.

Although to the humans the spike wolves and lizard parrots seemed distinctly monstrous, the inquisitors seemed to feel that the encounters were more or less "normal" events.

Not much different, Teg thought, *from the brushes I've had had with skunks, coyotes, even mountain lions and bears, on my more isolated field projects.*

The encounter with the piranha toads was completely different.

They'd headed out that morning carrying shovels and trundling a flatbed cart, in addition to their usual kits, for they felt sure they would find the entry to the main library building that day. To this point, there had been no sign of the towering doors depicted in their research materials, but bits of paving and an anomalously intact ornamental pedestal—now so smothered in vines that they'd taken it for a shrub until Meg suggested they check it more closely—had pinpointed the location.

Teg had wanted to start clearing right away, but Grunwold—who by benefit of his role as owner/captain of *Slicewind* had been landed with the role of organizer, if not precisely leader—insisted they had to head back to *Slicewind* before the spike wolves and other nocturnal creatures started prowling.

"If you humans had better night vision," he grumbled, "we could stay out, but you don't."

"At least you didn't say we're too old," Peg said, heaving herself to her feet. "I'm all for getting back and putting some heat on my lower back."

Back aboard *Slicewind*, once dinner had been made, and Vereez had been reminded that it was her turn to do the dishes, Teg and Meg sat in the table in the lounge poring over maps and drawings.

"I think that's where the entrance should be," Teg said, lightly penciling in a five-pointed star to mark the spot. "These landmarks should help us find it."

"It's a pity we lack photographs," Meg said. "With drawings there's always the chance of an artist's interpretation adding an element of inaccuracy."

"Photos can have the same problems," Teg assured her. "Angle, type of lens, even lighting can distort. That's why solid landmarks—like that statue you found depicting the Library's founder, Dmen Qeres—are so valuable."

Peg, who was sitting in one of the cushy chairs, a hot water bottle at the small of her back, her fingers busy knitting some fingerless gloves from a heavy material more like string than yarn, spoke around a yawn. "Just remember, Teg. We're not here to do archeology. We're here to find the doors."

Teg sighed. "I haven't forgotten. But . . ."

"We've already been in this world for eighteen days, since we told our families we were going on our trip," Meg said. "At a scale of seven to one, that's not even three full days. Nonetheless, we need to consider the passage of time."

"Promise, no letting archeological fervor distract me from our goal," Teg said, raising her hand in something vaguely like a Boy Scout's salute, although when she thought about it, she realized she might have gotten it mixed up with the Vulcan one, from *Star Trek*.

The next morning, Teg was up before first light, reassuring herself that the weather was not going to interfere with their expedition. She found Grunwold also awake, neatly arranging shovels, coils of rope, oil lanterns, and devices that worked much like flashlights, although the "bulb" was a magically enhanced crystal.

"I'll get breakfast started," she said. "Peg's in the shower, and Meg's getting dressed."

Meg emerged a short time later. "I'll pack us a lunch, just in case we don't want to come back here before dark."

Despite mild protests from Vereez, who even after a

long day would stay up for hours, and Xerak, who probably had a hangover, the three mentors and three inquisitors were on the trail to the ruins while the dew was still drying on the grass.

Once they were on the site, despite her promise of the night before, Teg couldn't help falling into her usual archeological protocols. She eased the likelihood of complaints by putting the three inquisitors to work in the area where the door was most likely to be located, then recruited Peg and Meg to help her create a fresh map using the few certain landmarks they'd found, then shading in details from the map they'd made using the brochures and books they'd gotten from Kuvekt.

Teg paced off distances, something she could do with close accuracy, and Meg handled the sketching. Peg climbed up onto the pedestal holding the statue of Dmen Qeres to get a better perspective of the scene and compare it to her map.

"There was a statue like this at my college," she mused aloud as she settled herself, "of one of the early deans or something. It was just like this—academic gown, the book open between his hands. I swear that even allowing for the fact that this fellow has a raven's head, the expression was just the same. Pompous and wiser-than-thou. It was like a challenge, y'know. People used to write rude things on the book's pages."

She stood on tiptoe, so she could look at the book the statue held, then read aloud, "'Underfoot is the priceless gem, keystone you require.' Huh, that's weird. Maybe I got the first word wrong? Shouldn't it be something like *wisdom* or *knowledge* or *education*?"

"Is that actually written there?" Meg asked, her voice oddly tight.

"Sure! You don't think I could make up something like that? When I took my turn writing in our dean's book, I quoted some of Jim Morrison's lyrics."

"What's strange," Meg said, closing her journal, in which she'd been sketching their site map, "is that yesterday, after we found the statue, I got up on the pedestal—I had Xerak give me a boost—so I could look at the book. I will swear that the pages were blank."

"Slide over, Peg," Teg said, trotting over. "I want to take a look."

"I'll hop down," Peg said, lowering herself onto her butt before making the drop to save her knees.

Teg clambered up, feeling the aches in her calves from the last couple of days' hikes. "Peg's absolutely right, Meg. Those words are here, but I completely believe you when you say they weren't yesterday. The inscription doesn't look nearly worn enough to have been exposed to weather for two decades, much less going back to when the Library was founded. Peg, would you get Xerak? We need a wizard's opinion."

When Xerak took his turn, leaping up with an effortless grace that was practically feline—*Or maybe I've just forgotten what it was like to be in my early twenties,* Teg thought ruefully—he was equally baffled.

"After Meg had taken a look," he admitted, "I did, too. The pages were blank and smooth. What's weird is that they're still smooth, like these words were painted on, not carved."

"Can you, uh, 'detect magic' or something?" Peg asked.

"I played D&D with my grandkids and their friends, and that's a pretty basic spell."

Xerak looked confused. "I thought you said you didn't have magic in your world."

"We don't," Peg said cheerfully, "but that doesn't mean we can't pretend. Can you detect any magic?"

Xerak closed his eyes and concentrated, then waved both hands and the tip of his tail. "There's something. Faint. Almost as if it came from inside the statue? That's not quite right, but it's the best I can manage."

"Maybe," Meg offered, "there was a spell in the statue, one that would provide inspiration if anyone climbed up and looked at the page. Maybe what you and I did yesterday activated the magic but, because of all the damage to the Library, the book took a while to provide a quote. That would explain why this doesn't make much sense. The mechanism could have been damaged when the Library was."

"Makes as much sense as anything," Xerak agreed, jumping down. From the way his tail kept lashing, Teg would have bet he wasn't at all satisfied. "Well, we've been moving dirt and rock, but you ladies win the prize for the most interesting find. Figures. Come see what we've uncovered."

While the three mentors had been mapping, the sweating inquisitors had cleared away sufficient of the encroaching vegetation to discover that here—as in so many places—the ground was broken and uneven. Foundation lines showed how part of a wall remained on their level, while the rest of the same wall marched on a good five to eight meters below.

"The doors, if they're here at all," Vereez said, panting slightly and accepting Teg's canteen with a grateful swish of her tail, "probably are associated with a part of the building that dropped down."

Teg knelt and inspected the buckled pavement, which was made from flat, hexagonal stones. "Down and possibly to one side or another. See how these pavers have shifted? According to the drawings in the brochures, there was an elaborate ornamental pavement leading up to the main entrance. This is part of that pavement, but torqued."

"Any sense which way?" Grunwold asked eagerly.

Teg shook her head. "Not with this small a sample, but if we clear some more . . ."

Peg marched over, grasped the handles of a small, wheeled flatbed cart laden with the vegetation the inquisitors cut away, and groaned theatrically. "Let's get to it!"

They worked steadily, taking a quick break for lunch, then getting back to work almost before they were done chewing.

Maybe it was the rumble of the cart. Maybe it was the general excitement of being near their goal, but none of them—not even sharp-eared Vereez—noticed the approaching menace until one snared Peg around her middle with its tongue.

She, very sensibly, screamed, then even more sensibly added, "Help! I'm being eaten by a piranha toad!"

The piranha toads were the size of a compact car, a mottled deep purple. They resembled a toad in that they were squat, as wide as they were long, and possessed of enormous mouths. These mouths boasted multiple rows of needle-sharp teeth, tightly spaced except for a gap in the middle through which the tongue—a cord of startling violet—snapped out.

Those teeth, Teg thought wildly, *must be the piranha part.*

"Feerranu!" Vereez shouted, turning around, the shovel she'd been using on some stubborn roots in hand. "But these are enormous!"

Not sparing time for a reply, Grunwold loped down the slope, machete in hand, heading toward Peg.

Meg—who was perched up on a heap of masonry where she could take notes without being in the way—called in a voice so calm and cool that she might have been announcing that the library would be closing in fifteen minutes, "Two more of the feerranu are emerging from the undergrowth, to the right and left of the one that has Peg."

"Let us know if you see others," Xerak yelled. "Vereez, deal with the one on the left. I'll take the one on the right."

"Got it!" The reply was more like a sharp yap than a word as, still holding the shovel, Vereez charged.

Teg paused, looking for her own opening. Digging while wearing swords had proven too cumbersome, so no one was wearing weapons, although Xerak had his spear staff. She didn't even have a machete, and the whisk broom she'd been using to clear pavement wasn't much of a weapon.

Grunwold had reached Peg's captor. Teg thought he'd smash it in the head. Instead he brought down the machete's blade in a carefully aimed strike and sliced through its tongue. Blood the ridiculous blue of raspberry popsicles showered forth.

Peg dropped, rolling frantically in an effort to get free from the binding tongue. Teg grabbed a shovel, and went to help her. After that, if it hadn't been for Meg's occasional calls of encouragement and direction, she would have had no sense of what was going on around her.

"Nicely done, Grunwold!"

"Xerak, if you're done bashing yours, I believe Vereez could use help. Two more of those feerranu just came out not far from her."

"Teg! Leave Peg be. There's one coming at you."

Teg swung her shovel blindly, felt it hit something that felt like an under-inflated tire, heard a grunt of . . . pain? Surprise?

Nearby, Peg was on her feet, her face blue with the piranha toad's blood, streaked with tears, but her expression was angry, not afraid. Teg got between her and the creature, smacking it directly in the mouth when it began to open its jaws, the coiled tongue visible through the gap in its teeth.

"Good hit!" Peg said. "I want a shovel, too. Fucking son of a bastard bitch tried to eat me!"

Teg flashed a grin at her. "Looks as if the inquisitors have things under control . . ."

Meg's voice cut her off. "Everyone, back up! Get up to where we were excavating. I see some qwesemu—spike wolves—in the forest. They're hesitating . . ."

No wonder, Teg thought as she'd worked her awkward way up the slope—a job made infinitely harder because she wasn't going to turn her back on the battle. The original three piranha toads were down, although still twitching. Xerak was using his staff to scientifically batter another. Vereez had reverted to the two-handed style of her training, machete in one hand, a steel trowel from Teg's dig kit in the other. Between her and Grunwold yet another piranha toad, this one an enormous specimen the size of a VW bus, was getting the worst of it.

Heru, who had been frantically circling over the battle, began to croak, "Lizard parrots! Lizard parrots! Lizard parrots!"

"No, you idiot!" Grunwold cursed. "These are piranha toads not..."

But the orange and green xuxu had not been wrong. A flock of the lizard parrots were gliding in, for once in agreement with each other. Whether they intended to scavenge or join the battle was unclear, but no one was taking a chance.

With a final slash at their deflating opponent, Vereez and Grunwold broke for the slight bit of open ground offered by the dig site. Xerak brought his staff down in a powerful two-handed blow between the piranha toad's eyes and did the same, not waiting to see if he'd killed or only stunned his opponent.

Behind them was the pit into which at least part of the Library had dropped. In front, the spike wolves were beginning to stalk stiff-legged, quills rattling, from cover. Above, the lizard parrots swirled, random members of the flock darting down to test their defense. The inquisitors positioned themselves to the fore, Xerak in the middle, Vereez to his left, Grunwold to his right. Grunwold had his spear now. Vereez was feinting with Teg's trowel in an adaptation of her usual two-handed fighting style.

Xerak, meanwhile was clearly preparing to do something wizardly. As on the night they'd stolen *Slicewind*, this involved an intricate dance, employing not only arms and legs, hands and feet, but tail. Teg, standing slightly behind and to one side of Vereez, forced herself to not watch the almost hypnotic motions. She didn't think the bulky piranha toads could get up here but the spike wolves and lizard parrots were another matter.

She saw motion in the growth to one side, something creeping along, stealthily taking advantage of the confusion to move in on their flank. Based on size and shape, it might be one of the spike wolves.

I thought Grunwold said those were nocturnal.

Grabbing her shovel more tightly, Teg prepared to swing. Maybe the creature saw the motion and decided to get the jump on her while it could. While still several yards away, it leapt, but misjudged the distance. Its jaws snapped harmlessly, inches from her face. Its body caught Teg squarely in the torso and knocked her back and into the dank depths.

Thought and Memory were walking up and down her, the way they did when they wanted to wake her up to feed them. Thought probed Teg's cheek with a cool nose. Memory gently nipped her wrist.

"Go 'way," Teg muttered. "I wanna sleep."

The cats persisted. Now someone was yelling. Hadn't

she gotten rid of the clock radio because she hated waking up to some DJ shouting? Better a buzz or electronic chirping.

"Teg! Teg!"

The voices were familiar. What was the book club doing at her house? They always met at Pagearean Books. Was it a holiday? Valentine's Day? They were going to have a small group, just Meg and Peg and her: the widow, the divorcee, and the luckless loser.

Memory nipped her wrist again. At the sharp pain, Teg remembered everything, including the spike wolf hitting her in the chest and her falling. She felt under her, realized she'd landed on a pad of accumulated plant matter, thick enough to be springy.

Should she move? What if she'd broken something? She didn't hurt too much, but would she hurt if she'd broken her back? Teg decided—for the moment at least—to settle for shouting. Though what if that spike wolf was somewhere near? Well, she guessed she'd learn if she could move then.

"Uh, hello!"

"Teg! Teg! You're alive!" Peg's voice.

Teg laughed painfully. "I think so. Maybe I'm just an echo or a talking xuxu like Heru."

"Don't move," Meg said, her voice even calmer than usual—a sure sign she was panicked. "Right after you fell, Xerak released some sort of electrical charge that made the lizard parrots decide the spike wolves were a better target than us. When the lizard parrots started attacking them, the spike wolves headed for the undergrowth. Most of the piranha toads are either dead or retreated when the spike wolves showed up. We should be able to get to our gear and come after you in just a few minutes."

"I'll wait here," Teg said, "at least unless something comes after me. Can I have some light? There's a little down here, but not a lot."

Peg's voice. "I'll get a lantern and lower it to you."

Teg lay as still as she could, fighting panic. It helped when the lantern was lowered and imaginary monsters were banished further into the surrounding shadows. Carefully turning her head, she saw that she was on a ledge at least two meters wide and quite long. The faded browns and greens of the accumulated leaves and less identifiable vegetation were sprinkled with fresh material from their cutting and sweeping above.

There was no sign of the spike wolf that had knocked her down here. Possibly it had managed to scrabble out, possibly it hadn't fallen, but had rebounded from her to vanish into the undergrowth. Above Teg could hear a smattering of her companions' chatter as they worked to rescue her.

Vereez was first down, then Peg, still grimy and stained with blue blood from her encounter with the piranha toad, but chattering about how she'd repeatedly qualified in first aid—and even second and third—when various of her children, grandchildren, and the like had been involved in various terrifying activities. Once they had assured themselves that Teg was unbroken, they helped her stand.

"You're lucky you don't have a tail," Vereez said, "or landing like you did, you might have a bad break."

"There's something to be said for unadorned butts,"

Teg agreed, carefully feeling her legs and sides, wincing occasionally. The vegetation she'd landed on had saved her serious injury—there was no doubt of that—but she had some interesting scrapes.

"Walk around a bit," Peg urged, handing Teg one of the flashlights. "We don't want you to stiffen up. They're rigging a sling to pull us up, since I, at least, have no skill in rope climbing."

"What!" Vereez teased. "Your third daughter didn't study it?"

Peg shook her head. "No, Esmerelda was more into domestic arts than gymnastics. She is an excellent baker, but not much of a gymnast. Now her Denise . . ."

Teg half listened as she paced back and forth, examining the area more by habit than by interest. Right now, she hardly cared about ruins and lost libraries. She wanted a smoke and then a long soak or maybe both at the same time. But the habits of a lifetime guided her eyes, if not her mind. At the edge of the ledge, she found herself slowing, then stopping.

"Peg, did you say they were rigging some sort of sling to help us up?"

"That's right."

"They might want to come down instead."

"What? Why?"

Teg motioned with the beam of the flashlight. "Because, if I'm not mistaken, down there are the doors into the Library of the Sapphire Wind."

The other three were down in record time, especially given they needed to bring the others' gear with them.

Meg, who had been lowered, rather than climbing, hurried over to where Teg stood examining the double paneled door by methodically moving the flashlight's beam from side to side.

"That's definitely it!" Meg cried in delight. "Look at those curlicues carved around the edges, the pattern near the lock panel. Those are exactly like the pictures!"

"Except," Teg said dryly, "those doors were part of a building that stood at the crest of a hill. These are— what?—ten meters down?"

"At least," Xerak agreed. "This ledge is a bit over four meters down, and I'd say that's twice as far. I wonder what happened?"

"I," Grunwold said, trotting over to join them, a coil of rope over one muscular shoulder, "wonder if we can get the door open once we're down there." He shone his own flashlight over to one side, illuminating a section of sturdy tree trunk. "That looks like a battering ram to me."

"Maybe that just fell down here," Peg said hopefully, then shook her head in negation of her own statement. "No, that would be more unlikely than . . ."

"An entire building dropping at least ten meters and staying intact?" Teg shrugged. "Speculation will only get us so far. Grunwold, do you think you can get us safely down there?"

Grunwold massaged the base of one antler thoughtfully. "I thought we'd start with Vereez and me going down to scout."

"But . . ." Teg began, then remembered the spike wolf that had knocked her over the edge, the piranha toads, the lizard parrots, and who knew what else that might be down there. She reluctantly nodded agreement to the wisdom of his suggestion. "All right. But I want to go down before you start poking around and messing up the site."

"It's not 'all right' with me," Xerak cut in. "I should go down instead of Grunwold, probably with Vereez. We both have more applicable magical skills."

"Grunwold, you're also stronger than either of us," Vereez said, "and the best at armed combat. If any of the creatures we left up top come down . . ."

Grunwold glowered, but he didn't argue. The descent was delayed while the remaining lanterns were lit. Then Peg was nominated to keep watch for anything coming down from above.

"Fine with me," she quipped. "I wouldn't trust Teg or Meg not to get distracted. Just don't forget to tell me what's going on."

"Keep the chatter down," Grunwold grumped, anchoring his rope to a projecting chunk of rock. "We can't hear ourselves think."

"I'm not surprised," Peg shot back, "with the sort of thoughts you're having echoing in your head. We need you calm, not sulky."

Grunwold looked astonished, then sheepish—his big ears drooping. "Sorry. But I'm honestly worried about what noise might bring. We're not in the safest of places."

"Point taken," Peg said. "I can wait to hear the exciting details."

Grunwold clearly wanted to protest when Vereez insisted on being the first one down, but he couldn't disagree that she was a good choice. She was the lightest, quick on her feet, whereas Xerak, especially with his staff in hand, was more encumbered. Vereez took a few steps across the bracken-strewn ground below.

"Solid stone pavement," Vereez called. "Probably the same mosaic pattern that we were looking at above."

Teg glanced back up, then down again, estimating distances. The hilltop had fallen away in stages, leaving this ledge first at four meters, then the lowest another six or seven meters further down.

And the doors stayed standing, she thought. *If I didn't already have ample reason to believe in magic, that might do it.*

Teg was all too aware that the day wasn't getting any younger. They'd put in several hours of work before the attack. She knew that good sense demanded they get back to *Slicewind* and safety before dark. She watched impatiently as Xerak joined Vereez and the two did some further checking of the area before approaching the two huge doors.

"They're locked," Vereez called up.

"No surprise," Grunwold replied. "Hey, Peg. Have any of your children or grandchildren studied lock picking?"

"Only of the most limited sort," Peg replied. "There was a fad a few years ago, and I admit, I joined in on the fun. I'd be happy to try."

"Let me go down there," Teg almost pleaded. "I'm not all that bruised up. Maybe I can figure something out."

She was in motion as she spoke and Grunwold, perhaps fearing she'd try to jump down if he didn't lower her, gave in without more than muttered imprecations about crazy humans.

Teg felt very strange, excited, almost elated, as if—beyond all common sense—she knew what she would find. Removing her whisk broom from her pack, she knelt—doing her best to keep from wincing when the bruises from her fall throbbed in protest—and began whisking clear the stone pavement in front and alongside the doors.

Absently, she could hear the others talking. The tree trunk had definitely been used as a battering ram—the end showed evidence of impact—but the door showed no marks, not even a chip in the glossy finish. Xerak studied the lock, tried the spell he'd used to open the warehouse back on Grunwold's family's estate, only to end up with scorched fingers. These wards were much stronger.

Vereez's voice. She'd been searching the rubble near the battering ram and discovered that someone had made a ladder. Many of the rungs had come loose, but Grunwold was certain he could fix them. Surely that would be much faster than making a new one.

Xerak again. Wasn't it getting on toward evening? They had a hike ahead of them, and what if the piranha toads or spike wolves were still around? He sounded worried.

Teg worked faster. Yes! She hadn't been sure—looking from above by flashlight wasn't much to go on—but the character of the pavement had changed. The hexagons had gradually been replaced with diamonds. At first these were merely elongated rhomboids, like those on playing cards, but then they became more elaborate, with carvings that suggested faceted gemstones. These pavers were colored, most a bluish slate, but some in beige, rose, and . . .

"Vereez!" she called. "Come over here. I have a use for those incredible fingernails of yours."

The young woman hastened over. "What?"

Teg pointed to a paver that, in the flashlight's glow glittered with mica. "Can you lift out that stone? Yes. That one. I think you'll find . . ."

Obediently, Vereez probed, first with the tip of her hunting knife, then with her fingernails. "It feels loose."

"Careful," Teg cautioned. "If this is what I think, it could come apart."

Vereez wrinkled her nose in puzzlement, but probed more carefully. At last, the top of the paving stone Teg had indicated came away, revealing a hollow within which lay a large key. Teg had feared that the key would have been cast from metal, which could have corroded, but this key appeared to be carved from dark green jade.

"'Underfoot is the priceless gem, keystone you require,'" Meg recited in an awed voice. "Excellent deduction, Teg! What made you think of it?"

"I'm not sure," Teg admitted. "Underfoot. Keystone. The fact that the majority of the pavers were diamond shaped. When I noticed the different detail, I started looking for one that was unique."

"Do we try the key right away?" Vereez asked eagerly, turning the key over and over in her hand, as if unable to believe it was real.

"We'd better not," Grunwold said, his disappointment evident. "It's getting late. We'll come back tomorrow, early. And we'll pack along the basics for camping, just in case we decide to stay the night. No idea how long it will take for us to find what we're looking for."

"Yes," Meg said, tucking her journal away with evident reluctance. "No matter how great was today's triumph, I fear our search is far from over."

❧CHAPTER SEVEN❧

The next morning, not even Vereez tried to sleep in. *Slicewind* didn't have a full bath, so Teg couldn't have her longed-for soak, but Peg gave her an amazing rubdown that included the use of a strongly scented oil that Vereez compounded. This burned away the worst of the aches, and let Teg get a good night's sleep. In the morning, she boasted some impressive bruises, but her excitement countered the worst of the pain.

Grunwold had repaired the ladder. As they hiked back, he and Xerak carried it between them, resting the ends on their shoulders and using it as a stretcher on which to carry additional camping gear. Vereez took point. Peg—Heru perched on her shoulder and looking behind—took the rear. Everyone—even Meg—carried at least a spear. Despite their precautions—or perhaps because of them—they saw nothing more threatening than some lizard parrots. These flew away when Heru croaked at them, making the xuxu puff out a triumphal fanfare through his crest.

The repaired ladder made getting to the door much easier. When the last person had clambered down, Grunwold carried it off to one side, then covered it with some of the leaves and bracken that had drifted from above.

"I wish," he said, standing back to inspect his work, "I didn't feel so certain that this is exactly what the people who left this ladder here did—and that they never made it back to retrieve it."

"There aren't any bodies," Teg reminded him, "and not a trace of bloodstains on the pavement. Stop thinking the worst."

Vereez was taking the key from where she'd been wearing it on a string tied around her neck. Teg had gone to sleep early, so she'd missed the discussion about who would actually open the door and who would stand ready in case something—no one was certain precisely what—came bursting out at them.

Now Vereez ceremonially handed the key to Meg. "All right, Librarian. Do your thing!"

Then she dropped back, strung her bow, and set an arrow to the string. Grunwold drew his sword and stepped up next to Meg. Xerak had been chanting something under his breath for the last minute or so.

Peg looked over at Teg and said softly, "When you pass beyond the doors of the Library of the Sapphire Wind. Ready?"

"And then some!" Teg agreed, clutching her machete.

Meg put the key into the lock, then used both hands to turn it. Grunwold was reaching forward to help her when she said, "No need, dear boy. It's turning. Be ready to grab the handle on the left, and we'll pull together."

But there was no need. As soon as the key finished turning there was a resounding click, and the doors began opening outward. Grunwold put a protective arm out to push Meg behind him, then they stepped back and rejoined the other four.

Initially, the doors parted to reveal nothing but a band of darkness so absolute it seemed solid. Only when the twin panels were flat against the stone of the building's front did they see that at the heart of darkness a shape was swirling into being. To say it was blue—the clean rich blue of a perfect sapphire—would be to do it a disservice, for the blue coruscated with sparks of every color in the spectrum, as well as a few that were only hinted at in dreams.

"A whirlwind?" Peg speculated. "But it's too solid."

"It's Sapphire Wind," Xerak replied, his tone hushed. "The Library's guardian."

"No wonder we didn't find any bodies," Grunwold moaned. "That thing could destroy us, then scour away the traces. Slowly, back away . . ."

Meg had been peering around him. Now she shook her head and slipped under his arm, moving forward a few paces. "It's inviting us in. Look how it swirls forward a little, then back, bending like a beckoning finger."

"Luring us in so it can kill us," Grunwold said, grabbing Meg firmly by one shoulder when she started to move closer. "It probably can't leave the immediate vicinity of the Library. Come away, you mad woman!"

Meg stared up at him with disdain. "Have we come this far to be turned away now? You heard the verse. Beyond those doors are the answers you seek. Are you going to quit because it turns out the Library is not deserted?"

Grunwold froze, unable to find a reply.

"I think," Vereez said, sliding her arrow back into her quiver, "Meg's right. Grunwold, if you want to stay here to protect our escape route, we'll ask after a cure for your father. No matter what, I'm going ahead. I've exhausted every other source, and I'm not giving up on my search."

"Me, either," Xerak said, his tone both wistful and determined. "My master . . ."

Grunwold stared at Sapphire Wind. "I don't think it means us well. I feel . . . But you're right. We've come this far. I'm not going to wait as rearguard and drive myself crazy wondering what's happened to you."

"Let's walk in step," Meg suggested. "The doorway opens wide enough to take all six of us abreast, with room to spare. I don't think one of us should cross before the others. That might leave someone out if the guardian is being very literal."

"Should we hold hands then?" Vereez asked, sheathing her twin swords. "We might as well show ourselves a united company."

"Sure," Xerak said. "I'll stand at the right end. That way I can keep my staff in my free hand."

"And I'll take the left," Vereez said, "since I am ambidextrous. Grunwold, it's a great deal to ask you to go in weaponless, but would you take the center, with Meg and Teg flanking you? Heru can ride your shoulder. Peg? If you would stand between Meg and Xerak, we'll have someone who can use a sword at either end."

"I am flattered by your confidence," Peg said, "but I can't imagine that we can cut a wind." She chuckled. "Although I'm nervous enough to break wind."

"Peg!" said Meg and Teg simultaneously, but apparently the translation spell wasn't up to off-color puns, so the three inquisitors only looked confused.

"Ready?" Vereez asked with a manic cheerfulness that fooled no one. "Then march! Right, left, right, left. Here we go!"

During the dozen steps it took for them to cross the diamond pavement, the vista before them began to change. The whirlwind continued its beckoning gesture, bending lower and lower until they could see into the top of its swirling vortex. This opened, becoming a tunnel that grew to fill the entire doorway.

"I told you it is going to kill us," Grunwold said, but he sounded cheerful. "At least it'll be quick."

Teg, gripping Grunwold's left hand, wondered if he'd take her trembling for fear. It wasn't. She was as excited as she'd ever been. This was the sort of adventure that teased at the hearts of all but the driest of archeologists, that was why—despite his tomb-robber, pot-hunter, massively unethical behavior—Indiana Jones was an icon so many archeologists embraced.

This was discovery writ large. When they came to the doorway, Teg didn't hesitate. She might even have pulled the others into the swirling blue vortex. Then they were walking through what felt like surf, if surf could be dry. Their feet sounded on pavement, then tile, then the silence of plush carpet.

Or maybe we're walking on air.

Then the sensation of tugging surf ebbed and ceased, the swirl surrounding them slowed, then vanished, and they stood in front of a desk upon which a sign neatly printed in several of the local languages stated: GENERAL INFORMATION.

Surrounding them was not just a grand foyer, but a temple to knowledge. Teg had visited the Library of Congress several times and had thought that nothing could excel the main reading room, with its elaborately painted domed ceiling and iconic statuary, but she suspected that in its prime, the grand reception area of the Library of the Sapphire Wind would have made that room look small and tawdry.

Overarching a vast open area was the astronomical skyscape that had continued to live in Grunwold's father's stories. This, through some miracle, remained intact, the stars glittering against a dustless black. What the remainder of the enormous room had looked like had to be guessed at, for it was a vista of destruction. Once-brilliant frescos were cracked or scored with burns. In some places the plaster had slid down and dissolved into slag. Mosaics that had once depicted poets reciting or musicians singing were so filled with gaps that they became the visual equivalent of a stammer.

Teg remembered the drawings in many of the brochures and journals that they'd purchased from Kuvekt, so she guessed that the crumbled heaps of pink and white stone were where various designated experts had sat enthroned, absorbed in research when they were not assisting visitors. What looked like the largest kindling pile ever must be the remnants of the beautifully polished cedar cabinets in which lesser—but still valuable—reference works had been kept. Priceless data storage crystals glittered in chunks underfoot. Fanning out from the information desk, some seats incongruously intact, others broken to fragments, almost to gravel, were the long tables and benches where visitors had studied or awaited consultation.

No one was standing behind the information desk, so Meg took it upon herself to walk around it, doubtless to see if there was a directory or suchlike stashed there. What she found—or rather what found her—was completely unexpected. Once she was fully behind the desk, Meg lowered herself into the chair and folded her hands in front of her. When she looked up at them and spoke, neither her voice nor her manner were her own.

"Grunwold, son of Sefit and Konnel, the latter once called Tam; Vereez, daughter of Inehem and Zarrq, adherents of Fortune; Xerak, son of Fardowsi, sometimes called 'Clever Fingers'—since before you were born, since when you were born, I have awaited your arrival."

"What the . . . !" Grunwold said, jumping back and drawing his sword with a metallic *shing*!

Xerak grasped his spear staff in a cross-body, defensive grip, the head beginning to glow with emerald fire. Of the three inquisitors, only Vereez kept her hands relaxed. She replied with the cool politeness of the socialite she had been trained to be.

"I am Vereez, daughter of Inehem and Zarrq Fortune. Tell me, is my friend, Meg, safe in your hold?"

"She is." The voice that responded was cool, breathy, and genderless.

"I am relieved to hear this. May I ask who you are? I have guesses, but why should we play at riddles?"

"I am Sapphire Wind, spirit of this library."

"That's what I thought. How could you have waited for me and Xerak and Grunwold? This library was destroyed before we were born."

"Precisely."

"So how could you await us?"

"Because you are the offspring of those whose conduct led to the destruction of this library."

There was complete silence. Not even Grunwold—who could usually be depended on for a profanity or outburst—could find anything to say. Finally, Teg took up the questioning.

"That's an amazing claim. How do we know to believe you?"

"And why," Peg cut in indignantly, "should these children be held responsible for something their parents did, even if they did do it? I certainly don't hold my children responsible for my actions—although they have a remarkable tendency to try to blame *me* for their mistakes, though that's neither here nor there."

Meg might have smiled or rolled her eyes at Peg's disorganized volubility, but Sapphire Wind only paused, as if trying to decide which question to answer first. At last it said, "I can show you what happened, but would you believe me even then? It is possible to lie with images as easily as with words."

"You," Xerak said, "knew our names. I suppose you could have overheard these from our talk when we were outside. But you knew our parents' names. That's interesting. I've been trying to remember, and I'm not certain we've spoke of our parents by name since we left Kuvekt-lial, and maybe not even then."

"That's right," Grunwold said, lowering his sword, although he didn't return it to its sheath. "I've said 'my dad,' or 'my mom,' but I certainly wouldn't have referred to him as 'Tam.' It's a family joke that he won't let even his parents call him that."

"There is a reason why your father has sought to discard that name," Sapphire Wind said, "and that reason is indirectly tied to the destruction of the Library. Will you let me show you?"

Vereez answered for all of them. "Yes, but—can you find some other way to talk to us? This using Meg makes me uneasy."

"If you will go through the door I will cause to open," Sapphire Wind replied, "there are means within to enable me to communicate."

"Let's do it," Grunwold said, returning his sword to its scabbard. "Hey, Wind . . ."

Xerak hissed, appalled by the informality, and Grunwold began again with an exasperated sigh, "O Great Sapphire Wind, caretaker of this ruin, we came here guided by prophesy, seeking the answers to questions. Will we have the opportunity to ask these?"

He tossed his antlered head at Xerak as if to say, "Satisfied?"

Sapphire Wind did not appear to notice this byplay. "That will be up to you. Come. More will be made clear when you have seen what I have to show you."

Heralded by a soft, white glow, a door slid open to the far right and rear of the reception hall. When Meg rose and began leading the way toward the door, the rest trailed after, reluctant yet eager. The door gave access into a room that had suffered much less damage than had the reception hall. A mosaic of white tiles lined the entire chamber. The ceiling was domed, and the walls curved, so that the impression was that of walking into a pearl. This illusion was perpetuated by several rows of seats set amphitheater style around the lower curve, anchored onto the wall so they seemed to float.

The focus of this peculiar theater in the round was a sculptured form that reminded Teg of the sort of baptismal fonts still found in old churches, although this one—except for being made from the same pale pearlescent stone as the mosaic that lined the sphere—looked more like a chalice. The chalice was situated so that its graceful stem rested at the base of the sphere. The chalice's cup was filled to a finger's breadth of the rim with a liquid that shimmered in purples, blues and yellows, like the oil that rises to the surface of a road after a sudden rainstorm.

"The Font of Sight," Meg said, her voice now her own. "I read several references to it in the brochures, but there were no drawings." She paused and reached out to touch Vereez lightly on one arm, and said softly, "It was sweet of you to ask after my safety."

"Did you think we wouldn't be worried?"

"Yeah," Grunwold added. "Who's to say that whatever grabbed you wouldn't go after one of us next?"

Vereez rolled her eyes and moved closer to Meg. "I guess we should take seats?"

Meg nodded. "Yes. Why don't we all arrange ourselves on the right hand side? That way none of us will view whatever image appears in the Font upside down."

"Sensible," Peg said, "which I suppose means that Grunwold will insist on sitting on the opposite side, just to be difficult."

Grunwold didn't deign reply, but he did sit with the rest of them. The seats were arranged two in the bottom row, then three, then four. Grunwold *did* insist on sitting in the rearmost row. Privately, Teg wondered if this was asserting his independence, or if he was a bit spooked by some sorts of magic. Maybe he was just being polite and sitting where his antlers wouldn't block anyone's view.

Meg and Vereez took the lowest two seats. Peg and Teg settled themselves on the next tier. Xerak vacillated for a moment, clearly wondering if he should sit with Grunwold, but then seated himself on Teg's other side, his fascination with the Font winning over whatever loyalty he felt for his often irritable friend.

"I wish I'd thought to get some popcorn," Peg was saying when the liquid that filled the font began to ripple and eddy. "Hmm . . . Liquid-crystal television?"

"Shut up." Teg elbowed her. "Or I'll make you go sit with Grunwold."

The images that appeared above the shimmering waters of the Font resembled those used in science fiction movies where three-dimensional holograms had replaced flat images. Teg guessed that this was so the image would be easily viewed from any part of the rounded chamber. The setting was what was surely the main reception hall of the Library of the Sapphire Wind. Although the images were presented completely without sound, no words were needed to comprehend what was happening.

A trim woman with the head of a silver fox came

through the main doors, looked around uncertainly, then went over to the information desk. The man sitting behind it—he had the head of some sort of brown-feathered hawk or eagle—wrote something down, handed it to her, then motioned for her to take a seat. She did so, removing a book from her bag and settling in to read with apparent lack of impatience.

Vereez spoke softly. "My mother? I think . . . She's so young, but . . ."

The image next showed the arrival of several other people. Each went to the information desk, each made a query, each was asked to take a seat and wait.

Grunwold identified a male with the head of a stag, much like his own, as his father, Xerak a young woman with the head of a tufted-eared squirrel as his mother. The remaining male whose lean, broad-shouldered muscular body was graced with the head of a polar bear, Vereez identified, her voice thick with apprehension, as her father. The final arrival was another woman—this one with the head of a snow leopard—who came in and sat next to Grunwold's father.

"I don't recognize her," Xerak said. "Do you two?"

"Not me," Vereez said, then paused. "Not to say for certain."

"I don't know her either," Grunwold said. "She's a real babe, isn't she?"

"Jerk," Vereez said. That she even responded to Grunwold's comment showed how rattled she was.

Although there was no way to tell the passage of time, Teg had the distinct impression that these arrivals had been spaced out over several hours. Over time, all five featured players were called to the reception desk. Then, either alone or with one companion, they were escorted into the stacks. As soon as their escort had left them, they began to behave in a very un-researcher-like fashion. One of the first things each did once the escort had left was don a necklace with an attached pendant, then tuck the pendant out of sight. When they did so, their images shifted slightly, each becoming tinted a light yellow.

"My guess," Xerak said, keeping his voice low, even though there was no soundtrack to interrupt, "is that those pendants make them 'invisible' to the Library's security. If you look, you'll notice many of the staff are wearing similar ornaments, although much more openly. Those five would now be perceived as belonging to the resident community."

"This isn't good," Vereez said, her voice rough with tension. "Not good at all."

The image pulled back, showing a cutaway view which revealed that, although the five had dispersed to areas apparently isolated from each other, they were now moving toward the same point: what the image cooperatively revealed as a door concealed behind an apparently immovable bookcase. Clearly, whatever they were looking for, it wasn't going to be found in one of the books, scrolls, or neatly racked data crystals.

What played out after that began as a neatly run heist. The five hid until the Library closed for the night, the visitors had left, and the majority of the staff had departed. Only a few diehard researchers remained, scattered in various study carrels. None of these were even close to where the would-be thieves had gathered.

Vereez's mother went over to the concealed door and began to make various motions.

"Amazing!" Xerak said. "That looks like a heavy-duty ward or trap-detecting spell. Vereez, did you know your mom knew things like that?"

"No." The single word was bitter. "Did you know your mother knew things like that?"

Because Xerak's mother was busily pulling out of an inside pocket of her coat a folder containing a tidy selection of lock picks. From various secret pockets and seams in her clothing, she removed an array of very nasty-looking darts, small knives, and what looked like a garrote.

"No," Xerak replied in a tone that had lost any sense of detachment.

The next five minutes or so made clear that all five intruders possessed both an impressive array of extralegal skills and a variety of concealed equipment. Since working magic pretty much made her useless for anything else, Vereez's mother was guarded by Vereez's father. That he wore a set of matched swords similar to those his daughter now carried provided a decidedly creepy link between past and present.

When Vereez's father gave the thumbs up, Grunwold's father and the unknown woman hauled back the edges of the bookshelf, revealing a staircase that descended steeply into the depths, then passed along a series of corridors lined with what looked like safe deposit boxes, each neatly closed and—presumably, since each had a keyhole—locked. While some of the boxes were quite small—hardly more than pigeonholes—others were capacious cabinets.

"I bet that's the artifact repository," Xerak said. "Those wouldn't have been kept on open shelves like the books."

"Rather an awkward route to use to get into it," Peg said.

Xerak laughed. "I'd have expected more difficulties, actually. Once you get beyond routine domestic magics, artifacts aren't things to leave lying about. Anything worth being put in the repository here would already be on the 'handle with care' list at most stores."

That the thieves were searching for something specific there was no doubt; that they were also open to taking anything of value they could carry was proven by their actions. The unidentified snow leopard woman and Xerak's mom cast about, quickly locating and opening a concealed compartment in which hung a neat row of keys. They each grabbed a key ring and started opening safe deposit boxes. Rings, pendants, small carved boxes of exotic wood or stone all vanished into pockets, pouches, and packs.

Each time something was taken, Teg expected an alarm to go off, but apparently the pendants the thieves had donned gave them carte blanche. Indeed, at first they were somewhat cautious, but soon they were grabbing whatever they could carry, as if they couldn't believe their own luck. Grunwold's father shoved several swords into his belt. Xerak's mother—whose figure was naturally svelte—began to look distinctly busty as she dropped item after item down her cleavage and into the folds of her blousy top. What amazed Teg was how much the thieves could take without slowing their progress or making themselves clumsy. Nor for one moment did they ever lose a certain preternatural alertness.

Eventually, Vereez's father found something he showed to Vereez's mother, who nodded. Then he dropped the item into one pocket. He signaled the others, and the treasure hunting ended without even a wistful glance at the wealth that remained.

"They've done things like this before," Vereez said, hurt seeping through her assumed nonchalance.

Grunwold replied with a casualness that deceived no one. "I think they were looking for something specific. When Zarrq-toh found it, they quit looting."

Xerak grunted a noncommittal reply.

Eventually, the thieves arrived at a cross corridor no different than many they'd passed without even hesitating. Vereez's father, who was in the lead, pulled up short, turned right, paced four steps, then pointed with the tip of his longer sword at a set of shelves. Again, Vereez's mother worked some complicated bit of magic. Again, when the magic was completed, Grunwold's father and the unidentified woman pulled apart a set of shelves to reveal a stairway leading down.

That no one had used this staircase for a long time was evident. Cobwebs laced the walls and hung over the treads like a peculiar holiday garland. Bright yellow-and-green-spotted triangular "beetles" the size of Teg's thumb scuttled away from the light. The treads were thickly furred with dust, the coverage marred only where water had dripped from sweating stonework.

But the thieves were undeterred. Xerak's mother took a torch and burned away the worst of the spider webs, at the same time examining the stairway to assure that nothing more dangerous than beetles awaited them below.

While they'd trotted confidently down the staircase that had led into the repository, this time the thieves were more careful. Xerak's mother led the way, searching each tread, each section of mortared stonework wall, for booby traps. Sometimes she found them, and everyone would still into preternaturally alert waiting while she disarmed them.

Sometimes elements in the traps were rotted or corroded, the threat they offered minimal, but she dealt with each one with care. The unidentified woman and Grunwold's father were obviously impatient, Vereez's mother and father were less so, possibly because whatever magic the silver fox-headed woman had done had clearly taken a lot out of her, and they were glad for her to have a chance to rest.

At the base of the stairway was a small foyer, on the other side of which was a heavy door that Grunwold's father opened only after Xerak's mother had carefully inspected it. Behind it—centered on a fluted pedestal in a room hardly large enough to hold all of the intruders—stood a small, oddly shaped item some ten or twelve centimeters in height, and quite narrow; perhaps two centimeters at its widest point.

The artifact was far less expensive-looking than any number of objects the thieves had already taken, made not from shining gold and glittering gems, but from polished bronze and a dark, smooth matte-black stone. The lowest section reminded Teg of a candlestick holder—although only four centimeters in height. It would have been difficult to make it hold even one of the small candles that are usually stuck atop a birthday cake. Onto the candlestick's spindle was fitted a sort of crenelated chalice cut from black stone. The spindle apparently passed through the crenelated chalice, extending a few centimeters above it, where it was capped by a minute sculpture of a songbird. Although intricate and elegant, the artifact on the pedestal hardly seemed to merit such extensive security and concealment.

Moving with surgical precision that in no way made for slowness, the team went through an elaborate procedure that—after spells were cast and special tools employed— enabled them to remove the artifact from its pedestal. When Vereez's father took a small ivory box covered with intricate carvings from one of his pockets, Xerak emitted a long, low whistling sigh.

"That's an enshrouding container. Even one that size costs a small fortune—if you can find someone willing to part with it or a mage's circle to create one. I bet that's what they were searching for in the upper part of the repository. What's going on here?"

"I think," Grunwold said, his voice gruff and tight, "our moms and dads are busy stealing something that they shouldn't even be near. And they are very good at what they're doing. I wonder what went wrong?"

The images had frozen during this discussion, as if Sapphire Wind wanted to make certain no one missed the least element in this revelation of past misdeeds.

Vereez said tartly, "If you two would shut up, we might find out."

Although no one would have said they had dallied on the way in, the moment the artifact was placed in the enshrouding container and Vereez's father had dropped it back into his pocket, the pace sped up. Protected by the unidentified woman, Xerak's mother led the retreat up the stairs, evidently scanning for traps or alarms that might have been activated by the artifact's removal. Sheathing his twin swords, Vereez's father knelt in front of Vereez's mother, who was nearly fainting from exhaustion, positioning her so he could carry her piggyback. Grunwold's father took the rear, sword in hand, alert for anything that might come after them.

Up the first stair the thieves went, along the corridors of the repository, retracing their steps with haste that never devolved into carelessness. When they were through the last of the hidden doors, they quickly rearranged their order. Now Grunwold's father and the unidentified woman were in the front. Vereez's father, still carrying her mother, remained in the middle. Xerak's mother dropped to the back.

Once again, Teg was struck by how polished their performance was. All of them knew their roles perfectly. Even the way Vereez's father carried his partner, her long fox's muzzle resting on his shoulder, showed no urgency or concern. He'd done this before. He expected to do it again. She, for her part, dozed, confident in the protection of her comrades.

So what went wrong? Teg thought, remembering the ruins that surrounded them. *For surely something went wrong.*

The thieves were nearing the star-domed reception room. Unlike when they had arrived, they were making no effort to be cautious. Apparently, they had been assured that the Library would be empty at that time, and that their pendants would take care of any magical security. The latter was certainly true. Several times they passed horrific creatures that sniffed at them and let them go by, satisfied that—despite the group's odd behavior—they had some right to be there.

However, the reception hall was *not* empty. At one of the long tables near the information desk a trio of scholars—one with the head of a blue jay, another with the head of a skunk, the third with the head of an otter—were in consultation. Books and racked data crystals were piled around their feet and over the table. Scrolls weighted open by inkwells, paperweights, and empty scroll cases were spread around them. The trio were all seated, reading, motionless except for hands that moved to take notes. Therefore, the thieves remained unaware of them until they were nearly on top of them.

Although they were not hiding, the carpeted floors and the soft shoes and boots worn by all five thieves must have made their progress nearly soundless. In any case, the two groups spotted each other at precisely the same moment. The reactions were very different. The thieves started sprinting for the door. The researchers though . . .

The skunk thumped his pen and it transformed into a staff. The blue jay reached beneath his robe and came out with a pendant that sent pale yellow light lacing out to tangle the legs of Vereez's father, who, burdened as he was, proved less agile than the rest. The otter pressed her hands flat on the tabletop and began to chant.

"Oh, shit!" Xerak yelled. "They're all mages!"

Even the overview provided by Sapphire Wind could not make precisely clear exactly what happened next, especially after various guardian creatures began to pour into the room. Grunwold's father and the unidentified woman used their swords with consummate skill, first cutting the yellow strands that bound Vereez's father's legs, then turning to hold off the guardian creatures. Vereez's father, still carrying Vereez's mother, raced for the exit. Vereez's mother was awake now. Taking careful aim, she shot a ball of blue-white light directly at the paper-covered table.

"Oh, no!" Xerak almost roared. "Excellent technique except..."

The blue-white ball hit, fountaining forth tiny lightning bolts and cascades of sparks. The papers turned to flame. Explosions shot miniature volcanoes of something far hotter than mere fire into the air to catch and burn every bit of wood, paper, and fabric.

The three wizards leapt back from the table. The otter's robes were on fire. The blue jay let his spell drop in order to grab hold of her and smother the flames. The skunk pointed his staff at the documents on the table and water gushed over them, but it was far too late to halt the spreading conflagration.

"...Inehem-toh must have gambled that they weren't reading highly magical documents." Seeing the puzzled expressions on the humans' faces, Xerak explained. "Think of dropping a match onto a heap of shredded paper and only after realizing that the paper has been soaked in oil."

"More than oil," Peg exclaimed, horrified. "Gunpowder!"

The fire was spreading now, raging over the tables, catching shelves of reference works. The five thieves continued fighting their way to the door. Vereez's father no longer had the luxury of carrying his partner, but he was doing his best to protect her. She slid a ring from her pocket and began using it to shoot bolts of putrid green liquid, that caused whatever it hit to sizzle and melt, at the monstrous guardians.

Nonetheless, one of the guardian creatures, perhaps attuned to whatever had been sealed in the enshrouding container—or to the container itself—ripped directly through Vereez's father's tunic, grabbing the container in its jaws and pulling hard.

The woman with the snow leopard head brought her sword down, severing the creature's neck. In its death throes, it chomped down, teeth crushing the ivory container and breaking the artifact within into pieces. There was a flaring of eye-searing blue-black light that, even seen secondhand, caused Teg's eyes to run and spots to blur her field of vision.

When she could see the display again, the five thieves were fleeing out the Library's main door, the three scholars were nowhere to be seen, fire was spreading, and earthquake-like forces were rattling the building.

"Thus," a voice hardly recognizable as Meg's declaimed, "the Library of the Sapphire Wind was destroyed."

The Font's image faded soon thereafter. The three humans and the three inquisitors stared at each other in shock and horror.

"Well," said Vereez, obviously trying to keep her voice light and completely failing, "I understand now why Sapphire Wind blames our parents for the destruction of the Library. I'm still not certain what that has to do with us, though."

Meg held up her hand. "Sapphire Wind is willing to clarify whatever it can, but it needs a means to speak. It has asked me if I will help it and I have agreed—unless that will be too disturbing for the rest of you."

"It will be disturbing, sure," Peg said, "but if you agree, and if no harm will come to you, then . . ."

Teg said, "It's up to you, Meg."

"Allowing Sapphire Wind to speak through me will be more efficient than charades or show and tell," Meg replied. "I will be listening, and even be able to ask questions, although not out loud. I feel we need to know more."

"But, Meg-toh," Grunwold said, his use of the suffix revealing the affection he'd been careful to conceal, "you're opening yourself to possession."

Meg smiled. "When we were attacked, none of you inquisitors hesitated for a moment to put yourselves at risk. How can I do any less?"

"When you put it that way," Grunwold said slowly. "All right, but if anything happens to you . . ."

He let his threat—which was, after all, somewhat empty, since not a one of them knew how to fight a bodiless magical creation—remain unspecified.

Xerak and Vereez nodded their reluctant acceptance of Meg's offer.

Without any more fuss than when it had borrowed Meg's voice before, Sapphire Wind spoke: "Meg wishes to know what happened to the inhabitants of the Library and the associated surroundings."

"Me, too . . ." Vereez said softly, doubtless dreading how many deaths lay at the feet of her parents and their allies.

"Not aware yet how limited my abilities would be in the future," Sapphire Wind continued, "I archived those who belonged to the community."

"Archived?" Teg said. "Can you clarify that?"

Meg's arm gestured in the direction of the foyer. "I had been given a spell that enabled me to save a person's life by storing that person within a magical artifact. It was intended to be an emergency measure. At the time—fuddled as I was for reasons I can explain—I viewed this as an emergency. The Library's staff and scholars reside within the stars of the celestial dome. 'Reside' is misleading. They are stored there, asleep. Gently dreaming."

"How many?" Xerak asked.

"Four hundred and twenty-three: this includes the Library staff, resident researchers, visitors, and those of the support community who lived near enough to the main Library buildings to be at risk of immediate demise. The inhabitants of the associated village were safe from immediate harm. Most of these fled within a few days as the area became too dangerous to safely inhabit."

"I've been wondering about those dangers," Peg said. "Over and over we've heard how dangerous this area is, but really it hasn't been that bad. We did have some trouble with the piranha toads and the lizard parrots, but really, the vicinity hasn't lived up to its reputation. I'd love to think it's because we were so well prepared, but I don't believe it. Did you have anything to do with how easy we had it?"

"I did," Sapphire Wind replied. "I have been waiting for either one of the extraction agents—repentant—or someone intimately connected to them to come to me.

When you finally did so, I protected you until you found this place. Even then I helped you to find the doors."

Teg gasped. "The spike wolf that knocked me over the edge! That was your doing? I could have broken my back or been killed!"

"It was a risk that had to be taken," Sapphire Wind said. "The rate at which you were discovering locations was such that I feared it would be weeks before anyone looked carefully below."

"After all that time . . ." Teg began, forgetting she wasn't arguing with Meg.

Peg put a hand on Teg's arm. "Sometimes, it's precisely 'after all that time' that it becomes impossible to wait. Let up, Teg. I want to hear why Sapphire Wind thinks it's so important that people connected to the disaster deal with the cleanup. I don't think it's just a matter of abstract justice."

"It isn't," Sapphire Wind replied. "When you were watching the vision, you may have noticed that, at the very end, the artifact the extraction agents were trying to steal was broken into three parts. Although the image did not show this, I have ascertained that the artifact was not destroyed, but instead separated into three components: the Spindle, the Nest, and the Bird.

"I have done my best to research what happened to these components, and could only find a partial answer. I am certain that one part remains here. The other two are not here. I believe that at least one of the missing components may have been taken by one of the extraction agents."

"That makes sense," Grunwold said grudgingly. "I

mean, they did have the artifact in their custody. When that enshrouding container was broken and the thing was crunched, they would have tried to grab what they could. That's what I would have done."

Sapphire Wind moved Meg's arm to point toward the Font of Sight. "Let me show you the end of the vision again and see what you deduce. I would not have you take such an important matter on my conjecture alone."

The vision began with the fading of the blue-black light, focused in on the five extraction agents, as Sapphire Wind had termed them.

Tact? Teg wondered. *I wonder if Meg had anything to do with that choice of words. After all, referring to the parents of people you want to help you as "thieves" may be accurate, but it's not going to make you friends.*

The snow leopard woman was on point, running to shove open the main doors. Vereez's father was once again carrying Vereez's mother as he ran full tilt for the doors. Grunwold's father was grasping one wrist, which was streaming blood, but he had stayed back to wait for Xerak's mother. She was coming up from a crouch. In her right hand, she held a long dagger, stained with gore. Her other hand was clenched tightly around something that caught the light for just a second.

"Fardowsi-toh is definitely holding onto something," Vereez said. "It could be part of that artifact, but it's impossible to be sure."

"If I had one piece of the artifact," Sapphire Wind said, "I could more accurately divine the location of the others."

"Can't you use the one that you say is here?" Xerak asked.

"It is close by," Sapphire Wind replied, "almost certainly somewhere in the Library, but I do not know precisely where. I have searched the rubble in the reception area to the best of my ability, but I did not find it. My natural form can move solid objects, but only in a limited fashion."

Teg was aware that all five of her companions were looking at her. "I'll check through the rubble out in the reception hall, near where the thing broke apart, but I can't promise I'll find anything, especially since Sapphire Wind has already searched through the area."

"But where else would the piece of the artifact be?" Vereez asked. "I mean, it couldn't have sprouted legs and walked off." She paused, considering. "I mean, it couldn't, could it?"

Sapphire Wind shook Meg's head. "I do not believe so. However, it could have been carried away by one of the Library's guardian creatures. For many years now, as I have caused the detritus in the reception area to be sifted through, I have come to believe that is the most likely solution. They were summoned to keep it from being stolen, you see."

"I am afraid I am beginning to understand," Vereez said. "If one of the guardians did take it, then it would have put it back, right?"

"That is my supposition," Sapphire Wind said.

Peg had seated herself and taken out her knitting, Teg thought as much to distract herself from the unsettling sight of seeing someone else talking through Meg as because she was restless.

Now, her needles still clicking, she asked, "Why haven't you simply checked?"

"Because I am much reduced from what I should be," Sapphire Wind said. "Ironically, while I can undo locks and disarm wards, I cannot open doors. I cannot compel the more intelligent of the guardian creatures such as would have been likely to retrieve, then attempt to replace, the component."

"And the doors are closed now?" Grunwold asked. "Who closed them? The extraction agents didn't."

"When the guardians were summoned, this also reactivated the wards in case there were other intruders elsewhere in the Library. Doing so caused open doors to close."

"But," Peg asked, "then how would the guardian with the bit of the artifact have gotten through closed doors?"

Meg gave an oddly boneless shrug. "I was not present, so I cannot say, but many of the guardians have hands, or a close approximation of such."

Teg moved toward the exit. "Sapphire Wind, can you give me more light out in the reception hall? If not, we're going to need to bring in the rest of the lanterns from *Slicewind*. Searching for a few small pieces of bronze is going to be hard enough without doing it by flashlight beam. I think we should reassure ourselves that the piece of the artifact isn't over where we saw it dropped before trooping off to the basement."

"Or not trooping," Xerak said, holding up a hand and gesturing for everyone to take a seat. "Grunwold, Vereez, we haven't really talked about what we saw, but we can't keep dodging it. Those were our parents. My mom. Grunwold's dad. Both of Vereez's parents. I didn't recognize the other woman. Did either of you?"

"No," Grunwold said.

"She looked a little familiar," Vereez said hesitantly, "but I can't say for sure. My parents entertain a lot, and by now she'd be over twenty years older. People change a lot in twenty years."

Xerak nodded, then continued speaking. "We could go after the piece that might or might not be down in the vault . . ."

"Guarded by monsters," Peg said helpfully.

". . . or we could go talk with our parents."

Vereez stiffened and Teg, remembering what she'd confided about her parents, how they'd taken her baby away without involving her in the decision, understood why.

"I think," Vereez said slowly. "I'd rather take my chances with monsters."

❧CHAPTER EIGHT❧

Grunwold, eager now that success seemed near, wasn't to be so easily balked, even by his crush. "C'mon, Vereez. I know you feel your parents have seriously held out on you, but they might know where the other pieces are—heck, they probably have them in one of their vaults. We could get the pieces, then we could come back here, retrieve the final piece, and get Sapphire Wind to wake up whoever can help us with our inquiries."

Xerak raised a hand. "Wait, Grunwold. I have a question for Sapphire Wind. You said you would explain how you can help us after we'd learned about the Library's destruction. We've learned. Now, how about some information?"

Again, Sapphire Wind spoke through Meg. "Forgive me for being tightly focused on my own concerns. I have waited a long time for someone who could help me." Meg sighed in a manner very unlike her usually controlled self. "If you had come in the days when the Library was functioning, you would have been sent to an appropriate specialist. However, today all the specialists are archived. I had only enough power to save them. I lack the power to free them—or rather, to free all of them. If you retrieve one piece—whichever piece—of the artifact, I will seek out and retrieve the most appropriate specialist, then convince that one to aid you."

Meg's right index finger rose in her familiar "one moment, please" gesture. After a brief pause, Sapphire Wind said, "Meg has asked, and I will answer. I could retrieve someone now, but I have no incentive to spend my limited resources for no gain to myself."

Vereez, daughter of bankers, nodded crisply, "That seems fair. So we'll look for the piece that you think is still here. Can you give Teg some light, at least?"

"I can provide illumination," Sapphire Wind replied, "for a limited amount of time."

"If Meg doesn't mind continuing to act as mouthpiece," Xerak said, "then while Teg does her checking, maybe you can tell us more about what we need to do to get you to help us."

Grunwold, his voice gruff, added, "Sapphire Wind, you do realize that the three of us are very little like our parents? You may be deceived by appearances, but none of us are skilled—uh—extraction agents. The school I attend is great at teaching a good basic curriculum, as well as various specialties useful in both agriculture and art. However, theft isn't among the courses on offer."

Sapphire Wind paused. "Yes. I knew this about you. I have been"—another pause, as if it searched for a word—"researching your families since I began to regain some power in the years following the destruction. I hoped that one or more of the extraction agents would repent and return. This did not happen. I hoped to gain confirmation if one or more of them had the missing pieces. I failed. Eventually, I pinned my hopes on your coming to me."

Teg continued out the door. "I'm not doing much good here. Let me go and see if, maybe, just maybe, part of that thingie got dropped in the reception hall when the extraction agents were making their retreat."

Peg put her knitting away. "I'll come help you. I've always been good at finding dropped contact lenses and stray earrings."

When they were alone, beginning what Teg suspected would be a fruitless survey, Peg said softly, "Teg, do you think that Sapphire Wind had something to do with creating the events that brought our young inquisitors here?"

Teg considered. "How? By its own admission, it is unable to leave this location."

"But it also admits it has been able to 'research.' What if it did something to make certain that when the three started searching, they wouldn't find anything unless they came here?"

"Interesting theory," Teg admitted. She knelt to inspect a glint of metal within a small heap of crumbled stone. "So no cure would be found for Grunwold's father's illness. Vereez's sister would stay lost. Same with Xerak's master. Sort of a curse, maybe? Seems harsh."

"From our point of view, maybe, but think of how Sapphire Wind feels. It saved hundreds of lives—but by trapping them. It's trapped, too. Stuck alone in this ruin except for some monsters."

"When you put it that way," Teg said, "I almost understand." She pulled a package of dental picks from a side pocket of her pack and probed around something caught within the matrix of burnt detritus that layered the floor.

"Did you actually find it?" Peg asked, her voice rising in hope and astonishment.

"No, wrong shape, but . . . Get out that inch paintbrush, will you? Use it to sweep off where I've loosened the muck."

Peg did, clearing as Teg continued to pry up detritus from around the shape. What Teg had found seemed to be a piece of jewelry, the center portion of which was an undistinguished-looking piece of pockmarked black stone set in gold. The gold setting included extrusions, so that the whole looked like a stylized sun with wavy rays. Upon closer inspection, Teg noticed that at the end of each "ray" was a stylized hook. The solar disk was bordered with multifaceted eyes, each of which was set with minute, glittering gems in a variety of colors.

"I recognize that!" Peg gasped. "That's the amulet the blue jay wizard held up, the one that shot out those yellow light ropes."

Teg grinned. "I think you're right. I wonder if it still works?"

"We'll ask Xerak—later. Let's see what else we can find."

Although they turned up the metal clasps of books long reduced to ash, nibs from pens, cracked glass inkwells, and other, less identifiable, detritus, they didn't find anything that could be a part of the broken artifact.

"I thought we might find the skunk's staff," Teg said, "or part of it."

"In stories, a wizard's staff is often bound to him," Peg said. "Maybe that's the case here. Or maybe it went back to being a pen and was burned to a crisp."

"Or is here . . ." Teg said, thoughtfully, looking at her collection of junk with new interest. "We'll ask Xerak."

They persisted in their search until Vereez came to get them.

"I'm guessing you didn't find it, right?"

Teg nodded and rolled stiffly to her feet. "And I don't think we're going to. At this point, I'd say either it's been moved or it rolled somewhere else in this room." She waved vaguely to indicate the vast space. "If that's the case, I think we'd be better off doing as Xerak suggested—going to find the other pieces and coming back later."

"How about you three?" Peg asked. "Have you come up with any brilliant plans?"

Vereez rolled her eyes. "We've gotten to the point where we're arguing stupid details. We've agreed we'll look down in the repository before we leave. The only question is do we start now or wait until tomorrow?"

"Now," Teg said, knowing the question was mostly out of consideration for her bruises and Peg's stiff middle. "Honestly, whatever was in the ointment you gave me yesterday has done an amazing job for my aches."

"Mine, too," Peg agreed. "I'm raring to go."

"My mother . . ." Vereez stumbled over the words, then pushed on. "She taught me herb lore. I . . ."

Teg didn't know if foxes could cry, but fox women certainly could and tears were flooding from Vereez's dark eyes and matting her fur. Teg pulled her close and hugged her tightly. Vereez leaned gratefully into the embrace for a moment, then sniffed hard and pulled herself straight.

"I always thought Mother knew a lot more than what she claimed about herb lore. I guess I was right, huh? She knew a lot more about magic in general than she ever let on. She and my dad . . . They've been . . ."

"Lying?" Peg suggested firmly. "I guess that's one way to put it."

"Is there any other way?" Vereez said, ears pinning back as sorrow surged into anger. "Is there? The way they talked about their lives, how they met . . . They met young, in college. Mom said she loved how Dad looked out for her . . . She never said that this was while they were pulling off robberies! I . . . I . . . I just don't know what to think!"

"Until you can talk to them," Peg said, "give them the benefit of the doubt. Maybe they were dishonest. Maybe they did things they later were ashamed of. Maybe they wanted to remake their lives, and maybe they meant to tell you someday, when they thought you would be old enough to understand."

"Maybe!" Vereez snapped—quite literally, as a fox might when biting through a rabbit's neck. "Or maybe they're just hypocrites, holding me up to standards of behavior that they never bothered with themselves."

Teg, remembering what Vereez had confided in her, stepped in before Vereez's anger led her to say more than she intended. "You both have good points. Vereez, think about it. Whatever your parents' reasons, you've now learned something that will be valuable to you if you need to make them answer your questions. Calm down."

Vereez's ears slowly began to perk again. "You're right, Teg. I did. Whatever reason they hid their past from me, they're not going to want it to get out now. Prominent bankers with a past as 'extraction agents,' as Sapphire Wind so politely put it. Hah!"

She looked ready to charge off that very moment.

"Hang on. You'll be in a far better situation to ask questions if we learn more about your missing sister from Sapphire Wind," Teg went on. "That may be why Hettua Shrine sent you here. Trust me. It's always better to save questions for those things you can't figure out on your own. Easier to trust the answers, too, if you have the means to cross-check."

Peg nodded. "Teg's tactics are sound. What's to keep your parents from continuing to deny they know anything? Better if you can ask something more to the point."

"You're right," Vereez said. "You're both right. I promise, no running off like a snake/chicken"—the translation spell garbled at this point, as if uncertain which word to supply and settling for giving both—"with my head bitten off. Shall we tell the boys to stop arguing and go after some honestly in your face monsters?"

"Not quite yet," Teg said. "I've found a few items I want to ask Xerak to check over. Who knows? They might be useful."

A few minutes later, Xerak was holding the blue jay wizard's amulet flat on the palm of his left hand, while holding his right hand over it, palm down. He finished chanting a long string of syllables the translation spell did not—or could not—translate. The amulet rose off his palm and hung, gently spinning, in the space between his palms. Xerak closed his eyes, concentrated hard, then let the spell lapse.

"It's been damaged," he said, holding it out to Teg, "but it should still work—at least as to its most basic ability."

"Which is?" Teg asked.

"See how the center of the amulet resembles a multilegged creature?" Xerak asked. "It's stylized, but it reminds me of a creature we call a geetark. They extrude liquid that solidifies into a sort of thread, and use that to trap their prey."

"We have an entire class of creatures like that," Teg said. "We call them spiders. Do your geetark really have eyes all around their body?"

"Of course," Xerak said. "Don't yours?"

"Nope," Peg said. "They only have eyes in front. When we first found this, I thought it was a stylized sun disk, so how about we call this a sun spider?"

"Well," Xerak began, "geetark don't have much to do with the sun. In fact, they're actually cavern dwellers, but . . ."

"Isn't there a type that is associated with volcanoes?" Vereez put in. "I remember finding that fascinating."

"Hold on," Grunwold interrupted. "Time later for comparative biology. Xerak, what will that amulet do?"

"It should shoot out binding ropes, just like Sapphire Wind showed us the blue jay wizard doing in the vision. There would be limits, according to how much magical energy the amulet has stored, but it could be a very useful addition to our arsenal."

Teg held it out. "Then you'd better take it. I certainly don't have any magical energy."

Xerak shook his head. "You don't need to have mana of your own to use this. That's the advantage to amulets and talismans. They store their own energy. You can use them as tools to do magic, just like you can use the 'flashlights' to make light."

He used the English word with self-conscious pride, having gone out of his way to learn it when he realized that the concept of the device, if not what made it work, was familiar to the humans.

"What else can the sun spider amulet do?" Peg asked.

"I can't be certain," Xerak replied, "without time to work a detailed analysis, and the facilities to do so. The spell I just did is my limit without additional material. At a guess, the amulet might be able to create or summon an actual sun spider, perhaps even one of a monstrous size. In the case of creation, the amulet itself usually serves as a"—the translation spell frizzled for a moment then settled on—"template. However, in most cases, at least some of the power for such a large working would need to come from the caster. Anyhow, with the amulet probably being damaged, and no longer allied with a specific wizard, I doubt it could either summon or create."

"Supplying magical energy is probably beyond me," Teg said, turning the sun spider amulet over in her hands, admitting to herself that she was reluctant to give her treasure to someone else. *Archeologists always have to hand over their finds. It would be so cool to keep one for once.* "Still, I like the idea of being able do a Spiderman with web shooters. That could be useful in an emergency. If you don't mind, I'll hold onto it."

Xerak was clearly confused, so doubtless the translation

spell had garbled what she'd said, but he seized on the important point. "Yes. You keep it. Save it for an emergency. In its current condition, it may only work once."

The young wizard looked tired, his mane limp and stringy. Remembering how Inehem had needed to be carried after she'd done complicated magic, Teg decided to hold onto the rest of her and Peg's finds—which doubtless were mostly junk—for later examination.

"All right," she said. "What's the plan?"

"Many of the areas we're going through," Grunwold said, indicating a rough map he'd drawn, "will permit us to walk two abreast, but we'd be crowded. So we're going to go single file. Vereez and Xerak will go in front. I'll take the rear."

He paused and Teg guessed that he wasn't happy about this, but had been argued into agreeing. Vereez continued.

"If you humans agree, we want Peg after Xerak, since she knows how to handle a sword. Teg and Meg will be in the middle. Spears are going to be a lot less useful in close quarters, so we're leaving all but Xerak's behind. We do have machetes if you want them."

Teg suggested, "Let me go right after Peg. Meg after me. Oh, and I have a question for Sapphire Wind."

Meg's head tilted to show that Sapphire Wind was listening, and Teg went on.

"If the creatures roaming through here are guardians, can you control them? You seem to be a sort of guardian yourself."

"I am and I am not," Sapphire Wind replied. "But, to

answer your immediate question, if we encounter actual guardians, there is indeed a chance I will be able to dissuade them from acting. However, there are many forces roaming this ruin that are not guardians but are, instead, magics released from their bindings."

"Like in the stories the inquisitors told us," Teg said. "Darn! I was hoping those were exaggerations."

"So were the rest of us," Vereez added with a tense laugh.

"Sapphire Wind is going to exit Meg," Grunwold went on, "but will accompany us in an insubstantial form. It will do what it can to divert guardians, as well as undo wards and locks. It will also serve as our guide."

"I," Xerak said, "will be able to perceive Sapphire Wind fairly easily. Vereez will be able to do so if she concentrates. The rest of you will, I fear, be unable to see it unless you concentrate hard. That's another reason for putting us up front."

"Meg may be able to see me," Sapphire Wind said unexpectedly. "She is, at least for now, attuned to me."

"I'm as eager as anyone to start exploring," Peg said, "but we've been on the go for a while, and I could use some lunch."

Remembering how beat Xerak had looked, Teg was quick to second Peg's proposal, although she was itching to go deeper into the building, where the chance of significant finds would go up. She remembered a project manager who had gotten so absorbed in the pit house he was digging that it took a second pointing out to him that above ground the snow was approaching white-out conditions to get him to stop.

I can certainly be less obsessive than that!

When they resumed their exploration, Teg carried one of the machetes. She placed the sun spider amulet in her left pocket, where she could easily grab hold of it with her free hand. Xerak had shown her how to activate the amulet, but she hoped she wouldn't need to use it. She might as easily tangle up her allies as an enemy—and she wasn't at all certain she could even make it work.

As Sapphire Wind led them in the direction of the repository, the rippling tide of destruction that had flowed through the Library eliminated any chance that the vision they'd seen in the Font of Sight would make their surroundings familiar. Bookshelves had toppled domino fashion, one knocking over the next. Fire had swept through, finding ample fuel in dry paper, vellum, and wood. Even though decades had passed, an acrid reek still hung in the air.

"Grunwold, you're going to need to come up here after all," Xerak said. "I'm going to need both your and Vereez's help to move some of this stuff."

"Right," Grunwold said. He lifted Heru off his shoulder, and held the mini pterodactyl balanced on one hand. "Peg, take rear guard. I'll have Heru watch behind you, but you'll need to be the brains of the operation."

Heru made a blatting sound that was anything but complimentary, but hopped over to sit on Peg's shoulder without protest.

Peg's eyes widened in momentary astonishment at finding herself so nominated, but nodded briskly. "Aye, aye, Captain."

Teg handed her machete to Meg. "I'd better help the

kids out. I'm good at seeing how things fit together. I may be able to save us from a collapse."

She was coming out from under where she'd been inspecting a chaotic pile of partially burned shelving and charred textbooks when she caught a flicker of motion as something emerged from a layer of ash atop a more-or-less erect shelf unit.

"What's that?" she asked, pointing. The motion had resolved into flock of flaccid yellowish-grey pancake creatures that were moving by slowly flapping their sides, rather as if they were bats that had figured out how to manage without the mouselike middle section.

"Abau!" Meg called. "Watch out! They'll blind you if they can."

How can she know? Teg thought, then realized that Sapphire Wind must have supplied the information.

There was no time for Teg to retrieve her machete—even if Meg wasn't already using it to poke at a hovering abau. Instead, Teg settled for a chunk of charred wood about the length of her arm. It wasn't a cool weapon, not the like coppery-bright, slightly curved blades Vereez was wielding, but it was enough to keep the things from reaching her face. Grunwold proved that his antlers weren't just ornamental when one of the abau got inside his guard. Xerak demonstrated that his spear staff wasn't just meant for magic, poking holes in the abau with almost surgical precision.

But Heru was the real hero of that particular battle. Gliding above the attackers, he stabbed out with his long neck, pinpointing an area on the creatures' backs that somehow disabled their ability to flap. Once they flopped to the floor, the abau were helpless enough that they weren't even worth squashing.

"Do we kill them?" Peg asked, her gaze darting between the feebly moving abau and the surrounding stacks, in case anything else unpleasant was awaiting them.

"If you do not," Meg said, "Sapphire Wind can establish control over them, and through them their associates. Abau are apparently among the Library's guardians, although not the most intelligent. Their usual job is to deal with accumulated dust and keep watch for vandalism."

Although the band was victorious against the abau, their next opponents were far more vicious. Under Teg's direction, Xerak and Grunwold had been working to shove open a door that had burned while about six inches open, its hinges transformed into slag, its wood heat-hardened. Once they forced the door fully open, they were able to move into a pleasantly spacious area that had probably been a reading room. There they paused for a break, seating themselves on one side of the nearest of the long tables that, with their associated benches, were the room's primary furnishings.

Teg was sipping from her canteen when she felt, almost as much as heard, a deep, rumbling growl. She glanced at the three inquisitors and saw that each had frozen in midmotion. Heru, who had just accepted half a cookie from Peg, froze, the crescent dangling ludicrously from his bill.

"What is . . . ?" Teg started to ask, when Xerak pointed with his spear staff. Teg's first impression was that the creatures were skulking out from under the long tables at the farther end of the room. Then, incredulously, she realized that the forms were materializing from shadows that unfolded to become four-legged monsters.

The new arrivals were the general size and build of a Doberman pinscher, with the same deep, broad chest, and trim but powerful hips. These monstrosities, however, were scaled like snakes and possessed heads akin to those of goats, with similar creepy, square-pupiled eyes, and sharp, short, very pointy horns. Five of them padded forth, their claws clicking against the stone floors. Their scales were varicolored, in hues ranging from black through bronze, into a golden tan. The one nearest to Teg was tiger striped in bronze and gold. When it snarled, it revealed fangs a tiger would have been proud of.

"Uh, Meg," Peg said, "can Sapphire Wind tell those dobergoats we're invited guests?"

Meg's lack of a reply, and the way she was gripping the chunk of wood she'd traded Teg for the machete, was a reply in itself. Either Sapphire Wind couldn't, or doing so was going to take time.

"Dobergoats?" Vereez said, slightly shaking her head as if the translation spell was doing something odd. "These *summiss* are very dangerous. Stay back, ladies. Xerak?"

"Working on it . . . Cover me. Gonna take a bit." He stepped back behind the front line, hands wrapped around his spear staff, muttering under his breath.

Teg thrust forward to stand between Grunwold and Vereez, machete firmly gripped in both hands. She was surprised to find that she was relatively calm, her focus on the growling creature stiff-legging toward her.

Tiger, Tiger burning bright, her back brain chanted. *Guess we're gonna get into a fight.*

The dobergoats charged as one. Vereez, better able to bring her twin swords into play in this more open area, distracted the two at her end. Grunwold took the two at the other. That left Teg with her striped "friend." Probably the only thing that kept her from getting charged and bitten right off was that the dobergoat was just smart enough to realize that she looked—or maybe it was *smelled*—odd. Instead of charging as its associates had done, it continued its methodical stalking.

Teg held her machete in both hands as she might have when clearing brush, and spoke at the creature. "Yeah, billy goat pup, I'm weird. I bet I'd taste really, really bad. You don't want to risk that or that I'll cut you when you're gagging on my taste."

The dobergoat growled more deeply. Teg had cats, not dogs, but she'd seen enough dogs in action—her dog-owning colleagues often brought them along on extended field projects—to recognize the signs of a pack creature letting the mob overrule whatever common sense it possessed. When it charged, she was ready, and swung at it with a will.

Her machete's sharp edge caught the dobergoat solidly at the join of shoulder and neck but, instead of biting deeply, it only nicked the scaled hide.

Great, not like a snake: thicker, heavier hide. Not surprised. Not surprised.

She knew no one was available to come to her aid. Xerak's chanting hadn't stopped. Vereez and Grunwold had opponents of their own. She could hear Peg shouting and Heru screeching. The dobergoat was continuing its lunge for her, going below the blade, probably planning to clamp its jaws around her left arm. Teg braced herself, determined not to scream, but a scream squeezed through her lips nonetheless.

No. That wasn't her. It was the dobergoat. Meg had walloped it solidly on the back, right above the tail, with her piece of burned wood. The tiger-striped dobergoat yelped, and backed away, tail between its legs in a very canine manner, eyeing its new weird opponent with a dangerous mixture of fear and fury.

"Thanks!" Teg managed to gasp, getting her machete ready for the thing's next rush. She spared a glance for the others. Heru had gone to aid Grunwold. Between the two of them, one dobergoat was down and probably not getting up again, while the other was backing toward one of the tables, bleeding from a bunch of cuts, including one near an eye that was probably Heru's doing.

Vereez was dealing with the largest of the pack, a muscular, tawny creature with brilliant green eyes. Peg was fencing with a mostly bronze diamond-backed dobergoat, not so much trying to harm it as to keep it from both herself and Vereez. As Teg watched in horror, it darted at Vereez's tail in a distraction tactic.

Shouting, "En garde, varlet!" Peg sprang forward, looking more like Errol Flynn than any many-times grandmother should, then skewered the creature where its foreleg merged into the torso. Teg expected the blade to bound off, but the point went in, the creature's own rush at Peg pushing its body halfway up the blade. The creature fell, apparently skewered to whatever it used as a heart.

Peg held firmly onto her sword, but it twisted from her grip as the creature crashed to the ground. Perhaps the death of its comrade infuriated the tiger-striped dobergoat. It rallied and came rushing at Teg and Meg. Teg dreaded that this time she was about to get badly bitten, but she managed to hold her ground. The square-pupiled eyes were focused on her, the dobergoat was gathering itself for a leap, and then Xerak shouted a single loud syllable that sounded something like: "Now!"

The air rippled, and four of the five dobergoats vanished. The only one that remained was the one Peg had killed.

Typically, Grunwold muttered, "About time!" but the look he gave Xerak was pure pride.

"What did you do?" Peg asked. She was holding her right wrist, and looking a little green, but her voice held her usual curiosity.

"Banished them," Xerak replied, reaching for his flask. "The way they appeared like that, they had to be summoned. I sent them back. Meg, ask Sapphire Wind if they're likely to show up again."

Meg, who had slid off her pack and was pulling out her first aid-kit, nodded. She paused, then said, "Sapphire Wind thinks not. We are in a restricted area, and those were meant to herd out intruders. Sapphire Wind will attempt to give us permission to be here."

"Herd?" Vereez said. "They looked like they were going to do a lot more than escort us out."

Meg sighed. "'Meant to.' Sapphire Wind did warn us that the damage to the Library systems would have had a deleterious effect on many of the guardians." She turned her attention to Peg. "You're holding that wrist, dear."

"I think I sprained it," Peg admitted sheepishly. "I

didn't expect my sword to go in so deeply, and when the dobergoat fell, it was heavy enough to twist the blade in my hand before I could let go."

"Let me wrap it for you," Meg said.

After Meg had wrapped the injured wrist, Peg insisted she was "just fine," but Teg, seeing how Peg left her sword sheathed until needed, rather than carrying it at the ready as she had before, had doubts.

"Do we quit for the day?" Vereez said reluctantly. "We seem to keep getting into fights, and I don't think it's going to get easier as we move forward."

"I think we should," Grunwold agreed. "Sapphire Wind has hopefully made sure the abau and the dobergoats won't continue to give us problems, so tomorrow shouldn't be a repeat, right?"

"Let's quit," Peg stated in her best "no-nonsense Mom" voice. "Xerak's hiding his exhaustion well, but he's beat. I'll admit, my wrist is aching. Let's call it quits for now and come back tomorrow, refreshed."

"Do we 'camp' here in the Library?" Teg asked. "I know we brought gear, but I'm not sure any of us would get a good night's sleep. This place is too dangerous. Even if we set watches, it's likely we'd keep getting woken up to beat off whatever comes crawling out of the rubble."

Reluctantly, the inquisitors agreed that hiking back to *Slicewind* made sense. Sapphire Wind promised they would have no difficulty reentering the building the next day. Indeed, Teg had the oddest feeling that the building watched wistfully as one by one they passed out through the doorway.

***

The next morning, much invigorated, the six returned to the ruins. This time Sapphire Wind opened the door for them, swirling and bobbing in obvious welcome.

Once they were safely inside and the doors closed behind them, Meg extended a hand toward the blue cyclone shape and made a beckoning gesture.

"Well, come along. You can't talk in that form."

"Did you rest well?" Sapphire Wind asked, using Meg's body. "I hope so. I will once again lead the way. Stay alert. I have patrolled the route we took yesterday, and it remains safe, but once we leave the reading room, I cannot promise safety."

"Never make a promise knowing you can't keep it," Peg said cheerily. A night's rest and a liberal application of yet another ointment from Vereez's med kit had done a lot for her wrist, although she still kept it snugly wrapped.

They reached the reading room without incident. In the way of such things, the distance they had labored to cross the day before now seemed impossibly short. After getting the door on the far side of the reading room open, they were faced with a large area in which partially burned books had fallen from tilting shelves into irregular drifts of pages, ash, and covers.

Meg moaned aloud, heard herself, and blushed. "I'm sorry. Bad memories. This looks like the children's section after school-visit days."

"If the children were pyros," Peg added, nodding agreement.

"Still," Grunwold said, "at least it doesn't look as if we're going to need to move fallen shelf units. Heru, glide through there and see if you wake up any monsters."

"Right, Grun!" the xuxu croaked, and launched itself from his shoulder. The occasional beats of his wings caused ash to billow. Vereez sneezed. However, even after Heru made a few daring landings atop bookshelves, nothing showed any interest, unfriendly or otherwise.

"Let's go," Xerak said, when Heru was back on Grunwold's shoulder. "Sapphire Wind indicates that we need to cross this room, then bear left."

The area to the left proved to be more or less a continuation of the ash-filled room, but when they came to the next turn, a heap of partially incinerated tomes had drifted to block the aisle. Xerak poked at them with the tip of his spear, but Vereez, impatient with this latest delay, hunkered down to grab hold of some of the larger books and toss them aside.

"Careful," Meg called, clearly appalled, "some of those might be repairable. I see intact sheets, entire intact segments!"

"Yes, ma'am," Vereez chuckled. Rather than grabbing and tossing, she picked up the next stack, and rose to set it to one side.

As she was setting it down, from a gap that had probably once been an aisle, shot a tubular shape the same ivory-yellow of good parchment. For a brief moment, Teg thought it was a scroll, but no scroll would have traveled arrow straight, nor anchored itself so firmly in Vereez's thigh. What was worse was that when the "scroll" hit, it started wriggling, as if trying to burrow deeper in.

Vereez, who was wearing heavy trousers under her tunic, turned, stared down at her leg in disbelief, then grabbed the "scroll" with both hands and tugged. The thing wriggled again, then bent so that its rear end poked at Vereez's hand. Teg saw the stinger that emerged and bent against the thick leather of Vereez's gloves.

"Satefent!" Xerak shouted. "Back up everyone. Those things are vicious."

He grabbed Vereez around her waist and half carried her away. By the time they'd retreated to the reading room, Vereez was swallowing whimpers of pain.

"I can't . . . get it . . . out!" she managed, spacing the words around tugs. "It's . . . digging in!"

Peg called from behind them. "I stomped another of those book worms, and that seems to be the only one left. I'm on my way."

"Grunwold!" Xerak ordered. "I'm going to pull the book worm straight. You slice it off, close as you can to the head."

Grunwold's large brown eyes were so wide that the whites were visible all around, but he dropped his sword and pulled out his belt knife without comment. Vereez let Xerak set her down on one of the tables, and take over her grip on the book worm. Her eyes were wild, and a thin line of foam from panicked panting lined her long fox's jaw, but otherwise she was admirably controlled. This didn't mean she rejected the hands Peg held out for her to hold, an action which effectively blocked Vereez's view of Grunwold's descending blade.

Teg wished she had an excuse to look away. Although Xerak had pulled the creature straight, so that it could no longer sting, the book worm was wriggling hard, reminding her of eels she'd seen pushing into mud or holes in reefs for cover. She swallowed a gag.

Meg said, "Teg, you watch the door we came through. I'll watch the other. This would be a perfect time for something else to sneak up on us."

Teg nodded, feeling guilty about the relief that flooded her. Right now, she'd be happy for a pack of dobergoats. They were at least honestly nasty. These book worms were insidious.

A few moments later, she heard a squishing sound and glanced back to see Grunwold stomping on the book worm, which was now oozing a greenish-blue ichor from one end, into a pulp on the floor. Then she made the mistake of looking over at Vereez. Part of the thing still wriggled, against her leg. Red blood mixed with the blue-green ichor and Teg felt her gorge rise. She didn't throw up—quite—but if she'd eaten a heavier breakfast she probably would have made a real mess.

"Orange bottle," Vereez managed through clamped jaws. "My kit."

Xerak found it, opened it, sniffed it, and nodded before pouring a little of the contents where the book worm's head met Vereez's thigh. This caused the jaws to unclamp, and the rest of the thing to drop to the floor. Before Grunwold stomped on it, Teg saw that the book worm had a mouth like a lamprey's, with numerous teeth set around a circular opening, with the added bonus of a long blue tongue that was red with Vereez's blood.

"My mother's formula, again," Vereez muttered.

Once her leg was bound up, Vereez insisted they continue on. Teg had a feeling the young woman was fighting some sort of battle with her absent mother. If Inehem hadn't given up, not even when she was so exhausted she couldn't walk, Vereez wasn't going to whimper and insist on going back to the ship, even with a fresh hole dug in her leg.

Creatures weren't the only dangers. Moving the remnants of the massive shelf units, furniture, and other, less identifiable, bits of detritus strained both muscles and tempers. Everyone acquired numerous bruises and scrapes. Grunwold only narrowly escaped having an antler tine snapped off when Xerak let go of his end of a huge shelf before Grunwold's head was completely out of the way.

Nonetheless, they succeeded in clearing a passage to the hidden door that—so the vision had shown them—would lead to the stairway down into the repository.

Once they had reached the hidden door that concealed the stairway down to the repository, Sapphire Wind collaborated with Xerak and Peg. Using a combination of magic and Peg's surprisingly impressive skill with a lock pick, they undid the locks and wards that had so exhausted Inehem when the extraction agents had made their incursion.

Then Sapphire Wind activated some low-level lights that illuminated the stone treads. These were not worn smooth with repeated use as Teg had subconsciously expected them to be, but were in good condition, with roughened gouges cut into the stone to reduce the chance of slipping. However, while the light helped keep them from missing their step, it also accentuated every shadow, so that Teg found herself bracing against attacks that didn't come. Her already strained nerves were jangling by the time they reached the repository.

"Damn!" Vereez said. The word was English, picked up from Peg and Teg. Meg rarely swore, considering profanity an indication of a lack of imagination.

Is it imaginative to swear in an alien language, though? Teg thought as she eased her way past Peg, between Vereez and Xerak, so she could get a better look. She realized that she was letting her archeologist's fervor dominate, but she didn't want everyone tromping ahead through the ruined area before she had a chance to assess the site.

As Teg had expected, the repository, which they had last seen so tidy and orderly in the vision supplied by the Font of Sight, was as wrecked as the Library's upper floors had been. Whatever force had rocked the Library had ripped the units that held the numerous safe deposit boxes from the walls. Additionally, there was evidence that something large and strong had pushed its way through since the collapse, shoving enough of the toppled safe deposit boxes erect to create a jagged and erratic pathway through the debris.

"I wonder how whatever did that got through the locks?" Vereez asked.

"Maybe it was down here all along?" Xerak offered.

Sapphire Wind spoke through Meg. "If whatever did that was one of the Library's elite guardians, the locks would not have stopped it."

That announcement caused a thoughtful pause in the general move forward, during which time Teg finished easing her way to the front.

"Is this area safe?" Peg asked, then forced a chuckle. "I guess what I mean is 'Is it any more dangerous than upstairs?'"

Xerak did what Teg was beginning to recognize as a lesser spell, because he made fewer motions before the spearhead on his staff started to glow with a dark amber light. He moved the spearhead back and forth over the area in front of him. Teg had crowded close enough that she could see when his tense muscles relaxed.

"Based on what I just did," Xerak said, pulling his spear staff upright and leaning against it, "I think we might be safer down here than we were above. Those safe deposit boxes were intended to keep whatever was stored within them not only from being stolen..."

Grunwold snorted what sounded very much like "Yeah, right..."

"... but to keep their magical energies from mingling with each other. For that reason, we shouldn't encounter creatures like the enhanced versions of dobergoats and abau we fought over the past few days, since they probably owe some of their abilities to rogue magical energies."

"Wait," Teg said. "You're telling me those were *natural* creatures?"

"Certainly," Xerak said, "all but the book worms. Those are typically found in large libraries, and are created to deal with vermin. I'll admit, the one that got Vereez was the largest I've ever seen."

Vereez added, "The dobergoats were nastier than their natural counterparts, but perfectly normal creatures. My parents have some that patrol the grounds of our House of Fortune."

Teg decided she really didn't want to know more.

"And what do you think made that?" Peg pointed again to the trail through the debris.

"Well," Meg said, clearly speaking for herself, not for Sapphire Wind, "we did have the theory that the reason neither Sapphire Wind nor Teg could find the piece of the artifact that we suspect was dropped by the escaping extraction agents was because something carried it away. I would say the probability that this is what happened just rose."

"Before we go charging off after it," Teg put in, "we should check for hazards."

Xerak nodded. "I can use magic. You use your archeologist powers. The rest of you will need to rely on common sense. I realize that won't be easy for Grunwold, but he can try."

Grunwold made as if to throw a chunk of masonry at Xerak, but his ears were perked and he was grinning. "I'll keep watch over the stairwell. We certainly didn't manage to deal with all the things haunting the upper floors, and, as Sapphire Wind just reminded us, some of the guardian creatures can open locks."

Thanks to whatever had come plowing through, they had to do minimal shifting of wreckage and moving of rubble to get through the area with the safe deposit boxes. Once they were beyond the numerous subsections built to accommodate ranks of boxes, the level of visible destruction dropped dramatically.

"Probably," Teg said, inspecting the join of wall and ceiling, "because these corridors weren't built, as such. It looks to me as if they were cut from the bedrock, then the stone was smoothed and dressed to make it look prettier. I'd love to know how they managed to . . ."

"Magic," Peg interrupted her. "By magic or by using

some magical critter. You're got to remember, Teg. Hortas or whatever are completely possible here."

"'Hortas'? Why does that sound familiar?"

"*Star Trek*," Meg said, surprising Teg more than a little. "Classic version. Episode called 'Devil in the Dark,' if I recall correctly."

She raised an eyebrow in a perfect Spock imitation. "Fascinating."

"I didn't follow most of that," Vereez cut in, "but if what you're saying is that these corridors should be structurally sound, then let's get going. I have a pretty good memory, and if we can't find our way to that place our parents went by conventional tracking, I think I can remember most of the turns those extraction agents took."

Vereez took point, with Xerak just behind her, and Teg replacing Peg as third. At first they did trail the marks left by what Peg dubbed the "stone plow," but eventually they had to rely on Vereez's memory. Sapphire Wind admitted, when queried, that it was feeling muddled, perhaps because it had expended considerable energy on locks, lights, and communication.

Meg said, "We probably shouldn't count on Sapphire Wind, so it can reserve its power for locks and wards."

At last Vereez showed them where a closed door blended surprisingly well into the surrounding stonework. "I think this is the door that leads to that second stairwell down. Is everybody ready?"

❧CHAPTER NINE❧

Teg longed for a moment to investigate whether the camouflage was managed with stone facing or paint or something arcane, but restrained herself. The tension in their little group was almost palpable.

Vereez said with forced calm, "Sapphire Wind, can you tell if this door has been locked or had any sort of magic worked on it?"

"I sense neither," Meg's voice replied. "As best I can tell, it has only been pulled shut. The latch is located right there."

A sparkle of blue-white light outlined where a lever lay flush against the door, rather after the fashion used for pocket doors in small apartments or mobile homes.

Vereez set her hand on it. "Everyone ready?"

Grim nods, surprisingly similar, never mind the difference in the shapes of the heads involved, gave her the reply. Xerak held up one hand.

"Give me a moment to ready mana in case I need to

quickly work a spell. The small workings I've been doing are beginning to tell on me."

Not even Grunwold expressed any impatience. When the spearhead atop Xerak's staff was limned in a pale, greenish-violet light, Vereez slid up the latch, revealing the downward stairway they'd seen in the vision in the Font of Sight. Interestingly, there was far less dust and fewer cobwebs than they'd seen back then. Their feet gritted some on the stone treads but no more, Teg assessed, than would be reasonable given the passage of something over a couple of decades within an enclosed space.

How long had this stairwell been sealed when the extraction agents came through? she wondered.

Stepping with care, they approached the door that over two decades before the extraction agents had struggled to open.

"Sapphire Wind says it can open this door for us," Meg said. "It also says it doesn't believe that the room beyond is untenanted."

Teg glanced around and saw the same thought on very different faces. *Whatever it is, it isn't going to like us breaking in.*

"Let Sapphire Wind open the door for us," Vereez stated, although the cant of her ears and her inflection made the statement a question. "That way none of us needs to get too close. Maybe we can get a look at whatever is inside before it gets the jump on us."

No one protested, but numerous weapons shifted to ready.

"When everyone is prepared, then," Meg said with

such calm it was impossible to tell if it was she or Sapphire Wind who spoke.

"Those of you in front," Grunwold grumbled, "remember to move so you don't block the door. Okay? Now, open it!"

With the faintest grinding of stone against stone, the door slid to one side, revealing the same small room, the same ornate pedestal that they'd seen in the vision in the Font of Sight.

Two elements did not match that vision. As expected, the top of the pedestal was empty. But none of them prepared for the horrific creature that coiled around the pedestal's base.

Long bodied yet bulky, the monster had elongated, many-toothed jaws, like those of a crocodile, and that creature's armored hide as well. However, its skull was more canine, with a higher forehead. Eight legs—each longer than those of a crocodile, and more heavily muscled than those of a dog—with spikes at the joints, lifted a heavy, broad-chested torso like that of a mastiff. The tail that balanced the long head and stocky body was tipped with a ball, rather like what Teg recalled an ankylosaur was supposed to have had. Worst of all were the all-too-intelligent eyes, huge and brilliant red, that studied the intruders from beneath ridged protective plates.

The fragment of the artifact they sought rested on the floor between the creature's front paws—or were those hands? Teg wasn't at all sure. What she was certain of was that this monster wasn't going to give up its prize—it looked like the bronze spindle on which the larger bit had rested—without a fight.

After a long pause for mutual staring, the monster gaped open its long jaws and spat a gob of particularly viscous saliva toward them. Either this was a warning shot or the creature had bad aim, for the steaming stuff plopped directly between Teg and Vereez, who were closest to the front. They leapt back as one. Vereez grabbed the edge of the door and slid it shut.

"So," Peg said, her tone so calm she had to be severely rattled, "what was that?"

"No idea," Grunwold said. "Xerak? Vereez? You've seen more than this simple farmer's son."

"I've never seen one of those," Vereez replied.

"Me either," Xerak added, "not even a picture in my master's vast collection of bestiaries. There's only one classification I can give it: unique monstrosity, magically created."

"A classification system that includes the unique," Teg said, trying her best to match Peg's calm. *We're the mentors after all, even if this world is not our own.* "That's a nice system indeed."

"So, how do we deal with Unique Monstrosity?" Grunwold said. "That room is too small and too awkwardly shaped for us all to rush it. Even if we could, the portion of the artifact it's holding might get broken."

"Additionally," Xerak added at his most scholarly, "we know the creature's spittle is either hot or acidic, or possibly both. If that stuff hits exposed skin, that would definitely hurt."

Teg had flipped the sun spider amulet into her palm and was staring at it. "What if I used this to shoot webs at its head? If I'm really lucky, I'd manage to rope its jaws shut. Even if I can't do that, it's certain to be distracted. Or," she continued, making as if to hand the amulet over, "you could use it, Xerak or Vereez."

Xerak shook his head. "I think Vereez and I should stay with the tools we're skilled with. If you're willing to try to web the thing's head, then . . ."

As they carefully laid their plans, Teg couldn't help but worry whether the monster was doing some planning of its own. Could it be eavesdropping? Maybe that nearly earless head was pressed against the door and it was chuckling to itself as it made counterplans.

She decided not to mention her paranoid conjecture. Overheard or not, they were going to need to give this a try.

When next Sapphire Wind was asked to open the door, Teg found herself kneeling on the floor to the left of the door, the sun spider amulet resting in her right palm. She'd tried to focus on it, as Xerak had taught her, and was aware of a faint buzz of energies against her skin. Despite her other, numerous, apprehensions, she felt a curious confidence that, when she activated the sun spider amulet, it would at least emit goo.

Vereez stood to the other side of the door, panting slightly, brown eyes bright and excited. Xerak and Grunwold stood back, long weapons in hand, ready to form the second wave. Peg held her sword, and Meg a machete, making up the third rank.

"Ready?" Meg asked softly. When answers came in the form of tense nods, the door began to slide open once more.

The crocodilian-headed creature was waiting, but this

time they didn't give it the leisure to spit and hack. Hooting and yapping, Vereez ran in the direction of the heavy ball at the end of its tail. At the same moment, Teg pushed her hand palm out, the sun spider amulet nestled against her skin. She didn't let herself think that what she was doing had anything to do with magic. This was a tool. Xerak had told her how to use it. Shooting webbing was no different from throwing a shovel of dirt out of a pit, blind, knowing where the wheelbarrow was and that she would, absolutely, beyond the faintest doubt, hit it.

She was astonished and delighted when thick creamy ropes of silken goo shot from the sun spider amulet and hit the monster along the line of its jaw. She didn't succeed in wrapping a perfect line of spidey silk and tying the jaw shut. Instead, what she did was more like walloping the teeth with a line of caulk or a wide bead of very stiff frosting. At least for this moment, that crocodile mouth lost its smile.

Vereez had landed squarely on top of the wrecking ball at the end of the creature's tail, her weight not only keeping the Unique Monstrosity from swinging the ball into action, but making it difficult for the creature to move forward. It growled in frustration, aware it couldn't turn to attack Vereez without making itself vulnerable to both Grunwold and Xerak.

As a compromise, the creature hauled itself into a seated position, holding the fragment of the artifact close to its chest with its left paw. Grunwold swung his sword, but the creature blocked the blade against its heavily armored right arm. For good measure, it spat bits of web goo at him. Before long, it was going to have its mouth clear. Then its spit would be dangerous, rather than just annoying.

"Teg, silk it again!" Peg yelled.

"Can't. Spider doesn't have enough juice," Teg replied, backing into the hallway to give Xerak and Grunwold room to maneuver.

She held onto the amulet though, playing with it the way one does a worry stone, her fingers moving restlessly over the contours of the rough stone at the middle as she watched the battle, wishing desperately that she had something better than a machete, although there was a question as to whether anything smaller than a bazooka would help.

The stalemate would soon be ending. The room was too crowded for Grunwold and Xerak to effectively attack the Unique Monstrosity. Even if one or the other retreated into the hall, the creature's armor had demonstrated that it was proof against both sword and spear. The Unique Monstrosity seemed to be resistant to Xerak's magic as well, barely reacting when he enhanced his spear thrust with a jolt of flame.

All that was keeping the Unique Monstrosity from gaining the advantage was the rapidly dissolving goo sealing its mouth, and Vereez's determined clinging to that wrecking-ball tail.

It may be two against one, Teg thought, *but that one has eight legs and is using the middle sets to keep the boys back. What to do? What to do?*

Suddenly, she got a really odd feeling that the sun spider amulet was trying to tell her that it just might have a little more goo in it. Then she had an idea, although whether it was hers or the amulet's, she wouldn't have been willing to bet.

"Xerak!" Teg shouted. "Go for its eyes! Grunwold, you cover him."

She'd suspected that the Unique Monstrosity was intelligent. Its tactics were just too good. Now she counted on the translation spell to make it understand what she was saying. When it winced, she felt sure it had.

Xerak summoned a new gout of fire to the tip of his spear staff. Grunwold moved to where he could parry any viscous spittle. The Unique Monstrosity raised its free hand to cover one of its large eyes, squinching the other shut as best it could. Xerak shoved forth his flaming spearhead and Teg shouted.

"Grunwold, go for the other eye! Leave me an opening!"

The Unique Monstrosity wasn't lacking in courage but, when both flaming spear point and Grunwold's sword flashed directly for those overlarge eyes, it shrieked. In a moment of panic, it raised its remaining forearm to cover its face. This brought its hands into view. Teg saw that the heavy armor that protected the digits limited their ability to grip. The spindle portion of the artifact was only loosely grasped.

Okay, sun spider, she thought at the amulet. *Let's grab that bit of metal right out of the Monstrosity's paw.*

A cord of spidey silk shot out, gobbed onto the bronze spindle, coating it. Teg hauled back, grateful for all those long, boring evenings on field projects where fishing had been one of the few amusements available. She'd developed a light touch, and once the spindle was "hooked," she pulled with just the right amount of force to pop the fragment of the artifact from the Unique Monstrosity's hand-paw.

The creature shrieked, an earsplitting sound that made Teg want to clap her own hands over her ears. Ignoring the danger of the sword and spear to its eyes, the monster lurched toward where Teg was trying to reel in her sticky line. Even the weight of Vereez on its tail only slowed the Unique Monstrosity, and Teg didn't think she could both recover the artifact and stumble out of the way in time to avoid the snap of those crocodilian jaws.

Then Peg shoved through and dove, sliding like a batter trying to turn a single into a double. With her left hand, she grabbed the bronze spindle, goo and all, then curled herself around it. Grunwold and Xerak leapt to protect Peg, and Teg—whose head was suddenly light—stumbled back. Had Meg not hurried forward and caught her, she would have fallen squarely on her butt.

As Meg lowered her to the floor, Teg heard Peg's voice, shrill with tension, but still holding matriarchal no-nonsense authority.

"I've got it and I'm keeping it. Come at me, Monstrosity, and I'll vanish back to my own world, and then what would you do?" She was reaching for the transport talisman on her wrist as she spoke, and the monster seemed to understand the threat. At least it stopped moving. "Good, whatever you are. Now, I want you to slow down and listen. You've been guarding this bit of artifact, right?"

The Unique Monstrosity slowly nodded.

"Very good," Peg continued. "Now, pay attention. We're not going to steal it. We're going to fix it. Do you understand that?"

Again a slow, heavy-headed nod.

"So we're on the same side, it seems to me."

No nod this time.

"Do you want the artifact fixed?"

Nod.

"Can you fix it?"

No motion. Teg wondered if the creature's neck wouldn't let it shake its head. Or maybe it had a more complicated thought to express and didn't want to say no. She felt about five drinks drunk, but managed to speak.

"Hold on, Peg. I have a question for it." The glowing red eyes turned to look at her. "Can you talk? I mean, when your mouth isn't all gummed up?"

The creature nodded enthusiastically.

Meg took over. "Shall we call truce then and discuss matters?"

Again a nod.

"Let's go back upstairs," Grunwold suggested. "It's not exactly comfortable, but it's better than here."

"And I," Peg said, accepting Xerak's help to get to her feet, "would definitely prefer a chair. You kids sure know how to make an old lady push her limits."

Teg had feared that their recovering the piece of the artifact would be a signal for every remaining guardian creature to attack but, perhaps because the Unique Monstrosity walked with them, perhaps because Sapphire Wind swirled around them, visible now as a faint sparkle in the air even to the nonmagically attuned, they met with no opposition.

On their way back through the artifact repository,

Sapphire Wind directed them to a pigeonhole where reposed an enshrouding container similar to the one that they'd seen broken in the vision. Once the artifact was stored in it, some of the tension crackling in the air ebbed, but Teg wasn't sure it had anything to do with the artifact being sealed away or just pure relief that the job was done.

When they were back in the reception room, everyone gathered around one of the long tables. Heru soared to take up watch on one of the high desks that commanded a good view of the corridors into the stacks. Grunwold went outside, returning with a bucket of fresh water so that the Unique Monstrosity could wash its jaws.

While Meg and Vereez treated a variety of small wounds—including a nasty scrape Peg had gotten on her chin when she had dived across the floor—Teg started laying out a sort of picnic. She found she was both ravenous and nauseous, which wasn't a pleasant combination at all.

Eventually, everyone but the Unique Monstrosity took a seat on a bench and selected some sort of refreshment, while pretending that having a very large monster washing its face a few yards away was completely normal. After a great deal of sloshing its jaws in the bucket, the monster spoke. To Teg's astonishment, it sounded completely human.

Well, completely comprehensible, anyhow, Teg amended, for the voice was deep and grating.

"My name is Emsehu. I am the son of Dmen Qeres, the man who built the Library of the Sapphire Wind," the Unique Monstrosity announced, "and I am the man who, albeit indirectly, am responsible for the Library's destruction."

"Hang on," Grunwold said, pausing in the middle of meticulously repacking one of the first-aid kits. "Are you saying you're the one who hired our parents to steal that thing from the Library?"

"I am. And 'that thing' has a name. It is called Ba Djed of the Weaver."

"Why did you need to steal the Ba whatever if the place belonged to your father?" Grunwold pressed, apparently unaware of the irony that he—who had stolen *Slicewind*—should be the one to ask this.

"The answer to that is complicated."

"And why do you look like that?" Grunwold persisted.

Peg cut in before Grunwold could continue his cross-examination.

"Grunwold, it has been a very stressful day for all of us. We all understand that. Even so, how about you let Emsehu manage more than one statement before cutting him off?"

Grunwold turned his ears sideways in obvious annoyance, then shrugged. "If you want. This was starting to sound like one of those long, boring tales. I thought I'd cut to the chase. Save time. Like that."

He busied himself with repacking the first-aid kit, and Emsehu continued.

"The Library of the Sapphire Wind was founded by my father, but I had no rights to it. You see, my father had one love—his scholarly, magical duties. This did not mean he was celibate, but he usually avoided 'complications,' which is how he referred to his occasional offspring. When his sexual liaisons did produce children, he dealt with them in what he felt was an honorable fashion, providing financial support for the offspring, and otherwise having nothing to do with him or her.

"I was raised by my mother, who told me she was a widow. Claiming that she was overwhelmed by grief that their time together had been so brief, she would tell me nothing of my father. I assumed that she would tell me when I was older, but she died in a boating accident when I was in college. Bereft of my mother, I became more eager to know something of my father. However, I could find no one who knew him.

"Desire to learn more of my heritage made me a better student than I might otherwise have been. After college, I went on to Zisurru University in Rivers Meet. I specialized in research spells, including dabbling in divination and rebirth lore. Eventually, I learned that my mother had lied to me. Not only had my father not died back then, he was still alive. It took more research to learn his name, but eventually I did so.

"With this new information, I found him easy enough to locate, for Dmen Qeres was one of the great wizards of his day. I did not presume to introduce myself to this great man, but I did win a post at the Library of the Sapphire Wind. These many years later, I can freely state what I barely permitted myself to admit then. I hoped that my father would take notice of me for my talents, make me one of his intimates, and rejoice when I confessed myself his son.

"But that didn't happen. I had ability and talent both, but Dmen Qeres was an old man who had already settled on his favorites. He had neither energy nor attention to spare for one of many eager young scholars who strove for his recognition. Eventually, disheartened, I left the Library to take work elsewhere. When I heard Dmen Qeres had died, I waited to learn if he had acknowledged any of the children of his body in his will. He had not.

"For some reason this last rejection—as I saw it— bothered me as none of the others had done. Perhaps it was because, if he were swiftly reborn, I would not have a son's claim on him. By now, I hardly know.

"My late father had left his entire fortune to endow the Library of the Sapphire Wind. With some perverse sense of entitlement, I sought employment at the Library once more. Even during the first time I had worked within those walls I had sensed that the Library held powerful secrets—but then isn't such the natural aura of all great libraries? This time my goal from the outset was to discover what those secrets might be.

"Eventually, I became aware that deep beneath the Library's repository was a hidden vault in which something of great value was kept, its aura masked by the various and disparate magics stored in both the Library's texts and the items in the repository. I grew wild with the desire to have whatever this was for my own, obsessed with the feeling that if I had it, I would also possess what had been my competition for my father's attention and affections.

"I will not say I was sane, but I was cunning. Rather than risk the theft myself, I hired a talented group of extraction agents to do so. I equipped them well. If in some part of my mind I expected them to fail—and me to learn from their failure—still I had not the least sense that I would be putting the Library in danger.

"After the Library's destruction, I made my way to the ruins and, using my research magic skills, attempted to learn what had happened to the artifact I had sought. In this way, I learned that the artifact my extraction agents had been sent to get was, apparently, still within the Library. I didn't realize then—indeed I was ignorant until now—that what I had found was only one part of a great whole. Sapphire Wind was not as generous with me as with you. Indeed, I did not realize the Library's prime guardian was still present and could be appealed to."

Meg spoke for the Library's *genius loci*. "Sapphire Wind did not trust you—nor think you could be bargained with as the Library bargained with us."

"Ah, that explains its actions. And the conclusion is probably valid as well."

Emsehu lapped water, more canine-seeming than crocodilian in this.

When Emsehu didn't resume speaking, Vereez asked, "But your transformation. How did that happen?"

Emsehu heaved a great sigh. "Once I was certain that my father's great treasure still remained here, I came to the ruins several times to attempt to locate and retrieve it. During my last attempt, I was wounded near to death. At that point, a twisted aspect of my father's magical protections made itself apparent. My dying was arrested and my spirit was channeled into one of the guardian creatures that the Library of the Sapphire Wind had been equipped with from its earliest days.

"These guardians were magical simulacra. Now I learned why some were more effective than others. I was far from the first to attempt to steal from the Library's treasures. Those individuals who died in the attempt were imprisoned in a simulacra, bound to use all their wits to protect what they would have stolen."

"So your living soul was enslaved?" Xerak asked, horrified. "That's the blackest of magic."

"There was a loophole," Emsehu admitted. "If an imprisoned soul wanted to be freed, all it had to do was die—via suicide or in combat or simply by willing it. However, the simulacra were enchanted with a strong self-preservation initiative. The two often clashed. In my case, since I was obsessed with finding and possessing my father's treasure, I discovered my fate did not disturb me. As a guardian creature, I could roam the Library at will. As such, I located a lesser guardian who had carried away one piece of what I knew was the great treasure. I slew that guardian and made myself the artifact's protector. My intention was to seek the other pieces but, probably because of the guardian impulse of the simulacra I now inhabited, I ended up focusing on keeping what I had, rather than attempting to gain more. Instead, I researched the history of what I had, which is how I learned its name."

"And what about now?" Grunwold asked with his usual gruffness. "We've got the 'treasure'—even if it's only part of the treasure. You all right with that?"

"I am resigned," Emsehu said. "In any case, as that peculiar monster you have advising you—the one called Peg—said, your goal is to fix what is broken. Perhaps I will wait until the treasure is whole again, then make my move."

Meg laughed. At least Teg was pretty sure it was Meg, not Sapphire Wind.

Meg said, "You are caught in the body of a guardian of this Library of which the Sapphire Wind is the *genius loci*. I suggest you don't try anything too clever, especially if you wish to continue living. You spoke of three ways your spirit could move on. The Wind assures me that there is a fourth. It can dismiss you, but it would prefer not to do so, since in this form you are useful, and dead you would be of little use."

Emsehu inclined his head. "I appreciate the consideration. I would prefer to continue as a guardian. For many, many years, my thoughts have been muddled. They are clearer now, and I find I have much to consider."

"Very good," Meg said, "as long as you serve faithfully, you may remain." Meg turned her attention to the rest. "Since we have shown ourselves faithful to our own bargain, Sapphire Wind will research and then release the person it deems most fit to aid us. Which question would we like answered first?"

Her lips shaped a small, amused smile. "Oh! Before we discuss that, let me add that I have also convinced Sapphire Wind of the wisdom of explaining to the archivee what the situation is, therefore ascertaining that whoever is awakened will be willing to assist us."

"Good thinking, Meg," Xerak said. "Thank you." He looked squarely at Grunwold and Vereez. "We could decide which inquisition has priority randomly, rolling dice or something, but in addition to looking for answers to our questions, we should consider the larger tactical picture. We will need a lead or assistance or something that will to help us find the other two pieces."

"And I suppose," Grunwold retorted bitterly, "that

you're going to argue that your beloved master would be our best choice. Well, just in case you're wondering, I'm not sure I could argue against you. I'd been thinking that having a powerful wizard on our side would be useful."

Xerak shook his head vigorously, his mane tossing with the violence of the motion. "Actually, I wasn't. I was thinking that we should learn everything we can about a cure for your father. Maybe if we brought Konnel-toh a cure, he'd be grateful enough to fill us in on what happened all those years ago—I mean, immediately after what was shown in the vision. And, well . . . Konnel-toh is seriously ill. We might not have time to mess about."

Vereez nodded agreement, but when she spoke there was acid in her tone. "I agree. Let's help Konnel-toh first. I was talking with Peg and Teg earlier about how now that we know the truth about our parents' pasts, we have some leverage over them. If we find a cure for Grunwold's father, we'll have a carrot. If not, there's always a stick."

Surprise widened Grunwold's eyes so much that he almost looked frightened. "You're serious? You'd choose to find a cure for my father first? Now that we know that he's, well, one of the villains of this piece, I wasn't sure that you'd agree we should making saving him a priority. Both of your inquisitions deal with innocents: a missing little girl or Xerak's master, who may have been kidnapped."

"Your father is no more of a villain than *both* of my parents," Vereez nearly spat. "In fact, if there's a real villain, it's my mom. If she hadn't been so stupid as to let off that spell that started everything burning and exploding . . ."

Xerak gently thumped Vereez between the ears with

two knuckles. "Vereez, you know firsthand how it is when you've done too much magic all at once. It's hard to make good choices. You're so tired, so disoriented. What's around you starts seeming a lot less real than the beating of your pulse in your head. I'm not excusing them for what they did—coming here with every intent to steal—but as for Inehem-toh's choice to throw that lightning sphere, I'm not sure I'd make any wiser choice in a similar circumstance—though I'd throw a fireball."

Peg glanced up from her knitting. "This is all good, but maybe we should get back to the question of who we're going to ask Sapphire Wind to awaken?"

Vereez bared her fangs in a bright, flashing smile. "You're right. I vote that we learn what we can about a cure for Grunwold's father."

Grunwold stubbornly shook his head. "I'm still voting for Xerak's master. We could really use his resources."

Xerak punched Grunwold in his shoulder. "Sorry, I'm with Vereez. And, listen, before we go any further, I think you'd better get something through that pointy head of yours. Uten Kekui is my *master*. He's not required to do anything for me. He might even require me to stop taking part in your inquisitions and get back to my studies."

Vereez looked shocked. "Surely he'd be grateful enough to offer to help us!"

Teg snorted. "If he needs to be rescued, as Xerak believes, he might be the opposite of grateful. He might feel a need to assert his authority."

Peg giggled. "Uten Kekui might not even want to be 'rescued.' Maybe he's off visiting his harem or something." When Xerak looked offended, she sobered. "I'm sorry,

Xerak. I know you're worried, but I was remembering . . . Never mind what. So, Grunwold?"

"All right," Grunwold said. "I'll make it unanimous. We'll ask for information leading to a cure for my father's illness. For someone who can give us the cure, if possible. After all, the faster we get the cure, the faster we'll be able to get on the trail of the second and third pieces, right?"

For all his aggressive tone, no one was deceived. Grunwold might have discovered that his father was a thief and a liar, but he hadn't given up on his hope that Konnel's life might be saved.

Meg held up one hand, then looked into the middle distance, communing with the Library's *genius loci*. Then she nodded.

"Very good. Sapphire Wind says that searching for the appropriate person may take some hours. It suggests that we go back to *Slicewind*, rest and replenish ourselves. Now that Sapphire Wind is once again in sync with the Spindle of Ba Djed of the Weaver, it will have the power to alert us—well, me—when someone is ready to speak with us."

"I'm all for going back to the ship," Peg admitted. "Between spraining my wrist yesterday, and today's valiant slide for home, I'm all out. Vereez, do you have any more of that muscle rub?"

"Plenty," Vereez assured her, "and if we run out, I bet I can compound some more."

Sapphire Wind's summons did not come until midmorning, by which time Grunwold had polished every bit of brass and wood aboard *Slicewind* that could be made to shine, and even Vereez had gotten enough sleep. Peg had also slept in, and reported that she felt much less sore. Meg had taken over the table in the lounge so she could have some privacy to write in her journal.

Up on deck, Teg spent some time discussing with Xerak what had happened when she had used the amulet, trying to get a sense for how she'd managed to tap that strange force.

"Could I have had that magical overload you were talking about?" she asked him. "I felt really weird after, both sick to my stomach and wanting to eat everything in sight."

"It's possible," Xerak said. "I wouldn't have thought that the amulet would have had enough stored mana to summon more silk, especially after the amount you used the first time."

"Me, either," Teg admitted. "Actually, after I caulked Emsehu's jaws, I was pretty certain that was that."

"Did you do anything to mesh yourself with the amulet?"

"Mesh?" Teg considered. "After I pulled back to give you guys room, I did keep running my fingers over it, like you do with a worry stone, y'know?"

Fleetingly, she wondered if the translation spell could handle the concept, if she should demonstrate, but Xerak nodded.

"May I see the amulet?"

Teg realized that she really, really didn't want to give it to him.

Which is all the more reason you should, chica. *Who knows? If you don't, you might end up muttering about "My Precious" and turning into a monster.*

She reached into her pocket and pulled out the sun spider amulet. If Xerak noticed that she handed it over with undue haste, as if she feared that any delay might make her change her mind, he didn't comment.

Seating himself on one of the lockers, Xerak cupped the amulet between his hands and muttered to himself. Then he held the amulet up to the light, so he could examine it more closely in the strong morning sunlight.

"Well, this is interesting," he said. "When I made my first inspection, I thought it was odd that the center of the amulet was made from such a rough, unattractive stone, especially since the setting is a high-carat gold, and the small gemstones are so intricately faceted. However, at the time, we had a lot more to think about, and it was just a relief to find that the amulet had at least limited function. Now I understand what the center stone is."

Teg had also been studying it, and she hazarded a guess. "It's a meteorite, isn't it? In our world those are rare and often valuable. Is it the same here?"

"Very much so," Xerak agreed. "Some types are particularly valued for use in magic, especially for items meant to resonate with the earth-oriented disciplines."

"Resonate?" Teg asked.

"As I do with fire," Xerak said. "Let me explain further."

He was just entering into a complex and, to Teg, confusing lecture about resonances when Meg looked up from the travel journal she'd been reading, and began staring into the middle distance in what was becoming an alarmingly familiar fashion.

"It's ready for us. Do we have any of those rich honey-nut clusters left? And any poffee? Sapphire Wind suggests a gift would be a good idea. And this person is likely to be hungry."

"We definitely do," Peg said, dropping her knitting into her bag and flexing her fingers. "I know just where they are. I'll add them to the supply pack."

With very little delay, the three humans and three inquisitors were making their way along the now familiar trail, alert but no longer apprehensive. When they opened the main doors and entered the reception area, they found that someone had evidently been clearing up some of the rubble. Near the information desk where they had had their picnic, a larger area had been cleaned up, the table had been polished, and more comfortable chairs replaced the benches. Seated at the head of the table, making notes on a slate with a piece of chalk, was an otter-headed woman who looked very much like one of the wizards from the vision in the Font of Sight.

She studied them through eyes that widened when she got her first good look at the humans. "Amazing! So you are the three who have come from another world to help set matters right?"

"We've come to help these three," Meg said with an autocratic gesture toward the inquisitors, "and if that involves setting matters right, then I suppose we are. And you?"

"I am Nefnet," the otter-headed woman said, "a specialist in matters of illness and—more importantly, for the sake of one of your young inquisitors—in their cures. Come. I have cleared seats around this table so we might more easily consult."

"If you don't mind," Teg said, "I'd like continue the

cleanup job. I'm used to listening and working at the same time."

"I'll help," Vereez said. Wordlessly, Xerak joined them.

Peg took one of the offered seats. "I'll sit. I'm still aching in muscles I'd forgotten from my flying tackle. Sit here, Grunwold," she said, patting the chair next to her and motioning to Grunwold.

Grunwold obeyed. After he had settled, he slid the package of honey and nut clusters across the table. "Here. I mean, thank you. We'd like you to have these."

Meg, who had seated herself on Grunwold's other side, inclined her head in a slight nod of approval.

Nefnet looked at Grunwold. "You're the young man whose father is ill? You do look rather like one of the thieves."

"Yeah, I do or did," he said gruffly, then realized that he probably sounded ruder than he meant. "I am. I'm sorry. He doesn't look much like me now. I'm still trying to fit the dad I've known all my life to all this new information."

"I understand," Nefnet replied. "Sudden revelations are very hard to take."

Teg glanced over, but the expression on the otter's face didn't seem to be sarcastic.

As Peg took out her knitting, she asked, "Are you a doctor, then?"

"I am not," Nefnet replied, "although depending on what ailed you, I might be able to serve adequately. Rather, I am a scholar who has taken an interest in various forms of illness, how they evolve over time, why they affect certain people and not others."

"Closer then," Meg said, "to what in our world would be termed a medical PhD."

Nefnet nodded, so the term must have translated. She turned to face Grunwold, although—quite clearly—she was fascinated by the humans, almost to the point of distraction.

"Tell me what you can about your father's illness."

Grunwold began by describing his father's symptoms, which sounded, Teg thought, something like Parkinson's disease, although with the addition of patches of numbness that had, apparently, been among the earliest symptoms. Whatever it was, it didn't sound good.

After asking several more questions of the sort meant to eliminate one option in favor of another, Nefnet said, "Do you know how long he's had this?"

Grunwold shook his head. "Not precisely. My parents didn't talk about his being ill until it became impossible to hide that something was wrong." He didn't conceal his bitterness. "That was just a few years ago. But from things they've said here and there, I've gotten the impression that Dad's been declining for several years. Now he's in bad enough shape that . . ."

He shook his head apologetically, clearly too choked up to speak.

When Nefnet began asking what Grunwold knew regarding treatments his father had tried, an interesting point emerged. Despite his evident wealth, Konnel had refused to consult experts, settling for a local healer who was only asked to treat specific issues, like a rash or very dry skin.

"I never knew why," Grunwold said. "Now, from what we've learned here, I wonder if he was worried that some of his past—let's call them exploits—would be discovered if someone looked too closely into his history."

"Indeed possible," Nefnet replied. "Obviously, you don't know a great deal about your father's younger years. Moreover, whatever you were told would be suspect. However, tell me what you know. Then I'll examine you."

Peg's knitting needles paused in midclick. Everyone else froze. Teg realized she was holding her breath.

"Why do you want to examine him?" Peg asked.

Grunwold looked down at the table, then raised his gaze resolutely. "Because I have it, too. I don't know how Nefnet guessed, but she's right. It's not very far advanced but, whatever it is that's killing my dad, I have it, too."

A general clamor arose, through which Nefnet said nothing, not even in response to direct questions. Grunwold finally raised a hand for silence.

"I didn't say anything because I was afraid of two things: that you'd think I was just looking for a cure for myself, which I'm not, and because I worried you'd think I might be contagious, which I don't think I am. Got it?"

"Why don't you think you're contagious?" Vereez asked, her tone one of curiosity, not accusation.

"Because as far as I can remember, my parents have never taken any precautions—and believe me, if she thought anyone else might catch whatever this is, my mom would take them. Xerak, remember the summer you spent with us?"

"When one of the servants came back from holiday with mange?" Xerak said. "Do I ever! That preparation your mom had everyone wash with stank like . . . like . . . like nothing else I've ever smelled."

His ears folded back at the memory. "And Sefit-toh wouldn't let us go anywhere or do anything fun until she had eradicated the mange from the estate—and what's worse, we didn't even have it! You were a complete grump but, now that I think about it, since we couldn't go anywhere, I did a lot of reading. That's when I started getting serious about studying magic. So I guess the quarantine wasn't a complete loss."

Grunwold snorted. "For you...I..." He stopped himself with visible effort. "The point is, my mother was always like that about anything she thought might spread. If she thought my father had something that might be contagious, she would definitely have taken precautions."

"So she—and he—knew something," Nefnet said thoughtfully. "Did you tell them that you had symptoms?"

Grunwold shook his head. "My symptoms only started a few months before Xerak and Vereez told me they were going to Hettua Shrine. I'd already decided that, since no one else seemed to be doing anything, I was going to find a cure for Dad."

He looked at them all. "Honest!"

Meg reached up to pat him on one muscular shoulder. "We believe you, Grunwold. Now finish giving Nefnet your father's treatment history, then let her examine you. If you need privacy, we can go do some cleanup. Certainly there's plenty to clear away before anything like repairs to the Library can begin."

For the first time since they'd met him, Grunwold looked vulnerable. "Please, stay. I've been hiding this for so long. I'm tired of hiding."

After a detailed examination, Nefnet seemed hopeful but she would not promise a cure—at least not for Konnel.

"For you, Grunwold," she said, "there is hope, because the disease has not had an opportunity to become as deeply rooted. For your father, all I can offer is a remission—and that only if you are willing to repeatedly provide the material from which the treatment will be made. I'll be honest, I'll need to draw some of the blood from the center of your bones, and getting that will be very painful."

She went on to describe what sounded to Teg—whose knowledge of medical procedures was scattered and eclectic—like a magically assisted bone-marrow transfer. Grunwold's own treatment would be simpler.

"Had your symptoms progressed to the point of muscle or nerve tremors," Nefnet said, "I would offer less hope, but I could find not the least trace of either of these."

This explained some of the very peculiar postures she had requested Grunwold assume, along with her insistence that he lie on the floor with small containers of various liquids distributed over his prone and supine form in turn.

Vereez asked impatiently, "How long before you can begin treating Grunwold?"

It was hard to imagine such an expression on an otter's amiable features, but nonetheless Nefnet's smile was cruel. "Had your parents not set in motion the destruction of this library, I could have begun almost immediately. However, now it will be necessary to see what remains of my books, equipment, and supplies. I will also need to check whether some of the plants in the gardens I tended have survived in a useful form."

"Don't," Peg snapped, looking far more ferocious than Nefnet, "you start blaming these young people for what their parents did—did, I remind you—before any of them were born. Got it?"

Nefnet looked as if she was going to snap back, then she subsided. "You're right, human. I apologize. Unborn children cannot be blamed for their parents' crimes. In my own defense, let me explain that for over two decades I have existed in a dream state where I was aware—even when the dreams were delightful—that something had gone horribly wrong. It is a miracle that I did not lose my sanity."

Meg's lips curved in a smile that held compassion, rather than amusement. "Sapphire Wind drained itself to provide those dreams to you and to all those it saved. Now the means to begin the recovery has finally come. Let's not let anger stop us before we have begun."

"If you give me a list of the plants," Xerak added, "I can check whether any of those you need are still growing here. My master felt a solid grounding in plants both medicinal and magical was an important part of a well-rounded wizard's education."

"I'll go with you," Vereez said. "I have some background in herbal lore, and I can guard your back in case a lizard parrot or piranha toad gets the peculiar idea that you actually look appetizing."

"And the rest of us," Teg said, "will help Nefnet locate the books and such she needs. I trust she will not protest?"

Frank curiosity regarding the humans won out over

Nefnet's anger. "I would welcome a chance to get to know more about you. And your help would speed matters along."

"We'll protect you, too," Grunwold said. "Even with Emsehu on our side, the library's not as safe it was."

❧CHAPTER TEN❧

After several days—and several nasty encounters with denizens of the Library and its environs—Nefnet announced that she was ready to treat Grunwold.

"I'll admit," she said, "my work was considerably accelerated by being able to draw on the full resources of the Library, rather than the limited portion that would have been available to me before. Since I was only a junior researcher, I had no idea what a wealth of knowledge was stored here. Even after the destruction, so much remains!"

Xerak nodded agreement. "I am coming to understand why my master mourned the loss so deeply."

Vereez was more impatient than Grunwold to move matters along.

Is it because she's coming to care for him? Teg thought. *Or is it because until we speak with Grunwold's father, we can't move on to the next phase of our project?*

When Nefnet had assembled her medications, Xerak assisted her in creating mingled magical and medical procedures that should not only cure Grunwold, but should enable his body to manufacture the materials that would be at the center of Konnel's treatment. Vereez acted as a sort of surgical nurse, handing over appropriate tools, tinctures, and decoctions as requested. The three humans supervised.

Though there's not much we can do if Nefnet opts for treachery, Teg thought. *Still, she doesn't know that. And who knows what Sapphire Wind might be able to detect? I think the Wind would tell Meg if it thought something hinky was going on. I'm still not certain whether Nefnet even wants the Library repaired—given the way she was eyeing some of the books and artifacts, she might prefer to scavenge for herself. But Sapphire Wind's goals and ours run in harness—for now.*

"Grunwold will sleep at least until dawn," Nefnet said, when the last stage of his treatment had been completed. "Every turn of the large sandglass, both his joints and the numb areas should be rubbed with the blue concoction. Every turn of the small glass, someone will need to open his mouth and rub this orange unguent on his gums and tongue."

She was rocking with fatigue as she spoke. Xerak was yawning so prodigiously that Teg found herself inspecting his fangs with new respect.

"We won't forget," Peg said, accepting the varied jars. "Compared to some of the illnesses I've had to deal with, this will be easy. I remember when my Tabitha had the chicken pox . . ."

She rattled on, telling a prosaic tale of cornmeal baths and mittens, even as she hustled Nefnet and Xerak to their respective sleeping places. Vereez settled herself near Grunwold's head, where she could see both sandglasses.

"I'll take first watch," she said. "I used so little magic that I'm wired from the mana I pulled up in case I needed it. It will take time to ebb. If you three want to look around, this would be a good time."

"I'll stay here"—Meg indicated the information desk—"and read."

"I wouldn't mind poking around a bit more," Teg admitted sheepishly, "but I'll stay here in the reception hall. There's plenty to look at."

She'd been working her way up through the various sage's stations. Since on the day of the catastrophe the sages had retired for the evening and had locked away their materials, much remained intact. Teg had to keep reminding herself that, despite the years that had passed, if all went well, the owners would be returning. She supposed that she would need to return the sun spider amulet as well, but since no one had suggested she do so, she would wait until Sapphire Wind was able to awaken its owner.

Grunwold's recovery took an additional three days, but once Nefnet was certain that the numbness was indeed retreating, Nefnet pronounced him cured.

"I suggest you let me check you over whenever you return here," she said, "just to be certain. Indeed, it might be wise if we arranged for you to come and see me once a year—sooner if any of the symptoms return."

Grunwold looked more relieved than annoyed at her suggestion. "I will." He reached up and rubbed one of his antler tips. "And my father? Can I take medication to him?"

Nefnet drew in a deep breath. "Although a part of me has no desire to see Konnel, I would prefer he came here for treatment. Your care was relatively easy. His will be more difficult. I have samples of your blood, hair, spittle, and feces so I can begin to create medication for him, but the medication will work better if I can inject some deeply into muscle groups."

"And if he won't come?" Grunwold said.

"If Konnel cannot face one of those who he wronged," Nefnet replied without pity, "then he has not earned treatment."

When Grunwold looked as if he might argue further, Vereez turned on him. "Don't! Just don't! You have your cure and hope for your father. Xerak and me, we're still waiting. Besides, I hate to say it, but the possibility of a cure gives us leverage."

Grunwold bent his head as if he'd planned to go for her with his antlers, but Vereez grabbed him under the chin and forced his head up.

"Idiot! I'm not saying you should withhold the cure. I'm saying that you can open the discussion of past events in, well, a positive way. Show you came here to find a treatment for him. Neither Xerak or I have that option. If we try to get information from our parents, there'll always be the underlying element that we're threatening exposure if they don't comply."

Teg remembered that Vereez had already confided her willingness to threaten her parents if needed, and admired the young woman's cunning.

Grunwold pushed her hand away, but didn't resume his attack stance.

"I'm sorry Vereez, Xerak . . . You're right. I'm stalling. I'm not looking forward to this heart-to-heart with my dad, but it can't be avoided. Sapphire Wind needs a second piece of that artifact, and it's likely that my father has some idea where it is. We can set sail as soon as *Slicewind* is readied."

"Then we can go as soon as we get to the ship," Peg said cheerfully. "While you've been recovering from Nefnet's treatments, we've been filling the water casks and laying in fresh supplies."

Grunwold looked astonished. "Where did you get supplies?"

Xerak shrugged. "The gardens had some good foraging, and we set snares. Peg's been cooking steadily."

Peg smiled. "And I've set aside some food to leave for Nefnet-va as well."

The researcher wrinkled her nose in a smile. "Thank you. In reviewing the artifacts in the repository, I located some that provide nourishment. Magical food may sustain the body, but is not usually very tasty."

"Are you sure you don't want to come with us?" Teg asked. "Emsehu and maybe Sapphire Wind will be some company, but I'd think you'll get lonely."

Nefnet shook her head. "I have been suspended for decades. Many of the older people I knew and loved will have died. Those who still live believe me dead and have had a long time to mourn me. I need time to adjust, to consider how I will deal with this."

"That reminds me," Vereez said, "we have one piece of

unfinished business. Sapphire Wind said that when it had one piece of the artifact, Ba Djed of the Weaver, it could use it to divine where the others might be. Well?"

For lack of someone to look at, she looked at Meg. As if preparing for a long discussion, Meg carefully seated herself. Then, between one breath and the next, Sapphire Wind spoke.

"I had not forgotten my claim. I will admit to an unwillingness to confess to failure."

"Then you can't find it?" Vereez's tone was heavy with disbelief. "I thought you wanted the thing."

"I do. However, I cannot pinpoint its location. I am only certain that it has not been completely destroyed. If it had been, I think the piece we have would have lost its virtue."

"Maybe we should take the one piece we've found with us," Vereez suggested. "Maybe if we were closer, it would move like a compass needle, point the right direction."

Meg's face went blank and she grew very still. Then right about the point where Teg was going to start checking her vital signs, Sapphire Wind spoke.

"I am reluctant to let the Spindle out of my care, but you may be right. Even if you learn who took the rest, they might deny the truth if you lack evidence. Then where would you be? Xerak, do you know spells for seeking?"

Xerak looked grim. "I absolutely do. Over this last year, I've become a specialist. You might say I've done a crash course in them."

"Then take the Spindle, but be careful. Its aura is very potent. If you handle it overmuch, you may suffer unpleasant consequences."

Nefnet opened her mouth as if she might protest, then

closed it. Again, Teg felt a flicker of distrust for the wizard. What did Nefnet intend to do, alone here among this wealth of magical resources? Teg wished she could warn Sapphire Wind to be careful, but would it even listen? After all, Nefnet belonged to the library. Teg and her friends did not.

They said their goodbyes soon after, and hiked back to *Slicewind*, escorted by Emsehu, whose presence assured that any local horrors would keep a good distance.

As they were tramping along, Grunwold said, "Just when I start fooling myself that what our parents did wasn't all that terrible—that Sapphire Wind's intervention saved the day by 'archiving' all those people—I get a sharp kick under my tail. I hadn't thought about what Nefnetva and all the others will face after they're unarchived. Even those who were lucky enough to have their families with them, still . . ."

"I know," Vereez said. "Every one of them will know someone who has died and maybe even been reborn. Over twenty-five years is a long time."

"More than we've been alive," Xerak said morosely.

"Please!" Meg interjected tartly. "Introspection is useful only to the point that it grants perspective. The three of us came to help you inquisitors to find answers to the problems that have held you back. We have managed to possibly find a cure for Konnel, but the price for that—as well as for using the Library's resources to solve the others—is that we have acquired two additional problems to solve. We have a great deal to do, and cannot spare energy for self-indulgence."

"Arrgh, maties," Peg said in a theatrical pirate accent.

"Hoist the sails and pull in the gangplank. We've some fast sailing to do."

The winds were with them, and they didn't make any stops on the way, enabling *Slicewind* to cover the distance back to Grunwold's family estate at a speed that rendered the forests and waters beneath into an impressionistic blur. Nonetheless, the journey seemed to go on forever. Grunwold was edgy, which he covered by being grumpy—or rather, grumpier than usual. Vereez was doing a poor job of hiding her excitement, while Xerak had begun to fret about the fate of his master. That meant he started drinking more heavily again, something he'd backed off on after they had landed near the Library and he had his first brush with the spike wolves.

More than once, Teg contemplated using her bracelet to return to her apartment and check on Thought and Memory, but she knew that she'd be running away, and that didn't seem fair. It didn't help her resolve to stay aboard that she was running low on the pipe weed (as Peg had dubbed it in honor of hobbits) that Xerak had bought her along with the pipe. No one—human or inquisitor—liked her cigarettes.

Grunwold had spent the entire voyage agonizing what time of day would be best to arrive at KonSef Estate, vacillating between sneaking in and making a bold return. In the end, he opted for the bold return, not because he felt any braver, but because the weather was turning nasty, and he didn't want to risk *Slicewind*.

"We may not be able to keep using her," he kept reminding them. "*Slicewind* is my parents' ship, not mine."

Another debate had been about whether or not to tell Grunwold's parents the truth about the humans. The humans put an end to this as soon as they realized the matter was being discussed.

"We're going in," Peg said. "We're your best proof to your parents that you've done something big."

"And we *are* your mentors," Meg added. "We must be present to provide support and advice, or we are not living up to our responsibilities."

On a stormy midmorning, Grunwold brought *Slicewind* down on the broad paved plaza in front of his parents' sprawling manse. The humans had conceded to the inquisitors' request that they wear their disguises.

"I'd never tell the kids," Peg said, settling her pronghorn antelope mask in place, "but I actually am glad to have something to hide behind. I'm more nervous about this than I was when I had a chance to sing at the Monterey Pop Festival."

"You never did," Teg protested, taking a final drag on her cigarette before putting on her mask. "I don't remember seeing you on any of the videos."

"I said I had a chance," Peg replied tartly. "I didn't say I took it."

Meg poked her badger-masked face around the door of their cabin. "Hurry. The inquisitors are debarking. Grunwold's mother just came out of the house."

Predictably, Grunwold hadn't been home five minutes and he was already involved in an argument. This time he wasn't the only one doing the yelling. A matronly woman with the head of a camel was in the midst of a full-scale rant.

"... and then, knowing full well how ill your father was, you not only left home, you stole *Slicewind*, then lured Xerak and Vereez off ..."

Vereez tried to interrupt, probably to say she didn't need to be lured anywhere, but the camel-woman—presumably Grunwold's mother—didn't pause.

"... to whatever madcap hijinks. I don't want to imagine what you've been up to ..."

She took a deep breath and Grunwold managed to get a few words in.

"Finding medicine for Dad."

"... but no doubt it will bring scandal." She stopped and took a ragged breath. "What?"

"While the rest of you were content to sit around and let him die," Grunwold began, his voice rising, "I went seeking a cure."

This raised a murmur through the crowd that had gathered. Teg still had some trouble reading expressions on the animal faces, but ears were another matter, and she thought that what she was seeing was positive. Whatever he'd done in the past, Konnel was popular with those who lived and worked on his estate.

Grunwold lowered his voice. "It's a complex matter. If you're done humiliating me, Mother, perhaps we could go inside."

Grunwold's mother put out a hand and touched her son lightly on one cheek. Now that she wasn't yelling, Teg could tell she was quite lovely, with huge dark eyes and amazing eyelashes.

"I ... I ... Yes. Come inside. Your friends, too." She stopped, noticing Meg, Peg, and Teg for the first time, taking in their masks. "I know Xerak and Vereez, of course, but these are?"

"Part of my story," Grunwold said firmly. "Meg, Peg, and Teg, this is my mother, Sefit. Mother, these are our mentors—how we acquired them is a long story."

Sefit looked dazed. "Yes. I imagine so. Let us go inside."

Grunwold scanned the crowd and singled out a pair of burly farmhands—only as an afterthought did Teg note one had the head of a wildebeest, the other of a beaver. "Abeh, Tenneh, get *Slicewind* under cover before this storm hits. I'm leaving Heru with the ship, so don't get too curious about our cargo. Got it?"

"Absolutely, young master."

Grunwold managed a tight smile. "Thanks, guys. I'll remember." Then he turned to Sefit. "Mother, after you . . ."

The room to which the mistress of the estate took them was in a tower that commanded a good view of the surrounding grounds. It also, Teg realized, was relatively secure from eavesdroppers. A desk heaped with paperwork stood near one window. A long conference table surrounded by ornately carved chairs dominated the center of the room.

By the time Sefit took a seat at the table's head, she had clearly regained much of her bad mood. "Sit down, all of you." Then she turned to Grunwold, who had placed himself at her right. "So you went seeking a cure for Konnel. I notice you didn't say you'd found one. If you came up with that just so . . ."

"I didn't," Grunwold cut her off. "I didn't find a cure,

but I did find a possible treatment. Much will depend on Father. Or, if he's not able to make decisions, then on you." .

"Tell me first," Sefit said, "and I'll judge if Konnel is well enough to see you."

For a wonder, Grunwold didn't argue. Instead, he launched into his tale, beginning with the visit to Hettua Shrine. This, in turn, necessitated Meg, Peg, and Teg unmasking. Teg thought it was some measure of how worried Sefit was about her husband that, after she accepted the humans' reality, she did not ask further questions, but pressed Grunwold to continue.

He made short work of their journey and the difficulties involved in finding an entrance to the Library. Only when he came to the point where Sapphire Wind insisted they view the vision in the Font of Sight, did he slow.

"Mother, how much do you know about Dad's past?"

Sefit's wide camel lips pursed in what was clearly a frown. "Not enough. He told me he was ashamed of much of what he had done, said he'd rather die than have the truth be known."

Grunwold winced. "That may be what he's been doing—I mean, why he hasn't tried harder to seek a cure. So, I'll give you a choice. I can tell you what we learned from the Font of Sight, or move to what we learned in the end."

Sefit closed her eyes, clearly torn. When she finally spoke, her voice was much gentler than it had been. "I told Konnel I was willing to live with his secret. I can't violate that now. Tell me what you can about the treatment without mentioning his past."

Teg was impressed. She knew she wouldn't be able to stop from prying. Prying, after all, was what she did for a living. Grunwold reached out and squeezed his mother's hand, the first affectionate gesture between them since his return home. Then he launched into his tale again, explaining how Sapphire Wind had told them it needed magical energy in order to awaken a specialist. He skipped over their heroics, and moved directly to Nefnet's diagnosis.

When he mentioned that he, himself, was in the early stages of the malady that was killing his father, Sefit was shocked. "You never mentioned that! Why?"

"Maybe because I saw no one looking for a cure," Grunwold said. "Maybe because . . ."

Sefit spat—literally, like a camel, although unlike a camel, she targeted a tidy metal spittoon. "You didn't go looking to help Konnel! You selfish little, lying . . ."

That was too much for Peg. She'd been sitting quietly knitting, only the rapid clicking letting on how upset she was getting.

"You stop it!" she yelled, getting to her feet so fast that she knocked her chair over. "No wonder Grunwold kept saying that he wasn't looking for the cure for himself, that he honestly wanted it for his father. He *knew* you'd accuse him. And why? Does attacking your courageous son make you feel better about how you've sat around for the last couple of decades letting your husband die by inches because he's afraid of exposing his past?"

Sefit pulled her lips back from large, yellowish teeth. "Are you saying that . . ."

Peg leaned forward on her hands so that she was nearly

nose to nose with Sefit. "Yes! Damn it, I am! I'm saying that for all your shouting and yelling, you're more afraid of learning the truth about Konnel and what that might do to your cozy life than you are of his dying. I'm saying you're a selfish, self-centered, egotistical..."

"Whoa," Teg said, getting to her feet and grabbing Peg, who looked as if she was about to take Sefit by the shoulders and shake her. "You've made your point. Don't make matters worse."

Peg remained tense, but she let Teg pull her back. When a wide-eyed Xerak righted her chair, she resumed her seat and even took up her knitting, although she didn't begin moving her needles until Sefit also sat. Stunned silence reigned until Grunwold broke it.

"Honestly, Mother. I went looking because I wanted to find a cure for him—not for any other reason. I knew I had years. You and Dad did a good job hiding how seriously ill he was but, once you had to tell us, well, it was easy to look back and see past events in a new light. Like how Dad stopped going without a shirt, or when he started to supervise, rather than doing work himself. Even my being sent away to school... That made sense in a way it hadn't before. I realized that whatever this illness was or is, it progresses relatively slowly."

Sefit nodded. "I'm sorry." She turned to Peg. "Maybe you're right. About my feeling guilty, that is. I reserve the right to disagree about the rest. I did argue with Konnel, try to get him to see healers, but he always refused. So I tried to make sure that nothing else would make him sick, because I wasn't certain how far his stubbornness would go."

"Now," Grunwold said, "let me finish telling you what we've discovered."

He did, concluding with how Nefnet had been able to heal him and how she was, even now, compounding medications that should slow the progress of the disease in Konnel, even reverse some of the worst of the later symptoms.

"But Nefnet-va insists he come to her, which is why I didn't wait and bring the medication with me."

"Why . . ." Sefit trailed off. "That has to do with your father's secret, doesn't it?"

"It does."

"You'd better see him, then."

She rose and motioned for Grunwold to come with her, but he shook his head.

"All of us or none. They already know the worst, and I want them to hear what Dad has to say firsthand, so they don't think I'm holding anything back."

Sefit sighed, but she didn't argue. "Fine. All of you wait here. Konnel is going to insist on at least sitting up in bed, and getting him ready will take a while. I'll brief him while I do what's necessary. At the very least, he should be prepared in advance for your strange new friends."

After Sefit had departed, Grunwold looked at Peg with something between astonishment and gratitude. "I'm not sure if I should thank you or ask if all this is too much for you. I thought that Meg was the wise one, Teg was the nosey one, and you were the funny one, but you've snapped a few times recently."

"I *am* the funny one," Peg replied complacently, "until I get pissed off. Then I'm the mean one."

"I'll remember that," he said with sincerity. "Listen, all of you. Take it easy on my dad, okay? Whatever you think about him or what he did, he's dying."

"I second Grunwold's request," Meg said, "for absolutely unsentimental reasons. Konnel has held his secret even from his wife and, despite how meek she acts when speaking of him, I would say she spent a good many years trying to get it out of him. This is not a man who can be browbeaten. He must be convinced to help us."

When they were summoned to Konnel's room, Sefit met them on her way out.

"I have repeated to him what you told me," she said. "I told him that this was not the time for long confessions. He can decide what he wants to tell me—including nothing at all—after he's spoken with you."

She paused, then gave Grunwold a tight hug. "Good luck!"

Konnel little resembled the handsome stag warrior whose exploits they had seen in the Font. He shook, even when sitting—as he was now—wedged into his chair by pillows. He was gaunt, probably, Teg thought, from dehydration and malnutrition, as much as from his malady. Getting food into him wouldn't be easy. He'd spill much of what was put into his mouth, and she doubted he could risk chewing anything too solid, so much of what he ate would be soft. His coat, once a rich reddish brown, slightly darker than Grunwold's, was dull and patchy.

But his large brown eyes were still alert and commanding and his voice, when he spoke, had surprising force, even though his intonations were weak and every word quavered.

After they were seated in a half circle of chairs, positioned so that Konnel could see them all without more than minimal movements of his head, Grunwold handled introductions. Then, taking a deep breath, he went on.

"So, Dad, Mother said she told you what we've done, where we've been."

"And so you know," Konnel said softly, "about my less than illustrious past, about how what we did led to the destruction of the Library of the Sapphire Wind. What would you think if I told you that even what happened that day was not enough to cause us to retire?"

"I'd believe it," Vereez said. "Because my parents are stubborn, and they wouldn't want to admit something had scared them into quitting."

"Did you already know about their past then?" Konnel asked.

"Not a bit. They may have quit stealing—or at least turned to finance—but that doesn't mean they changed completely."

"Xerak?"

"Not even a little," Xerak said. "Although as I grew older I did wonder if my parents' antiques business sometimes turned a blind eye to where things might have come from. But if I considered why, I thought they were naïve about the more sordid side of the world. More fool I."

"I wondered," Konnel said, "because we'd all sworn not to say a word, not even to our nearest and dearest. You see, among those we killed..."

Grunwold started to interrupt, but Konnel stopped him with a raised hand.

"...were specialists in many arcane arts. After the Library of the Sapphire Wind was destroyed, their friends, students, families all swore vengeance. Silence was our only protection—that and the fact that the area was so horribly disrupted that no one successfully penetrated into the ruins for many years. Only in the last few years have any made claims I might have believed, but none until you got inside."

"We had help," Grunwold said. Teg could tell his usually twisted sense of humor was coming back. "Dad, I want you to stay quiet and listen while I tell you what happened. You might say I have some good news and some bad news."

By the time Grunwold—assisted here and there by the others—had finished his narrative, Konnel's eyes were bright with unshed tears.

"All these years," he said, "I have believed myself guilty of mass murder. I don't care that those we wronged may yet come for vengeance. Maybe I'll be afraid later, but for now all I feel is gratitude."

"Grateful enough to help us?" Vereez asked bluntly. "Sapphire Wind says it will help me and Xerak with our searches, but that it cannot without the remaining pieces of Ba Djed of the Weaver. Can you give us a lead?"

Xerak added helpfully, "The vision showed my mother turning and grabbing what looked very much like a piece of the artifact. Did she? Does she still have it?"

"She did, and I do not know." Konnel held up a hand. "Bear with me. It is my turn to tell a tale. I am not as fragile as Sefit believes, but talking at length can be an ordeal."

"Should I ring for some refreshments? Medicine?" Grunwold asked.

"Some spiced taga tea for me," Konnel said. "Order whatever your friends would like as well."

Grunwold departed to place the order, and Konnel turned his attention to the three humans. "I would very much like to know more about you but, sadly, that will need to wait. Someday perhaps, I can invite you for a long visit. However, I can thank you for helping right wrongs you had no part in creating."

Peg patted him on one blanket-covered knee. "It's been our pleasure. Really. Not all the bits, I'll admit. Some of the creatures here are more terrifying than I ever expected to meet, especially at my time of life, but on the whole . . ."

Meg nodded. "Yes, I definitely prefer this to retirement."

Grunwold returned then, pushing the refreshments cart, sparing Teg from finding something to say that wouldn't sound trite. She didn't have a lot of experience dealing with terminally ill people—especially ones who, as best as she could figure, were about her own age. The realization was sobering and unsettling both.

As his son poured him a cup of taga tea, the scent of which evoked citrus and spice—something like lemon and ginger, if the lemon had the bite of grapefruit and the ginger just a hint of catnip—Konnel began his tale.

"I believe you said that Sapphire Wind referred to us as 'extraction agents.' We never used that term, but if we had thought of it, we certainly would have. Certainly, that's how we thought of ourselves—not as mere thieves or burglars. We were all in college together, although not all in the same year. I think our first 'extraction' was when

Ohent wanted to take back a gift she'd given to a fellow who dumped her shortly after—and who didn't have the good manners to return the present.

"It was a great deal of fun, not just the removal itself, but the planning, the practicing. Our plan called for several of us to climb up a rope, but that's not as easy as it sounds. We messed about for days, but in the end every one of us could scurry up and down like sun spiders."

He paused, took a deep draught of his tea, and sighed, his gaze on a long-ago self, far distant from the man who—although he strove to hide it—was having difficulty lifting his cup.

"Later, there were pranks. Then Inehem did poorly on an exam. She was certain the instructor was punishing her for ignoring his flirtations. He never returned tests, to eliminate the risk of the questions being shared with other students. She couldn't do anything about that particular test, but she was permitted a retest. We stole it in advance and when he told her that once again she had failed, she claimed to have memorized many of the questions during the test and that her answers had been correct. Of course, she had memorized them, simply not during the test. She threatened to take him to his department head. He backed down.

"That was our first taste of power. It would not be our last. In fact, 'removals'—as we began to call our exploits— began to shape what we studied. Inehem had been uncertain about her studies of magic. She was sincerely interested in finance as well. Now she buckled down. Zarrq, aware how vulnerable magic left a person, devoted himself to being her protector. Fardowsi continued her formal history and art studies, but she began to practice lock picking and related skills in her spare time.

"I had no gift for magic, but muscle, fighting skills, and a wide range of purely practical skills, such as sailing, driving a team, and the like became necessary as our jobs became more complex. Ohent learned a few magical tricks, but—like me—she became a weapons specialist and generalist. We all finished college with at least reasonable grades, and with loaded bank accounts about which our parents knew nothing. Zarrq and Inehem made some shrewd investments from the start. If we'd had a way to explain our little fortunes, we could have taken it easy."

Vereez laughed. "As if you would have. I never wanted to be the little socialite my parents had me set up to be, but I didn't know what else there was. One thing this trip has taught me is that I am my parents' daughter in at least one way. I like the excitement, the challenge, the not knowing what tomorrow will bring."

"So," Teg said, seeing that Konnel was beginning to look tired now that the pleasure of memory—and possibly of telling about exploits he'd had to keep secret for decades—was no longer sustaining him. "Shall we take it as read that no matter what jobs all of you were officially doing after graduation, 'removals' were your actual jobs?"

Konnel nodded gratefully. "I will say this for us. We did try to choose removals that wouldn't leave us hating ourselves. I will admit, though, that line became greyer and greyer as time went on. When we were approached by the man who proposed the Sapphire Wind job to us, we accepted his justification without doing much checking. The challenge was what excited us.

"He told us how when his father had died, his stepmother had sold off personal items that had been promised to his children. Our client had only been a child at the time but, when he became an adult, he had traced some of these items to the artifacts repository of the Library of the Sapphire Wind.

"He claimed that he had attempted to purchase these artifacts back from the Library, but had been turned away. Later, he himself had worked at the Library for a time, but had failed to find a way to extract the items he desired. Therefore, he had inside knowledge, but he needed the help of professionals. That's how we acquired the pendants that would enable us to be seen by the Library's guardians as members of the staff. He also gave us detailed maps, and told us what he could of the usual routine.

"We laid our plans carefully. Each of us visited the Library separately, so we would be familiar with the building from more than maps. We set the date for the retrieval for over a holiday, when many of the residents would be away, but the Library would still be open. We planned for every contingency we could and trusted to our long-time teamwork for the rest. When the day of the heist came, we did very well, until, suddenly, everything went wrong all at once."

Peg asked so conversationally that there was no way to take offense, "You didn't start wondering when the final item your client wanted you to take was so carefully locked away?"

"Wondering? No. Not really. For all we knew, there were dozens of those small, high security repositories. If anything, that last bit made his story about having been refused the opportunity to repurchase the items more believable. The items in the pigeonholes weren't exactly common, but they were the sort the Library regularly let researchers use or even loaned out. If this was a unique item, though . . ."

Xerak, who had been listening with his eyes closed, so still that if you didn't know him you'd think he was dozing, asked, "What happened afterward? Did you all get away? We recognized our parents, but not the snow leopard woman. Is that Ohent? She didn't . . ."

"Die? No. As far as I know, Ohent is still alive. What happened immediately after was that we got ourselves out of there. We'd arranged a fast transport and, even as the earthquake was spreading, we were already gone. Then we reported to our client that we'd succeeded—but only partially. We handed over the pigeonhole items he'd requested, returned the Library talismans to him, and accepted a partial fee with good grace. We'd walked out of the Library with a good many negotiable items, so we knew we'd make up our expenses and even turn a profit.

"The one thing we didn't hand over was the fragment of that last artifact. Fardowsi hadn't told us yet that she had it. Inehem knew—she'd sensed it—but they both decided to keep quiet about it. I think Inehem, in particular, was beginning to wonder if we'd been told a tale seeded with just enough truth to make it work.

"It took a few days for news of what had happened at the Library to get out. As you saw yourselves, it's in an isolated area and wasn't exactly a tourist destination."

Teg saw Vereez beginning to fidget, so she anticipated

her question. "And what happened to the fragment Xerak's mother took? Does she still have it?"

"I don't think so."

Konnel must have caught Vereez's impatient motion, although she quickly stilled it, for he held up his hand.

"It's complicated. Fardowsi loaned the artifact—a small bronze bird—to Inehem, in the hope Inehem could learn something about its nature. By now we suspected that the artifact it had been part of, and that alone, had been our client's goal. He knew he couldn't handle the protections set on it, and hired us. Inehem learned little, except to confirm that the artifact had not been ruined, but that without the rest, the Bird was incomplete. She returned the Bird to Fardowsi. Not too long after, Fardowsi began to have terrible nightmares which she blamed on the Bird. We scoffed.

"I'll admit, I was the worst scoffer. I didn't notice how quiet Zarrq and Inehem were on the subject. I offered to take custody of the Bird. In time, I had nightmares so similar to those Fardowsi had experienced that Ohent said I was unstable, that what Fardowsi had said had influenced me. But when Ohent took custody and she, too, began to experience similar nightmares, well . . . We knew we had to take precautions."

"Couldn't you just lock the Bird up," Xerak asked, "in an enshrouding container, like the one you found there in the repository?"

"We did and that helped," Konnel replied. "But only for a time. The enshrouding container acted as a mute but within a few weeks, whoever was acting as custodian would begin to have nightmares. Eventually, Ohent offered to

become full-time custodian. She'd fallen on hard times—
had never been a saver like the rest of us. Or, I'll be honest,
as inclined to work hard. So we all contributed to a trust
fund that Vereez's parents administer."

"You trusted this Ohent not to sell the Bird? Or just
throw it away?" Peg asked.

"We did," Konnel said. "As far as I know, Ohent has
kept her part of the bargain."

"Going back to an earlier point," Meg asked, "what did
you tell your client? I would think your relationship with
him would be an uneasy one. After all, he might resent
your destroying what he viewed as his heritage, yet he
actually gave you partial payment."

"That we could prove he sent us in to steal gave us
some protection." Konnel shrugged, the stiff motion an
inadvertent parody of his son's familiar gesture.
"Nonetheless, we were aware he was a potential threat,
so we kept track of him until his . . . death."

There was something in the way Konnel said the word
that made them all look at him.

"Death?" Teg asked.

"Presumed death," Konnel amended. "Our client kept
returning to the Library, even after it was nothing more
than increasingly dangerous ruins. He put together
several expeditions that came back in tatters. Then one
came back without him. They said he'd been killed, and
they'd fled. Even if he reincarnated immediately, which
we didn't think likely, it would be decades before he'd be
any sort of threat. He might not retain his memories,
making him even less of a threat. Basically, we considered
ourselves safe from him."

"Well, that's useful to know," Meg said with a firmness that made clear she didn't think now was the time to discuss Emsehu's actual fate. "Let us return to what we need to do next."

"It sounds as if we need to find Ohent," Vereez said, "and ask her to give us the Bird portion of Ba Djed that she has in her custody. Where is she?"

"I don't know," Konnel said. "But your parents should, since they send Ohent her stipend."

"Will Ohent just hand the Bird over?" Xerak asked. "Shouldn't we have some sort of document saying it's all right with the rest of you?"

Konnel nodded. "That would probably be a good idea. Writing is difficult for me, but if you compose an appropriate document, I'll sign it and add my seal."

Vereez looked satisfied. "Since we're stopping in Rivers Meet to see my parents, we can get a similar letter from them, and from Fardowsi-toh. I saw pens and paper in the conference room. Let me go and rough something out for you to approve, then I'll write it fine and you can sign it."

As she hurried out, Grunwold said, "Dad, I'm sorry I stole *Slicewind*, but I didn't feel I could ask permission."

"With your mother and I planning to ship you to the brickworks, no, probably not." Konnel looked amused rather than annoyed.

"Do I need to steal it again," Grunwold asked, "or will you and Mother give me permission to take it?"

Konnel started laughing. "I'm almost tempted to lock *Slicewind* down and see if you really could steal it from me ... But that would be stupid. The faster you're done with these searches, the faster you can get on with your lives. Sefit will argue, but I think I can convince her that you need *Slicewind* more than we do."

Xerak's brow furrowed. "Should we take *Slicewind*, Konnel-toh? Shouldn't you travel to the Library as quickly, and easily, as possible?"

"We have another flying ship," Grunwold cut in indignantly. "*Cloud Cleaver*. It's roomier than *Slicewind* and much more comfortable. Not as fast, though, or as maneuverable."

"Ah, the life of wealthy plantations owners," Xerak said. "I've lost count of the boots I've worn through in my journeys. I should have come here sooner."

"That's right," Konnel said. "I heard something about those journeys from your mother."

He would have likely asked more, but Vereez came trotting in. "Here's a draft, Konnel-toh."

Konnel read it, then smiled slyly. "When you write the signature line, put my full name, then 'Tam.' That's what I went by in those days. I dropped the nickname when I decided to become respectable. That will make Ohent certain it comes from me—and will reassure the others as well that it's not some clever forgery."

"So that's why you didn't like us to use your middle name," Grunwold said. "It was too close to the name you were leaving behind."

"That's right. Now, despite Vereez's eagerness, there is no way you're leaving today. The weather is horrible. Moreover, I will need time to finally confess my past to Sefit. When we are done with that, I—or I expect she— will need a full briefing as to what to expect in the vicinity of the Library ruins: hazards and the like."

The three inquisitors looked at each other, then Vereez nodded, a bit reluctantly.

Good, Teg thought, *that gives us time to decide if we tell him that Emsehu is there, or if we let our Unique Monstrosity reveal his own story if he chooses. I think I favor the latter.*

"That makes sense. Shall we leave you and call Sefit-toh?"

Konnel held up a hand, almost managing to hide the tremors. "One more question. Do you want me to send a message to your parents to alert them that you're coming, and offer my support?"

Vereez considered, then shook her head. "Thank you, but no. Please, think how you would have felt if you knew Grunwold knew about your past and you couldn't see him right away to learn his reaction."

"Very well. I will not mention your visit to anyone. Now, if you would call Sefit. Oh, Grunwold, if you don't mind your mother's inevitable fit of temper, I'd like you to stay. You're a grown man now, and it's time we include you in important conversations."

And just like that, Teg thought, *Grunwold is an adult. He may have claimed that status for himself by his actions, but his father's acknowledgment means no one will be able to challenge his claim.*

❧CHAPTER ELEVEN❧

When they left the next morning, Grunwold took
Slicewind's helm long enough to pilot them out of sight of
the KonSef estate. Then he turned the wheel over to Peg,
went down to his cabin, and collapsed into his bunk
without bothering to undress. He even snored through
Xerak pulling off his boots.

"Grunwold didn't sleep at all last night," Xerak
reported when he came up on deck. "After the meeting
with Sefit, he went and sat with his father. Some of his
cousins came up, and they had a sort of muted family
reunion."

"I don't think Grunwold slept much on the way here
from the Library either," Teg said. "Every time I came on
deck for a smoke, he'd be up here, either at the wheel or
polishing something."

"He had a lot to worry about," Xerak said. "It wasn't
exactly fun, but talking with his dad went better than I'd
hoped. Now that we have the full story, things should go
a lot easier from here on out."

"Did Konnel tell the rest of his household about his past?" Peg asked. "Those cousins you mentioned?"

"Not yet," Xerak said. "He promised Grunwold and Sefit-toh that he would tell those who might be shocked if the news came out, but he wants to get treated first."

"Reasonable," Peg admitted. "My kids always knew I had been a bit wild when I was younger, so learning the details wasn't too much of a shock, but the only Konnel his family and retainers know is the hard-working, prosperous landholder. Learning he'd earned his seed money as a more-or-less glorified thief would be a lot to dump on them right before leaving on a trip."

When they arrived at Rivers Meet, Vereez piloted them to a different docking facility, one her parents apparently didn't own, since she had to pay for the berth.

"I'm not as confident as Xerak that things will go smoothly. This way, if my parents decide to be difficult, we can retreat to the ship. I'm also going to stock up our supplies before they have a chance to cut my line of credit."

"Why are you so worried, Vereez?" Xerak asked. "Because your folks are so very hung up on being respectable?"

Vereez only shook her head, and refused to say more but Teg, recalling parents who shipped their pregnant daughter off to go through her pregnancy in isolation, only to never see the baby, thought Vereez had reason to worry about how her parents might react. Teg had also been thinking how young Ohent, as seen in the Font, had looked vaguely familiar to Vereez. Could Kaj be Ohent's son? If Ohent had come asking for money, maybe an advance on her trust fund, that would explain the uneasy dynamic Vereez had sensed, even through her obsession with the handsome visitor.

Because, Ohent could put a lot of pressure on Zarrq and Inehem. She alone of all of their little band of thieves doesn't have a social position she'd worry about losing.

Impatient as she had been to confront her parents, Vereez kept her vow to stock *Slicewind* with both necessities and luxuries. Then, like a general marshalling her armies for review, she inspected all of their attire, tweaking sashes into place, straightening collars, insisting that Xerak clean and shine his already pristine spear staff.

Then she led them down to where a fancy, semi-open carriage was waiting for them. It was of the sort that seated them facing each other, three on a side. The carriage was drawn by four creatures something like frilled lizards, although longer legged and much friskier. Their scales were a glorious sunset orange.

"The House of Fortune," Vereez said to the driver, who possessed the head of what Teg thought was a tapir, although she wasn't completely certain. "The residence. Take the riverside promenade, please."

"That's the longer route, Customer-kir," he said, not able to resist a twitch of his mobile nose in what was probably greed.

"So I am aware," Vereez said haughtily. "Drive on."

The driver snapped a long whip in the air over the draft lizards' backs and they moved out, their steps matched and their gait so sinuous that the carriage glided along the street.

Aware that the driver would definitely be eavesdropping, everyone was silent during the journey. For the humans, this was no particular burden, and Teg, at least, was glad her mask would conceal her reaction to so many new and exciting sights. During their last visit, they had gotten a brief look at Rivers Meet, but that had focused on shopping districts and public forums. Now they were seeing a larger view of the culture: houses as well as businesses, parks where sports teams played. Once they drove past a school or daycare, where children as adorable as those in a Disney cartoon frolicked on a playground not too unlike those Teg had played on herself.

The three inquisitors watched the passing scene less intently, although Grunwold had recovered enough from the stresses of the last several days to nudge Xerak when a particularly sensuous girl with the head of an ermine strutted by, clinging to the arm of a buff youth with the head of a falcon. Xerak looked unimpressed. Teg wondered if their young wizard was finally beginning to worry about his own eventual confrontation with his parents, or at least with his mother.

Intellectually, Teg had known that Vereez's family was rich but, when the carriage turned off the riverside promenade, taking what she thought was another street, and she realized that this was actually a private driveway, and the massive mansion in front of her was Vereez's home, she reassessed her estimate up by several grades.

I'd been thinking multimillionaires, as in maybe tens of millions and most of that tied up in investments. This is hundreds of millions, with money to squander.

Suddenly Teg was afraid in a way she hadn't been even when they'd been attacked by spike wolves and piranha toads. That—even when she'd been knocked off the ledge—hadn't seemed quite real. This, though, she understood: the power of wealth and what it could buy.

Surreptitiously, she touched the bracelet on her wrist, reminding herself that she didn't need to get to some Lantern Waste or ride the Hogwarts Express in order to escape.

I'm like Dorothy with the ruby slippers, and if it gets to be too much, well, there's no place like home.

"Cozy little place," Peg said. For once, she had not pulled out her knitting, although Teg was willing to bet that she had some yarn or string hidden in one of the formal robe's voluminous folds.

Vereez laughed and waved to one of the gardeners, who bowed and waved back. "Actually, when I was growing up, it was cozy in a strange way. My parents have offices here. Unlike many of my friends who saw their parents only for a few hours in the evening, if then, I ate breakfast or lunch with one of them most days. Dinners they often used for business entertainments, but if they could, they included me."

Grunwold nodded. "I remember when we'd visit you. It was tremendous fun running up and down the hallways, climbing in the dumbwaiters, sneaking down the servants' stairs to the kitchen to get treats."

Xerak said dreamily, "I remember the libraries . . . So organized and yet so full of surprises. And those deep window seats, just perfect to curl up in and read away a rainy afternoon."

The carriage had drawn to a halt and the driver, obviously having realized that Vereez wasn't a mere visitor, was infinitely more respectful as he helped them out, accepting his payment as if Vereez was doing him a favor.

Maybe she is. Maybe her parents own the taxi service and she doesn't need to pay if she doesn't want.

Vereez had directed the carriage to leave them not at the main door, but at a side entrance.

"For the family," Vereez explained. "The other is for business and big parties."

"Nice to be family," Peg said, adjusting her mask.

Family door or not, Vereez didn't need to pull out her key and let herself in. The carriage had hardly begun to pull away when the door was opened by a tall, lean man with some sort of rodent's head—a ferret, maybe. Teg wasn't sure. Based on the numerous samples of daily wear she'd seen during their drive, she was fairly certain that his attire was some sort of livery.

"Vereez-kir," he said, making an efficient bow and motioning for a couple of young men to gather up the various bits of baggage, "welcome home. Your apartments are, of course, ready for you, but may I know how many guests we are to have?"

"Five," she said, motioning for them to enter. "Is the Hetnet Suite available? If so, I would like it for these three ladies."

"It is," the butler said. "If you don't mind waiting a short while, I will make sure the linens are fresh."

"That would be fine. They can come to my suite while we wait."

"Yes, Vereez-kir. I recognize Grunwold-lial and Xerafu

Akeru-va. We can accommodate them in the Sword Suite, or in private rooms, if they would prefer."

"Hi, Leyenui," Grunwold said, dipping his head in greeting. "I don't mind sharing a suite with Xerak. And I remember loving the Sword Suite, even if we did get in trouble for trying to take down that set of ornamental swords."

He laughed. Leyenui didn't have the highly mobile ears that Teg had come to rely on as emotion indicators, but something about how completely immobile he kept his whiskers and ears made her think that the butler did not have as pleasant memories of that particular escapade.

"Very good. Those rooms are ready for immediate use. Your parents had visitors who left only yesterday."

"Are my parents at home?" Vereez did a very good job of hiding any anxiety she felt.

"Unhappily, they are out, lunching with clients. However, they are expected back shortly. Would you like me to let them know you are here?"

"Yes. Thank you."

Throughout, Vereez was very much the lady of the house, not rude or distant, but very clearly someone who could request whatever she wanted and expect it to be done. The difference between her current demeanor and the raffish character who took her turns at *Slicewind*'s wheel, or argued with Grunwold or Xerak, gave Teg a great deal of insight into the girl who had fallen for Kaj.

She was used to having what she wanted. I wonder if, on some level, that made her believe that wanting was, in and of itself, sufficient excuse for doing whatever she felt like. I've grown very fond of our three young inquisitors but, on some level, they're all just a little spoiled—or maybe "spoiled" isn't the right word. Privileged?

After, Leyenui gave orders as to the disposition of the luggage, then went off—not hurrying, but very efficiently—to spread the alert that the "young mistress" had returned unexpectedly, bringing five guests. Vereez did not take them immediately to her suite.

"He said it is ready," she said softly, her voice holding an amused chuckle, "and I am certain it is. However, I know that either he or the housekeeper will want to make certain. I'll take you for a turn in the garden to give them time."

She began with a path around an ornamental pond. "Those," she said, pointing to some insects rather like a cross between butterflies and dragonflies that flitted over the pond, "are hetnet. The suite you're staying in is decorated with them as a motif, so if you don't like them, let me know and I'll shift your room."

"They're beautiful," Meg said. "Their wings are shaped more like those of a dragonfly, but with the intricate patterns of a butterfly. That one on the pink flower reminds me of a monarch, but in ice blues and white."

Peg bent to look closely at another. "My grandson Salvador has been collecting butterflies. I remember we always have to be careful not to brush the powder from the wings."

Vereez laughed, sounding truly delighted. "The same is true with these!"

"Then let's call them 'powderwings,'" Peg said, "to remind us to be careful."

As they walked along the carefully kept paths between

flowering shrubs and knotwork herbal plantings, the three inquisitors reminisced about the games they'd played in a childhood that was, really, not so long ago. Many of these games had taken place down along the riverfront, where there was not only a boathouse, but an elaborate treehouse.

When they were far enough that they could look back at the mansion, Vereez pointed. "See there, where the large balcony is? That's the Powderwing Suite. It has three separate bedrooms, but only a single bathroom. You won't mind sharing?"

"Have we before now?" Peg asked. "I don't recall our having trouble aboard *Slicewind*."

"Good. I wanted you to have a suite where you could go without your masks. The balcony is deep enough that it's hard for anyone to see into the rooms, unless you stand right up to the windows."

"Considerate of you," Meg said. "These masks are comfortable enough, but after a while, peering through eyeholes does become trying."

"The servants always knock," Vereez continued, "but I am going to tell Leyenui that you are to be left to wait upon yourselves. If you keep the door locked, you should be fine. It's not that I haven't come to appreciate your appearance, even find it lovely, but the smaller stir we create . . ."

"I agree," Meg said, as the other two nodded. At Grunwold's family estate, they'd stayed in the office tower, so that their strange appearance wouldn't need to be explained. Concealment was becoming standard operating procedure.

No heroic entry as the long-awaited "daughters of Eve" here, Teg thought ruefully. *Definitely not Narnia.*

Not long after they had walked back to the mansion and had a chance to freshen up, Vereez's parents returned. Inehem and Zarrq were recognizable as more mature versions of the people from the vision in the Font of Sight. Zarrq was, if anything, more powerfully built than he had been in the days when he effortlessly carried his wife through various perils. Inehem's figure was more voluptuous, her fur slightly more silvery than it had been.

I wonder if her coat has lightened with the years or if she uses cosmetics.

Inehem and Zarrq embraced their daughter, greeted Grunwold and Xerak as family friends, and looked at the three masked visitors with apparent curiosity.

Vereez had decided to take advantage of their undoubted interest regarding what she had learned at Hettua Shrine to get right to the point.

"These are Meg, Peg, and Teg," Vereez said. "They're part of our story."

She launched into the tale, beginning with how Grunwold had joined herself and Xerak, then moving on to what had happened at Hettua Shrine. When she reached the point where they had taken advantage of Hawtoor's napping to begin the summons on their own, Inehem and Zarrq exchanged quick glances. Teg wondered what they were thinking.

Is it "She's so like we were?" or "How could she? Didn't we raise her better?" I've known quite a few people who enjoyed being wild in their youths, but who believe that their own children should behave quite differently.

As had Grunwold, Vereez saved having the three humans unmask for the appropriate part of their story. Konnel had been fascinated, but Teg had the sense that Vereez's parents were uneasy. Vereez apparently caught this, too, stumbling over a few sentences before resuming the easy flow of her narrative.

When she reached the part about going to the Library of the Sapphire Wind, there was no doubt that Inehem and Zarrq were not pleased. Whereas Konnel had been relieved to have his secret out at last, there was no doubt that they were unhappy—and worse, that they were angry.

Uh, oh, Teg thought. *I don't think they're going to help us. I hope that "not helping" is all they intend to do.*

Although clearly edgy, Vereez had the poise to continue her tale as if she wasn't aware of her parents' building fury. She concluded by producing a copy of the letter Konnel had signed. "He says you should know where to find Ohent and, through her, the piece of the artifact you—well, Fardowsi-toh—took away when you all left the Library. Konnel-toh agrees that we should return it to the Library."

Zarrq held out an elegantly manicured hand. Like the polar bear whose head he possessed, his skin was black—not the dark brown that is usually called "black" in humans, but a jettier hue.

"If I might see that?" He took the letter, read it, nodded, and handed it to his wife.

Then Inehem made a few quick gestures. The signature glowed a pale green. "Authentic."

Inehem returned the letter to Vereez. "So, why should we assist you in this?"

Vereez looked startled. "Because the shrine sent us to the Library of the Sapphire Wind, and the Library's *genius loci* gave us this task. We need the artifact if we are to get the answers we desire."

"There is another part missing," Inehem commented coolly. "You could search for that first. My understanding is that with two parts this Sapphire Wind could pinpoint the third. Perhaps you should assert yourselves more, rather than expecting us to make things easy for you."

Vereez replied with matching chill. "We *have* asserted ourselves. Winning that first part was far from easy. We're not asking for you to do anything but give us an address. We'll go to Ohent and ask her to give us the piece. It would help if you would give us her location and a letter similar to the one Konnel-toh gave us, that's all. I'd think you'd be eager to assist us."

"Why? Just because Konnel is consumed with guilt, should we feel the same? Perhaps he wouldn't have felt that way if he wasn't ill—and ill by his own careless action."

"What?" Grunwold didn't so much speak as the word exploded from him.

"Didn't Konnel tell you that part? How he came to catch the illness that is killing him?"

"He didn't. I didn't ask. It didn't seem important," Grunwold managed.

"But it is. Did he lead you to believe that after the debacle at the Library we retired from our work as extraction agents?"

"No."

"Well, at least Konnel was honest about that. We

continued to take on extractions for some time. However, the team was not what it had been. Ohent and Konnel, in particular, had lost their nerve. We were on a delicate job for an alchemist who had hired us to retrieve some materials from a facility that had been badly damaged in a failed experiment. I've often wondered if Konnel was unsettled by some similarities in the setting to the Library after that job went wrong. For whatever reason, he was careless."

Intent silence invited Inehem to continue. She did in the dreamy tones of a "once upon a time."

"We'd been given a list of things our client wanted, with the understanding that anything else we took was a bonus. An attractive jade jar caught Konnel's eye." Inehem shaped something about the size of a soda can in the air with her hands, then went on. "He grabbed it without making certain that the seal was intact. It wasn't. He managed to dodge most of the contents when they spilled out, but some splashed on one of his upper pants legs. He didn't worry much at the time, but later he realized that some had soaked through to his skin. That location was where the first numb patches occurred.

"I helped him with research after, and there was some indication that more than an infection was involved. There might well have been a curse. And curses, as you know, have a nasty tendency to pass on through family lines. Nonetheless, Konnel went ahead and married, then started a family. Really, I have no problem understanding why he feels guilty and desires to expiate that guilt."

Zarrq added in his deep, rumbly voice. "We, however, feel no such guilt."

"Not even that all those people might have been killed?" Xerak asked in astonishment.

"No," Zarrq said. "They chose to create a hazardous environment, as well as maintaining an attractive nuisance. If we could get through their security, then what happened is as much their fault as ours."

Peg stirred restlessly but, where the hippy chick might have argued, the older woman understood that these people were very different from Sefit and Konnel.

Vereez asked, clearly choosing each word carefully, "So you will not give us Ohent's location?"

Zarrq and Inehem exchanged glances, then Inehem said, "I think not."

"Will you give us a letter to show her if we locate her on our own?"

"We will not," Zarrq said.

"What," Vereez said, "if we decide to leak what we have learned about your past ventures? I'm certain that your business associates would hesitate to work with proven thieves."

"Proven? How would you prove it?"

"I could give the same account I've given, then bring Nefnet-va forward to confirm it."

"And if we denied?" Zarrq asked. "It has been over two decades. Even if you had spells done to confirm this Nefnet's identity, we could balance with rumors that those were faked."

"And dear child," said Inehem with fake sweetness. "Have you thought that any rumors you spread would hurt Konnel and Fardowsi far more than they would us? Financiers have a certain reputation for ruthlessness. I suppose the risk of exposure doesn't matter much to Konnel. He has a semi-independent kingdom there, but Fardowsi's business would suffer. People would always wonder just how she acquired her 'antiquities.'"

Zarrq laughed. "In a few words, she'd go from being a respected antiquarian to a former thief and probable fence."

Something in his inflection made Teg wonder just how law-abiding Xerak's mother really was. From the expressions on her associates' faces, she wasn't the only one wondering.

"In fact, Vereez, dear," Inehem said, "your father and I really think you should give up on this search of yours. We hoped that going to the shrine would be enough, and get this out of your system. However, since Sapphire Wind has chosen to manipulate what should be a neutral element to its purposes, we must protest. You will stop here."

"But my . . . sister!"

"You have no sister," Zarrq said firmly. His tone made clear that if she persisted, he would say precisely for whom she searched. Something predatory in how he held his sleek, white-furred head added, *Do you really want your friends to know about your shameful behavior?*

Vereez's ears, to that point sharp-pointed and aggressive, melted into puppyish dismay.

"I . . ."

"Your friends are welcome to spend the night," Inehem said, her tones honey-sweet with victory. "And then tomorrow you will bid them farewell and wish them luck in finding Xerak's master. We will discuss your future when we're just family at home together."

Grunwold and Xerak had been listening with barely disguised astonishment. Now Xerak spoke soothingly.

"Vereez, maybe you should listen to your parents. Maybe they do have your best interests at heart. Remember how they warned us not to play in the boathouse when the river was flooding? Sometimes parents do know what's best."

He then turned to Inehem and Zarrq. "Give us a chance to talk to Vereez. I'm sure we can help her to understand why you think continuing is unwise. As for me, since we've had a change in plans, if you don't mind, I'll go and visit my parents later this evening. I fear my mother may share your views, but I should at least ask her for a letter. If we can't get any help from her, then maybe we need to go back to the Library and consult with Sapphire Wind as to other leads."

"Of course, Xerafu Akeru-va," Inehem said. "We know how important your search for Uten Kekui is to you. I am sorry that we cannot help, but Vereez's delusion cannot be further encouraged."

"May I go to my suite now?" Vereez asked, her voice shaking and her eyes bright with unshed tears.

"Yes. In fact, I think," Zarrq said, "and I am sure your mother agrees, that it would be best if you remained there until you have calmed down. Your friends can visit with you there."

In your detention cell, Teg filled in.

"Fine!" Vereez's ears pricked again for a defiant moment. "I hadn't ever realized how ruthless you both are. Thank you for this lesson. I won't forget it."

With that, her ears collapsed, she leapt to her feet, and

she stormed from the room. Grunwold and Xerak waited until the humans had put their masks back on. Then, without a word to their hosts, they also left, Peg hurrying after, doubtless to keep them from doing anything foolish.

Meg paused in the doorway. "Thank you for your hospitality. I have children of my own—older than Vereez, true—but I remember how difficult they can be at her age."

Teg nodded, figuring that Inehem and Zarrq could interpret the gesture as they wished.

"Let's go see Vereez," Xerak said once they were all in the hallway. "I can wait to visit my parents until she's been calmed down."

Vereez had left her door ajar. When they let themselves in, she was half-collapsed in one of the cushioned chairs that furnished the suite's "living room." Raising her head from her hands, she waited until Teg had closed the door and the humans had unmasked.

"They're serious," she said. "I can't believe they care so little about exposure but, for whatever reason, they're willing to risk it to keep me here."

"Perhaps," Meg said, taking a seat on the chair opposite Vereez, "they are more concerned about what will happen if Sapphire Wind 'unarchives' the remainder of the Library's population. We saw Nefnet's reaction. Do you believe for a moment that among the hundreds of people who have lost over two decades of their lives, that none will want revenge?"

Peg moved to the chair next to Meg's and took out her knitting. Teg perched on the arm of Meg's chair, while Grunwold paced restlessly around the room. Xerak settled for working out his frustrations by alternately thumping the butt of his staff and dragging it through the carpet's thick pile.

"I hadn't thought about that," Vereez admitted, "but right now I can't say that I blame them. By 'them' I mean the Library's people, not my parents."

"Don't be so hard on your parents," Peg advised. "Frightened people do stupid things, and although they seem very cool and sophisticated now, I'm not sure your mother is all that far from the panicked young wizard who threw that lightning globe. They may ease up if you give them time."

"I don't..." Vereez was beginning, when Xerak interrupted with a violent gesture of his spear staff.

"Okay. I've put up a quick ward against eavesdropping. If Inehem is trying to spy, she's going to get a variation on Peg counseling patience, but I can only maintain the illusion for a few minutes at most. Vereez, do you want out of here or are you giving up for now?"

"Out."

"Fine. Can you guys get her out of here and to the river? I can have a boat waiting. From there she and I can sail to meet you at wherever you care to take *Slicewind*."

Grunwold looked worried. "Out of here? The House of Fortune has passive security like a bank's. It won't be set to keep us in, but you can bet Vereez won't be able to take a step out of this suite without setting off all sorts of alarms."

Peg was grinning. "I have a plan. It won't even involve getting Vereez to the river." Peg looked at Vereez. "Do you think your parents will care if most of us leave early for *Slicewind*?"

"No, I don't. I suspect they'd be glad to have you gone." She looked sulky. "They'll probably figure I'll be easier to manipulate if most of my friends have dumped me."

"Excellent!"

Xerak signaled that his protection against eavesdropping would be going down any moment.

Peg rose from her chair and went to sit next to Vereez. "Now, dear, let me show you how to knit. There's nothing like knitting to calm the nerves."

Peg's plan, explained in notes and doodles she scribbled while ostensibly teaching Vereez to knit, was just insane enough that it might work.

Implementing the plan began that evening, after dinner, when Grunwold and Vereez got into a ferocious "argument," with Vereez advocating telling everyone in the world about what "flea-bitten shiftless thieves" their parents had been, and Grunwold shouting that his father was dying and he wasn't going to have him remembered for the few things he'd done wrong, rather than for everything he'd done right.

The pair were passionate enough that Teg felt certain that anyone snooping—magically or otherwise—would be convinced. The exchange ended with Grunwold insisting he wouldn't sleep under the same roof as Vereez. Meg and Peg had gone with him back to *Slicewind*, while Teg remained behind to comfort Vereez. Xerak left at the same time to go see his parents.

A tearful Vereez had asked Teg to sleep in her suite, and Teg had complied. After the household had settled for the night would be time for Part Two.

At what Peg liked to call the "pee-hours of the early morning," Teg rose from her bed and, without turning on any lights, headed into the opulent bathroom that was part of Vereez's suite. Her heart was thudding and she really *did* need to pee. As she was doing so, Vereez padded in after her.

"Oh," she said in a sleepy voice. "Sorry. I'll just wait while you finish."

"I didn't mean to wake you," Teg said, hoping she sounded natural.

She reached up and pulled the chain that would open the gravity-fed flush, then moved to the sink and turned on the water. After quickly washing her hands, she reached for her talisman bracelet and rubbed the strands, muttering the activation charm.

This was the dicey part. Well, the *first* dicey part. What if the spell didn't work? What if all the magic they'd encountered when fighting the various protectors in the Library had deactivated it? Hadn't Hawtoor said the bracelets would work best in a low-magic area or something like that? More reasons why her talisman bracelet wasn't going to work were flooding Teg's mind when the door appeared, just as it should. Teg twisted the knob, then she and Vereez (who reached behind her to turn off the water), stepped through.

They appeared in Teg's bedroom, startling Thought and Memory, who were sitting side by side, looking out the bedroom window. They took one look at Vereez, hissed, then melted under the bed. Teg felt a pang of guilt, but she was also feeling the pressure of time.

A quick glance at the window showed that it was night

here, a clock confirmed the hour was about two in the morning. That was a relief, because Teg had been worried that (despite Meg's careful calculations as to the best time for them to make the crossing) Felicity the cat sitter might be visiting. Also, it meant that they wouldn't need to wait for the streets to be quiet, and they could head over to Meg's. Teg pulled the shade down and then flipped on a light.

"We have a little leeway before we need to check in, since time passes more slowly here, but we have a lot to do." Teg hurried over to one of her dressers, and pulled out a hooded sweatshirt. "Try this on. It's one of the oversized ones I keep to wear over my bulkier field gear. Hopefully, the hood will be large enough to hide your nose."

Vereez had automatically caught the sweatshirt in one hand, but she was staring around the room, her brown eyes wide. She bent to take a closer look at Thought and Memory, who were now peeking out, eyes wide in astonishment. Thought hissed, and Memory pulled back under the bed. Teg hunkered down so she could pat Thought.

"Don't be an idiot, cat," she said affectionately. "Surely you've seen a girl with a fox's head before."

Vereez was still looking avidly around Teg's bedroom, her gaze travelling over all the things Teg took for granted: the electric light, the glowing readout of the digital clock, the tightly woven artificial fiber carpet, the photographs, back to the cats.

"Vereez, can you understand me?" Teg asked. One of their concerns had been that the translation spell wouldn't carry over. They'd been prepared to communicate via charades if they must.

"This really is another world," Vereez replied, her voice hushed. "I believed, but I had no idea *how* different it would be."

"You'll get a closer look at part of it. We're going to need to walk over to Meg's, because I can't have my car vanishing from the garage." Teg got down on her stomach and reached under the bed to pat Memory, who rubbed against her hand. Then reassured that her cats had forgiven her, she rolled over and got back to her feet. "Let's see if that hood is enough to hide your snout."

It wasn't but, in combination with a wraparound scarf, someone would need to look closely to see anything but Vereez's large brown eyes.

Downstairs, Teg got coats for both of them out of the front closet, making sure that Vereez's was long enough to hide her tail. Vereez was already wearing trousers and boots from her own wardrobe that would pass well enough. The final touch was a walking stick left from when Teg had sprained her ankle a few field seasons back. She handed this to Vereez.

"Walk with this. If anyone comes to talk with us, bend over it, like you're old and infirm."

A short time later, trailed right up to the door by now actively inquisitive cats, Teg and Vereez stepped out into the cold winter night.

Not for the first time since Peg had outlined her plan, Teg was glad it was February, so bundling up would be more reasonable than not. Peg had wanted to be the one to take Vereez through, but she had been forced to admit that it was possible one of her numerous family members would have decided to house-sit for her in her absence. Meg hadn't thought that anything in her wardrobe would make a good disguise for Vereez, while Teg's wardrobe was widely varied both in style and sizes.

And having grown up poor, I do tend to hold on to things. I just hope I don't become one of those hoarders. Of course, it's not as if my undearly departed relatives left me a boatload of family heirlooms.

Teg reached for the phone and punched in Meg's number. When the machine picked up, she left the prearranged message. "Hi, this is Tessa. We're leaving now. It's 2:15."

Since they couldn't precisely coordinate times, this was to give Meg something to check when she came through. Now she'd know they had made their escape. Leaving the door open between worlds hadn't seemed like a good idea, so Meg would check periodically.

Now to hope her bracelet works, that they got Slicewind moved, that Vereez's parents still think we're both sound asleep in her suite. That Xerak . . .

Checking to make sure that she hadn't left anything out of place that would alarm Felicity when she came by, Teg unlocked the door and led her much-bundled companion out into the street.

Teg's house was in an urban neighborhood, within walking distance of the shopping center that included Pagearean Books. Meg lived on the far side of the same shopping center, in an apartment building that catered to seniors. It wasn't quite a retirement community, but it did offer a few additional services. She'd carried her keys with her Over Where, and now they rattled in the pocket of Teg's winter coat.

Vereez was fascinated by everything from the concrete sidewalks ("Is there a ritual reason they're divided into such regular rectangles?") to the streetlights ("Why are they so high up? Are you afraid someone is going to steal the light source?").

During the hours after the others had left, Teg had coached Vereez about some of what to expect under the guise of telling her stories to distract her from her supposed fury at Grunwold. Therefore, the first car that went by made the fox woman jump, but didn't frighten her. That was reserved for a motorcycle. As it roared toward them, Vereez dropped her walking stick and reached for the swords she wasn't wearing.

"Easy!" Teg said, retrieving the stick and handing it to her. "That's just a sort of two-wheeled car."

Vereez looked shamefacedly at Teg. "Sorry. But that huge white eye, and the horrible sound, and the smell! How can you stand to live here? There are so many acrid smells!"

"The stink's even worse in the summer," Teg assured her. "But, remember, humans don't have as sharp a sense of smell as you do. When we were driving through Rivers Meet, I noticed how clean the streets were, even though you use draft animals. I wonder if that's because your people can't 'overlook' mess."

"Maybe . . ." Vereez was definitely not convinced, but too fascinated by her surroundings to enter into one of their more usual debates.

When they reached the shopping center, Teg left

Vereez outside while she darted into an all-night convenience store to buy a few cartons of cigarettes. On impulse, she bought some chocolate bars and a few other treats she thought the inquisitors would enjoy sampling.

Teg emerged to find Vereez gone. She was about to panic when she saw the bundled figure leaning on her cane in front of a fast food restaurant a few doors away. The eatery was closed for the night, but the window's decorations showed clearly in the streetlights.

"I thought you said you don't have our sort of people here!" Vereez said accusingly.

Teg looked where Vereez was pointing, puzzled. The restaurant's window had been painted with a depiction of the shop's mascot: a dashing tiger-headed man balancing a tray of burgers, tacos, drinks, and fries.

"That's just fancy, imagination, whimsy," Teg protested.

"But there, too!" Vereez said accusingly, pointing toward a sporting goods store in which a poster showed anthropomorphic representations of the Taima University's mascot facing off against that of its archrival. Teg had to admit the wolf-head man could have been a cartoon representation of the riverboat captain who'd taken them downriver, while his owl-headed opponent could have been a particularly buff cousin of Hawtoor's.

"Really," Teg persisted, taking Vereez's arm and steering her along, "it's just fancy. As we told you, one of the things we've found very strange about your world is that you people have characteristics that match creatures in our world, but your own animals and plants—at least as far as we've been able to tell—are similar but different."

"So those aren't real?" Vereez insisted, pausing to look

in the window of Pagearean Books, in which a display featuring books by Sandra Boynton and Richard Scarry showed a wide array of anthropomorphic animals.

"Not a one," Teg insisted. "Please. We've got to get moving. Not only might Meg be waiting, but the shopping center's security guard may come over to make sure we're not potential vandals."

"Do you think it's because you all look so alike that you need to invent other sorts of people?" Vereez asked, allowing herself to be steered along. "It's as if you feel the lack, even though you don't know our type of people really exist."

"Interesting theory," Teg conceded. "Anthropologists— like me—usually explain the prevalence of animal totems, which are found in some form in just about every human culture, as a desire to take on the perceived qualities of the animal. Sports team mascots are almost always creatures who are swift and dangerous—not necessarily carnivores, although often they are, this despite the fact that the last thing that would be acceptable in most sports would be to physically maim or eat the other team."

"So what are a fox's perceived qualities?" Vereez asked.

Teg considered. "Cleverness verging on sneakiness, I guess. The Japanese *kitsune* is often depicted as looking much like you—a beautiful woman with the head and tail of a fox. I believe she can turn either into a fox or a human, but when she's a human, she has to be careful to remember to hide her tail."

"Tails," Vereez said seriously, "can be a problem. Still, I wouldn't want to do without mine."

When they reached Meg's apartment building, Teg had

Vereez wait on the sidewalk while she tried the key Meg had given her for the front door. It worked fine, and they breezed through the foyer, to the bank of elevators. Another advantage of this late hour was that the front desk wasn't manned after midnight, and the building's ground-floor convenience store was also closed.

Luck seemed to be with them. An elevator car was waiting. They were inside and Teg was pushing the button for Meg's floor when someone called out, "Hold the elevator, please!"

Teg considered refusing, but she knew that these doors didn't close quickly and had a very acute sensor so they would spring open if any of the building's slower-moving residents caught a cane or trailing bit of clothing while getting aboard. Instead, she motioned for Vereez to turn slightly away, then she hit the Open Door button.

A man came running up. Despite the cold, he wasn't wearing a hat. Teg guessed he was somewhere between her and Peg in age, maybe a recent retiree who'd downsized to an apartment. He wasn't bad looking, with a touch of iron to hair that was otherwise still dark, and weathered skin still bright from the cold.

"Thanks!" he said.

"What floor?"

Please don't let it be seven. Please don't let it be seven.

"Six, please."

As Teg punched both buttons she thought thanks to the gods who protected fools. The elevator doors seemed to take forever to close.

"I don't think I've seen you before," the man said.

"Oh, I don't live here. I'm visiting a friend."

Even as she said the words, Teg realized how lame they sounded. Who visited someone in a retirement community so late?

Fortunately, the man assumed that Vereez was the friend in question. Bent over as she was, wrapped in scarves, the young woman was doing a fair imitation of someone far older.

"It's a nice place to live," the man said. "I moved in right after Christmas."

The bell pinged and the elevator stopped. The man got out with a cheerful, "See you around!" Teg managed to keep from sagging against the wall until the door was completely shut. Vereez began to giggle just as the elevator door slid open on Meg's floor.

"Hush! Here's where we get off. Take my arm and keep doing your bent-over old-woman act. It'd be just our luck to have the local insomniac out pacing the corridors."

Vereez complied, but Teg could still feel her shaking with suppressed giggles as they traversed several halls to reach Meg's apartment. When they were inside and the door locked behind them, Teg switched on the light. Either Meg wasn't here yet or they'd missed her first pass.

Vereez looked around eagerly as they stepped into a large area that doubled as a dining room and entry hall. The coat closet Meg had chosen as her portal was to one side, so they'd do best to wait here.

"Is this Meg's family?" Vereez indicated a neatly arranged group of photos on one wall.

Teg nodded. "Her late husband, Charles. Her son, also Charles, and her daughter, Judy. Below, that group picture, is Charles, his wife—Sandy, I think—and their two children. Judy was married once, briefly. I gather it didn't work out."

"They don't live near?"

"No. Charles and his family are in New York City. He does something with stocks. Judy is in Los Angeles, California. I think she works with a movie agent or something."

Those short sentences necessitated a lot of explanation and pulling out a map of the United States. Before Teg was well into what a movie was, and what an agent did—a subject about which she only knew something because of a novel they'd read in book club—Meg had opened the closet door and was leaning through.

"Excellent! You made it! I was worried when I made my first check, but I thought I was probably early."

Behind Meg, *Slicewind* in full sail could be glimpsed. Grunwold was at the wheel, Xerak and Peg hovering nervously nearby. Vereez and Teg hurried through and Meg closed the door. Teg noticed that she didn't look back.

The sun was high overhead, a visible reminder of how much faster time passed here. As Teg and Vereez stripped off their winter clothing, Teg gave a quick summary of how things had gone. Vereez kept interrupting to tell Xerak and Grunwold about the oddities of the humans' world. The young men were definitely interested, but they were distracted, too.

"Did you have trouble getting away?" Teg asked. "Any complications?"

"No, the plan went smooth as silk," Peg said, with understandable pleasure, since it had largely been her creation. "As far as we know, Vereez's parents haven't yet twigged to her departure."

"But what do we do now?" Vereez asked. The adrenaline was clearly fading, giving way to edginess. "We're no further along in finding Ohent than we were— further, maybe, because my parents may try to prevent us."

Xerak's whisker's twitched in a feline smile. "Yes and no. I did exactly what I told Zarrq and Inehem I was going to do, and visited my parents. I had a somewhat different reception from either you or Grunwold."

"Oh?"

"Make yourselves comfortable," Xerak said, seating himself on the deck and leaning against one of the lockers, "and let me tell you a tale."

❧ CHAPTER TWELVE ❧

"I gave the others only a thumbnail sketch of what happened when I visited my parents," Xerak began, "because I didn't want to have to go through this twice."

"And he's been gloating," Grunwold added, checking *Slicewind*'s heading, then giving Xerak his full attention. "If it hadn't been for Peg and Meg, I would have thumped him."

Xerak's snort showed what he thought of that, but he was too pleased with himself to take any real offense. When everyone was settled and Peg's knitting needles were clicking away, he began.

"Something that Inehem said started me wondering—especially that bit about how my mother's reputation might be damaged if the facts about her past came out. It wasn't so much what Inehem said as the way she laughed when she said it. I started thinking, and realized that a good many things I had wondered about my parents' business since I was a boy made perfect sense if, in fact, in addition to being a talented antiquarian, my mother was a fence."

Xerak waved a hand to indicate that he wasn't going to go into any of the things he'd speculated about, then continued. "So, after I left the House of Fortune, I stopped at a place I use as a message drop, then headed to my mother's shop. I set up a few simple scrying spells before I arrived. Once I was inside the shop's security, I activated them. The spells I'd set weren't long lasting—those probably would have been blocked—but they were enough to confirm the existence of several secret compartments, just the sort of places to hide items of dubious provenance."

Peg started to ask something, but Xerak shook his head and held up his hand to stop her.

"Ask me about the complexities later, if you really want to know. Leave it that Mom hadn't been sloppy. Only someone who was a mage who was also a member of the immediate family could get around her protections, only—really—me.

"Armed with that information, as well as what we'd learned from Sapphire Wind, I asked my mother if she'd speak with me in private. No doubt, Mom was ready for me to ask her again for funds to assist with my search for Uten Kekui. Instead, I confronted her with what we'd learned, then added that I'd confirmed that she was obviously using the shop for transactions that were less than completely legal. While she was still poleaxed, I demanded that she help us locate Ohent."

"Did you tell her that my parents had refused?" Vereez asked.

"No. Mom seemed to take for granted that while I was speaking with her, you were speaking with them. Anyhow, it turns out that your parents aren't the only ones who have stayed in touch with Ohent. Seems that Ohent hasn't quite given up the business of taking things that don't quite belong to her. Basically, she's a part-time tomb robber.

"Apparently, Ohent discovered that in the vicinity of a necropolis, the dreams that have plagued her as the custodian of the Bird of Ba Djed don't bother her as severely, possibly because of the number of spells and charms that are used to protect the mausoleums from malign influences. At first, Ohent just lived nearby and took work on a landscaping crew. Then, one day, she more or less happened on a nice urn and . . . Well, you could say my mother was kind enough to oblige an old friend fallen on hard times."

"Do you know which necropolis?" Vereez asked eagerly.

"I do and we're sailing that way. I picked up some maps, and Grunwold's plotted us a course that will bring us there in a few days."

"Wait, why would there even be a necropolis?" Teg asked. "I thought you people believe in reincarnation. Why would you have cities for the dead?"

"Because some people think they're a good idea," Xerak answered. "I'd say the belief in reincarnation is pretty much universal—there's too much evidence to deny the reality. However, there are different theories as to how reincarnation works. Some common questions include how long it takes for a spirit to be reincarnated;

whether anything the living do can influence how much of their previous lives the reborn remember; whether the living can assure that the reincarnated person returns in his or her own family or at least in the same region; and whether posthumous rituals can strengthen the chance that a reincarnated person will retain abilities gained in a past life. Those are a few of the most common issues."

"Wow!" Peg said. "That's a lot more complicated than Christianity's debates about Heaven, Hell, and Purgatory. So, how do the necropolises tie in?"

"They're usually built by people who believe that the actions of the living can influence elements of the reincarnation cycle. In most cases, mausoleums are maintained by those who want to draw the spirit back to a region or family. They believe the used-up body still has a tenuous connection to the departed spirit."

Grunwold nodded. "Also, those who want to try to make sure memories and abilities are retained will use the corpse as a link when they attempt to feed the departed spirit energy or whatever."

"Whether or not there is a link," Vereez added, "is probably the most hotly debated existential issue."

"Existential, not theological?" Teg asked.

"What do gods have to do with it?" Vereez asked, genuinely puzzled. "Gods are for crops, moral guidance, explaining how things got started, stuff like that."

Meg's tone was very gentle as she asked, "So none of your religions say that gods have anything to do with whether or not a spirit is reborn?"

"Not whether," Vereez said. "I hear some religions say that how you live might have an impact on how you're reborn or how quickly, but most people consider that pretty primitive thinking. Rebirth happens no matter what."

"That's so different," Peg said. "I'm not sure how I feel about it."

"So, what does your religion say about rebirth?" Vereez asked, ears perked in interest.

Peg's reply came slowly. "That it doesn't happen. You live once, then you die and go to an afterlife. Which afterlife depends on how you lived your life. That's basically it."

Vereez was as astonished as if Peg had said that you only ate one meal, and that was it. Teg and Meg weighed in with examples of different human religions, including those that believed in reincarnation. Their descriptions complemented each other: Teg's being more anthropological, Meg's drawing on both theology and history.

Despite religion being one of the three big no-nos of polite social discussion (the other two being money and politics), the conversation remained very civil. Peg, Meg, and Teg were used to such discussions, because all three "no-nos" came up quite often at book group. For the three inquisitors, human religions were just another facet in how weird human cultures were.

Afternoon tended to be when everyone was awake, since whoever had been on night shift had gotten some sleep. Unless someone craved privacy—and that someone was most likely to be Meg, who took advantage of either the stern cabin or Vereez's not being in use to go write—everyone tended to gather above deck if the weather was fine.

This was one such day. Peg and Vereez were finishing up a round of fencing practice.

It's a good thing, Teg thought, *that they were using wooden swords, because Vereez hasn't stopped fighting phantoms ever since we got her out of the House of Fortune. Even so, Peg's only just parried a few too-solid hits.*

Meg and Teg were cutting up various meats and vegetables that Peg would later turn into a stir fry. The style of cooking, if not the seasoning, was known Over Where, and on one of her quick trips home, Peg had grabbed some spices, as well as soy sauce and sesame oil.

"We're a day or so out from the necropolis," Grunwold commented from where he was overhauling the cargo winch while supervising Xerak as the young wizard reluctantly washed the deck nearby. "Anyone have a plan for how we're going to find Ohent, since Xerak's mother didn't have an address? Ask around for a woman we only have seen through visions—visions that show her as a pretty hot young thing, not a crazy old lady?"

"Hey!" Teg said, tossing at him the butt end of a stalk of something that looked like rhubarb but tasted more like green beans. "Watch out before you start insulting old ladies. I think all three of us are older than your parents and their friends."

"I wasn't insulting," Grunwold said, obnoxious as usual. "I was being practical. Okay. Maybe calling Ohent 'old' would be an exaggeration. How about solidly mature, and probably definitely crazy? Remember she might not even be using the same name. My dad isn't."

"How many people live at the necropolis?" Meg asked, closing her journal. "Should we expect a thriving community or a few pilgrims?"

"Something in the middle," Xerak replied, pausing to wring out his mop. "There will be enclaves where those who share a philosophical outlook are welcomed, where they can receive counseling as to how to best accomplish their goals. However, the map also shows a small town with stores, a few hotels, transportation services, and the like."

"Ohent is more likely to be living in the town, then," Peg said. "Or at least known there, right?"

Xerak nodded. "Known. Maybe not living in town, though, especially if she's a tomb robber. Neither the enclaves or the town would be convenient for someone who makes her living looting the dead."

"Ohent could have another job," Teg suggested. All this talking about tomb robbers was making her uncomfortable. She knew plenty of people who thought that this was precisely what archeologists did for a living. "Porter. Running a small shop. Maybe working at a hotel. She could still be doing grounds keeping."

"Mom didn't make Ohent sound like the most responsible person," Xerak said, "but maybe she has family who look out for her."

"So, as to scouting for Ohent," Grunwold said, pulling them back to the topic with the same firmness that he used to keep *Slicewind* on course. "How obvious should we be about who we're looking for? Do we go around to the various shops and hotels, and say, 'Hi, we're looking for an o—for a woman in her middle years with a snow leopard's head. She might be a little crazy, and she might answer to the name Ohent.'"

"You forget," Xerak said. "We have the Spindle of Ba Djed. I've kept it in its enshrouding container until now, but when we get to the necropolis, I can take it out and use it to track Ohent—or at least her part of Ba Djed, which is what we really want."

"What's to keep you from having nightmares and going crazy?" Grunwold asked. "You're enough of a problem already."

Xerak shrugged. "I have a theory about those nightmares. I think that Ba Djed resents having been broken apart and stolen. If it realizes that we're trying to help it rejoin, well...I might have visions, but not necessarily nightmares."

"That makes sense," Vereez said, excitement and anger warring in her voice. "Why would it be nice to people who broke it into pieces? I wouldn't be."

And Teg, thinking of a fourteen-year-old who had had her daughter taken from her at birth, understood Vereez's anger was about more than her recent brush with captivity.

"Xerak," Teg asked, "do you think you're the only one who can use the artifact for tracking? You're certainly the most magically trained, but Vereez has some talent, and even I was able to use the sun spider."

She trailed off, not wanting to sound as if she thought she was on par with Xerak. Xerak wasn't offended, though.

"You have a good point, and it would be better if more than one of us could safely associate with the Spindle, if necessary." Xerak turned to Vereez who was now putting away her practice swords. "I've been wondering . . . How much magic did you study?"

"Not much, really," Vereez said with a shrug. "I was told I didn't have much talent, but I picked up a few things here and there, mostly from friends."

"You were told," he repeated, "by . . ."

"My parents," she said, "they said that the tests . . ." She stopped and her ears flattened against her skull. "Oh. My parents. My parents who seem to want me to be nothing more than an ornament. My mother who was apparently a competent wizard when she wasn't much older than I am."

"Don't get pissy," Xerak said, "but I think Inehem was more than competent and, after some of the things you've pulled off in the last few weeks, I think that if you'd received more training, you might be almost as good as I am."

"Almost?" Vereez's ears perked and she put on a haughty expression. "Don't puff yourself up, Tangle Mane. I might be better."

"Maybe," Xerak said in a tone that made clear he didn't believe it.

And I don't think this is arrogance, Teg thought. *I wonder if Xerak's magic is so powerful that it's more a handicap than a benefit. From what he said earlier, about learning to create spells without any formal training, there's no way anyone could have hidden his abilities from him.*

Xerak was continuing. "However, I would be willing—more than—to teach you, and Teg, too. My master said that there's nothing more dangerous than a wizard who suspects he or she has ability and messes around trying to figure out how much and what form it takes."

"Me?" Teg said. "I mean, I managed that sun spider webshooter amulet thingie, but that's different from being a wizard."

"Maybe," Xerak said again. "Maybe not. You certainly got more out of it than any of us expected. We won't know if we don't check. The necropolis is still a day or so's flight from here. Vereez already knows the basics, so she's going to be ahead of you. Still, I might be able to teach you enough that you can at least feed mana into the webshooter thingie, as you call it, without crashing afterward."

Grunwold, who for all his skills in other areas apparently had accepted that he was decidedly unmagically talented, huffed. "And what good will this do any of us? I mean, a couple of days' tutoring might pass the time and keep Teg from stinking up the air with her cigarettes, but do you really expect a couple of novices to be any help?"

"I gave up 'expecting' a long time ago, Grunwold," Xerak said, not bothering to hide his sadness. "Did you expect what has happened to us since you decided to go to with me and Vereez to Hettua Shrine?"

"No. Guess not. Sort of. I mean, I did find a way to help my dad."

"Lucky you," Xerak said, and his voice sounded far older, filled with the many disappointments he usually took care to hide. "And I'm glad. Really. I like Konneltoh. I even like you, most of the time. But if you think the rest of our search is going to suddenly get easy . . ."

"I don't," Grunwold admitted. "Maybe I just wish it

would." He tossed his head, and pointed to the mop, "Now, back to work. Don't think I haven't noticed that you're slacking."

Over the next several days' travel, Teg worked hard with Xerak until she felt confident that she could reliably activate the sun spider amulet. She remained less than confident that being able to do this made her any sort of wizard. Vereez was still boiling over with tension from her parents' attempt to hold her prisoner, so she wasn't in anything like a suitable frame of mind for the quiet meditation exercises that were the only way that Xerak— a novice himself not long ago—knew to test for affinity with various sorts of magic.

One of Teg's lessons was practicing how to get the most out of the sun spider amulet's webshooter ability.

"Since the amulet has a limited ability to convert mana into webbing," Xerak explained, "targeting is crucial. I've set a target on the stern locker. Let's see what your optimum distance for accuracy is."

"And don't miss and gum up my woodwork," called Grunwold from the wheel.

"Aye, aye, Captain," Teg shouted back, then concentrated.

She was so tightly focused on the amulet and the target that she didn't see the cat until he pounced directly on the newly created strand, then squalled in indignation when he discovered his paws were now stuck to the webbing.

"Thought!" she exclaimed in automatic indignation, then repeated more slowly. "Thought?"

Xerak was staring in blank astonishment. Grunwold

turned from the wheel. Meg and Vereez looked up from their respective books. Only Peg, down in the galley doing something miraculous for dinner, wasn't aware that something remarkable had happened.

"Thought?" Xerak repeated. "What is a 'thought'?"

The longhaired grey-brown tabby hissed at him, clearly blaming Xerak for the condition of his paws. Teg made a quick motion that severed the strand from the amulet, then dropped the amulet into her pocket as she hurried across the deck to confirm that the new arrival was indeed her cat. Any doubt she might have had—which was minimal—vanished when Memory in all her shorthaired golden glory began weaving herself between Teg's ankles, definitely pleased with herself.

"Thought," Teg said to Xerak, recognizing from his inflection that the translation spell had—as was often the case with names—not translated the word, so the leonine wizard was not being suddenly philosophical, "is one of my cats. Memory, here,"—she pointed with an elbow—"is the other."

Vereez who had, Teg suspected, been brooding, not reading, set her book down and hurried over, looking livelier than she had since they had returned from her escape.

"It is, isn't it? I remember seeing them in your apartment. Hey, there. Remember me? Let me help you with that nasty stuff on your toes."

Vereez made a little gesture with two fingers and something between a large spark and a tiny lightning bolt shot out and hit the clump of webbing, causing it to dry and crumble.

"Does that feel better?" she crooned. Thought, after glancing reproachfully at Teg, rubbed against Vereez's extended hand.

"Cats?" Xerak said. "Are those animals from your world? They look sort of creepy."

Teg reflected that, in a world where the animal-headed people seemed to draw their types from her world's wildlife, a creature with what Xerak would see as a "person's" head would indeed be creepy. Unlike most domestic animals, cats were definitely closer to their wild counterparts. Grey-brown, longhaired Thought was close to a lynx or bobcat. Shorthaired, golden Memory might be a little lioness or puma.

"I think they're darling," Vereez said. "How did they get here?"

"Good question," Teg said, plopping down onto the deck and letting Memory climb into her lap.

"Is this the first time?" Meg asked.

"Yes . . . Wait!" Teg stopped. "After I fell off the ledge, down to where we found the doors into the Library, when I came around, I thought they were with me. Later, they were gone, and I thought I'd been hallucinating. Since then, there have been times, especially when I was asleep, that I thought one or the other was sleeping with me—they do at home—but I put that down to sort of muscle memory or to my brain making excuses for how it feels different to sleep in a bunk on a moving ship."

Heru soared down from his perch up on one of the crosstrees and landed on Grunwold's shoulder. From there, he leaned down, studying the two housecats with a mixture of interest and apprehension. Thought studied him back, yellow-green eyes narrowing in predatory speculation.

"Don't even think about it, bucko," Teg advised him. "That xuxu isn't one of your rubber dinosaurs."

Thought huffed, then, tail high, strutted over to her. Teg reached out and stroked him, picking the last of the dried web goo from between his fluffy toes.

"How do you think they're getting here?" she asked.

Meg pointed to the legs of Teg's cargo pants, which were now lightly adorned with cat fur. "When we made our bracelets, we created the yarn by rubbing the combined fur and hair against our trouser legs. I wouldn't be in the least surprised if you inadvertently mixed in some cat hair when you made yours."

"It's as good a theory as any I can come up with," Xerak admitted. "We've wondered over and over why people from your world came in answer to our summoning spell. As far as we know, you're the first, at least for Hettua Shrine. There aren't even legends about people like you. But there must be a connection, and maybe your cats are exploiting that. You haven't been back as often as Meg or Peg, but you were recently there with Vereez."

"Maybe that made them curious," Vereez said, looking pleased. "Or maybe your studying magic so diligently did something they could exploit. But I'm with Meg. I bet it has something to do with the bracelet."

Teg looked at her bracelet, wondering which of the metallic strands might be transformed cat fur. Then she shrugged.

"Well, as long as you folks don't mind, I certainly don't.

I know time passes more quickly here than there, but I have felt bad about leaving them alone so much."

There were general noises of welcome, and one annoyed squawk from Heru. After that, for the rest of the voyage, Thought and Memory bopped in and out on some schedule of their own, vanishing with equal ease, even sometimes when they seemed to be enjoying themselves quite a lot.

"I bet your cat sitter is due," Peg speculated, laughing. "I've never known a house cat whose tummy clock wasn't set to meal time."

Teg was in the *Slicewind*'s bow, taking advantage of a strong tailwind to smoke an actual cigarette, rather than her marginally more acceptable pipe, when the necropolis came into view. At first she couldn't believe her eyes, thinking that this must be an optical illusion.

She motioned for Peg, who was knitting nearby, to come up and join her. "Do you see what I see?"

As she came forward, Peg had started singing the Christmas song, but she broke off with "way up in the sky ..." Her mouth hung open in an "oh" of delight and disbelief. "Meg! Stop scribbling in that book. You've got to see this!"

Meg closed her journal and hurried forward. She looked along the line of Teg's pointing arm, then started. "Pyramids! A desert with ranks of dozens, maybe hundreds of pyramids!"

"What did you expect?" Grunwold asked from the wheel. "We said we were going to a necropolis."

"In our world," Meg retorted tartly, "there are as many

different forms of burial and burial art as there are religions and cultures. However, some of the most famous are the Egyptian pyramids. This necropolis makes the grouping at Giza seem a poor example indeed."

Xerak padded forward to join them. "This is an impressive group. My understanding is that pyramids are preferred for mausoleums because they channel and enhance energy. That makes them useful for sending messages to spirits that have not yet been reincarnated."

"That makes sense," Peg said, "but do they sharpen razor blades?"

Xerak blinked his large golden eyes at her. "I've never asked. Do they in your world?"

"Some people claim they do," Peg said. "My first husband, Don, had a little pyramid he swore kept his razor blades sharper than if they just stayed in the box. Of course, he also claimed that if he wore a special hat, his favorite teams would be more likely to win."

"Did they?" Xerak asked.

"Not that I ever noticed."

"Is that the town you mentioned?" Teg said, indicating a cluster of buildings along the necropolis's easternmost edge with a river visible beyond.

"That's it," Xerak said. "See down there, over to the west just a little? That would be one of the enclaves. Given the blue roof tiles and the irregularly spaced obelisks, I'd say that's the Banquet of the Past. They're one of the groups that claims that the proper rituals will assure that the dead remember more of their past lives and abilities. Over there is probably dedicated to the Posthumous Reminders."

"Big place," Peg said. "I'm guessing those Banquet of the Past people do very well, whether or not they get results. Is there a special reason this necropolis is in a desert? I ask because the culture Meg mentioned—the Egyptians—also built their pyramids in the desert."

Vereez said, "Useless real estate. Cheaper, and no one is likely to try and take the place over."

"If you wouldn't mind stopping gawking," Grunwold called, "I'm going to be bringing *Slicewind* down. Get to your stations. I may need you to work the sails."

Despite his request, Grunwold didn't need the least bit of help. He had chosen to bring them in near a sort of RV park between the edge of town and the river, where an eclectic and improbable selection of vehicles were berthed. Teg stared in fascination at a gigantic dinosaur-like creature that seemed right out of *Star Wars*; a stagecoach drawn by deep-chested, axe-beaked avians; a floating craft that reminded her of a banana-split dish suspended between four round, fat balloons.

In comparison to these, *Slicewind* looked positively normal.

After Grunwold glided their ship onto the river for a nearly splash-free landing, Vereez insisted on using her credit line to pay for a berth several days in advance. Teg guessed Vereez was waiting to see if her request was refused, which would be a good indication of how her parents felt about her recent behavior. However, if they'd cut her off, the bank branch here hadn't been informed, and Vereez seemed to think the bank would have known.

They'd decided to live aboard *Slicewind*, rather than taking rooms in a hotel. Not only would this make concealing the three humans' abnormalities easier, but people would be less likely to notice their comings and goings. On the day they arrived, there was time enough for Xerak to use some of his searching spells to check both the town itself and a couple of the closer enclaves, but the Spindle provided no indication that the Bird was anywhere nearby.

Although he made light of it, Xerak was clearly worn out by the arcane search. Not even Grunwold—who liked to tease both Vereez and Xerak for being content to take it easy when he would have been out and about—pushed Xerak to try harder. Instead, Grunwold worked off his excess energy by taking the three humans on a tour of a showier portion of the great necropolis.

Vereez stayed behind—to study, so she'd said—but really, although no one actually mentioned it, to watch Xerak as he slept, in case the nightmares Konnel had told them about manifested after his recent use of the Spindle. So far, the necropolis's neutralizing ability seemed to be working, but since Xerak's scrying would be actively working against the charms and wards that permeated the area, no one expected this to last.

Given Grunwold's still-apparent crush on Vereez, Teg wondered that he didn't object at the attention she was lavishing on the other young man.

But maybe he's being smart. Her moods have been all over the place since we left Rivers Meet. Better to bide his time until she's not so prickly or inclined to burst into tears.

The necropolis proved to be a fascinating place. From the air, it had seemed like Giza on a grand scale, complete with a river to double for the Nile and ample sand. Up close, the differences were more apparent. Unlike the Egyptian pyramids, most of which had long ago lost their ornamental exterior stonework, on these it was intact. However, the architects had not been interested in smooth, polished exteriors. Instead, every pyramid—no matter whether a towering structure many stories high or a small building, not much larger than Teg's modest house—was finished with carved panels.

"Even I can see this isn't like Egyptian art," Peg said. "The bodies are more naturally done—not so much of that twisting of the torso, head in profile stuff—but there are similarities. I can't put my finger on what."

"I suspect some of the apparent similarities," Meg offered, "may be a result of the medium. Carving into stone can limit certain elements and make perspective more difficult. Nonetheless, I do understand what you mean. They do 'feel,' if not Egyptian, then Middle Eastern."

"Part of the Egyptian feeling comes from the loving detail lavished on what we'd think of as unimportant elements," Teg offered. "Plants and animals, especially, are given so much attention. I'm reminded of Babylonian carving as well. There's a muscular vitality to so many of the people and animals."

Later, when Grunwold went off to buy them all cool drinks, Peg said, "I didn't want to talk about this in front of the inquisitors, but do you think that these buildings were influenced by our world?"

"Possibly," Teg replied, "but what about the reverse? The Middle East is where some of the oldest human civilizations grew up—and not only the Egyptians, but the Babylonians, as well, often had animal-headed creatures in their mythology. If it wasn't for the art, I'd say it's just a universal human desire, a need to connect to people like, but not like, us. What if that desire has its roots in a time when there were people like us but not like us who visited?"

"Very Jungian," Meg said. "A collective unconscious memory of actual events, rather than of archetypes? I doubt we shall ever know. Even if there was a connection, it was a long, long time ago, and, for all their magic, this world's records don't seem to be any better than ours."

"Wait," Peg said. "Don't our records go back thousands of years?"

Meg smiled gently, and Teg chuckled.

"Yes and no," Meg said. "They do, but are fragmented."

Teg nodded vigorous agreement. "The more we learn, the more what those 'records' mean is reshaped. Every culture tends to interpret those that came before in the context of their own present."

"Got it," Peg said. "Some of the things I've read about, say, what the sixties were like are completely different from my experience, but if only one issue of, oh, *Life* magazine survived, that would be taken as canon."

"And that's just a few decades ago," Meg said. "Imagine the distortions that could happen over centuries."

The following day, Xerak was up and eager to be about. Based on some vague dreams, he suggested they move their search into an area that was undergoing a peculiar sort of gentrification. Since the spirit was believed—

known, Teg reminded herself—to be immortal, no special reverence was paid to long-dead bodies. General belief (and this *was* belief, not certainty) held that a spirit was usually reincarnated within a century.

Therefore, if after a century had passed, a particular tomb had gone unvisited or the funds for its care had been exhausted, the area could be purchased by a new client. Sometimes the old pyramid was refurbished; sometimes it was completely razed and a new, grander structure erected in its place. This explained why, even though the necropolis had been in use for centuries, the structures were in such good condition.

The district in which Xerak slowed and finally halted was dominated by an enclave whose teachings had become unpopular in the last few decades. Grunwold called it the Enclave of Eternal Nagging. Xerak offered the more official name: Posthumous Reminders.

"Their creed goes something like this," Grunwold said. They had, so Xerak could do his search spells without being quite so obvious, retired to the shade of one of the many gazebos that were built in the intersections of roads within the necropolis. "You die, but you've forgotten to tell your family something—like where the good silver is hidden or something. These people claimed to be able to help you contact the spirit of the departed—the more recently departed the better—and help you get an answer to your question. The answer comes in the form of dreams, which—if you can't figure out what they mean for yourself—they promise to help you interpret."

"And this is unpopular why?" Peg asked. "I'd think these people would be minting money."

"About thirty years ago," Vereez said, "that's how it was. See how grand these pyramids are? Families were entombing everyone here, so they could consult them not just for the sort of things Grunwold was talking about, but about bigger issues. In some cases, it was as if the dead continued running their families, even after they should have been getting ready for their next lives."

"I bet the field was split on that one," Peg said. "Some people must have loved having the status quo maintained, while others must have felt as if they were in a choke hold."

Xerak was lying on the gazebo's stone floor, replenishing his strength with what he said was watered wine, although from the aroma, a lot of the water must have evaporated in the heat.

"That was one problem," he said. "Another was the serious issue of whether spirits were resisting rebirth because—even if they did manage to be born into the same family—they didn't want to risk a demotion or loss of influence."

Meg gave a thin smile. "I can imagine how that was received. Didn't you say that many of these enclaves base their philosophies around whether a reincarnated spirit can remember some aspect or ability from its past? They wouldn't have liked this resistance to moving on at all."

"Resources were getting tied up, too," Vereez said. "People would claim that something couldn't be sold or repurposed or whatever because the not-yet-reincarnated spirit had forbidden it. Up to that point, property rights had automatically passed at death. Now those laws were being challenged."

"Who knows what would have happened?" Grunwold

said. "In the end, though, the enclave lost influence in a single day."

He glanced at Xerak, as if expecting he'd take up the tale, but the young wizard had put aside his wineskin, taken up the Spindle, and pressed it to his chest, his hands folded over it, both to conceal it and to channel its vital force. His eyes were half-shut but, by now, they all knew the difference between drowsing and scrying.

"Xerak could tell you better than I can how it was done," Grunwold went on. "Some wizards were involved. I know that much. But I guess the end result is all that really matters. They demonstrated absolutely that the Eternal Nags were cheating—not always, but enough and on some really crucial points."

"The credibility of the cult of Posthumous Reminders was shot," Vereez agreed. "My parents..." Her voice stumbled, but she went on determinedly casual. "My parents always held this up as a test case for how important it was not to attempt to alter reality to one's own advantage."

Peg asked, "Seems as if the Eternal Nags are doing better these days, or is this some other sect moving in?"

"They're recovering," Grunwold said. "The scandal is receding. The faction that survived the purge has had time to get across the idea that just because some of their members got greedy and cheated, that doesn't mean they're all greedy cheats."

Xerak groaned and shoved himself up to a sitting position. "I've done as much as I can from here. We'll head west and north, toward the interior of this quadrant. Then I can try again."

As they walked, it became evident that they were

moving into one of the areas where a lot of construction was going on.

"Y'know," Grunwold said, "if my dad's old friend has taken to reselling artifacts, this would be the sort of place I'd expect to find her."

"Isn't anyone monitoring the construction sites?" Teg asked, horrified.

"A monitor can't be everywhere," Xerak said. "And if someone . . . Vereez? What's wrong?"

The young woman had pulled up short and was now dropping back to where she would be partially hidden.

"I think I've spotted your 'someone,'" she said very softly. "Remember how I told you that our parents' old friend looked maybe a little familiar? She visited our house a few years ago, brought her son with her. Over there, with the head of an African painted dog, pushing a wheelbarrow. That's him. That's Kaj."

Canine head or not, Kaj exuded a raw sensuality that Teg found herself reacting to. *Not too old and dry,* she thought, laughing at herself. *I wonder if I should trade my lynx mask in for a cougar.*

Kaj was working shirtless, showing off a muscular human-shaped torso whose light fur—hardly more than natural human body hair—followed the golden brown into darker browns and blacks just touched with the white of his canine head's longer head hair.

Where Grunwold and Xerak were still somewhat gangly and boyish, Kaj was definitely a man. If several years ago, when he'd seduced Vereez, he'd exuded this same raw masculinity, Teg found it unbelievable that

Inehem and Zarrq hadn't been more careful to chaperone their daughter.

But maybe she was still their little girl to them, he just the son of someone they'd known since they were hardly more than kids themselves. It's amazing how often it's the ones who were wild themselves who overlook that their children are growing up.

"That's Ohent's son?" Xerak said, perking up. "Wow! He doesn't take after his mother, does he?"

"He does in a way," Peg said. "He shares with the younger her we saw in the vision a confidence in his body—and an awareness of its impact on others."

"Do we talk to him here?" Meg asked. "Perhaps wait until he is on break? Or would it be better if we attempted to follow him back to where he's staying and confirm that Ohent is also there? Parents and their grown children do not automatically live together."

"Good point," Xerak said. "I'll track him. Grunwold looks too much like his father. Kaj might recognize Vereez, and you three with your masks would be immediately noticeable."

"Promise not to go talk to him or Ohent without us?" Vereez demanded.

"Promise."

"I'll have Heru stay near you," Grunwold said, stepping back into cover, then waving for the mini pterodactyl to come down and join them. "That way if you need to send a message, you can do so."

No one said, "Or if something happens to you, he can let us know," but from the rapid nods it was evident that everyone was thinking it.

Xerak didn't protest. He started to wave the rest of them back, then stopped. He took out the small pouch in which he had been carrying the enshrouding container that held the Spindle and handed it to Meg.

"You folks had better keep this. We already know that Ohent was once an extraction agent. I don't want to risk her trying to take this from me."

Meg nodded and tucked the enshrouding container away. "Good thinking. Are you certain you're not too worn out from scrying to track?"

"I'll be fine," Xerak assured her. "My plan is to find a nice shady spot and wait. Since Heru is staying with me, he can follow this guy—what's his name again, Vereez?"

"Kaj." The single syllable came out so clipped and tight that Teg didn't think she was the only one to notice the tension in it.

"Right. Kaj. Heru can follow Kaj if his work takes him out of my line of sight. We'll be fine. Go back to *Slicewind* and rest."

They did. The humans went below, where they could take off their masks. Grunwold stayed on deck, doing things with sails and lines to pass the time. Vereez vanished into the tiny cabin near the mast that had been assigned to her and closed the door firmly behind her.

"Whoo-hoo," Peg said softly. "A little drama there, I think. A past crush?"

"No doubt," Meg said. "And even I am not so old as to wonder at it. This Kaj is a most elegant specimen."

Teg only nodded, feeling silence was the best way to make sure she didn't let even a little of Vereez's secret slip out. She wanted a smoke badly but, although it had been agreed that she could risk taking off her mask above decks after dark, as long as she stayed below the side rails, daylight had been deemed too risky. She took out her pipe and stared at it, estimating the hours.

"Really," Meg said, "I must admire how tenaciously you cling to an unpleasant habit. Here you have had a wonderful opportunity to give it up."

"I don't see you giving up coffee," Teg said, for, as with the pipe weed Xerak had found for her, the local "poffee" was close enough to substitute for coffee, "or Peg her knitting."

"Neither of which will contribute to our risk for lung cancer or a host of other ills," Meg replied with an analytic calm that was worse than any more emotional rebuke. "However, we can't have you edgy later. Perhaps you could put on that hooded sweatshirt Vereez wore upon your return and go above."

"Thanks, Meg. I just might."

Grunwold only rolled his eyes—a very expressive gesture with his huge brown deer's eyes—and moved to cover her when she crept up the ladder.

"Wind's off the starboard quarter," he said, "so if you sit behind that sail locker, it should carry the smell away."

She did, relaxing and puffing at her pipe. Eventually it went out and she dozed, waking only when Heru announced his return with a loud, raucous squawk through his crest, before shifting to words. Maybe because he'd had a lot of practice this trip, his speech was much clearer.

Or maybe I just understand better, Teg thought. *Weird, now that I think about it. Why didn't the translation spell*

simply compensate for Heru's different pronunciations?
Is it because it was important that we understand that, for
Heru, this is a learned language, that he has an accent the
others do not?

"Xerak says, 'Come at twilight, where this wonderful
xuxu, so wise, so elegant, so filled with clever
thoughts—'"

"Yeah, right. Sure he said that," Grunwold interrupted.

"He did! He did! I insisted on the form!!"

"I bet you did. Where are we supposed to go?"

"To the vicinity of the cottage of the groundskeeper for
the enclave of the Eternal Nagging, the Posthumous
Reminders. There is an abandoned cottage nearby where
Xerak will wait. I have seen it, I can show. Xerafu Akeru,
wizard most powerful, asks that you bring for him a
change of attire—the turquoise robes with scarlet trim,
he says, since he is not at his best after a long day in the
dust. Also, his comb and brush, which are in the blue-
dyed leather case."

The others had emerged from belowdecks as soon as
they heard Heru's voice, and now Peg said, "I know which
ones Xerak wants. Our boy's a definite dandy lion, isn't
he? But he has a good point. We should dress to make an
impression."

⁅CHAPTER THIRTEEN⁆

Going out at twilight all dressed up did not attract any comment. Many of the enclaves held receptions in the evening hours. Vereez insisted on paying for them to take a carriage to within a short walk of their destination, saying that if they were going to try to make a good impression, they shouldn't undo it by arriving with their hems inches deep in dust.

All of them had taken care to look their best, but Vereez was particularly elegant, so elegant that the simple floral broach she wore pinned to her collar seemed tawdry by contrast.

I bet Kaj gave her that. What's the message she's sending? Teg thought. *"Look. I've kept your token all these years?" Or, "See how cheap this is in comparison to my wealth?" Maybe Vereez doesn't even know herself. She says he never wrote her or visited, so even admitting she still has it says more than she may realize.*

Maybe Vereez had had a similar insight for, when they ducked inside the abandoned cottage where Xerak was

363

waiting, Teg noticed that the broach was gone, and a much more suitable ornament had been pinned in its place.

Xerak briefed them as he changed. "Kaj left work, then came pretty much directly home. I let Heru do the close following, so I doubt he knew he was being observed. I've been watching since I sent Heru to get you. It's possible someone could have slipped out the back, but I don't think so."

"Walled garden!" Heru added. "Not much used. Cluttered!"

"Which house are we talking about?" Grunwold asked, making shushing noises at the xuxu, who came over and nipped one of Grunwold's antlers in pretend protest. "Wouldn't they have seen us come here?"

Xerak shook his head. "Kaj's place is over there, that house with the faded blue paint. Looks to me as if, when the Posthumous Reminders were doing well, they built an extended complex, probably for servants or maybe for supplicants they wanted to stay nearby. Except for the one Kaj went into, all the houses are empty now. I chose this one because it has a good view of the blue house, but neither the doors or windows of this place should be easily visible from over there."

He indicated the window he stood near. It was partially overgrown with a flowering creeper that reminded Teg of honeysuckle, although the leaves were glossier and the flowers a bright purple.

"If one of you wants to take over for me," Xerak continued, "I'll finish getting ready. Maybe Heru would watch the back door again?"

"On it, wiz," Heru said, tweaking Grunwold's ear and

flying out the door. Teg noticed that the mini pterodactyl carefully circled around, keeping to cover. Vereez promptly moved to take over Xerak's post at the window.

Xerak enlisted Peg's help getting his mane untangled and properly combed. While this was being done, they finalized their plans. Vereez insisted that she be the one to take point.

"After all, I've met Ohent, even if I didn't realize how important she was then. Who knows? Maybe she'll think I'm bringing her more money from my parents."

"Doubt it," Xerak said. "For all Inehem and Zarrq are wealthy, they're letter-of-the-contract types. Ohent would be more likely to believe my mother was sending her payment for some consignment."

"But," Vereez retorted, "as far as Ohent knows, you know nothing about the more, uh, 'colorful' part of your mother's business."

"If you two don't stop bickering," Grunwold said, "I'm going to race over there, bang on the door myself and tell Ohent—if she's even there—to hand over the Bird. You'd think you were hoping to marry the woman!"

Vereez couldn't blush, but the flickering melt of her ears gave away something of her embarrassment. What was interesting was how Xerak's gaze dropped to the floor and how he nervously straightened his collar.

Oh . . . Teg thought. *That's interesting. I wonder.*

Peg's eyebrows rose, but she didn't comment, only ran the wide-toothed comb one last time through Xerak's mane. "There, young man, you're presentable again. How about Vereez first, with you behind? You're taller than her anyhow."

"Get a foot in the door," Grunwold advised. "Or your spear staff, Xerak. We can't be sure of our welcome."

When Vereez knocked on the worn wood of the door, no one answered for longer than seemed reasonable given the apparent size of the dwelling. She was about to knock again when the door swung open.

Kaj stood there, still bare chested. His work trousers had been replaced by a pair of pants cut off at midthigh and left unhemmed. He held a wooden spoon in one hand. A fragrant aroma, not unlike curry mingled with apple, drifted out around him.

He stared at their elegantly attired group for a long moment, his gaze lingering on the three masked humans, then returning to Vereez.

"Yes?" he began, then stopped. "Vereez? Is that you?"

Kaj's surprise was genuine, uncolored by either shame or pleasure. His only emotion seemed to be a hint of chagrin at being found so informally dressed, occupied with such a domestic task.

"Did you bring a message from your parents?" he asked, motioning for the group to come inside, then closing the door. "My mother is . . . sleeping. If you'll wait in the front room, I'll see if I can wake her."

Vereez had entered when invited, paused as if hoping for some additional recognition, but when none came, she moved into the front room as directed. Based on the elegant moldings and ceiling ornamentation, the room had probably once been an elegant receiving parlor, but now it clearly served as what Teg had grown up thinking of as a "sitting room." There were two comfortable chairs, each with reading material piled up next to them.

On his way out, Kaj paused to light an oil lantern that hung where it would give each chair equal illumination.

Sitting in either of those chairs—so clearly the private terrain of the residents—would have seemed an invasion. Wordlessly, Grunwold cleared a padded wooden bench of an assortment of jackets, sweaters, and pillows to make space enough for the three humans. Vereez took a seat on a large ottoman, started pleating the hem of her tunic, realized she was doing so, then sat unnaturally still. Xerak lounged gracefully onto the floor, while Grunwold— refusing Peg's mute suggestion that he clear off another stool—leaned against the doorframe.

They could hear Kaj mounting creaking wooden stairs, bare feet padding, then the soft murmur of voices. Vereez's and Grunwold's ears both visibly pricked, but judging from their disappointed expressions, they couldn't make out what was being said. Eventually, one pair of footsteps descended the staircase.

"My mother is making herself . . . presentable," Kaj said. "If you don't mind, I need to get back to my cooking."

"Do you need . . ." "Can I . . ." Vereez and Xerak spoke simultaneously.

Kaj looked bemused. "I've got it covered. Do you want water or something? No? Then excuse me."

He left, pointedly closing the kitchen door behind him.

"I was only . . ." "I simply thought . . ." Again Vereez and Xerak spoke over each other.

The ease with which they could hear footsteps overhead, and Kaj rattling and clinking in the kitchen, made the visitors unwilling to talk, so they sat quietly, their finery a glaring contrast to the shabby respectability of their surroundings.

"Maybe . . ." Xerak was beginning, when creaking stair treads announced Ohent's descent.

Head to toe, she was concealed beneath a veil draped over her head, drifting down in loose folds to brush against the floor. The fabric balanced on the cusp between opaque and translucent, the dusty lavender, almost grey, material revealing that there was indeed someone beneath, but obscuring details. Tiny copper disks weighted the edges, ringing softly against each other with each step.

Ohent entered the room with a cautious tread, as if not trusting the floor would still be there each time she raised and lowered her foot. When Grunwold pulled back to give her room to pass, the shadow in the shawl paused to look at him for longer than seemed necessary, then ghosted to settle in the chair nearer to the window.

"I was dreaming," she said. "Not of you, or so I thought. Maybe of you. Why have you come here? Kaj thought you might have brought money. I do not think this is so. This is not the time for money, and it was made clear to me long ago that time will matter."

Vereez took a deep breath, then spoke. "I don't know if you remember me. I am Vereez, daughter of Inehem and Zarrq. There, in the doorway, is Grunwold, son of Konnel. Down there on the floor, the wizard, he's Xerak, son of Fardowsi."

"You may remember me better as Senehem," Xerak said. "That's the name my parents gave me."

"Little Senehem, become Xerafu Akeru, the undutiful

son, the dutiful apprentice. Ah, yes. I have heard . . . What
brings you three here, children of my old friends, my not-
quite enemies? And are you not to introduce the three
masked ones? They are not your parents, that much I can
smell. Beneath the perfumes and incense, their scent is a
little . . . odd."

"Show her the letters," Grunwold suggested gruffly.
"From my dad and Xerak's mom."

Vereez removed copies from the neat, embossed
leather folder she had carried. The hand that not-quite
emerged from beneath the veil was gloved, the tips
perforated so that fingernails—or claw tips—could
emerge. Ohent snagged the folded letters, unfolded them,
and turned toward the lantern light to better read what
was written there.

"Konnel says you have a tale to tell that will interest
me, a request to make that he urges me to grant. I taste
relief in his script. Fardowsi is less pleased, but she, too,
urges me to listen, to aid. Shall I?"

Her question was addressed as much to the air as to
any of them, but Vereez said softly, urgently, "Please. We'd
be grateful if you did."

"How grateful, I wonder? Only one thing connects me
to those two, to the other two who are conspicuous in that
their treasured only child is here but no scented missive
on heavy paper. Only one thing . . . Why after so long?"

"If you'd listen to what we have to tell you," Grunwold
said impatiently, "you'd know."

"You have your father's looks, from back when I first
met him, but your mother's manner. Still, I am curious.
There, I have admitted it. Tell me your tale."

Ohent let the letters slide to the floor, settled back in her chair with a rustling of fabric, jingling of thin copper disks. Then, as Xerak—who had been chosen in advance to start the story—opened his mouth, Ohent raised one hand to stop him.

"Kaj! Take the pot off the stove and come here. I know you will listen, you might as well be present."

The kitchen door opened and Kaj padded in. He carried a tray on which rested a fat, round pitcher that beaded moisture, and a selection of mismatched, although quite elegant, glasses.

"Zinz tea," he said shortly. "Talking's dry work." He set the tray down, poured for himself and his mother. "Help yourselves. There's more."

Xerak acted as if this barely civil offer was courtesy itself and, after pouring himself a cup, began the increasingly polished account of how they had gone to Hettua Shrine, and what had happened thereafter. As in other tellings, at the appropriate point the humans were introduced. Ohent and Kaj only nodded, accepting this evidence, and Vereez took up the tale.

When Grunwold told how they'd stolen *Slicewind*, Ohent chuckled appreciatively, but that was the only reaction from either mother or son through the account of how they'd searched for the door into the Library, and how Sapphire Wind had revealed the role that Ohent and her fellow extraction agents had played in the Library's destruction. They ended with Xerak explaining how Sapphire Wind had insisted that without the return of Ba Djed of the Weaver, it would have great difficulty supplying answers to the inquisitors' questions.

Throughout the long and sometimes erratic retelling, Teg watched Kaj carefully. She was getting better at reading the reactions of people who had animal heads. They didn't blush or flush or pale, true, but their ears gave away a lot, and Kaj's ears were large, along the lines of a wolf's or fox's, rather than small and buried in a mane like Xerak's. Also, their eyes narrowed in apprehension, widened in surprise, just as a human's did. If she was reading him right, Kaj was not surprised by this story—not even the bit about how his mother had been part of the destruction of the Library.

The three inquisitors had taken charge of telling those parts of the tale that specifically applied to them. Xerak and Grunwold had hidden little, but Vereez had chosen not to tell how her parents had attempted to take her prisoner, nor, precisely, what her personal holdback was, only that her parents had not approved and that was why she had no letter from them.

"So . . ." Ohent said. "Bribery helped sway Konnel. Threats worked to persuade Fardowsi. But nothing would sway Inehem and Zarrq. I need to consider that, don't I, dear son?"

"Yes, Mother." There was a weight of old arguments behind those two words.

Ohent turned her attention to the three inquisitors and their mentors. "So, you have come here to request that I give you the portion of Ba Djed—that's what you called it, right?—that I hold in trust, so that you may go back to the Library of the Sapphire Wind and receive the guidance you seek."

"That's right, Ohent-lial," Xerak said.

"I," she said, in apparent non sequitur, "have dreamed of stolen lore, of an ever watchful, blank-eyed guardian. For more than twenty long years, I have dreamt that. Now I know why. Calling, calling, calling . . . Can you tell me why I dream of darkness, of dust, of scents that I have never even imagined, that I have never smelled in the waking world? Of beaten gold and polished glass, of carved stone creatures with the faces of . . . Hmm . . . With the faces of hound-nosed cats, whiskerless, hairless but for where they are too, too horribly hairy, silken threads coursing like water, erupting . . ."

She began to laugh maniacally. Kaj rose, went into the kitchen, came back with a weird rattle, an egg-shaped thing that held all manner of oddities encased in fine mesh wire. He shook this right next to where, obscured by the veil, Ohent's ears should be. The noise was like nothing Teg had ever imagined, cacophonic harmony, a hint of a pattern lurking beneath raw, abrasive noise.

Kaj folded his ears close to his head, but otherwise gave them no warning. They waited, hands pressed to their ears. As Teg's head was splitting and she was about to bolt from the room, Ohent's hysteria began to ebb. Kaj shook the rattle more violently, then, when he saw Ohent was calming, left without comment, presumably to stow the noxious rattle somewhere.

"Is she often like this?" Xerak asked horrified, when Kaj returned.

"Just about every day," Kaj said. "It's better for Mother if she's either completely drugged when she sleeps—so far under that she has no sense even of time—or if she doesn't sleep at all. Otherwise, she dreams of things, of events. I'm not sure what she sees that upsets her so much, but there's no question that after a point she becomes unable to handle whatever it is."

"My mother," Xerak said, "thought that the dreams were Ba Djed insisting on being reassembled. Does your mother cope better when she's awake?"

"Better," Kaj replied, "unless something causes her to remember, then she can go off..." He shrugged, wordlessly saying *as you saw just now*.

"What did that rattle do?" Peg asked.

"Grounded Mother in the here and now," Kaj answered. "It took a long time to figure out the best way. Sound seems to do it, but the sound we need is so abrasive that... Well, let's just say that Mother's peculiar therapy is one of the reasons we're living here in a near ruin on the edge of a necropolis."

Ohent had been sitting very still, but now she stirred. "I am not so much insane as besieged, but there are times when the walls I have built collapse and I am mad. I admit it. I have difficulty holding a job that involves working with others, for I do not know who will say what that will demolish my frail fortifications. Thus the once great 'extraction agent' is reduced to laboring as a groundskeeper in such a sorry place. But my pathetic plight is not what brought you here. You came to take from me the Bird that I have given more than two decades of my life to caging. I am wondering what my price should be."

"I thought you'd be glad to be rid of it," Grunwold said in exasperation.

"Perhaps I should be, but for decades now my life has

been defined by this role. And what would I do without the support payments? My health is ruined by the drugs I take to sleep or to keep from sleeping. I am no longer young and lithe and strong, so even if some old friend"—her gaze lingered on Xerak—"might hire me to acquire trinkets for her store, say, I would not be able to take on high-paying jobs for a long while, maybe never. My son has already taken up grave robbing. Shall I ask him to add more crimes to that merely to support his mother?"

Kaj looked uncomfortable at this blunt admission of his side activities, but not in the least ashamed.

"Your father, Grunwold, was paid in miracles for his assistance," Ohent stated. "Why should I take less?"

Grunwold lowered his head so that his antlers pointed forward. "That's the second time you've accused my father of being bribed. My father didn't demand miracles, and you know it. We would like your help, but I'm not going to stand here and listen to you . . ."

Ohent laughed, a cracked, shrill sound. "Peace, little buckling. Peace. I am glad Konnel will have a chance at recovery. I am sorry he will not be cured. We were . . . very close for a time. Although, well before the time we accepted the Library extraction job, that intimacy had ended, we parted friends. But Konnel's recovery does not profit me, nor my son."

Ohent ran a fingertip claw up and down the copper disks along the edge of her veil, so they chimed musically, and fell silent.

"Do you want money?" Vereez asked. "Even if my parents view their part of the bargain settled, I might be able to pay you. I have some small money of my own."

"Invested, no doubt, by them, and so easily 'lost,'" Ohent said.

Vereez's ears flickered back. Apparently, although she had dreaded her parents putting her on short allowance, she hadn't anticipated this.

"Nonetheless," Vereez continued defiantly. "We three, we'd promise to do what we could to give you some financial support."

Xerak and Grunwold nodded tacit consent to this informal contract.

"That's sweet," Ohent said, and there was no sarcasm in the words. "But I think that Kaj and I could do quite well on the stipend, especially if I didn't need to take so many drugs. I think there's something I would like more than money or security."

Vereez leaned forward, ears perked. "Yes?"

"I want my granddaughter."

Kaj looked confused. Vereez's ears pinned back flat.

The room became so completely silent that even the chitter of some sort of night creature in the not-quite honeysuckle seemed loud.

"You know?"

"I know."

"They *told* you?"

"They did not, but I know my son. He has his virtues, many of them, but keeping his—hands—off pretty girls, especially pretty girls who adore him and follow him about, has never been one of his gifts. Your parents might have turned a blind eye to your pursuit of Kaj. They hated having me visit, you know, because they feared a chance word from me might give away upon what foundations their House of Fortune had been built. When Fardowsi mentioned that she was surprised that you'd been sent away to study, given how your parents adored you, I made some inquiries. I am not what I was, but I still have friends."

"Oh . . ." Vereez's gaze was fixed to the worn carpet.

"So your 'sister' is . . ." Grunwold said, his voice terribly soft, holding no trace of its usual acerbity.

"My daughter," Vereez said, trying to sound blunt, but only managing to show how sad she was. "I've never even seen her. They took . . ."

She started weeping. Teg paused, wondering if Kaj would react, but he stood frozen, apparently stunned by this revelation. She slipped off the bench and knelt beside Vereez, holding her as her sobs grew more violent.

Kaj glowered at his mother and stalked from the room. Xerak started to say something, but Peg shushed him.

"Give Vereez time. This is a surprise to you, but to her it's an old wound ripped raw."

Ohent had leaned back in her chair, her veils obscuring her reaction—if any—to the scene. Certainly her voice, when at last she spoke, was unchanged.

"I wondered if she had agreed to give up the child. I see not."

Meg said, "Vereez has been searching for the child to the best of her abilities for years, but all she has met with were dead ends. We have some reason to believe that Sapphire Wind may have done something to obstruct the flow of information."

"That wind might not have had to blow too hard," Ohent said. "From what you have told me, your impression of

Zarrq was of a devoted guard to his wizard wife. When we were in the field, that was certainly his role. However, when we were setting up a job, he was the master of both information and disinformation. Hiding the location of an infant given away at birth would be nothing to him."

"But his own granddaughter?" Peg's tone was indignant. "Give her away just to keep scandal from touching his little girl?"

The copper disks rang loudly as Ohent shook her head. "Oh, no. That was the least of it. He might even have found a way to keep the child in the family, perhaps present her as the daughter of a friend or relation who had died in childbirth. Probably relation," she added thoughtfully, "that would cover any chance resemblance as the child grew. No, what he and Inehem could not bear was that because my son was the father, we would be drawn together again."

She started to say more, laughed shrilly, then forcibly silenced herself. Teg wondered what Ohent had been about to say. Did she doubt—as Vereez herself had done—that Kaj would care about the offspring of a, for him, casual encounter?

"I, too, did my best to find out what had happened to the child," Ohent said, "and had as little luck as Vereez. But I would like the little one found. If she is not happy where she is, I would like to have her to care for."

That brought Vereez's head up out of her hands. "You?"

"Why not, young lady? You think I would be a poor caregiver? I have not fed my son on a diet of lies about my past as have my oh-so-respectable former friends. Think on that."

Vereez scrubbed at her eyes with her fists, then groomed the fur smooth until only dark tear trails remained against the russet.

"Finding my daughter has been my goal from long before I went to Hettua Shrine, so I have no problem with that part of your request. Giving her to you, to anyone..."

"Perhaps," Xerak interrupted, "we should start with finding her. There's one insurmountable difficulty. Ohent, you say your price for giving up the Bird of Ba Djed is our finding this child. However, the Library's price for helping us to find her is the artifact."

Grunwold added, "It's more complicated than that. Access to the pieces of Ba Djed isn't Sapphire Wind's fee. The artifact is a tool it needs to heal the damage done to it so it can do the search in the first place. If you won't give the Bird to us, we can search by more conventional means, but I don't think we'll do any better than Vereez already has. She may not look it while she's sniveling, but she's smart and determined."

Vereez glanced at Xerak and Grunwold, as if not certain how to express her thanks for their support, but her words were for Ohent. "The boys have spelled it out. If you won't compromise, we're stuck. We might as well go back aboard *Slicewind* and aimlessly sail the world looking for Xerak's missing master."

"Compromise?" Ohent said the word as if this was a card game and someone had changed the bid.

Vereez nodded decisively. "Come with us to the Library. Let Sapphire Wind use the two bits of Ba Djed of the Weaver to help us find my daughter. You can stay at the Library and keep an eye on your bit, or we'll do our best to make sure your Bird—nightmares and all—is returned to you. Then, after we find my daughter, you surrender the Bird to Sapphire Wind, then we all decide together where the child's going to live after that."

Peg cleared her throat. "Have you considered the child might be happy where she is?"

Vereez swiveled to look at Peg. "I have. If she is, my blessings on her and whoever is raising her, but if something has gone wrong, if my parents put her in some sort of strict academy or horrible orphanage where she's miserable, then I'm getting her out."

Ohent shoved back her veil and for the first time they saw her unobscured. She was right. The powerful warrior who they had seen in the Font of Sight was gone, all but for the sapphire-blue eyes. Those shone now with the same clear light and sense of purpose.

"You have a deal. I will come with you. We will learn the fate of the child. I swear by the faith I have given to my guardianship of the Bird that if my granddaughter is well kept and happy, I will not attempt to change her life."

"Done," Vereez said, and reached to clasp the hand that her child's grandmother extended to her.

"Kaj, come back in here," Ohent called.

He did, expression impassive, arms folded over his chest.

Ohent looked at her son. "It would probably be a good idea if you come with us."

"Would it?" Kaj asked. Teg didn't blame him. Grunwold was openly glowering at him. Xerak was looking . . . befuddled? And Vereez wouldn't look at him at all.

"You know what to do when I have one of my seizures,"

Ohent replied. "If you don't want to come, you'd better write up instructions for my new caretakers."

Kaj considered. "I'll come. The job I was working on is almost done. I can explain I have a chance to get my crazy mother medical help. They'll understand. They might even pay me a little extra as a luck bonus."

Ohent's whiskers twitched in what might have been a smile. "Very well. I think your coming along will be the best for all of us."

They departed the next morning. Xerak and Grunwold had given the bow cabin over to Kaj and Ohent. She, more than anyone else aboard, needed private space. When she wasn't being plagued by her personal demons, Ohent could be interesting, even informative. When she was having one of her fits, she was impossible. It wasn't hard to understand why drugging her to unconsciousness had become the coping tactic of choice.

But the tension between Vereez and Kaj was what really made *Slicewind* feel too small. If Vereez had entertained hopes of one of those "young lovers separated by evil parents reunited" moments, she wasn't getting it. Kaj didn't avoid her, but neither did he seek her company—or so it seemed.

The second night out, Teg was on late shift with Vereez. Grunwold and Xerak were asleep in Vereez's cabin. The night was calm, and after headings had been checked, Teg withdrew forward of the hatch to light her pipe. She had a feeling Vereez might want to do some confiding, and fussing with a pipe provided a great excuse to think before speaking.

Teg was still packing the bowl when the silhouette of a sharp-eared canine head poked up from belowdecks. Even had Vereez not already been present, Teg would have had no problem distinguishing the difference between the painted dog's larger, shaggier ears and longer muzzle from the fox's more compact features.

In order not to ruin the crew's night vision, minimal lighting was the custom, so Kaj emerged as much shadow as substance, then prowled over to the wheelhouse. This was somewhat better lit, so that the pilot could check compass headings.

Did Kaj think Vereez was so preoccupied with her duties as pilot that she didn't notice him? His bare feet did slip quietly over the smoothly sanded boards. Or did he believe that her lack of acknowledgment was tantamount to an invitation? For whatever reason, he padded up behind her, wrapped his arms around her trim waist, and nuzzled against the side of her face.

Teg froze in place, feeling her face heating up in embarrassment. As always when preparing a smoke, she'd moved to where the wind wouldn't carry her scent. Kaj didn't know the ship's routine, and might well believe he was alone with his once-upon-a-time lover.

Should I excuse myself? But Vereez knows I'm here. I'll take my cue from her.

Vereez's first words were, to Teg's ear, equivocal. "I used to dream about how your arms felt around me."

Kaj's chuckle was as smoothly sensual as the rest of him. "No need to dream. I'm here, arms—and the rest of me."

"Why didn't you ever answer my letters?"

No pause, which to Teg was as suspicious as a long pause would have been.

"I knew your parents wouldn't approve of us. I worried that they'd intercept a letter and you'd get yelled at."

"You could have written me through one of my friends. I told you which would be sympathetic."

"Until you and your pals got into a tiff over something. Then they'd have a hold on you. Silence was the only way I could protect you."

"Ah . . ." Vereez leaned her head back against his shoulder.

Taking this as an invitation, Kaj moved one hand to stroke her belly. The caress would have passed in a PG movie, but Teg had to restrain herself from squirming.

"Kaj, why didn't you come see me when you were in the city?"

"In the city? Oh, you mean when my mother came to see Xerak's mother. I did once. You were gone. I didn't get any letters from you after that, so I thought you didn't want to see me anymore."

He delicately licked the edge of one of Vereez's ears. Her hands tightened around the steering spokes of the wheel. One of his hands was dropping below her beltline, the other rising toward her breast when Vereez spoke again.

"But I wrote. After I was back in Rivers Meet, I did write. Didn't you get my letters, then?"

Kaj was clearly getting distracted. Teg could hear his breath coming faster. Even though he was part in shadow, she sensed his hips were moving as he adjusted his grip. Both of the young people were still fully clothed, but Teg would bet anything that Kaj was very skilled at removing any impediments to his desire.

I'm not going to sit here and watch him screw her, not physically, not emotionally. Maybe Vereez thinks I'm too old to care or another species, so it doesn't matter what they do in front of me, but . . .

"I didn't get your letter, no. But, darling, why are you thinking about the past? We're here. We're now. Right?"

He cupped his left hand tightly around Vereez's breast, bent to slide his right hand across the front of her crotch, down between her thighs. He was moving his right hand up, toward the clasp of her belt, when Vereez spoke very coolly.

"Then who cashed the check I sent?"

Kaj halted in midgrope. "Check?" There was a long pause during which he pulled slightly back, as if realizing how ridiculous his advances now looked. "My mother must have. You know she isn't exactly, uh, scrupulous where it comes to mine or thine."

"Sorry. That won't do. I paid for in-person confirmation. No matter how good a forger your mother is, she couldn't forge that."

Kaj let his hands drop, stepped back. "It's been years. I don't remember."

"I could handle that you were the type to seduce vulnerable fourteen-year-olds. After all, I didn't fight you off. Far from it, I'll admit, I encouraged you. I could even handle that you would dump me cold. But that you would come up here, behave like this. Lie to me."

Teg had to admire how quickly Kaj changed tactics. "What else could I do? Tell you that I was a selfish prick?

Admit that even though I knew it was hopeless, I couldn't resist you? Yeah. I dumped you, but I did it to protect myself."

"Yourself?"

"I knew you'd dump me eventually, either because it was your idea or your parents forced you. I was a coward, all right? I wanted you, but I knew I couldn't have you, so I kept my distance. There. Satisfied?"

"Maybe." Vereez's tone was noncommittal, but she didn't invite Kaj any closer. "I'll think about it. For now, we need your mother's help, and she needs you. That means you and I are going to need to work together. After that, after I've found our daughter"—the stress on "our" was slight but definite—"after that, maybe we'll talk. For now, keep your distance."

For once, Kaj's suavity vanished. Eventually, making a sweeping bow, he said, "As the lady wishes," and vanished belowdecks. The sound of the wind against the hull and in the sails covered the sound of him returning to the cabin he shared with Ohent. Vereez waited a few moments, left the wheel, and checked below.

"Teg, he's gone," she said softly. Then, when Teg had emerged, still unlit pipe in hand, Vereez continued. "Sorry about that. I thought he might try to be seductive, but I didn't think he'd be so fast with his hands."

"Then you knew he was coming above decks?"

Vereez nodded, then flattened her ears. "I suspected he would. I made sure Kaj knew I'd have night watch, but I overlooked mentioning that there would be two of us. We haven't been sailing together long enough for him to realize that we typically have two people to a shift."

"Well, you'd told me he was hot stuff but . . ." Teg made a fanning gesture.

Vereez mimed panting. "I know. I don't remember him being so polished, but five years would give him a while to refine his approach."

"So you don't . . ."

"Think he's been pining over me all this time?" Vereez snorted inelegantly. "Not one bit. I might have believed it if he hadn't tried to put his magic wand into play, but if he thought he needed that . . . Well, he probably never realized how crazy I was about him."

"Was?" Teg said the word very delicately.

"There's a little bit of me that still is. But, no. I don't think he was making a play for me: Vereez. I think it was for Vereez, the wealthy financiers' only child and probable heir. Maybe he figures that if they've not cut me off yet, after everything I've done lately, then they'd even accept him as a son-in-law."

Teg looked at her pipe. "Mind if I light this?"

"Nope. You don't even need to go back to your hidey-hole. I'm getting used to the smell. It's not so bad. Maybe I'll take up smoking."

"Don't," Teg advised. "I'm thinking about quitting. You don't want to discourage me, do you?" Once she got the pipe drawing, she said, "Are you just stringing Kaj along to make sure he and his mom cooperate?"

"I . . . I wish I could say absolutely yes, but I'm not sure. He is my daughter's father. He has been amazingly faithful to his poor mother. There's good in him. I'm just not sure it's good for me."

Teg personally believed that whatever good there was

in Kaj would never be good for Vereez. On some level, he'd always believe she was that malleable fourteen-year-old. He also knew that Vereez had been pining over him these last four or five years. Vereez needed time to let the reality and the fantasy resolve themselves.

If he wasn't so sexy!

When Teg found herself wondering what it would feel like to have that lightly furred body pressing against her, how two faces so differently shaped managed something like a kiss, she realized she'd better distract them both.

"Do you think Sapphire Wind will be able to help us?"

"I think so." Vereez paused. "I've been thinking... We've gotten caught up in something a lot more complicated than I realized. We were lucky with Nefnetva. I think she resents us, sure, but she's a healer. Her inclination, calling, whatever, is to fix things. I can't believe everyone who was archived will stop at resenting. Some are going to want more."

"Revenge?"

"At least compensation, but revenge seems likely. This was a research facility for wizards. Meeting Xerak might have given you the wrong impression, but most of them aren't nearly as sweet."

"Xerak's monomaniacal," Teg said thoughtfully, "and he has a serious drinking problem, but, you're right, he's definitely sweet."

"There's a lot more to Xerak than his search," Vereez said. "What sort of people are the wizards in your world— that Dumbledore and Gandalf and Merlin I've heard you three mention?"

That led to a long digression, during which Teg

explained that these weren't real people. Happily, this world also had a tradition of fiction as separate from folklore and mythology, so the foundation was there.

"So," Vereez said, "even though there aren't any real wizards, you still understand that wizards' power can go to their heads, make them less than wise, no matter what the term implies. I know that Konnel-toh told us that the extraction agents scheduled their attack for a holiday when most of the Library was more or less closed and many were away but, even so . . ."

"I don't want to make you worry more," Teg said, "but even 'normal' people can cause trouble. The nonmagical librarians, researchers, even cooks and cleaners have had twenty-some years taken from them. As soon as someone puts the idea into their heads that they're 'owed,' well, you, Grunwold, and Xerak may not have much of an inheritance to look forward to."

"I've thought about that," Vereez replied. "What I'm trying to decide is whether I think they'd be justified. I mean, my father was right on one point. A magical library is, by definition, a dangerous place."

They talked until dawn began to pale the stars. Their attempts to find an equitable solution for the Archived were hampered in that—as Vereez herself was the first to admit—her knowledge of legal precedents was limited. Teg was fascinated, although not completely surprised, to find out that damage caused by magical workings gone awry was a recognized element in this world's legal system. People working with magic routinely signed waivers against reasonable risks.

"But," Vereez said as the odor of breakfast began to

seep up from below, "what people can realistically expect, and what they feel they're owed, are not always the same thing."

"I know," Teg said. "When we run a field school, people sign waivers indicating that they're aware that archeological digs can be dangerous places—but the dangers we're talking about are from rock slides or earth subsidence. If the Mummy emerged and started eating people, I don't think that would be covered."

"The Mummy? Never mind. Tell me later," Vereez said. "I'm not saying I forgive my parents for locking me up, or for trying to keep us from finding Ohent, but I'm beginning to understand why they didn't want their past misadventures opened up again."

❧CHAPTER FOURTEEN❧

"If everyone feels up to the hike over to the Library," Grunwold said as he steered *Slicewind* high over the broken terrain bordering the ruins of the Library of the Sapphire Wind, "I'd like to bring *Slicewind* down in that meadow near the lake so we can flush the cisterns and take on fresh water."

Heads nodded agreement all around, and Peg said, "Somehow, hiking over seems more polite. I know that we were told we could berth closer to the Library, but that was when we were already in the area. This time Sapphire Wind won't know to expect us."

Ohent emitted a shrill laugh. She'd become increasingly edgy the closer they drew to the Library, mostly remaining in the bow cabin, muttering loudly enough that the sound, if not the words, could be heard in the galley and lounge.

"I'd be happier if we walked over," Ohent confessed. "I've been having terrible nightmares. Whether it's my conscience or something else, I can't say, but I'm in no rush."

"Then that's settled," Vereez said from where she was leaning over the side rail, looking at the terrain below. "We should touch down in about an hour, with plenty of daylight left."

The meadow grass had mostly rebounded from their prior visits, but when Teg debarked she noted that Grunwold had hit their prior marks close enough that the difference was barely discernable. Once they were all ashore and *Slicewind* had been secured, Grunwold continued in command mode.

"I'll take point, as before, with Xerak right after me. Teg next, then Meg, then Ohent. Kaj, I think it would be best if you were right behind your mother."

Kaj signaled his agreement with a single short nod. During the couple of days' journey from the necropolis, sparring practice had resumed. Kaj had admitted that he didn't know how to use a sword, but he had proven a fair hand with both a light club, not unlike a police officer's baton, and a staff. Although no one really expected trouble, today Kaj carried both.

"Peg, you after Kaj. Vereez will serve as rear guard."

No one protested, so they set off. After their several treks between the meadow and the Library, the trail had come to seem familiar, even welcoming, but today Teg felt uneasy. The green tangle seemed too still, devoid even of the chatter and buzz of those avians and insects that knew they were too small to be endangered by the large bipeds. She noticed that Heru, who usually took off to forage and scout, was perched on top of Grunwold's pack, his head drawn down between his wings, long beak darting back and forth as he peered suspiciously from side to side.

She wasn't the only one feeling uneasy. Whenever they came upon anything unfamiliar on the little-used trail, Grunwold would probe it with the tip of his spear. Most of the time the bits of greenery concealed nothing, but once a sort of land squid, roughly the size of a cottontail rabbit, darted out from the leafy cover, squiggled away through the duff, and vanished into the underbrush.

"Tetzet!" Xerak stared after it in open fascination. "I thought those were extinct!"

"Maybe they were," Vereez said. "Who knows what got loose when the Library was destroyed? The repository might have had just about anything in it."

Vereez had hardly finished speaking when there was a sound like thunder, distant to the ear, yet paradoxically close enough that Teg was sure she felt the vibration. She darted glances left and right, noting that the leaves were trembling, too.

That wasn't my imagination.

At the sound, Grunwold started backing up, his arms spread wide as if to physically push the rest of the group back. Heru flew up, squawking protest. Footsteps quickened as everyone obeyed Grunwold's wordless command. Teg walked slowly backward, alert for the source of the strange disturbance. As Xerak threw his head back and sniffed the air, the point of his spear staff began to glow a deep amber.

Kaj coughed. "What is . . . making that reek?"

Teg sniffed experimentally, getting the usual vegetative

scents, augmented with that of freshly turned soil, accented with something like newly dropped cow manure mixed with rotting fish.

Freshly turned soil . . .

She shouted, "Something's coming up from underground!" as the ground began shaking beneath their feet.

The little land squid had been sort of cute. What erupted from the trail in front of them was anything but. The creature looked something like a long-trunked sea anemone, except that, instead of delicate fronds, it possessed a wealth of very solid tentacles. Still rising, the monster was already taller by half again than Grunwold, the tallest of their company, even without his antlers.

While the little land squid had moved horizontally, utilizing its tentacles to propel itself along, this creature was employing some of its tentacles to thrust itself up from below. As it rose, it braced tentacles on the surface, stabilizing a very sturdy central column. When the creature shook itself violently to toss off the loam, it revealed a main torso shaded a brownish grey, in contrast to the tentacles, which were in myriad shades of green ranging from spring pale to evergreen dark. If the tetzet had eyes, Teg couldn't locate them, but she was willing to bet its mouth was somewhere at the top of its trunk.

"Hoo-boy," gasped Peg, "the love child of Cthulhu and an Ent. Run away?"

This last was said in imitation of the Monty Python knights, but Teg felt certain Peg's proposal was no less genuine for all of that.

Grunwold had switched his grip on his spear, raising it

to shoulder height. He was pulling back his arm, readying to throw, when Xerak leapt up and dragged the spear off target.

"You can't kill it! That might be the last tetzet in existence!"

"We saw a little one," Grunwold countered irritably.

"That only *might* be a younger version," Xerak protested. "It might be a completely different variety. Who knows what young tetzet actually look like or how long they take to mature? We don't know all that much about tetzet, other than that none have been seen alive for at least five hundred years. There's even speculation that they might have been intelligent enough to be trainable. There are relief carvings at the ancient palace of Amyn that have been interpreted as showing tetzet being used to move timber and other bulky freight."

"I can certainly believe that thing can move bulk," Grunwold replied dryly, his gaze fixed where the tetzet continued to block the trail. "So what do you suggest? That we make our way through the trees, and put ourselves at the mercy of the spike wolves, piranha toads, and whatever else is out there?"

"I vote . . ." Peg started to reply, but what Peg would have voted for or against was lost when the tetzet whipped out a long tentacle, caught Xerak around the midsection, and dragged him rapidly toward it. Caught off guard, Xerak lost his hold on his staff. Teg, next in line, caught the staff before it hit the dirt, but she was hardly aware of doing so, her attention fixed on Xerak and the tetzet.

Xerak's arms were free, and he was trying to pry the tentacle from around him, but he wasn't having much luck, possibly because, as Teg noted with horrified fascination, the young wizard was clearly trying not to hurt his captor. The claws that she'd seen pop many a cork out of many a bottle were not digging into the tentacles, nor was the lion-head wizard using his formidable fangs to bite.

Showing no gratitude for Xerak's restraint, the tetzet lifted Xerak off the ground, then snaked out another tentacle to bind his legs and tail. The ground around the tetzet rippled slightly, suggesting that there were other tentacles beneath the loose soil, ready to grab anyone who came close.

"We can't rush it," Grunwold half muttered, "and among us we have two spears, three if we count Xerak's staff."

Teg glanced at Xerak's staff, and noted that the amber light in the head was still present, although fading slightly.

"Xerak, can you . . ." she was beginning when the tetzet flashed out another tentacle.

This one passed through the space between herself and Grunwold, darted to avoid Meg, then circled around Ohent's upper body, pinning her arms to her sides. The tetzet started reeling Ohent closer, but this time met with far more resistance.

Howling in outrage, Kaj leapt forward, grabbing hold of the tentacle at a point in front of where it wrapped around his mother, then digging in his heels. He lacked Xerak's claws, but muscles developed by lots of hard labor proved equal to this weird tug of war.

"Get my mother loose," he snarled, snapping his jaws at a tentacle that made an exploratory dart toward him.

Ohent wasn't helping matters, unless laughing in

increasing hysteria could be said to be some sort of discouragement to her captor. Oddly, it was Xerak who seconded Kaj's command.

"Get Ohent free. The tetzet's after the pieces of Ba Djed. I can feel it trying to get the Spindle, but its hold on me is defeating its purpose."

Teg could see what he meant. The tetzet had Xerak's body, from the underarms down, so tightly wrapped that the enshrouding container with its arcane contents was buried behind its own coils.

I just hope it doesn't decide to squeeze Xerak to a pulp or to rip him into convenient bite-sized morsels.

Peg and Vereez were trying to uncoil Ohent from the tetzet's tentacle. Grunwold took a trial poke at the tentacle that held Ohent, but stopped when she screamed:

"It's squishing me!"

Meg came up next to Teg, motioning to Xerak's spear staff. "This creature seems beyond what the sun spider amulet can handle. Could you possibly use Xerak's magic?"

In answer, Teg completed the question she'd been about to ask when the tetzet had grabbed hold of Ohent.

"Xerak, can you use your spear staff if I help you? There's still a lot of glow in the spearhead."

Despite his precarious position, Xerak frowned and shook his head. "I don't want to kill it."

"So don't kill it," Grunwold snapped at him, "but don't let it kill you! There's only one idiot like you, and in my books that makes you an endangered species, too. I'm not going to let you go extinct."

Xerak laughed, and Teg realized that the young wizard

had been keeping himself calm by focusing on something less personal than his immediate danger.

Then, too, beneath his superficial arrogance, Xerak has a tendency to undervalue himself, to see himself only as his beloved master's faithful student, a student who has continually failed in his search.

Despite the byplay between Xerak and Grunwold, Teg was aware that the others were making progress freeing Ohent. Vereez was using her twin swords to discourage any tentacles that attempted to get an additional hold on Ohent, while Peg and Meg worked on untwining Ohent from the encircling coils. Kaj combined keeping the tentacle that held his mother from dragging her toward the tetzet's trunk with a steady stream of soothing words.

"Take it easy, Mom. I've got this. I'm strong enough to keep this monster from getting you." As he repeated the words over and over, like a charm, Ohent not only stopped shrieking, from the fragments Teg caught, actually started helping.

Teg became aware that Xerak was now addressing her.

"Teg, I'm too close to the tetzet for throwing fire at this thing to be a good idea, but maybe we can use my magic to distract it enough that Grunwold can help me get loose. I felt the tentacles loosen up a bit when the tetzet went after Ohent, again when Grunwold poked it, so here's what I want you to do."

His explanation became intricate and arcane, but Teg thought she got the basic point. Xerak finished up by saying, "Grunwold, I'll need to stop pushing down the tentacles to concentrate with Teg, so don't panic if it gets a few more loops around me."

"I won't," the other grumbled, "but if it breaks your stupid neck, all bets are off. We can't let it get that thrice-cursed Spindle, after all."

"Fair enough. Ready, Teg?"

"Ready!"

Teg was more scared than she wanted to admit. Folklore, legend, and fantasy fiction were packed with cautionary tales about what happened to anyone who tried to use a wizard's staff.

That's without the wizard's permission, she reminded herself, *without his permission.*

Without further pause, she eased the inner self she was just learning to recognize into the hum within the staff that she knew was Xerak's own mana. It helped that he was her teacher, so she knew it well. For a fleeting moment, Teg thought she understood a little better why Xerak was so devoted to Uten Kekui. This sharing of mana was a little like singing in parts, a little like staying in step while performing a complicated dance. It was selfless and yet selfish, because as the blending took shape, Teg felt more acutely who she was, because she knew what in the combination wasn't herself.

There wasn't time to dwell on the sensation. Grunwold was shouting something. She couldn't pull herself far enough out to manage to understand the words, but she knew that Xerak was probably in trouble.

There. I can feel the fire rising. There. Over just behind the tetzet, right at the edge of the trail. The tree that's drying out. I bet the tetzet cut the tree's roots when it buried itself in the trail. Now, ready, aim ... Fire!

A bolt of white-hot fire jetted from the spear point

along the trajectory Teg had chosen. It missed the tetzet, caught the dying tree, and set it ablaze. The smoke and smell of green wood burning filled the air. The tetzet, silent to this point, trumpeted panic from high among its fronds.

Teg's vision blurred, and she sank to her knees. Like an image seen through a rain-streaked windowpane, she saw Grunwold racing forward to grab Xerak, pulling him loose as the tetzet sank down into the hole in the trail. She leaned her head against Xerak's staff, felt the faint hum of his approval, then toppled to one side in a dead faint.

When Teg came around, she thought that her head was resting in Xerak's lap, that he was spooning water into her mouth. To her surprise, when she fluttered her eyes open, the person tending to her was Kaj.

Why does he somehow feel like Xerak? came a thought, vanished almost as soon as shaped.

Kaj's voice, gruffer than usual, said, "You okay, Teg? Drink this, if you can."

He lifted her, propping her up, put something to her lips. Whatever it was tasted atrocious, but her body wanted it, even as her throat tightened and she gagged, so she forced it down and began feeling better.

"Vereez and most of the others are putting out the fire," Kaj said. "I got nursemaid duty for you and Xerak, because my mother wouldn't let me leave her."

"Ohent okay?"

"She's going to have some interesting bruises, but yeah, she's okay."

"Kaj saved me," Ohent said proudly from where she

leaned against a nearby tree. "He's more extraordinary than anyone realizes."

"And the Spindle and the Bird?" Teg asked.

"Both safe," Kaj assured her. "The tetzet seems to be gone, swum away underground or something like that."

"It's gone," Xerak confirmed. Turning her head, Teg found he was leaning against a tree not far away, his spear staff back in his custody. "I wonder how the tetzet happened to be here. I was sure they were extinct."

"We may never know," said Meg, coming over, soot streaked but looking quite satisfied. "If I were to speculate, I'd say that the tetzet may have been one of the original guardians of Ba Djed, released when the Library was destroyed. I suspect—and this is only supposition— that the tetzet somehow caught the 'scent' of the Spindle when we traveled this way on our way back to *Slicewind*. For lack of anything else to do, it settled in to wait to see if the Spindle came through again. We shall need to ask Sapphire Wind if it can somehow discourage a repeat performance."

"Amen to that," Peg said cheerfully as she trotted over to join them. "But all's well that ends well. Right? Teg, do you think you can manage to walk? So far no spike wolves or piranha toads or other of this area's charming denizens have come calling, but . . ."

"Give me a hand up," Teg said. "Whatever Kaj fed me has done wonders."

"It's a stimulant," Vereez called from where she was stomping out a few remaining sparks. "You're going to feel like a divinity for about two hours. Then you're going to sleep really, really well."

"Then let's get going," Teg said, finding that Vereez was correct. If she'd had wings, she'd have joined Heru in the skies. "Otherwise, you folks are going to end up carrying me when I crash."

They reached the doorways of the Library of the Sapphire Wind without further incident.

As the wide portal began to swing open, Teg found herself remembering the second verse of the rhyme supplied what seemed so long ago by Hettua Shrine:

All of this and more you will find
After you pass through the doorways
Of the Library of the Sapphire Wind

She laughed softly to herself.

"What's so funny?" Peg asked, while Meg tilted her head in a wordless echo of the question.

Teg answered, "I was remembering the rhyme. We certainly found out a lot, but I don't think any of what we learned was what our holdbacks expected. I wonder what we'll learn next, and where it will take us?"

"Good question," Meg said softly. "The only thing I feel certain about is that Over Where hasn't finished surprising us yet."

MEMORY
TPB: 978-1-4767-3673-0 • $15.00 US/$18.00 CAN
PB: 978-0-6718-7845-0 • $7.99 US/$9.50 CAN

KOMARR
PB: 978-0-6715-7808-4 • $7.99 US/$9.50 CAN

A CIVIL CAMPAIGN
HC: 978-0-6715-7827-5 • $24.00 US/$35.50 CAN
PB: 978-0-6715-7885-5 • $7.99 US/$10.99 CAN

DIPLOMATIC IMMUNITY
PB: 978-0-7434-3612-0 • $7.99 US/$9.50 CAN

CRYOBURN
HC: 978-1-4391-3394-1 • $25.00 US/$28.99 CAN

CAPTAIN VORPATRIL'S ALLIANCE
TPB: 978-1-4516-3915-5 • $15.00 US/$17.00 CAN
PB: 978-1-4767-3698-3 • $7.99 US/$9.99 CAN

GENTLEMAN JOLE AND
THE RED QUEEN
HC: 978-1-4767-8122-8 • $27.00 US/$36.00 CAN
PB: 978-1-4814-8289-9 • $8.99 US/$11.99 CAN

". . . filled with a satisfying blend of
strong characters and wry humor."
—*Publishers Weekly*

Available in bookstores everywhere.
Order ebooks online at www.baen.com.

LOOKING FOR A NEW SPACE OPERA ADVENTURE?

Praise for
CATHERINE ASARO

"Asaro plants herself firmly into that grand SF tradition of future history franchises favored by luminaries like Heinlein, Asimov, Herbert, Anderson, Dickson, Niven, Cherryh, and Baxter . . . They don't write 'em like that anymore! Except Asaro does, with . . . up-to-the-minute savvy!"
—*Locus*

"[Bhaajan], who starts out keeping an emotional distance from the people in the Undercity soon grows to think of them as her community once more. Asaro . . . returns to the Skolian empire's early history to tell Bhajaan's story."
—*Booklist*

"Asaro delivers a tale rich with the embedded history of her world and bright with technical marvels. Her characters are engaging and intriguing, and there is even a bit of romance. What really touched my heart was Bhaaj's interaction with the children of the aqueducts. I spent the last fifty pages of the book sniffling into a tissue."
—*SFcrowsnest*

"I'm hooked, both on her writing and her Skolian universe. This book had everything I wanted: strong characters, a new and unique world, and a plot that isn't as simple as it first appears." —*TerryTalk*

About Catherine Asaro's Skolian Empire saga:
"Entertaining mix of hard SF and romance."
—*Publishers Weekly*

"Asaro's Skolian saga is now nearly as long, and in many ways as compelling, as *Dune*, if not more so, featuring a multitude of stronger female characters." —*Booklist*

"Rapid pacing and gripping suspense."
—*Publishers Weekly*

KNIGHT WATCH

A new urban fantasy series from
TIM AKERS

KNIGHT WATCH

After an ordinary day at the Ren Faire is interrupted by a living, fire-breathing dragon, John Rast finds himself spirited away to Knight Watch, the organization that stands between humanity and the real nasties the rest of the world doesn't know about.

TPB: 978-1-9821-2485-4 • $16.00 US / $22.00 CAN
PB: 978-1-9821-2563-9 • $8.99 US / $11.99 CAN

VALHELLIONS

When a necromancer hell-bent on kicking off the end of the world shows up wielding a weapon created by Nazi occultists, John and the Knight Watch team will go to great lengths—even Minnesota—to find out who's responsible and foil their plans.

TPB: 978-1-9821-2595-0 • $16.00 US / $22.00 CAN
PB: 978-1-9821-9258-7 • $9.99 US / $12.99 CAN

Praise for Akers' previous novels:

"A must for all epic fantasy fans." —*Starburst*

"Delivers enough twists and surprises to keep readers fascinated . . . contains enough action, grittiness, magic, intrigue and well-created characters." —*Rising Shadow*

"Full of strong world building, cinematic and frequent battle scenes, high adventure, great characters, suspense, and dramatic plot shifts, this is an engaging, fast-paced entry in a popular subgenre." —*Booklist* on *The Pagan Night*, starred review

Available in bookstores everywhere.
Order ebooks online at www.baen.com.